Peabody Public Libr
Columbia City, IN

FICTION SHERMAN
Sherman, Jory.
The Baron range / Jory
Sherman.
1st ed.

DEC 2 98 DISCARD

W9-ATK-688

THE BARON RANGE

By Jory Sherman from Tom Doherty Associates

The Barons of Texas
Grass Kingdom
Horne's Law
The Medicine Horn
Song of the Cheyenne
Trapper's Moon
Winter of the Wolf

THE BARON RANGE

JORY SHERMAN

Peabody Public Library
Columbia City, IN

A TOM DOHERTY ASSOCIATES BOOK
NEW YORK

This is a work of fiction. All the characters and events portrayed in this novel are either fictitious or are used fictitiously.

THE BARON RANGE

Copyright © 1998 by Jory Sherman

All rights reserved, including the right to reproduce this book, or portions thereof, in any form.

This book is printed on acid-free paper.

A Forge Book
Published by Tom Doherty Associates, Inc.
175 Fifth Avenue
New York, NY 10010

Forge® is a registered trademark of Tom Doherty Associates, Inc.

Library of Congress Cataloging-in-Publication Data

Sherman, Jory.
    The Baron range / Jory Sherman.—1st. ed.
        p.   cm.
        "A Forge book."
        ISBN 0-312-86349-7
        I. Title.
    PS3569.H43B36   1998
    813'.54—dc21   98-19404
                                                                         CIP

First Edition: September 1998

Printed in the United States of America

0 9 8 7 6 5 4 3 2 1

This one's for that splendid triumvirate:
Tom Doherty, my publisher,
Bob Gleason, my editor,
and Nat Sobel, my agent,
with my deepest gratitude.

We are not granted wisdom;
We must locate it ourselves,
after taking a journey that no other can protect us from
nor travel for us.

—MARCEL PROUST,
*translated from the French
by the author*

Cast of Characters

The Box B Ranch

Martin Baron—patriarch of the Baron Family
Caroline Baron—Martin's wife
Anson Baron—son of Martin and Caroline
Juanito Salazar—Martin's Argentine friend
Mickey Bone (Miguel Heuso)—Lipan Apache Indian
Ken Richman—Martin's friend, drummer
Jean Gates—Ken's girlfriend

Box B Ranch Hands

Pepito Garza
Fidel Hernandez
Chato Manzana
Ramon Lopez
Paco Serra
Alonzo (Lonnie) Guzman—cook
Joselito Delgado

The Rocking A Ranch

Benito Aguilar—ranch owner
Pilar Aguilar—Benito's wife
Lazaro Aguilar—blind son of Pilar
Matteo Miguelito Aguilar—Pilar's older son
Luz Aguilar—Matteo's wife
Delberto Aguilar—young son of Matteo and Luz
Esperanza Cuevas—helps raise blind boy

Simon Currasco—ranch hand
Federico Ruiz—ranch hand

Others

Jack Killian—drifter
Maureen Ursula Killian—Jack's wife
Roy Killian—son of Jack and Ursula
Jerome Winfield—fisherman
Rob Coogan—sailor
Sam Cullers—pirate
Hoxie Hockstetler—pirate
Lars Swenson—pirate
Cuchillo—Mescalero Apache chief
Culebra—Cuchillo's son
Ojo—rides with Cuchillo
Jim Shepherd—barber
Peebo Elves—tracker
Dave Riley—soldier
Dream Speaker—Mickey Bone's mentor
Charles Goodnight—trail blazer
Sam Maverick—cowman

THE BARON RANGE

1

ANSON BARON WOULD never forget the night the big storm hit that part of Texas where the lands of the Box B lay. The storm seemed to sum up all the turmoil he felt inside, and the rage he felt toward his father. And it was the night that Mickey Bone left the ranch, stealing away in the darkness without even telling Anson's father, Martin, that he was leaving, or why he was leaving. At that time, no one knew why Mickey had picked up and lit a shuck for Mexico. No one except the Argentine, Juanito Salazar, and he never told anyone the real reason. He just told Anson that Bone wanted to find his own people and become an Indian again, a Lipan Apache.

But Bone's leaving like that left a bitter taste in Anson's mouth, and it would be many months before he would know the whole truth of that night and why Mickey had abandoned him. Anson had wanted to ride away with him and become an Apache himself. He had wanted to leave the wrath of his father and never set eyes on him again.

It was at one of those times during those hard days on the Box B that Anson Baron thought about killing his father, Martin. He was at that age when a father's harsh words cut deep and at a time when Anson was self-conscious. His muscles were filling out and the urges he had first experienced three or four years ago were stronger now. These urges were both masculine and confusing, and when his father

Peabody Public Library
Columbia City, IN

humiliated him in front of the vaqueros or the Argentine, Juanito Salazar, the anger rose up in Anson with a searing heat that surged
through his brain like wildfire.

But after Mickey rode away, Anson had left Juanito's casita and
gone to the big house where his parents, Caroline and Martin, lived,
the house on the hill called La Loma de Sombra, Shadow Hill. Even
though he did not want to see his father that night, he had no place
else to go. Juanito had told him to go home, and he knew there must
be some reason for the Argentine to say that.

He heard his parents arguing as the rain fell, clattering on the roof
with a maddening din. It seemed to the boy that his folks argued a lot.
He knew his mother, Caroline, was unhappy. He thought it might be
because she was with child, which was confusing enough at his age. He
thought his mother was too old to have another child. After all, he was
nearly seventeen and had gotten used to being an only child.

The argument broke off, and Anson heard his father's footsteps
pound on the hardwood flooring. He thought he heard his mother
crying, but he could not be sure because the sound of the rain on the
roof drowned out all but the loudest sounds. He looked out the window of his room and saw how dark it was and wondered about Mickey
Bone riding through all that rain and hoped he had sense enough to
seek shelter, which of course he would because Mickey was an Apache
and knew how to live on the land in all kinds of weather. He felt a
loneliness that seemed strange to him, felt that a part of his life had
been taken away and things would never be the same again.

Then he heard distant thunder and the house seemed oddly silent
all of a sudden.

2

THE ADOBE WALLS of the casita erupted into frantic drumbeats as the first gusts of the north wind blew lances of hard rain out of the black clouds of night. The man inside felt the pressure change inside the adobe, and the candle on the table flickered with the on-rushing air through the cracks in the windows. Shadows shifted around the room as if they were sentient beings born of shadow and darkness.

Juanito Salazar, the Argentine who had helped Martin Baron build the Box B Ranch, listened to the rattle of rain and the howl of the wind. His brow furrowed, he got up from the table and went to the north window. He had known the storm would be a big one, with much rain, but when he heard the far-off rumble of thunder and saw the clouds light up in the distance, he had even more reason for concern. It was not the threat of flash floods that concerned him now.

He strode from the window toward his front door. Quickly he grabbed his serape soogan off the peg jutting from the wall near the door of his casita and pulled it over his head and onto his shoulders. He put on his hat and went out the door. Then he ran toward the Baron house on La Loma de Sombra, not far away. His feet splashed in the puddles filling small craters, puddles that danced with the silvery daggers of rain.

Lamplight coppered the windows of the Baron house as Juanito raced for the back door. Rain pelted him with the ferocity of flung sand, stung his eyes. Already, he thought, the dirt under his feet was turning to mud.

The back door opened before Juanito reached it and Martin Baron emerged like some dark wraith, wearing a slicker. Behind him, his son, Anson, carrying two rifles wrapped in oilcloth, closed the door, the blackness of night swallowing him up in his dark hat and slicker. A moment later the door opened again slightly, and Juanito saw that Caroline Baron stood there, just out of reach of the rain, her face too shadowed to see. Juanito sighed inwardly. He could almost feel the sadness of Caroline's eyes as she watched her husband and son leave the house, leave her alone once again.

"Are you thinking what I'm thinking, Juanito?" Martin said.

"The gather."

"This'n's goin' to be a reg'lar Texas cloudbuster," Martin said.

"We'd better get to La Golondrina quick," Juanito said.

"How many men we got out there watchin' the herd?"

"Only two. Pepito and Fidel."

"Christ," Martin swore. "Well, let's get to the barn and saddle 'em up."

"What's wrong, Daddy?" Anson asked, raising his voice so that he could be heard above the rattle and splatter of rain. "How come we got to ride out in this rain?"

Martin didn't answer his son, but headed for the barn, his long strides leaving Anson and Juanito behind.

"All those cattle we were going to take to New Orleans are in one pasture on La Golondrina," Juanito said. "If they stampede, they'll tear down the mesquite fences and could come this way and flatten everything in their path."

"Cripes," Anson said. His voice was still changing pitch on him, cracking at times of stress. His words came out as a screechy cackle as he tried to keep up with Juanito and not drop the rifles. A hard gust of wind struck him broadside and he teetered for a split second in midstride, held in momentary check by the force of the blow.

Anson looked to the north, saw the white thunderheads pulse and glow with internal charges of lightning. A few seconds later he heard the muffled crescendo of booming thunder. And when the light disappeared from the clouds, he was once again plunged into darkness. He could barely see the barn through the driving rain, and by the time he reached it, his father and Juanito were already inside. He paused for a moment before going inside, then heard the slam of the back door as his mother closed it hard against the night and the storm.

3

—■—

Pepito Garza rode around the far edge of the herd bunched up on La Golondrina grass. He had no lantern, for the wind had blown it out, and he strained to see through the darkness and the sheets of rain that marched across the plain.

"Fidel," he called, and the wind snatched away his words as if they were sodden rags. Needles of rain stung his eyes when he tried to peer through the watery folds of night.

Pinpoints of light pierced the dark clouds to the northwest. To Pepito they almost looked like signal lanterns flickering on and off in a dust storm, but moments later, he heard the distant throb of thunder like Apache tom-toms or the muffled rumble of an earthquake.

The cattle grazed uneasily in the darkness, some starting to move around restlessly, aimlessly, as if they sought a leader among them who might reassure them. For now, Pepito was that leader. Yet he knew that no soft songs would soothe the restless beasts once the thunder and lightning drew closer. He called to Fidel again.

From the far side of the large herd, Fidel Hernandez called out in reply.

"Ven," Pepito responded. "Ven pa' 'qui. Pronto."

"Ya me voy," Fidel called, and his voice was distant and thin as if he were in a faraway ravine.

Pepito crossed himself and steered his horse toward the moving cattle, his senses heightened at being so close to those long raking horns. His small horse seemed dwarfed by the rangy bulls and steers and cows that loomed up in the darkness. A distant flash of lightning illuminated the main herd, and Pepito saw that they were all on their feet, moving toward something he could not see.

He thought of the big longhorn bull Amador, which he had last seen that afternoon near the watering tank at the far edge of the large pasture. Amador was a natural leader, a dominant bull with huge cojones that dangled like weapons from his loins. He thought of Amador and knew he must somehow find the herd bull and keep him calm.

"*Es muy malo,*" Fidel said when he rode up. "*Estoy muy nervioso.*"

"*Yo tambien,*" Pepito replied. "I am looking for Amador."

"Ah, it would be better if he were a dog and you could call him."

"That one would not come even if he were a dog."

"Do you think they will run, Pepito?"

"They will run wherever Amador runs."

"Will Amador stay, then?"

"I do not know. If a lightning bolt hits near him, he is liable to fly."

"I think that it is true." Fidel looked at the distant sky. The black thunderclouds were laced with forked lightning for just an instant and then seemed to pulse with a raw energy. Seconds later, they both heard the still-muffled boom of thunder.

"Do you count the seconds?" Fidel asked.

"I have counted fifteen."

"Twelve kilometers, then."

"*Quizás.*"

Fidel acted jittery as the two men rode through the herd, whistling to himself, talking in a quavery voice to the cattle they passed. Pepito was careful to avoid any closeness to cattle with horns that could sweep him from the saddle if they panicked. His horse stepped gingerly through the clusters of longhorns as if it were walking among prickly pear.

The wind shifted and circled, swirling around the two men, forcing the cattle to shift direction so that their rumps were headed into the brunt of the blow. There was a different mood to the herd now. Some of the cows began to bellow longingly. The steers, startled, began to nudge one another and lock horns with others as if to incite them to fight or to run.

Lightning splashed the sky with light to the northwest. This time the thunder took fewer seconds to reach the ears of the Mexican out-riders wending their way through the scattered herd of longhorns and mixed breeds. The bellowing of the cows grew louder and more frequent; the steers seemed to drift in and out of the herd like lost creatures summoned from the night and the wind.

Pepito held his hat down to keep it from blowing off and spurred his horse away from a young steer raking the air with his massive horns. Fidel guided his horse to the safe side of Pepito, his mount jittery beneath the saddle, every muscle in its shoulders quivering like gelatin.

"They are going to break, Pepito," Fidel said.

"Where the devil is that bull Amador?"

"There, over there," Fidel said, but he was only hoping. He did not know.

"Listen," Pepito said. "I hear something. Do you hear it?"

A ripple of distant thunder blotted out all sound for a moment as Fidel tried to hear what Pepito had heard. Then, in the brief silence, he heard hoofbeats, riders coming at a gallop across the plain. He could not see them, but he knew it was not the sound of cattle running.

"Yes, I hear horses coming," Fidel said.

"They are very close, but I cannot see them."

A jagged scrawl of lightning across the sky threw the cattle herd and the land into stark relief. For a split second they saw the three riders, like phantoms, emerge from the darkness only to disappear again as the thunder pealed like majestic timpani above them.

The rain slashed at them and raked the cattle herd with a stinging ferocity as the wind picked up and hammered down at them from the northwest. The two Mexican herders bent over until the wind lessened, and then Pepito turned toward Fidel. "I will ride on."

"Yes, I am going," Fidel said, and turned his horse to the east and rode away from the milling herd that was now closing up and huddling with one another for protection against the raking rain.

4

DID YOU SEE those two riders, Juanito?'' Martin asked.
"Yes. That was Pepito and Fidel."

"The herd was clumped up."

"For now," Juanito said and ducked his head as the rain drove at them in blinding sheets and the darkness closed about them like an iron maiden in the rumble of thunder.

Anson, riding behind his father and Juanito, hadn't seen a thing, only the jagged forks of lightning breaking the sky like cracked glass. Then he saw a dark rider appear out of the rain like some windblown wraith and heard Fidel's voice above the watery din.

"*Patrón*, Pepito says to come quick. The herd has much fear and he thinks they will break if we do not find Amador."

"We are on our way," Martin said, and they followed Fidel to the herd and found Pepito making his way through the cattle like a blind man in a thicket bristling with thorns.

"You found Amador yet?" Martin yelled.

"No. I do not see him."

"We'll fan out. Anson, he'll be the biggest bull in the herd. You cut straight up the middle. Use your cow sense and be damned careful."

"I know what he looks like," Anson said. Then he wondered what his father meant by "cow sense."

"Juanito, let's you and I go on the other side of this bunch. Everyone be careful. If that lightning and thunder gets any closer, the herd may hightail it. Fidel, you start cutting out those spooky steers and Pepito, you keep going where you're going."

The men split up. Fidel started working his horse through the herd, cutting longhorn steers from the back, driving them out into the open. The horse worked well in the thickening mud and the steers began to bunch up to one side of the main herd.

Martin and Juanito rode slowly through the herd, veering to the left, trying to spot one longhorn that stood out from the rest. It was pitch-dark and the rain drenched them while the wind tore at their slickers with ferocity, as if it had teeth and claws.

Lightning stitched intricate mercuric patterns in the clouds. Thunder crescendoed, its powerful rolling rumble only a few miles away from the cattle herd, and there was ominous warning in its somber undertones. The rain pummeled the creatures moving across the grassland in a deluge that threatened to wash them all away.

Water rushed across the plain until it was hock-high on the horses and cattle. The longhorns bawled at every crack of thunder and bunched together in milling confusion, their horns clacking when they touched like the clicking of arrhythmic castanets.

"There, over there," shouted Pepito above the rain, and Martin sought out the object of his exclamation. Bolts of lightning raked the sky and drenched Amador with light. He stood alone beyond the herd, his massive horns stretching out from his boss with majestic grace, his front hooves planted in mud and water above his ankles, his head low as if ready to charge any being that ventured into his *querencia*, his calico hide sleek and shiny in the sudden sizzle of light as if he had magically emerged from some watery pool at the dawn of creation.

"Juanito," Martin called. "He's ready to bolt."

"I see him," Juanito shouted, already shaking out his rope, his horse pushing against the rumps of cattle to forge a path through the herd.

Martin unfastened his own rope from the saddle, shook out a loop and drove spurs into his horse's flanks. His horse bunched its muscles and surged forward through the pack of longhorns, toward the place where Amador stood glaring in the darkness, poised to swing those massive horns at anything that approached him.

Fidel slipped his rope from the lashing on his O-ring with wet fingers that lost their grip on the braided hemp. His rope uncoiled and one end dropped to the wet ground with a splash just as lightning fractured the sky and thunder boomed simultaneously less than a mile away.

Amador lowered his head and charged straight at the snake writhing with a sudden gust of wind in Fidel's hands. Fidel saw the bull coming at him and pulled desperately at the rope as if that might save him. He felt the sudden jolt as the bull rammed the chest of his horse, and he felt the saddle slip out from under him and saw the gargantuan back of the bull slide beneath him as his horse went down. Then he released his grip on the rope and there was only air between him and the ground.

The horse screamed in terror as its legs crumpled under him and he lost his balance against the pull of gravity. A mighty horn slammed into the head of the horse as it collapsed, smashing the skull like a ripe melon, spraying blood and bone into the rain and the wind. Amador kept charging, churning the downed horse under its feet, turning its head to search for the next enemy as lightning danced across the sky and thunder upon thunder boomed like a battery of cannon from the black fortress of the sky.

Martin saw Fidel's horse go down and Amador's cloven hooves trample the animal after his horn had bludgeoned its brain to pulp. Then he saw the bull change course and head in his direction like a juggernaut.

The storm moved in over La Golondrina like some creature from ancient Norse mythology, hurling lightning bolts and booming thunder. One stroke of lightning speared from the sky with blinding speed. Before the bolt struck the ground, it stabbed a large steer in the rump, fried a path along its spine and twisted down one leg, peeling the hide from its flesh like a paring knife cutting a spiral around an apple. The steer bawled in pain and leaped into the air, shivered with the shock and dropped to the ground stone dead.

That was enough to send a signal through the milling herd. Those cattle nearest to the downed steer scrambled in all directions as if a bomb had exploded in their midst, scattering like a flushed covey of quail. As if on cue, the entire herd hurtled into motion all at once as lightning laced the skies and thunder shattered their eardrums.

Anson, in the center of the herd, felt his horse speed up beneath him and he grabbed the saddle horn to keep from being ejected from the saddle. Cattle, their long horns raking everything in their path, burst into motion all around him and surged toward some unknown destination as if they were one being with a single mind. He found himself being swept up in the stampede like a cork on a mountainous wave, the ocean surging beneath him with a terrible force. The tip of a horn dug into his horse's flanks just beneath his calf. His horse veered to the left, the herd packed around it and it was carried along on the immense tide of cattle, crushed on both sides, unable to break free.

What good does "cow sense" mean when it's like this? Anson thought as the herd picked up speed.

The dark clouds seemed even lower and the rain fell even harder, hitting the ground and raising the water level by inches until the cattle were splashing through knee-high puddles.

Anson tried to break away. He tried slowing the horse, hoping the herd would surge past him, but he felt a jolt as cattle struck his horse's rump and then had to keep up with the herd or get gored or run over. It seemed to Anson that he could hear men shouting above the roar of the rain and the loud rumbles of thunder. Lightning razed the sky almost constantly now and the thunderclaps followed close on the heels of every burst of radiant light.

"There they go!" shouted Martin, and Anson felt the herd surge to the left and pick up speed. The cattle broke away from him as the horse turned right, bucking against the flow of horns that clacked together and separated as the herd found its direction. "Anson," his father called.

"Yo," Anson replied.

"Look out."

Anson had his hands full guiding his horse out of the melee and could not answer. He wove his way through the stampeding herd that now swayed at right angles to his position. He wondered what his father meant by "There they go!" Where? All Anson knew was that he wanted to get away from them. The pounding in his ears was more deafening than the thunder now and the snaps of lightning all over the sky lent an eeriness to the scene that made him think he was in a living nightmare where nothing was real and everything was real at the same time. He felt helpless to change any of it, unable to wake up and leave the dream behind on the shores of sleep.

He saw Juanito out of the corner of his eye. Juanito was riding toward him in slow motion, his horse blotted out by the sea of cattle madly running to the north as if whipped on by the thunder and lightning.

Anson dodged two steers that swung toward him and kicked the horse with his spurs to avoid running into another bunch that loomed out of the night like ghostly cattle from hell. Juanito finally reached him, running his horse alongside to protect Anson's flank. Cattle flowed around the two men as bolts of lightning lit their wet faces in brief tableaux.

"Where's my daddy?" Anson asked.

"He was trying to stop Amador, but he is all right," Juanito said.

"Where are the cattle going?"

"They broke through the mesquite fence. They are heading toward La Loma de Sombra."

"The house?"

"Yes. Come, we must flank them on the west and try and turn the herd back."

"That's impossible," Anson said loudly as the thunder pealed.

"Then we must do the impossible. Come. Follow me."

Juanito wheeled his horse and rode through knee-high water through the stragglers in the herd, heading westward. When he reached an open spot, he spurred his horse into a gallop. Anson followed him, hoping his horse wouldn't step in a gopher or prairie dog hole and send him flying.

The herd sloshed through the water at a fair clip, so it took Juanito a long time to reach the head of the stampede. Anson looked for his father, but could not see him. He heard yelling from somewhere off to the east, but could understand none of the words.

Juanito drove his horse at the leaders on the fringe of the herd and slowly began to turn some of them into the rushing sea of wild-eyed longhorns and mixed breeds. Anson flanked Juanito and started doing the same, lashing at them with his lariat shortened to the length of a bullwhip. Finally the cattle began to turn. As they bunched up, they milled and stomped the water with their hooves. Leaderless, they became confused.

Then as Anson was beginning to relax, a massive burst of lightning and a gigantic thunderclap jolted the herd to turn on him and he had to ride out of their way or risk being trampled. Out of the corner of his eye, he saw Juanito switch his horse into a 180-degree turn and gallop out of harm's way.

"There will be no stopping them now," Juanito panted as he rode up alongside Anson's horse.

"What do we do now?" Anson asked.

"Ride ahead, if we can, and try to head them off before they reach the rancho at La Loma de Sombra."

"That's a long ride, Juanito."

"And where else would we go, *amigo mío?*"

The storm continued to rage and the herd was in full stampede, blindly following Amador. Anson watched them race by, slowed only by the water underfoot, and wondered if they could manage to get ahead of such an out of control herd. His horse was tired, and so was he.

Martin rode wide of the onrushing herd, flanking it on the right. Ahead of him, Pepito broke out a loop, swung his wet lariat over his head as he closed in on one of the lead steers. Martin saw the vaquero in relief at every flash of lightning, a spectral figure on horseback chasing after a ghostly herd through shimmering sheets of rain.

Pepito threw the rope and it soared over the horns of the steer, settled under one side, caught the tip of the other. He reined his horse back and the rope tautened. The horse backed down on its haunches and the steer jerked sideways into the oncoming herd.

The steer went down and those behind it crashed into the rope and stumbled. The rope jerked out of Pepito's hand as Martin rode up on him in the slashing rain.

"Did you get Amador?"

"No. I could not reach him."

"Come on."

Martin's horse leaped ahead as the rider put spurs to its tender flanks and Pepito prodded his own horse to follow. Martin jerked his rifle from its scabbard as his horse dodged cattle in full gallop through high water.

Anson saw dead cattle lit by lightning and his horse jumped over the downed mesquite fence on the heels of Juanito's horse. Some cattle had gotten tangled in the fence, where the herd was slowly trampling them to death as they struggled to rise from the brush. Anson could hear their cries as he rode by, but was helpless to save any of them.

Juanito neared the head of the herd. Off to his right he saw Martin and Pepito closing in on Amador, but they seemed to be riding very slowly as if their horses' hooves were caught in quicksand, and then he realized that he too was being slowed by high water. His horse swerved as one of the mixed breeds faltered and went down on one leg. Cattle barreled into the stumbling cow and she rolled over with the impact, bawling as she struggled to right herself and was knocked down hard until her head was underwater. She never rose up again and the water turned red as hooves slashed into her flesh.

Anson rode wide of the herd, trying to get out of its way and catch up to Juanito. He saw the cow go down and Juanito's horse shy away from it, swinging wide to the left. In the dancing light of lightning he saw his father well ahead of him, riding toward the head of the stampede, right into its path. He called out, but knew that no one could hear him over the explosive rumble of thunder. Rain bit into his eyes, stinging them raw, and he felt as if he were in some endless nightmare, powerless to break free of the mindless herd splashing through chest-high water.

Martin drew close to Amador and struggled to get close enough for a shot. His horse needed strong hands on the reins to avoid going down or faltering. He tried to draw a bead on the lead bull, but he could not see through the knifing rain and the bounce of the horse made it difficult to hold his rifle tight to his shoulder. The barrel bobbed up and down and swayed from right to left.

"Come on, boy," Martin said to his horse and dug his spurs in deep. The horse struggled against the rising water and gave it all the bottom it had. In between the rumbles of thunder, Martin heard another sound, one that made his blood turn gelatinous with the cold rush of fear that coursed through him. Then Amador did a strange thing.

The big longhorn bull veered toward Martin as if to charge him, and the entire herd swung on Amador's fulcrum. Martin's horse reacted and shied to the right, nearly unseating Baron. The horse stumbled on uncertain footing and Martin thought he was going to go down.

"Whoa up, boy," he said in a calm voice. "Steady."

At that same moment, Martin saw his chance. He brought the rifle quickly to his shoulder and took aim at Amador. He led him a few inches and squeezed the trigger. The flint struck the frizzen and threw sparks into the pan, but the powder was wet and did not explode.

"Damn," Martin cursed, and sheathed his rifle as he turned his horse away from Amador.

And that saved his life, for he heard the roaring again in the silence following a thunderclap and then his horse was rearing and struggling against a strong current. Martin was swept back toward the rear of the stampeding herd and no longer felt the ground solid beneath him as his horse breasted the surge of water that fanned out from the main current of a flash flood.

Juanito reined in his horse before Anson did and turned it away from the wall of water he saw coming toward the front of the herd. Anson saw him wheel and then, behind Juanito, he saw the huge swell of muddy water roaring down on the herd.

"Flash flood!" Juanito yelled, and waved at Anson to turn back.

In horror, Anson saw Pepito's horse rear up as lightning struck a water oak and the tree blazed with fire, silhouetting the vaquero. The water struck Pepito's horse as it stood on its hind legs. Then animal and man disappeared in the deluge. Anson's throat tightened in fear as he reined his horse far over in a tight left turn. He caught a glimpse of Juanito riding toward him just before his horse turned, and then he felt the water slide under his horse and he was floating, the horse pawing the water to stay afloat. Behind him, the oak tree blazed and sputtered in the rain.

Anson looked around and saw Juanito and his horse swimming by and cattle all scattered and flailing the rising waters for their lives.

"Head for high ground," Juanito called, whipping his horse with the trailing ends of his reins.

"Where?"

"Follow me."

It seemed hours before Anson reached land that was not flooded. Juanito's horse stood on a little knoll, watching the cattle drift past. Snakes coiled and slithered all over the knoll and then disappeared back into the water as Anson rode up, his ears still ringing with the sound of thunder.

Anson looked back and saw his father's horse breasting the waters, veering to avoid the nearby cattle. He no longer felt anger toward him. "Thank God," he said. "Did you see Pepito?"

"Yes," Juanito said. "Too bad. Fidel did not make it either."

Dead cattle floated by, their heavy carcasses bobbing up and down in the water.

"I'm glad we're alive," Anson said.

"Yes, that is a good way to look at it. Life goes on, even when there is death."

Martin Baron's horse climbed from the water onto the knoll. Martin did not say anything as they all looked at the cattle floating by, and Anson knew that his father was crying, although he could not see his tears in the rain.

5

———————

ANSON BARON HAD just turned seventeen years old the week after Mickey Bone rode away from the Box B just before the big storm hit that part of Texas, slashing the land with flash floods, ravishing the cattle and the fields, drowning several head of prime crossbred beef that Juanito Salazar had raised from Argentine and longhorn stock. Anson still thought of Mickey often and wanted to talk about him to his father, but Martin Baron did not like Bone and would not say much about his leaving except "Good riddance."

"Why didn't you like Mickey?" Anson asked his father the day after the storm and the cattle stampede was over. The wind had blown part of the barn roof away, collapsed the posts of the main corral, overturned watering troughs and feed bins. The barn was still filled with standing water and Anson had been pushing the water and mud out with a makeshift rake that had no teeth, just a flat board nailed to a mesquite stick. The barn reeked of urine and horse apples and sunlight angled through the hole in the roof.

"I didn't trust him. He's an Apache." Martin was currying a young colt that was still skittery from the storm. He held the animal fast with a rope halter while he ran the currycomb over its muddy sorrel hide.

"But he didn't live with 'em."

"He's livin' with 'em now, ain't he?"

"I—I guess so."

"Well, there it lies, son. Do you need to get burnt to know what fire is?"

Anson, a dark-haired, hazel-eyed young man, looked at his father, tall and sunburned, and felt a distance grow between them again. Lately, his daddy had been riding him hard, treating him like a little boy in front of the vaqueros and Juanito. And his mother, Caroline, seemed uneasy around his father, and he often heard them arguing at night after he had gone to bed. Something was wrong and he didn't know what it was, but he wished his father wouldn't treat him like a child. Not when he was ready to grow up and be a man.

Anson pushed a wad of horseshit and mud out the back door of the barn, scooted it to a pile he had made. He lingered in the sunlight, free of the heady musk inside the barn for a few moments. The light wind tousled his hair and he liked the feel of it—silky fingers caressing his scalp, ruffling the open-throated shirt he wore. If he had his choice, he would be riding with Mickey Bone, going with him back to his tribe, the Lipan Apaches, living free, just him and his horse. He did not feel welcome in the house anymore. His mother was acting funny and seemed to be sick or mad all the time and afraid of something she would not name. His father was distant, angry at everyone and every-thing, snapping at him as if he was a cur dog.

"Don't dillydally," Martin said to his son.

Anson stiffened at the rebuke. Sometimes he felt like a slave. The va-queros had more freedom than he had. At least none of them had his fa-ther riding them all the time, cussing them out, giving them stupid orders. He went back inside the barn and pushed the flat trowel through the mud and straw and droppings, grunting as the load piled up.

Martin finished currying the colt and led him into a stall.

"We'll geld this one," he told Anson.

"When?"

"Soon as we get this barn cleaned up, a new roof put on."

"What about New Orleans? You said you'd take me on a drive."

"The stampede pretty much fixed that. We'll have to get a gather together again sometime."

"How long?"

"You ask a lot of questions for a runt."

"I ain't no runt," Anson said quickly.

"Well, no, I guess you aren't no more. Still wet behind the ears, though."

Anson suppressed his anger, said nothing.

"I been thinking about selling the boat," Martin said after a long silence. He looked up at the missing roof, squinted at the column of

light. "We could use some cash money. Your mother's been after me
to get rid of it. It has been a-settin' there in Matagorda for a time."

"How come you never let me sail with you, Daddy?"

"Never thought about it. Didn't know you wanted to." He had
sailed the boat for a long time to finance the ranch, hauling goods up
and down the Gulf Coast.

"I'd like to."

"Well, we could run up to Galveston or New Orleans, see if we
might find a buyer."

Anson stopped pushing the wooden blade. His face brightened.

"Me and you, Daddy?"

"I could use a hand."

"You'd show me how to sail?"

"Wouldn't do you no good if I sell the boat."

"I don't care. I'd like to learn how."

"I guess I could show you a thing or two. Things old Cackle Jack
taught me."

"I 'member you talkin' 'bout old Cackle Jack with Mother. What
happened to him?"

"He died."

"How?"

"We got caught in a storm in the Gulf. Cackle Jack made a mistake."

"Was he a good friend?"

"The best a man could have. I miss him like hell sometimes. 'Specially when I'm out on the boat."

Anson's senses quickened. This was a side of his father he hadn't
known. For a second or two he thought his daddy was going to cry.

"Was he as good a friend as Juanito?"

"They don't come no better than Juanito. Just different, that's all.
Cackle Jack and me were like father and son. Juanito's more like a
brother."

"I wish I had a brother."

Martin laughed. "Maybe you will one of these days."

Anson knew his mother was in a family way, but he hadn't thought
beyond that. He might have a brother or a sister. It wasn't something
he felt like talking about much. "When can we go out and sell your
boat, Daddy?"

"Why, I guess when the work is done here we can go give it a look."

Anson beamed. He was ready to leave right then. But at his father's
warning scowl, he took up the wooden rake and began pushing debris
out of the barn into the sun, where he wished he could stay all day
dreaming his young dreams.

6

JUANITO SALAZAR STOOD up in the stirrups watching the Mexican with Yaqui blood scout the ridge near the line shack at Frontera Creek. He admired the way Chato Manzana could track, the way he hugged his horse so that he presented no target to any waiting Apache. But Chato was half Indian himself, his mother Yaqui, his father Spanish. Years before, Juanito knew, Chato had been captured by the Comanches when he was a boy. They called him Pug Nose, which stood for years until the Texans fought the Comanches and freed him, sent him back to Mexico, where he was treated like an outcast because he was more Comanche than Mexican. They saw his nose and called him the same name as the Comanches had—Chato, or Pug Nose.

It was a tragedy in a way, since Chato did not remember his parents, who had been killed when he was taken prisoner. When the Comanches took away his Mexican name, they reduced him to a slave, and now that he bore a Mexican name, from the family that had adopted him, Manzana, and a first name that had been translated from the Comanche, he was even more removed from his roots. But that was the way of the New World, Juanito knew. He himself was an Argentine, but he had seen this Texas land and it had grabbed his heart, as it had grabbed Martin Baron's.

Just before the big storm, Chato had ridden up to the Box B headquarters at La Loma de Sombra and said that he had seen Cuchillo, the Mescalero Apache chief responsible for many depredations in the Rio Grande Valley, at the Frontera Creek headquarters. Martin knew that Cuchillo was on the rampage, but was powerless to stop him. Instead, he had hoped the Apache would attack him, since he had a cannon, a four-pounder, hidden in the barn. But the storm had stopped Cuchillo somewhere on his raid, and Chato figured he might be near Frontera Creek.

Now Juanito watched as Chato guided his horse along the shallow ridge above the scattered adobes that comprised the Frontera Creek section of the Box B. He reminded the Argentine of the jaguar in his native country. Chato moved his horse slowly along the ridge, hanging over its side so that you couldn't tell from this distance whether you saw a long horse or a horse with rider.

Chato stopped, motioning for Juanito to ride up. Juanito tapped spurs gently to his horse's flanks. The lean Arabian mare moved toward the ridge, its ears stiffened to sharp cones, twitching back and forth. He called her Scheherazade and she was black as anthracite, with big brown eyes and just the slightest blaze of white on her forehead.

Scheherazade climbed to the top of the ridge and Juanito reined her up when he came alongside Chato. The little adobes looked almost golden in the dazzling sunlight, their square corners etched sharply by the shadows. Droopy flowers in clay pots hung disconsolately around the doorways. It looked, Juanito thought, like a miniature ghost town. Not even a dog was to be seen.

"The creek rose above the banks," Chato said in Spanish.

"That is true. Do you see any sign of Lopez?" Ramón Lopez was the foreman. He and his son and his wife watched over the Frontera herd and property.

"No, I do not see him. There is water in the adobes."

"Let us ride down there and see if anyone is alive." Juanito had a queer feeling in his stomach, as if he had drunk from an alkali well. "I told Ramón not to build his adobes so close to the creek."

Chato said nothing.

It was very quiet. A water snake slithered away from one of the adobes as the two riders approached. The corrals were empty and the little garden that Lopez's wife, Conchita, had grown was under four inches of mud. Green stalks, bent to the weather, could be seen curving out of the mud like the tentacles of some sea creature.

Juanito would have expected to see some sign of the Apache depredation, but he saw no dead bodies or signs of a fire, no indication of any destruction by anything other than water. The soil was smoothed clean by the wash of the creek through the tiny settlement, that was all.

"*Hola*, Ramón," Juanito called.

There was a long silence in the dead air. The adobes looked like little earthen tombs on some stark plain where once life had teemed. It was as if the villagers had vanished into thin air.

"Listen," Chato said. He gripped his rifle, ready to bring it to bear at a moment's tick.

"Is that you, Juanito?" called someone.

"Where are you, Lopez?"

"I am coming," Lopez yelled back. A few moments later, Ramón, his wife, Conchita, and their son, Jacinto, accompanied by two young vaqueros emerged from the brush down the creek, a place that had not been cleared of mesquite. They looked to Juanito like the tattered remnants of a decimated gypsy band who had lost their homes and all their belongings. Their faces were smeared with mud, their clothes saturated with it. The men carried old flintlock rifles held together, stocks and barrels, with rawhide. Conchita looked a thousand years old, her hair stringy and matted with clay, her eyes red-rimmed from lack of sleep. The men looked little better.

A clutch of small children emerged from the mesquite thicket looking like beggars on some street in a faraway country. Their eyes seemed too big for their skulls and their dirty clothes were tattered and wrinkled.

"*Qué paso?*" Juanito asked of Ramón. "Were you driven away by Cuchillo?"

"There was a fight," Ramón said. "The Apaches. They came out of the trees, but we were ready for them. They could not see us. Our casitas were too scattered for them to come in close and they could not see us all. It was a trick we had planned for them."

"I do not see any dead here," Juanito said.

"We killed two of them, and they took them away. One came back after Cuchillo and the others had left. We shot this one, and I shot his horse. And then we had much rain and we had to leave. I think we can find this wounded Apache. He and his horse were swept away in the flood"

"What happened then?" Juanito asked.

"The water came flooding into our houses and we ran away into the mesquite. We thought Cuchillo might come back like the other one, but he did not. I do not know where he went. But we hid ourselves and waited in the thicket. If the Apaches had come back we would have been ready to fight them."

Peabody Public Library
Columbia City, IN

Juanito looked at Ramón and the other vaqueros. They were truly brave men, he thought, good soldiers. With their old rifles, they had fought off Cuchillo and killed two of his men. And they had possibly wounded or killed another.

"You have done well, Ramón, you and your vaqueros. You are very brave. Show us where you saw the wounded Apache go. Chato and I will track him."

"I think maybe he is dead," said one of the vaqueros. "There was much water, so much that one could not swim in it. It was like a little ocean."

"We will see if he is dead," Juanito said.

"And, if he is alive, we will kill him," Chato said, a chilling tone in his voice.

"We will clean up our homes and bring the stock back in," Ramón said.

"Ten cuidado," Juanito told him. "Take care."

Chato and Juanito rode off in the direction Ramón had pointed, the Apache in the lead, scanning the ground for signs that he might read. The two men carried their rifles across their pommels, thumb on the hammer, index finger inside the trigger guard.

The ground was still wet from the flooding. Debris was strewn everywhere—branches, plants, pieces of cloth and wood and clay utensils from the adobes. The ground was smooth where the creek had washed over its banks, the earth flowing in the direction of the raging waters that had swept overland the previous day.

Chato began to range back and forth over the course of the flash flood as Juanito followed, unable to spot anything but deer and turkey tracks and the occasional imprints of javelinas, doves and rats. In low places, pools of water stood shrinking under the heat of the sun.

Juanito kept watching for any signs of an ambush. He still did not know where Cuchillo had gone during the storm and suspected that he might be nearby. And if he was missing a man, he might come back for his wounded. Or he might also lie in wait for anyone who might track such a wounded man.

The trail wound in and out of the brush, and Chato found signs that the horse had gone down, floundered to get back up again.

"The blood washed away," Chato said, "but horse bad hurt."

"How about the Apache?"

"Hurt bad, too. Look." Chato pointed to a place where a man had dug into the mud with his fingers. Probably, Juanito thought, to pack his wound, or wounds. The digging had been done off to the side of the path of the flooding, possibly after the waters had subsided.

"How old is this track?" Juanito asked.

"Three, four hours."

"So he did not go far after he rode off."

"He wait for blood to stop."

Juanito looked back over his shoulder. So the wounded Apache had waited near the adobes after he had been shot. Probably heard everything that went on. Probably knew that Ramón and the others had gone away to hide.

There were signs, too, that the wounded Apache had tried to cover his tracks. Chato pointed out where brush had been cut with a knife and the tracks wiped away with leaves, like a broom. His trained eye could spot such things. He was slow and careful, sometimes riding around a place where the tracks were plain. Juanito appreciated Chato's attention to such things, for the skin on the back of his neck prickled at every fresh track that emerged seemingly from nowhere. He was a fair tracker himself, but Chato was uncanny.

Chato found another place where the horse had gone down. There was an impression in the earth that showed the wounded Apache had had a difficult time getting the horse back up. Several yards later, moccasin tracks showed that the Apache was no longer riding the injured horse. And as Chato pointed out, the horse was becoming difficult to lead. In several places the horse had stood long enough for its weight to sink the hoofprints deeper, and it was dragging one foot when it started up again.

Later on, there were signs that the horse the Apache rode was stumbling. Once or twice Juanito saw places where the horse's knees had left impressions. Chato rode on more slowly than before, circling the tracks, making little sound. Juanito followed warily, his senses attuned to every breeze, every breath of his horse. It seemed that hours had gone by, but he knew that that was only an illusion. The tracks seemed fresher, bolder, more pronounced, the longer the two men rode. Far off in the distance he heard the cry of a crow, and then Chato flushed a rabbit, which startled Juanito.

He wondered if the rabbit had gone into hiding because the Apache had passed close by only moments before, or if the Apache was still hours away, perhaps gaining strength as he walked. It was then that Juanito noticed that they were well away from the creek, heading in a southwesterly direction.

When they came to a shallow draw that wound through the mesquite, Chato reined up his horse. He waited for Juanito to ride up to him, then turned in his saddle. "We cannot see ahead, but I think we will find the horse there," Chato said.

"Why do you think that?" Juanito asked.

"Look at that place there. The horse went down and dragged his hindquarters a little ways. Then he got up again, but I do not think he could have walked much farther.''

Juanito saw the place where something heavy had made a bowl-like depression in the sandy bottom of the draw. And there were signs that whatever had fallen there had been dragged or pulled itself for several yards before getting up again. There were clear hoofprints after that, disappearing around the bend in the draw.

"Do you think the Apache is in there?" Juanito asked.

"No. I think the horse is in there. The Apache would not stay with it."

"What would he do?"

"He would kill it and go on, I think."

"Maybe we should ride around it and come in from the other end," Juanito said.

"I will go in from this side."

The two men parted company. Juanito circled the draw and came in from the other end where it was again shallow. He saw the horse, a pinto pony that would probably run fourteen hands high when standing. Then he saw Chato ride around the bend and come into view.

Chato dismounted and examined the brown, white and black paint horse as Juanito rode up close.

"It has not begun to smell yet," Juanito said.

"No. The horse has not been dead long."

"Did he cut its throat?"

Chato bent down and looked at the large slash in the horse's throat, just above the chest. The windpipe had been severed. The hair was matted down on the neck where the Apache had knelt on it to hold it down as it convulsed in its death throes. He lifted its head by its long black mane and the slash in its throat opened wide.

Juanito's stomach churned. "*Bueno*, it is dead," he said.

Chato rolled the pony over so that its belly faced Juanito. As it rolled, the belly opened wide. The pony had been slit from breast to anus. It made a hollow, rubbery sound as it came to rest, its sides jiggling. It was then that Juanito saw the entrails piled up on the other side of the pony, the intestines coiled and gleaming blue-gray in the sun, a cloud of bluebottle flies swarming over the heap.

Chato reached inside the empty belly of the pony and felt around with one hand. When he withdrew his arm, it was splotched with blood.

"He took the heart and liver," Chato said. He wiped his arm on his breeches—*whap, whap*—and stood up.

"Some reason?" Juanito asked.

"He ate them while they were still warm."

"The Apaches do that?"

"He wanted the horse's strength."

"We have to run him down."

"I know."

Juanito knew that Chato would make no judgment. He too felt bad about the Apache. But he was an enemy. He had to be found. If he fought back, he would have to be killed.

Chato mounted his horse. "Did you see the Apache's tracks when you rode up?"

"I was not looking for them. Sorry."

"It is no matter. We will find them."

The two men rode out of the shallow ravine. Chato picked up the Apache's tracks, sure enough, and Juanito felt ashamed that he had not been more alert. They were quite plain to see.

The moccasin prints led into the brush, along a game path that might have been present for thousands of years. The path wound through the mesquite and over dunes in sandy and rocky terrain. The spoor was sometimes difficult to follow, but Chato always found signs where the Apache had passed.

And now the trail grew warmer as Chato examined bent grasses that were still trampled down, some still quivering.

"He is close," he said to Juanito.

"I know." Juanito's heart was thundering in his temples.

Then they saw the blood trail, so fresh it glistened in the sun like barn paint. Juanito took in a quick breath and gripped his rifle until his knuckles drained of blood. He could almost smell the Apache now, almost scent his sweat, the gushing wound in his side leaking his life's blood. Large splatters of blood doused the bare rocks and stained the grasses where the wounded man had passed.

Chato reined up. He stared straight ahead at something Juanito could not see. Juanito stood up in his stirrups and that's when he saw the Apache. He was sitting against a tree, partially shaded by the leafy branches. And he was chanting something in low tones. Spiders bristled on the back of Juanito's neck and his stomach knotted.

"That is Ojo," Chato said. "He has but one eye."

"You know him?"

"I have seen him before, riding with Cuchillo."

"What is he doing?" Juanito asked.

"He is dying."

Chato rode closer. Juanito followed warily, his spurs cocked to jab into Scheherazade's flanks and send her flying away from danger.

The air bristled with a strange tension as Chato and Juanito rode closer to the dying Apache. It was then that Juanito realized Ojo had turned his back on them.

"Watch out," Chato murmured.

Ojo whirled around, a rifle in his hands. Before Juanito could move, Chato fired his rifle point-blank at the Apache. Juanito saw the Indian's bare chest twitch slightly and then blood ooze from it as he went slowly to his knees. His finger ticked the trigger of his rifle. A puff of smoke spumed from the pan as the powder flashed hot silver and then the ball whistled overhead like some wasp on a path to an unknown destination.

Ojo knelt there for a moment, staring at the two men with sightless eyes frosting over with the final glaze of death. Blood was still flowing from his previous wound: a bullet had apparently gone straight through his abdomen. It was a hideous wound, with a large, tattered hole at the exit wound. Ragged pieces of flesh hung down and the meat inside had ruptured, forming a bloody doughnut. Sanguineous rags lay at the Apache's feet. Then he pitched forward, still clutching his rifle, falling on it with a dull thud.

"He is dead," Chato said.

"If that is what you say."

"Should I take his scalp to show Señor Baron?"

"No, he would not like that."

"I will cut off his head."

"No," Juanito said. "That is not necessary."

"It is what one does with a snake."

"Just leave him, Chato. Let us ride away from here and return to the ranch."

"Cuchillo will find Ojo."

"I know," Juanito said. "This is far from over, this thing with the Mescaleros."

"Maybe it will never be over."

Juanito said nothing. He looked at the dead Apache, so pathetic now, so lifeless. Yet so brave. So merciless. How did one defeat such a people? How did one even begin to fight an enemy who was such a part of the earth that he was seldom seen and disappeared like smoke when he finished fighting?

"Go with God," Juanito said in Spanish as he and Chato rode away. *"Vaya con Dios."*

7

B ENITO AGUILAR WATCHED as his wife, Pilar, bathed the blind child, Lázaro. She dipped a cloth in an iron pan that stood heated on the stove. Lázaro was naked and Benito thought how perfect he was in every respect, except for his sightless eyes. Lázaro was not his child, but fathered by his brother, Augustino. Truly, he thought, this family was cursed. He had killed both Augustino and his sister-in-law, Victoria, the widow of his older brother Jaime, who had been killed by Apaches. Victoria later married Benito's younger brother, Augustino. Victoria was barren, but wanted a child by Augustino, so she had forced Pilar to bed Augustino and carry his child.

He wanted to hate Lázaro, but he could not bring himself to loathe the poor blind boy. And Pilar loved Lázaro, so Benito tried hard to show affection toward him.

It was early morning and Benito sat on the edge of his chair pulling on his boots made in Matagorda. The room was dark, since Pilar had not lit any of the lamps in the kitchen. She had stopped doing that weeks before. He supposed it was because she felt guilty about seeing when Lázaro could not see at all. She spoiled the boy, seemed to want to enter his world of darkness. He had noticed that she had become frugal with lamplight. But it was a minor irritation. If she wanted to be blind like the boy, that was a small thing, not worth mention.

He had dressed earlier, eaten a breakfast of tortillas, *biftec* and red beans soaked in *salsa casera* his wife had made from the tomatoes, chilies and herbs she grew in their garden. He wiggled his toes and stood up, satisfied that the boots would not pinch, for they were new, traded for in horns and hides, for he, like many of the other ranchers, had little money for such necessities.

"What will you do this day?" Pilar asked him.

"Pray," Benito said.

Pilar, who had aged so much over the years, looked up at him, her face framed by black hair streaked with ribbons of gray. It broke Benito's heart to look at her. In a way, now that she had the syphilis, she was as afflicted as Lázaro. Matteo hadn't understood and Benito knew the boy hated him. Someday he was sure to return to the Rocking A and demand retribution. If only he could explain to the boy how it had been, how Victoria had treated Pilar like a slave, a surrogate for her own mad desires to mother a child. Jaime, his older brother, had been the one with luck. The Apaches had killed him and he died a merciful death.

"What will you pray for?" Pilar asked.

"For our souls, my precious."

"I have prayed enough for both of us."

"It was just a joke, Pilar. My soul has long been consecrated to hell."

"Do not talk that way, my husband. It is not something to joke about."

"I know. I am just tired, *nada más.* Tired of fighting the land, of raising the cattle, of fighting the Apache and the Comanche, the bandits who ride up from Mexico across the Río Bravo."

"This land is paid for *en sangre,* Benito. Blood! You must see that it produces wealth for you and me, for our son, Lázaro."

Benito winced. Of course the blind boy would inherit the Aguilar lands—if they had not all been sold off before Lázaro grew to manhood.

"Some of the cattle have the pinkeye," he said. "I want to keep the rest of the herd from becoming infected."

"Be careful you do not get the disease yourself," she said.

"Why? Because it would make me blind?" He hated himself for that little cruelty, but he could not pass up an opportunity to open Pilar's mouth, let her speak what was in her heart. She talked mostly to the boy of late, seldom to him, her husband.

"There are worse things than being blind," Pilar said.

"And what would these things be? Having the syphilis?"

"Benito, you do not need to be cruel. And you should not speak of such things in front of Lázaro."

"What should I speak of? The black leg. It is a disease of cattle, like the pinkeye. Syphilis is a disease of the human being."

"Cállate," Pilar said. "Be quiet."

"Should the boy not hear of these things? How will he be a man? Have you told him that he has a little worm inside him that will eat his flesh until he becomes like a leper, and after that, the little worm will eat into his brain until he goes mad?"

"Benito, must you be so cruel?"

"I do not mean to be, Pilar. But you hide the truth from the boy. Even if he had eyes, he would never see through the darkness you throw over him like a cloak."

"It is not necessary that he know about ugly things."

"Y porque no? Is blindness a gift, then? As long as one can not see a thing it does not exist."

"I do not mean to say that," Pilar said.

"You make Lázaro feel that he is special, that God has given him blindness so that he may become a curandero, missionary, a messiah, perhaps."

"El es muy especial." Pilar never raised her voice as she laved her blind son with the hot cloth. She began to dry him, crooning to him beneath her breath as if he were a small child. Lázaro seldom spoke when Benito was in the room. As if he understood that there was some barrier between him and his father.

"Yes, he is special," Benito said wryly. "Like the cattle with the pinkeye. They cannot see and they become very dangerous, attacking every sound with their long horns."

"Ten cuidado, my husband."

"I will be home after dark, Pilar. Will you light a lamp for me so I do not have to stumble to my bed in the darkness?"

"Cómo no?" she said.

"Be a good boy, Lázaro," Benito said to the boy.

"Yes, Papa," Lázaro said.

As he left, Benito strapped on his pistol and grabbed his pouch and powder flask, along with his rifle. Always the weapons, he thought, always the danger. Always the Apache.

8

PILAR DRESSED LÁZARO quickly after Benito had left. The light was just seeping through the kitchen windows, spreading over the counters and the table like a thin cream.

"There," she said to her son, "you are immaculate and dressed in fine clothes."

"Thank you, Mama," he said. "Was Papa mad at you?"

"No."

"Was he mad at me?"

"No, my son. He loves you."

"Not like you do."

"Well, a mother's love is different."

"Special?"

"Special." She smiled.

"What is the syphilis?" he asked.

"It is not something to concern you. Papa was just talking. He is worried about the cattle."

Lázaro turned to his mother, smiled crookedly. She touched his face with her hand, caressing his cheek with the backs of her fingers. "You are very handsome," she said.

"Someday I will make you and Papa proud of me."

"I know you will, my son. Someday you will be a grandee. You will own much land and you will have a beautiful wife and be happy."

"I do not want you to ever go away from me, Mama."

"I will never leave you, Lázaro."

But even as she said the words, she did not know if she believed them. She would grow old and die someday. Would Lázaro truly grow to be a man and be able to live in his world of darkness with so many evils to fight, to overcome?

"Good," he said. "I love you, Mama."

"And I love you, Lázaro." She squeezed his hand and they walked out the back door to gather eggs even as the rooster was crowing at the rising of the dawn. And there were tears in her eyes as she thought of leaving the boy behind when she died. Leaving him all alone, at the mercy of the world. And behind her dread of Lázaro's fate was an even larger fear, one she and Benito had never discussed. But she knew that one day this fear would become a reality that they all must face. And the memory of another son loomed large in her mind. Matteo Miguelito, from her own womb, but not Benito's son. She had seen the hatred in his eyes before he had gone to Mexico. The hatred and loathing. Yes, Matteo Miguelito would be back someday, to claim what was rightfully his. What would happen to her beloved Lázaro on that day?

Pilar shuddered to think about it.

9

THEY EMERGED FROM the mists of morning by ones and twos and threes, like resurrected beings. They joined together in some mysterious way until they were a band once again, as if some secret signal had passed between them after the storm had scattered them and decimated their ranks. Mythical pieces of some slain giant come together again after the storm had passed, melded into one magnificent fighting unit once again by the sun. The Apaches rode their ponies as one being, in perfect unison, back toward Frontera Creek. Not a word was spoken among them, but all away from the empty space where a pony and rider had once been, where a friend and fellow warrior was no more.

Cuchillo had been driven away by the storm and the flooding, but he was not one to leave his wounded or his dead behind him. He returned to Frontera Creek with his braves and saw that the vaqueros were back in their casitas, cleaning up. They were all armed, carrying rifles and machetes and some standing guard. They had not regrouped their horses in the corrals and the cattle were scattered through the brush like deer.

He wheeled his horse from his concealed vantage point above the line camp and his braves turned their horses as if they all were on a single wheel and followed him as he picked up the tracks of Juanito

and Chato and Ojo. Cuchillo had been on such spoor before, and he
rode with a heavy heart, for he could read a blood trail as well as any
man raised with the earth and sky and all creatures brethren to him.

A day passed before Cuchillo read the signs in the sky and knew
that they would find dead things on their journey.

There were many buzzards in the sky and on the ground where
Ojo had slain his horse and eaten the animal's heart and liver. And
coyotes had been at the corpse during the night and early morning.
He ordered his braves to pile stones on the remains of the horse. Then
the Apaches rode on, staring at the circling buzzards riding the air
currents.

Cuchillo came to the place where Ojo had been slain. They scared
the vultures away and saw that the little dogs had fed on their com-
padre during the night, tearing at his flesh and bones, leaving a hideous pile of human remains and scattered, half-gnawed bones. Like a
man reading a map, he studied all the signs until he had absorbed all
the terrible secrets of the earth. They had found the dead pony and
Cuchillo had seen what happened there and now knew the whole story
of Ojo's last moments as a man before he became a spirit once again.

"We will bury this warrior with his brave horse and lay with him
the sacred objects of our people and the tools of war," Cuchillo told
the others. "We will not mention his name again, but we will hear it
in the wind and in the call of the owl. Ojo died bravely and his hair
was not taken. We will tell his widow where he lies and that he faces
the east. Go and do these things. Bring his pony to this place and pile
the rock high so that the coyotes and the buzzards will feed no more
on the flesh of our brave friend."

And when this was done, and the smokes had been offered to the
great spirit and tobacco to the four directions, the Apaches rode away.

Cuchillo's son, Culebra, rode with his father and asked him about
death.

"What happens when a man dies, my father?"

"There are many stories, my son. But I like one that I heard some
moons ago, one that satisfies me like no others."

"What is that, my father?"

"It is said that the Great Spirit lives inside each man, and when
the man dies, the spirit returns to the Father of All. A little spirit joins
a big one. We cannot see this spirit, but it is like the breath and it
leaves on the wind of death."

"I do not understand it."

"That is why I am going to tell you what I heard from one who is
not of our people, but it makes sense to me."

"Who told you this thing?"

"It was one of those whining, begging Lipan Apaches."

"You take this man's word?"

"It was not his word. It was told to him by another. The other was one of the men who killed our brother two suns in the past."

"I am very confused, Father."

"The one they call Mickey Bone talked with me some moons ago. He wishes to go back to his people, the Lipan, the Querechos. He was once called Miguel Hueso."

"I know the man," Culebra said.

"We spoke of death and he told me what he thought it might be. If we cannot see spirit, he said, then we must speak of things we can see in the mind."

"And what were these things?"

"Bone said that when a man dies, it is like the rattlesnake shedding its skin. It becomes new again. But, he said, death was more than that, more mysterious, and so I listened to him."

"And then what did this Bone say to you, Father?"

"He said that death was like a rattlesnake shedding its skin, only what emerges is not a snake, but a bird, and it flies off into the hidden world and all we see is smoke where it disappears. That is spirit, and maybe we hear the bird sing for a time, but once it has flown away it can never be heard or seen again in this world."

"That is a good way to see death," Culebra said.

"I hope you will tell your grandsons what I have told you."

"But you heard it from a Lipan, the filth of the world."

"Bone was only a messenger. He heard this thing from another as I have told you."

"And who is this other, Father?"

"You know this man too, but you have not spoken to him, nor have I had words with him. He is the one from far away who knows the heart of the wild cattle and brought the cattle from far away to make new cattle for Martin Baron. Bone thinks he is a curandero, a kind of holy man who heals the spirit, not one who heals the body. He says that he knows many words and has read the talking signs in the paper skins they call Bibles."

"He is the one who is not a Mexican, but looks like one and speaks the same tongue."

"Yes. He is called Juanito Salazar and he is from a place where they grow silver in the mountains. It is called Argentina in the Spanish tongue."

"Ah," said Culebra. "And do you think this Juanito is a curandero?"

"I do not know. But he is very strange and he speaks of unknown things like a wise man speaks. Bone thinks he is a medicine man."

"But if he killed our friend, then we will kill him."

"Yes, Culebra. We will kill him. Like Baron, like Aguilar, he is our enemy. We do not want him here, so we must take away his life."

"I would like to cut out his heart," said Culebra, who had not yet learned all there was to learn about war.

Cuchillo said nothing, but his lips pursed a little, as if he was smiling.

10

ROY KILLIAN FINISHED milking the Guernsey, flexing his fingers to take away the hurt and the stiffness. A pair of flies performed aerial acrobatics as the cow switched her tail from hip to hip. Roy slid the stool away and picked up the bucket. Old Nellie gave five gallons a day when she came fresh, and Roy's mother made butter which she sold to townspeople.

He carried the bucket to the house, listening to the trill of a meadowlark beyond the empty clay field across the road. In the distance, spirals of smoke from chimneys in Fort Worth hung in the sky. His mother, Ursula Killian, was already at her day's washing behind the house. A black kettle sat on the fire, the water boiling, steam rising in the air to join the morning mist.

Suddenly Roy stopped. Across the flat black plain, he saw a lone rider emerging from the mist. The rider looked vaguely familiar, but a person wrapped in the cobwebs of memory, well out of range of Roy's remembrance.

"Ma, somebody's comin'."

"Probably more washing." Ursula stood over the kettle, stirring the clothes through the hot water. A chunk of lye soap kept bobbing up in the froth, then disappearing into the steamy depths. She looked up, shaded her eyes from the rising sun.

"I don't see no wash," Roy said.

"Maybe someone come to buy a pie," she said.

Ursula and Roy eked out a sparse existence from the worthless land her husband had bought fifteen years before. Fort Worth was growing and building, and people needed their clothes washed and bought her apple pies. The orchard covered better than two acres, but the trees were stunted and gnarled and only pretty when they blossomed. The pies she made now were from apples harvested the previous fall and kept in the storm cellar, where spring water seeped through the cracks in the adobe brick and kept it cool.

"Well now, I wonder who that could be," she said to no one.

"Something familiar about him, that's for sure."

"I don't recollect that horse," she said. Then she saw the dog and something stirred in her, caused a pang deep in her stomach. "Nor that hound."

"Looks like a mongrel dog," Roy said.

The two stood there and watched the rider approach. He seemed in no hurry. As he drew closer, Ursula squinted her eyes as if to pierce the veil of mist and see the man's face.

"Lordy, who can that be?" she asked, not expecting an answer.

"Some stranger," Roy said.

Ursula stared at the rider, watching the way he sat his horse, a dark sorrel she had never seen before. Then she gasped and her breath caught in her throat. "It's a stranger, all right, Roy. May I be struck plumb dead if that ain't your daddy."

"My daddy?"

Roy's memory stirred. He conjured up a red-haired man from long ago—fifteen years, he guessed—who had a soft, deep voice and who came and went and brought him toys and clothes from town. He had not thought of his father much in the past few years. His mother thought his father might be dead. Someone had told them that his uncle had died, hanged by some Mexicans in the Rio Grande Valley, a few years back. Ten years, maybe.

"It 'pears to be. Lordy, I can't believe my eyes. But I know the way Jack sets his horse, and he's always got him a dog or two. Wonder what he's come back for. Back from the dead, likely."

Roy stood there stunned, frozen into immobility by the specter of his father, a man he hardly knew.

"Urs," the man said as he rode up into the backyard.

"Jack."

"You must be Roy," Jack Killian said. "Don't you recognize your daddy?"

"I reckon he don't know you, Jack," Ursula said. "We thought you was dead."

"Damned near, a time or two."

Jack swung out of the saddle, fished in his saddlebags, brought out a pair of bundles. He handed one to Ursula, one to Roy. The dog lay down underneath the horse, its tongue lolling between its teeth.

"Nice dog," Roy said.

"I call him Dab."

"Dab?"

" 'Cause he's got a dab o' this and a dab o' that in his blood."

At the sound of its name, the dog retrieved its tongue and cocked its head.

"What happened to them other three dogs you had, Jack?" Ursula asked.

"An Apache kilt 'em."

"Seems you lost a lot the past few years. Your folks and all."

At the mention of his parents, Jack's face darkened for a second and he swallowed hard to keep his feelings down. "Seems like," he said.

"Where'd you get Dab?" Roy asked.

"He got me. Started follerin' me out of Waco one day a year ago, comin' up to my campfire at nights."

"He looks as bedraggled as you do," Ursula said without rancor.

"Brung you something from Fort Worth," Jack said, changing the subject. "Some cloth for you, Urs."

Ursula did not open her package. She just kept staring at her husband, shaking her head. "Well, I swan," she said. "You ain't changed a bit."

"Some," he said. "Hardy's dead."

"I know. Hanged."

"Yes, hanged. For stealing horses."

"Same as you, Jack."

"I don't do that no more," he said.

Roy hefted the bundle in his hands. It was heavy. He opened it eagerly and his eyes widened when he saw what his father had brought him. He lifted the holster from the wrapping and smelled the new leather, marveled at the gleaming pistol.

"Gawdamighty," he said.

Jack grinned. "That's a brand-new Colt Army .44," he said. "I've got powder, cap and ball for you in my kit."

"My own pistol," Roy breathed. "To keep?"

"Jack," Ursula said, "what have you gone and done?"

"I met a man down on the Brazos who's going to drive cattle up from Texas to Fort Sumner. He hired me on and I wanted to come and get Roy to go with me. He's growed now, and time he got to be a man.''

"Just like that, huh?" Ursula said. "You go off to God knows where and don't write nor come by and you just ride up and want to take away my boy.''

"I'll leave you some money, too, Urs. I know the boy's probably a help to you.''

"You sonofabitch," she said. Then she threw the bundle of cloth at Jack and ran toward him, fists clenched. She began striking him on the chest as he held her arms. He did not duck or try to avoid the blows.

"Ma, don't," Roy said. "Leave him be." He looked at the pistol again and strapped on the holster. "Daddy, I'm a-goin' with you.''

Ursula stopped beating on Jack's chest and turned to her son, her face contorted with disbelief. "What did you say, Roy?"

"I want to go away with my daddy.''

"You fool," she said. "You're both fools. Crazy, to boot.''

Jack stood there, his face devoid of expression. The years dropped away as he looked at his grown son.

"You ride into town with me and you can pick out your horse and saddle, Roy.''

"Boy, I'd like that," Roy said.

Ursula looked at her son, then at her husband. "Before you go, you bastard, do you want to come inside and have some breakfast? I'd like to hear what you done with yourself all this time away.''

"Why, sure, Urs, I could put away some fodder. Maybe some of that good coffee you make.''

"Oh, you remember my coffee, do you?" she snorted, ending the phrase with a "humph.''

"I remember a lot of good things, Urs.''

She blushed then and turned away, walking toward the house, still shaking her head.

"That iron looks good on you, Roy," Jack said. "Feel comfortable?''

"It feels real good, Daddy. Thank you. I'm much obliged.''

"Can you ride a horse?''

"I sure can.''

"Well, we're going to ride a long way, you and me.''

Roy smiled. His father turned and strode toward the house. The horse stood there, reins drooping, and Roy looked at the horse for a long moment before he ran to catch up with his father.

11

C AROLINE BARON SAT on the divan in the front room, staring
blindly at nothing. She was only half listening to Martin. Her
mind had started to drift when he started talking. She knew it was
important to hear what her husband was saying, but she could not
quell the thoughts that rose up in her mind, the guilt she felt, the
insistent flap of remorse like a loose shutter in a rainstorm banging
the window frame.

She had relived that day in her mind over and over and still had
no explanation of her behavior, why she had succumbed to an urge
so elemental it surprised her. Some dark place in her heart had been
illuminated that day, some deep longing for the forbidden, she supposed, that had lain dormant all her life and had so suddenly risen up
inside her that she had no defenses. A man and a woman. Alone with
each other. Martin gone and Anson as well, and the closeness of him,
the musk of his manly scent. The overwhelming longing to give herself
to this man. The secrecy of it and the desire to taste the forbidden
fruit.

So sudden. So achingly beautiful. As if the two of them were locked
away in a garden out of time and space, just the two of them, and who
would ever know? Just a man and a woman. Wanting each other and
taking the chance in the quiet of her room, in the softness of her bed.

Martin's bed, too. Filled with roses for a time and full of his scent and Martin's and the exquisite scent of them both in her nostrils made her dizzy and faint just to think of it, the wickedness of it, the sheer delight of that wickedness even now and the shamelessness of infidelity. Even for that brief moment, just that one time. That one sweet time and now her head swam with it and she could feel the warmth in her loins, the touch of him, his fingers on her shoulders and back, his lips caressing her neck, and the perfect shape of them together on her bed, one into another and then just one—one being, one soul, one long flow of honey—and the raw words of sex humming in her ears, the liquid Spanish and the harsh English, and just the words made her back arch and pull him deeper inside her and lose all sense of decency and faithfulness, for that was what a man could do to a woman. She had lost all will, all shame and all pride just to give herself to such a man and to take from him until she swam in a dark warm sea and dug her talons into his back like some beast of prey, wanting to hold him and to keep him, to make him die in her arms so she could hold on to him long afterward and just keep him, keep him, oh, and she burned for him again and again in her dreams and in Martin's arms.

"Caroline? Caroline?What's the matter?" Martin's voice, breaking through the terrible reverie. Her hands flew to her face and she knew she had broken out, that the blood rush of her lust had flashed on her face like some crimson stain.

"I—I feel faint," she said.

"You haven't heard a word I've said, have you?"

Caroline shook herself back to the present, calmed the rolling seas of her mind until she could feel the hotness flow out of her face and neck and descend finally to her breasts, and she pulled her dress tighter to her so that her shame would not show through the buttons and Martin would not be able to see his handprints on her bosom, the handprints of a thief and a lover, the handprints of a savage, like she.

"I—I'm sorry, Martin. I—I had some discomfort."

"Are you all right?" Martin asked in a worried tone.

"Yes, yes, just fine. What were you saying?"

"I said I've decided to sell the boat. We need the money and I've little time for freighting anymore."

"Why, that's good, Martin. You've been talking about selling your boat for some time."

"I'm taking Anson with me. I'll teach him to sail while we try and find a buyer for the *Mary E.*"

"Anson?" Her heart seemed to flutter like some soft moth caught against the windowpane. "Both of you?"

"Yes," Martin said. "Why? Is there something wrong with that?"

Caroline struggled desperately to compose herself. Suddenly her world seemed to be turning upside down. She fought for control of her emotions, battled to gain some lost ground.

"I—I just thought you weren't going to go away again."

"Not to New Orleans. Not right away. I'm just going to sell the boat. I think I can find a buyer real quick."

"But if you take Anson. . . ."

"Juanito's going with us, too."

"Juanito?"

"Yes. We'll sail up to Galveston, maybe to Corpus. Let Anson get his sea legs."

Caroline felt claustrophobic, trapped. She would be left all alone again. She searched for something to hold on to in the raging sea of her emotions. She looked up at the set of longhorns above the front door, remembered when Martin had brought them into the house, all polished up by Carlos, the butt ends wrapped in colorful swatches of a Mexican blanket. He had put them up there to remind himself of why he had come to this country. Now the room was filled with mementos of the hard days they had endured on the ranch: a branding iron by the fireplace, branches of dried mesquite in a vase on a hand-hewn table by the window, a pair of old spurs hanging next to a worn bridle and bit, her first straw broom leaning in a corner, ashtrays made of longhorn hooves and brass, Martin's old rifle on the mantel with its huge Spanish lock and frayed pouch for lead balls, a powder horn from a longhorn tip. So many things that belonged to the land and none from the sea—no compass, no sextant, no barometer, no ship's wheel.

"Martin, you're just not thinking," she said. "I'm going to have this baby and here you go, traipsing off again."

"The baby's not due for some months, Caroline. Besides, this will be a chance for me to show Anson something about sailing. He wants to learn."

"I don't want Anson to be a sailor," she said flatly.

"Something wrong with that?" Martin bristled.

"No, of course not. It's just that he—he's not like you."

"What in hell do you mean by that?"

"I mean, he—he's different. He doesn't know the sea. I don't want him to go where it's dangerous."

"Jesus Christ, Caroline. It's dangerous anyplace he might be. This is just nonsense."

"No, it isn't, Martin. I don't want you to leave me alone."

"Carlos will look after you. The Mexican women. You won't be alone."

She wanted to scream at him, to shake him until he understood the terror she felt in her heart. She wanted to make him see the darkness welling up in her, the fear that gripped her whenever he went away. The storm had stopped him from taking cattle up to New Orleans and he had promised that he would not leave her again, at least until after the baby was born. But now he was ready to go out to sea and play with his boat like a little boy.

Caroline clenched her fists in rage. She glared at Martin and hoped he could see the murderous light in her eyes. Was he so blind he could not see the terror in her heart, the dread that stalked her day and night?

"Carlos is barely able to speak English," she said tightly.

"So? You speak enough Spanish to get by. Caroline, look, we'll only be gone a week or so. I promise. The *Mary E* is a sound boat and she'll bring a quick sale and a good price."

"Can't you just send Juanito to sell your old boat?"

Martin's face twitched as if she had slapped him. "I built that boat from scrap with my bare hands, Caroline. It was just a hull and I made her into a sloop."

"I know your feelings about your boat, damn you."

"I'm trying to make the best of a tough situation, Caroline. Can't you see that?"

"You promised you wouldn't leave me alone anymore."

"I never promised you that. I can't be underfoot every minute of the day."

"You can be a husband," she said, blurting it out before she had thought it through.

"What do you mean by that?" he said, a perilous edge to his voice. "You got a complaint about me?"

"I—I didn't mean it that way, Martin. It—it's just that, with the baby and all, I'm—I'm afraid to be left alone."

Martin rose from his chair, the anger showing on his face. The muscles of his neck bulged, the veins in his throat pushing against the skin like blue snakes ready to strike.

"God damn you, Caroline, grow up. You ain't got your mamma to tuck you in no more. I've been a good husband to you and now you make me feel like I'm a prisoner, that I can't go anywhere unless I have your permission. Well, it doesn't work that way and it's not going to work that way. I'm taking Anson and Juanito to Matagorda and I'm going to sell my boat and pay some of these men who've been breaking their goddamned backs for me these past few months, and if you don't like it, you can run right back to Mama and Papa where you'll feel safe and protected."

She felt the fury of his displeasure and the force of his words drive her back inside herself, into that corner of her being where she felt safe, where she could hide from the dread.

Martin stalked from the room. She heard a door slam in the kitchen and then the silence rose up about her and she heard a board creak and tick for a second and she sat there numb and broken inside, more afraid than ever, desperate to cry out to Martin, to draw him back to her and have him hold her and caress her and whisper into her ear that he would never leave her, that he would stay with her, even though the child she was carrying inside her was not his.

A few moments later, she heard the plaintive notes of a guitar and then the voice of one of the vaqueros singing a *son huasteco*, one of the folk songs that told of a man gone wrong for the love of a woman, arrested and put in jail, then hanged before his weeping lover in the town plaza.

Caroline wished she had a song to sing that would tell of the hurt she felt inside, of the guilt she felt over what she had done and could not speak of for fear of losing all that she had, all that she ever cared about. *Martin is not the father of my child.* She heard the words uttering silently in her mind. And then she began to weep until the night filled up with her sobbing and became an undertone to the sad notes strummed on a faraway guitar.

12

MATTEO MIGUELITO AGUILAR looked across the room at the man who had just come into the cantina. There was something familiar about him, but he could not remember where he had seen him before. His clothes were dusty and wrinkled; his hat looked as if it had been dragged behind a horse. He wore an old flintlock pistol tucked into his belt and carried a pouch and powder horn. He wore spurs on his battered boots, small-roweled and rounded, like a vaquero's, and the heels were hardly worn at all.

Matteo knew the man was not a Mexican, although he wore the garb of a vaquero. His hair was black and straight and his cheekbones burned with the blood of Yaqui or Apache. The man must have balls, he thought, to come into a Mexican cantina. Alone, at that.

The man ordered mezcal at the bar. He dropped some pesos on the boards that clanked as they struck together. The barkeep, a rotund Mexican wearing a grimy apron, did not look at the man, but grabbed a glass and poured it full, then snatched up the pesos and returned to his conversation at the end of the bar with two women and a rheumy-eyed *campesino* from Sonora.

The cantina was almost empty. One other table was occupied by two horse thieves who wore wide-brimmed straw hats and spoke the gutter language of illiterates. Matteo had come in to meet a man who owed him money and to get away from the house where he lived with his wife and son. She was an ambitious woman who constantly nagged him, complaining that she lived in a hovel when they were entitled to be rich. But he owned a fine house in Matamoros, and he knew it was temporary. He would go to his family's ranch and claim it when the time came.

The man at the bar turned and looked for a table. On an impulse, Matteo motioned to him and pointed to an empty chair at his own table. The man hesitated for a moment, then strode toward him.

"Sit down," Matteo said in Spanish.

"Many thanks," the man replied.

"Do I know you?" Matteo asked. "Your face is familiar to me."

"You were just a boy when last I saw you, Matteo."

Matteo's face darkened. "That was a long time ago."

"Yes."

"What do you call yourself?"

"Mickey Bone."

"I do not know anyone by that name."

"Miguel Hueso." Mickey sipped the mezcal and kept his eyes on Matteo as he drank.

"Yes. The mestizo. You worked for Baron. You do not work there anymore?"

"No."

"Ah, there was trouble."

"No. I am looking for my people, the Lipan Apache. The Querechos."

Matteo leaned forward. Perhaps this was the man he was destined to meet at such a time in his life. Now he remembered him, for even when he was a boy, Hueso was a man who was spoken about. He was a mysterious man, a half-breed Apache, part Yaqui, perhaps, who had been raised by Mexicans. He was a man born to be with cattle. A tracker, a good shot. His father had spoken of him often.

"The Lipan are all gone, or else begging on the streets of Laredo and Juarez or hiding in the mountains. You do not want to find them, Mickey."

"I think I do," Mickey said.

"They can give you nothing."

"They can give me back my spirit. It is scattered to the winds. I am not a white man. I am not a Mexican. I am not even an Apache anymore."

"Where did you get these thoughts, my friend?"

"Do you know Juanito Salazar? The one who is from Argentina?"

"Ah, yes, that one. He is very wise, they say. I remember seeing him with Martin Baron when my mother would talk to them and sell them land.''

"Yes, Juanito is a very wise man. He seems to know the heart of an Indian, although his knowledge is very old, from another time, perhaps.''

"I know nothing of this," Matteo said. "He is just greedy like the rest of the gringos.''

Mickey swallowed half of his mezcal. "I do not think so," he said.

"He does not know your people. He must have had a reason to send you away.''

"He did not send me away. He said that I must follow the journey of my heart. He said that if my people called to me in my dreams then I must find them and go to them and find out who I am.''

"That is a strange thing to say. Will you have another drink?''

"I just stopped in to taste the mezcal before I ride on to the south.''

"Well another drink, then. Two is better than one, eh?''

"I will have one drink with you, Matteo. If you will answer a question from me.''

"The string is attached, eh? Very well, ask your question and I will answer it." He lifted an arm and beckoned to the barkeep. "Two more," he called out.

The low-ceilinged cantina was dimly lit, with a dirt floor covered with sawdust, tobacco spit and urine. The bar itself was just a wide board resting on a pair of barrels, with no stools. The tables were made from scrap lumber, the chairs from half-barrels covered with worn cowhide and brass tacks. Three lanterns shed the only light in the dimly lit room. If the catina had once had a name, it was now gone from memory and the paint on the false front washed away by wind and rain.

The barkeep brought the bottle of mezcal and poured two drinks. He swept up the coins Matteo had laid out for him.

"Now, Mickey," Matteo said when the barkeep had gone back to his conversation at the far end of the board bar. "What do you want to ask me?''

"Why did you leave the Rocking A?''

"You do not know?''

Bone shook his head.

"My uncle Benito murdered my mother and stepfather. And then he told me the *mentiras*, the lies. He said that Victoria was not my real mother. He said that Pilar, his wife, had given me to the light.''

"You do not believe this?''

"No. I think Benito would have killed me, too. So I ran away. I have taken a wife. I am just waiting for the day when I can go back and kill them all, Benito and Pilar and that little blind *hijo de puta* Lázaro.''

Bone drank the mezcal and studied the face of Matteo. He saw etched there all the hatred of the years in exile. Swirling in the depths of Matteo's brown eyes he saw pain and anger mingled with the resolve to avenge his mother's death.

"When will you do this?" Bone asked.

"I do not know. I want to have power when I go back to the Rocking A. I want to have money, lots of money. I will do this, Mickey. And someday I will go back there and kill my uncle and his wife, those *mentirosos.*"

"Then that is what you must do," Bone said. He could understand it. Matteo felt cheated out of his birthright. Sometimes he felt the same way, as at this very moment. He wanted to find his people and learn from them who he was, who he might have been if he had not been captured by Mexicans and raised in another culture.

As if reading his thoughts, Matteo asked Bone: "Do you know your father, Mickey?"

"No. I do not remember him much."

"I remember mine. Jaime Aguilar was a great man. And he was married to a noble woman. My mother wanted us to have the biggest and best ranch in Texas. She helped my father obtain the Spanish land grants. It was only hard times that forced her to sell some of the Aguilar lands to that gringo Baron.''

"He will buy more from Benito, I think."

Matteo's eyes flashed and he clenched a fist, then smashed it hard onto the table until the glasses clattered like dice in a cup. "No! Baron will get no more land." The others in the room paid no attention to this outburst, did not even look up.

"And if he does?"

"Then I will take it back. Mickey, I have been talking secretly with some Apaches I met. They are men who come to my small ranch down south and I give them beef and tobacco. They will help me when I take back my father's ranch."

"Apaches are like the leaves that blow in the wind, Matteo. They do not believe anyone owns the land. They believe the Great Spirit gave it to them and that they are the ones who should watch over it. They do not like houses that do not move, that block their hunting trails. They believe the land belongs to them and the buffalo, and if they do not fight to get it back, they will be like the buffalo, gone forever."

Matteo laughed harshly. "That is why they do not own land, why they will never have anything. They will be driven off like the buffalo."

"I think this is so," Bone said. "I know it. They do not yet know it. But I too am Apache."

"You are no longer an Apache. You have crossed a line. You are like the Mexicans who are no longer Spanish. You must mix in with the races that own the land, the Mexicans and the *norteamericanos.* That is how you will survive. I will take back all the land that was once my father's."

"Baron will fight you."

"I know. But if I have the Apaches on my side, he will not win."

"The Apaches may not help you. And if they do, they will only turn on you and take back what you have taken."

Matteo laughed again. "We will see, eh? Maybe they will become my children. I will feed them and take care of them and they will work, become vaqueros."

Bone finished drinking the mezcal, wiped his mouth on his sleeve. "Well, I am leaving now," he said. "I wish you good luck."

Matteo stuck out his arm, grabbed Bone by the wrist.

"When I go back to the rancho I want you with me, Mickey. I will make you a good offer to come and work with me." He released his grip on Bone's wrist and sat back in his chair. He held up his glass to the light and nodded at Bone. "You and I will be *ricos.*"

"I may not come back from that place where I go."

"You will come back. You have had a taste of the beef that grows on that land up there. You can never get the taste out of your mouth. You will come back with a wife of your own and you will want to live on the land so that you will not blow away like the leaves that drop from the oak trees in winter."

"I do not know."

"When you go to the mountains and find your people, look at how they live. Ask them if they know of me and how I treat them. Then make up your mind."

"You have talked to the Lipan?"

"Yes. Some of them are tired of begging, but they are afraid of the Mexicans. They are thinking of going up north where they might be treated better."

"I will see them. I will ask them what they think."

"Good. Then you come to see me and we will go back to the Rocking A together. You will never have to worry about a home again."

Bone looked into Matteo's eyes for several seconds, but he could no longer read what was in them. He knew only that Matteo was a formidable man. He had grown from the skinny, big-eyed child who had run away in the night. He had grown into a man and he would surely take back what had been taken from him.

"I will see you, Matteo," Bone said simply, and turned away.

"I am sure you will, Mickey." He watched Bone as he left the cantina and smiled. He knew it was no coincidence that Bone had come here on this night. He believed in fate and he believed in his own destiny, the promise his mother had made to him.

"You will inherit this ranch," she had said, "and you will be the most powerful man in Texas. People will respect you and pay you tribute. You will be a very great man someday because Aguilar blood flows in your veins. Do not ever forget that."

And Matteo Miguelito Aguilar never had, never would.

13

U RSULA LOOKED ACROSS the table at her husband, Jack Killian, a man she hardly knew anymore. But she felt the powerful tug of him, the magnetism he generated even after all the years they had been separated. He seemed changed somehow, but she did not know in what way. He was older, of course, but there was something in him that she could sense but not identify.

"You look well, Jack."

"I am well. Yes."

"It's been a long time."

"Yes, I'm sorry."

"You sent us money from time to time."

"When I had it to send."

"Roy missed you."

Roy hung his head, embarrassed. He had been watching his mother and father, dazed that they were sitting at the same table together, still elated that his father had given him a pistol and was going to buy him a horse.

"Did you, boy?"

"I wondered where you was, Daddy, I sure did."

Jack laughed, tousled his son's hair. Roy drew away slightly.

"Still don't know me, do you?" Jack said.

"I have to get used to you, I guess."

"You'll have time for that."

Ursula broke in. "Do you have to go into Fort Worth right away, Jack? Can't you stay the night?"

Jack looked at his wife, surprised. He looked around the room, a small space between the front room and the kitchen. There was not much that had changed. He had built the sod house with sweat and muscle, had furnished it with cheap furniture built by Mexican carpenters. Ursula had decorated the house with what she had: scraps of cloth, a rug she had bought since he'd gone, little knickknacks here and there. It was a cool, comfortable place.

"I wouldn't think you'd want me around that long."

Ursula looked coyly at him, drawing herself up straight in her chair, tilting her head slightly. "Why, Jack, you been gone a long time. A woman doesn't forget her man just like that. Stay the night, please."

Jack looked at his son, then back at his wife. He seemed to regard her curiously, as if they had never met. She knew he was wondering about her, how she might have changed, how it might be to lie in bed with her again, and she could feel his warmth across the table, and once again longed for his loving arms.

"I reckon it won't hurt none to stay the night. Get an early start in the morning."

"Good," Ursula said, her smile radiant. "Roy, why don't you put up your daddy's horse and grain him?"

"Rub him down if you want, Roy," Jack said.

"Sure, Daddy. I'll take real good care of your horse. He's a mighty fine-looking gelding. What's his name?"

"I call him Nomad. Do you know what that word means?"

"Kind of like a gypsy," Roy said.

"Close enough. It means wanderer. Maybe a desert wanderer. Like me."

Roy got up from the table. His mother gave him an indulgent smile, hoping he would take a long time to put up Jack's horse. "Don't hurry none, Roy," she said. "You take real good care of Nomad."

"I will," Roy said and dashed from the room. The front door banged shut a few seconds later.

"It's good to have you home, Jack. I missed you. Worried about you."

"I treated you bad, Urs."

"We don't need to talk about that now. Since you're staying, I'll fix you a good supper like I used to and we can talk about old times. I want to know what you've been doing with yourself."

Warily Jack Killian leaned back in his chair and brought the coffee cup to his lips as if he wanted to put space and objects between him and Ursula. He glanced sidelong at her as if to assess whether or not he was being judged. Ursula softened her look and smiled at him in reassurance.

"I guess not much, when it's all toted up," he said. "Maybe I was trying to find something."

"And did you find it?" Ursula asked softly.

"I didn't know what I was looking for, exactly. Maybe something I had inside all the time, or what I was made of."

"You always knew what you were made of, Jack. You took up with a pretty bad bunch."

"I reckon," Jack said, leaning forward. He did not feel so threatened now. Ursula thought that he looked as if he detected a glint of understanding in her eyes, and she wondered if he might have discerned something in the way she asked questions. Perhaps she appeared more sympathetic than he might have expected. She hoped that he accepted her curiosity as coming from a friend, not an enemy. "I thought they was good boys, but then I seen what they was doin' to Hardesty. He went plumb loco doin' the bad things."

"And you?" Ursula asked, her eyebrows curving to arches.

"A man gets out there beyond the law, Urs, somethin' happens to him. He don't notice it at first, but one day he's gone and done somethin' so bad it makes him sick inside. He knows he's done wrong, maybe not by any law that's wrote down, but wrong for him, and he gets to knowin' his days all have numbers on them and the numbers are gettin' smaller. Finally he knows if he don't go somewhere and make things right, he ain't never goin' to get another chance."

"Is that what happened to you, Jack?" Ursula's voice was very quiet.

"Not all of a sudden. I had some pure mean in me that had to get out or wore off and I just kept goin' deeper and deeper into badlands and I was plumb hell-bent on killin' something, me or somebody else, and I got to where I didn't much give a damn."

"And then," Ursula almost whispered.

"And then," Jack said, letting out a breath so that it sounded like a faraway wind building up, "I run into some men with dreams of building a big ranch, the biggest ranch in the whole world, and I guess some of what they were doing made me see how damned worthless I was."

"Worthless?"

"I wanted to kill a man I didn't even know. Worse, I don't think he was the right man. I mean he might have been the man who hanged my brother, Hardy, but he might not have been. I was going to kill him anyway because I had gone so far beyond the law that I thought maybe I was the law and I could do any damned thing I wanted."

"Maybe you're too hard on yourself, Jack. You didn't kill him, did you?"

"No, but not because I didn't want to. I wanted to and I was stopped from killing him. I was driven out of a place that took me in when I had nothing. My horses had been stolen, my dogs killed brutally. I had nothing but a rifle and no good sense when a man named Juanito Salazar came and fed me, and his friend, Martin Baron, gave me a place to stay, a horse, a job. And then gave me back my life."

"What do you mean?"

"He gave me a choice. To live and give up on killing a man, Benito Aguilar, or to ride away."

"And you rode away," Ursula said calmly, but there was tension in her voice. She knew what she felt was more than curiosity, more an urgent gladness that Jack was going to open his heart to her, show her his soul.

"I rode away, but I should have stayed, Urs. I rode away because I was full of hate and hurt. I wanted to avenge Hardy's death, or thought I did."

"But that wasn't the real reason, was it, Jack?"

"No. I really wanted to kill myself, I think. I had lived in a dark world so long I couldn't see any light. I couldn't get out of my own damned cage. I had been so far beyond the law, I didn't know what the law was no more."

Ursula sighed. "My," she said.

"I rode as far away from the Box B ranch as I could, but I kept feeling the pull of that land. And that Juanito had told me some things that made me think. And I thought and thought and rode and rode and I didn't know where I was going. And I didn't care."

"What things did this man tell you, Jack?"

"Juanito talked about life, but he talked about it like no man had ever talked about it. He made it seem a precious thing, almost holy, you know? He said life was all there was and it was everything and it never stopped with death, but went on and became something else forever."

"He sounds like a preacher."

"No, he never preached, it just come out of him like breath and sunk in deep, and it seemed real ordinary, yet way beyond ordinary, and I could see that he took life serious but wasn't afraid of death. Now, *that* was something I never seen before."

"You're not afraid of death, are you, Jack?"

"I don't know, Urs. Sometimes I am. Until I met this Juanito, who is from Argentina, I thought death was just the end of everything. You died and didn't have no memory and it was all over. So I guess I didn't care."

"But Juanito told you different," she said.

"Sort of. It just kind of came out of him in little ways, hardly noticeable unless you thought about it. And when I was riding away from my own death, I kept thinking of all that he said and trying to put it together in my mind, trying to put it all in one piece so I could see what all it was."

"And did you?" she asked, her voice almost breathless, so soft she could hardly hear it herself.

"Not right away, and not even now. But enough of it so that I knew Juanito was probably right, that life is not something that just happens for a time, but has been happening before time and goes on beyond time."

"That's pretty deep," she said.

"I know, and it don't make sense sometimes. Only if you could hear Juanito talk and how he says these things, then you know he's right on the mark."

"So you changed," she prompted.

"I guess so. I ended up on the Brazos and met Charlie Goodnight, and he had that same fire in his eye I seen in Baron's. He hired me on and it was like going back to the Box B, only I was some smarter, I guess, and I got to thinking maybe life was pretty good without revenge and without stealing. Maybe some men was right in putting down roots and staying put and I was wrong in being footloose and hell-bent and maybe I should slow down and learn some things."

"And you did."

"I reckon. I got to thinking about you and Roy and what I had give up and then Charlie said he had this idea to take cattle and drive them a long ways and sell 'em and then someday open up trails all over and take beef from Texas to places where they didn't grow none. I liked that notion, so I said I'd like to scout for him since I had rode that country where he was going, and he said I could have the job. I told him I wanted to bring my son down to go with me and he said that was all right. So here I am."

Ursula reached over and touched the back of Jack's hand, tapped it gently. "I'm glad you came," she said. "I'm glad you're taking Roy with you. Maybe it was meant to be."

"Urs, I'm damned sorry I stayed away so long."

"Well, you're back now. Water under the bridge."

She drew her hand back and picked up her tin coffee cup. She brought it to her lips, regarded Jack over the rim with a sense of wonderment. She wanted to pinch herself or yell out her happiness, but she had the feeling that Jack was sitting on the edge of his chair like a bird perched to take flight at any instant. She did not want to startle him, scare him away. He would leave again soon enough, and this time it would be different. She would not have Roy to keep her company, to keep her mind off the terrible loneliness she felt every day and every night.

She wished that she could just draw him into her arms and keep him from leaving. But, she knew Jack was uneasy, uncomfortable, even though he had changed. He was a man used to the wilderness, the freedom of the open places. He was like a wild thing, she knew, not yet tame enough to pet or feed by hand. She vowed to step carefully so that he would not jump and run away before she had the chance to make him feel at ease.

"Do you want your coffee warmed, Jack?"

"Good coffee. I'll take some."

Ursula arose from her chair and walked the few steps to the kitchen. She returned with the coffee pot, poured it carefully into Jack's cup so that the grounds would not flow out as rapidly.

"It's Arbuckle's," she said.

"The best. Long time since I've had really good coffee. Some of the stuff the cookies made tasted like it was made with iron filings."

Ursula laughed. "You can taste the cinnamon in Arbuckle's."

"That's right." Jack sniffed the tendrils of steam that rose from his cup. Ursula filled her cup and took the pot back into the kitchen, set it on the wood stove, next to the smoldering fire box.

She paused by the kitchen window and looked out at the apple orchard she and Jack had planted. She was using apples she had dried last winter for her pies, but the trees were blossoming and there would be new apples in the fall. She had started a peach orchard and planted some persimmon trees in the years Jack had been gone, but they had not matured yet. And, she had tried to nurture Concord grapes without any success. The vines hung lifeless beyond the orchard next to the pig sty she and Roy had built so they could raise meat for the winter and now there was a smokehouse with hams curing in the mesquite smoke.

"Would you like some ham for supper, Jack?" she asked when she returned to the table.

"You got pork? I ain't et none in many a moon."

"We've been raising pigs. We got a smokehouse, too."

Jack eyed her curiously. Ursula smiled. There was so much he did not know about her, secrets he would never know, if she could help it.

"You surprise me, Urs. You done well by yourself, you and Roy."

"We've managed."

"More than managed, I'd say. You bake pies and sell them. I'll bet you make some fine cider, too."

"I have some in the spring house. Would you like a taste?"

He waved a hand in the air. "No, you might spoil me."

"I'd like to do that, Jack."

Jack squirmed in his chair. "Some time, maybe. I really want to go on this cattle drive with Goodnight."

"I know you do. And, it'll be good for the boy. Make him grow some."

"You've done right well with him, Urs."

"Why, thank you, Jack. He's been a right nice boy. A big help to me."

"I guess you can manage for a time without him."

Ursula suppressed a smile. Men were so gullible and Jack was no exception. "Sometimes the soldiers come out to help," she said. "I do their laundry and they like my pies."

"Soldiers?" Jack said, his eyes blinking like semaphore lanterns.

"From the fort. I get most of my business from the soldiers."

"Well, yeah, I guess you would," he said lamely.

"Real nice boys, too," she said, with a saccharine tone that was deliberate. "Always willing to help a lone woman with the chores, bringing us cut wood for winter, blankets and such."

"What such?" Jack asked.

She recognized the nervous twitch in a neck muscle that had always given him away.

"Oh, whatnots. Cloth and thread and beads, lye soap. Little things."

"You might want to watch what them soldier boys bring you. Them things might have a lot of strings stuck to 'em." The drawl, too, told her that Jack did not want to hear that other men might be interested in her. She was sure that he still thought of her as his woman, even when he was far away.

"Oh, I'm careful, Jack. I know my bounds."

"I'm mighty glad to hear that."

"Still, they do seem to know the way to a woman's heart. Why, sometimes they'll come out of a summer evening and bring their guitars and jews' harps and serenade me and Roy. Real nice voices, too."

"I doubt they come out here at night to serenade Roy," Jack said sarcastically.

"Oh, Roy really likes it when they do that. Sometimes he hums along with them. The songs that he knows, of course."

"What songs?"

"Oh, 'Green Grow the Lilacs,' and some of the old hymns."

"The soldiers sing hymns?"

"On Sundays they do."

Jack shifted his position in his chair and sipped some coffee. Ursula could almost see the thoughts in his brain churning around, twisting one way and then another, turning over and over like a chunk of meat roasting on a spit. She had to steel herself to keep from breaking out in laughter.

"God, the soldiers ride way out here on Sunday nights? They must be soft. Why in hell aren't they out chasing Comanches? Christ."

"Now, Jack, don't get riled. They fight Indians and do a lot of hard work. But sometimes they don't have nothing better to do and they are always nice to keep me and Roy company. No harm in that."

"No harm at all," Jack said, but there was a thinness to his voice that belied his sincerity.

Ursula said nothing. She finished drinking her coffee.

"Anything I can do around here?" Jack asked. He seemed even more uncomfortable.

"I've got some washing to do. You can either keep me company or visit with Roy. I'm almost finished."

"I think I'll see what Roy is up to," Jack said. He pushed his chair away from the table, swallowed the last of his coffee.

"You might want to bring your things inside, put them in our bedroom," Ursula said pointedly.

"Yeah, yeah," Jack said, a gravelly husk to his voice. "I better do that, I reckon."

Ursula smiled indulgently, trying not to gloat. She felt almost like a black widow spider inviting its mate into her webbed lair. She knew that once the female spider had finished mating, she killed the male, wrapped him up in a silk cocoon and feasted on him at her leisure. But she wasn't going to kill Jack. She was just going to take him to her bed.

She set her cup down and walked toward the front room, with Jack following behind her. She deliberately swayed her hips so that he could see that she was still very much a woman. She stopped briefly at the front door and glanced back at her husband.

Jack looked like a man who had been caught while watching a woman taking her bath.

Ursula smiled coyly at him and pranced out the door, a becoming bounce to her step, a startling confidence in her mien.

And Ursula smiled with satisfaction as she heard Jack clear his throat a few steps behind her.

14

THE *MARY E* bobbed at anchor in the harbor at Galveston, swaying gently on her moorings, graceful as a swan, a bright white sloop glistening in the afternoon sun. Other sailing ships were at anchor or were being unloaded at the docks, but none stood so proud as the small vessel, her tattletale whipping in the wind, her sails furled, her mainmast jutting up into the blue sky like a battle lance. Gulls wheeled in the air and terns shrieked along the shoreline, the busy city sprawled inland, teeming with carts leaving the docks, packed full of fish and trade goods from New Orleans.

Martin thought of how much he owed that vessel he had mostly built with his own hands. The *Mary E* had helped him survive the harsh years on the Box B and made it possible for him to buy land from the Aguilar family and build a house for his wife and son.

Martin, Juanito, and Anson had sailed the *Mary E* up from Matagorda, had rowed the dinghy into port that morning as the sun burnished the water of the bay so that it shone like gold in some alchemist's cauldron.

Martin felt a tug at his heart when he looked out at his boat and pointed her out to the man standing next to him. Anson too felt a nostalgic pang. He and his father had sailed for five leisurely days, Martin teaching him how to handle the rigging, set sail, steer by the stars and the sun. Anson's legs were still quivering from the experience.

During that time, Anson had felt closer to his father than ever before. And his father seemed a different person away from land, almost a part of the boat as it sailed on a close reach before the wind, curving so swiftly through the blue water that he felt they would capsize. But the *Mary E* hugged the waves and performed like a champion with Anson's father at the helm.

"Well, what do you think of her, Jerry?" Martin asked.

Jerome Winfield was an old friend of Martin's he had met in Galveston years before when he was sailing the *Mary E* up and down the Gulf. Jerry had worked on several boats, dreamed of owning his own someday. He was a few years younger than Martin, but older than Anson.

"I've never seen her look better. All spruced up." Jerry was a blond young man, rugged, slender, with piercing blue eyes and a quiet smile. "Who's that on board?"

Martin waved to the boat. Juanito waved back.

"You don't know?" Martin asked.

"That isn't Juanito, is it?"

Martin laughed. "Who else?"

"Well, I'll be damned. I haven't seen him since you two were last in New Orleans. Does he still have his boat?"

"No, he sold his a long time ago. Like I should have."

"You like that Texas land, huh?" Jerry asked.

"Well, it's claimed me, pretty much."

"And you have a son. Anson, your father is a pretty good sailor."

"I know," said Anson, a slow smile breaking on his face. He drew himself up proudly and thought of that first night at sea in the Gulf, just he and Juanito and his father, all alone in the dark, with the stars so close he thought he might touch them. They were under full sail with a light breeze blowing, the moonlight glinting silver on the water and the wake churning a phosphorescent green, like some magical bubbling spring. He felt as if he had been plunged into some strange new world where there were no trees, no cattle, no land, no coyotes, not even an armadillo or a roadrunner.

"Well, son, what do you think of the sea?" his father had asked him.

"I love it," Anson had replied breathlessly. "It's so peaceful."

"Now it is," Juanito had said.

"What do you do in a storm?" Anson asked.

"Ride it out," his father replied.

"How?" asked Anson.

"You tell him, Juanito."

"You reef all your sails, Anson," Juanito said. "Throw out a sea anchor, kind of like a canvas balloon that fills with water instead of air. And then you find out what kind of man you are as the seas rise up against you, higher than the decks, and the boat pitches and wallows in the troughs of the ocean. You tie the wheel down, if you can, and hold on and think of good weather, calm seas."

"If it gets too bad and you can't pump out the bilge, you bail," Martin added.

"It sounds scary," Anson said.

Martin had looked at Juanito and smiled. Juanito had begun to laugh.

"What's so funny?" Anson remembered asking.

"Juanito doesn't believe in fear," his father had said.

"You don't get scared, Juanito?"

"If you know who you are, there is nothing to fear," Juanito had said.

"I know who I am."

"I mean inside you. The real you. The one who watches you."

"I guess I don't understand, Juanito."

"There he goes," Martin had said. "You'd better listen to him, Anson. He knows more than any man I've ever met. I'm not sayin' you'll understand him, but he knows a heap of things about life."

"Everything you see, everything you experience," Juanito said, "is what you create in your own mind. If you carry fear with you, if you think as a fearful man, then you will be afraid."

"You're saying if I don't believe in fear, then I won't ever have any."

"Something like that," Juanito said. "The Buddha said that our life is shaped by our mind. He wrote that what we think, we become."

"Who is this Buddha?" Anson wanted to know.

"A very wise man who knew the true meaning of life."

"I never heard of him."

"He was a wise man in ancient times. He said that joy follows a pure thought like a shadow that never leaves. So think happy, be happy. A storm is a chance to experience nature, to be part of it, to learn from it."

"Is that true, Daddy?" Anson had looked to his father for confirmation.

"I guess so. Juanito's way makes more sense than getting rattle-brained every time a storm comes up. It makes sense when you think about it some."

Anson had thought about that conversation ever since that first night. He knew that Juanito wasn't just a happy-go-lucky man, but a man who thought about things and lived his life the way he thought it ought to be. It was still hard to understand all the things Juanito had told him when they were out in the Gulf, but his curiosity had been piqued. He would chew over some of Juanito's talk for a long time, he supposed.

"Want to go out in the dinghy and look her over, Jerry?"

"You bet I do, Marty."

"Anson, go on and pull the dinghy up close to the dock."

Anson ran out on the dock and got in the dinghy. He pulled it snug against the dock, waited for his father and Jerry to step in. They sat down a moment later.

"Well, Anson, row us out to the *Mary E*," Martin said.

"Aye, aye, sir," Anson said as his father pulled the line inside the boat. He grinned as the oars dug in and he pulled away from the dock and turned the boat. He thought it was a fine life being a sailor. No chiggers, no mosquitoes, no Apaches. He couldn't understand why his father would leave the sea for such hard work as raising cattle.

None of them noticed the man standing in the shade of an awning jutting out from a small fish market set back from the embarcadero. He watched the three men in the dinghy leave the dock and struck a lucifer on his boot heel, lit a small cigarro, sucked the smoke into his lungs and blew it out of a mouth full of gold teeth.

He turned to the man standing next to him wearing a striped shirt and flared trousers, a large black belt with a flintlock pistol hanging from the side by its flange.

"Well, looks like Jerry's going to buy him a boat, Hoxie."

"He picked him a purty one, Sam."

Sam Cullers slapped his companion on the back. "Go get Lars and tell him to get the rowboat ready. We'll go out there tonight before Winfield gets back aboard."

"Sam, you are a larcenous sonofabitch."

"I'm only goin' after what's owed me, Hoxie."

"Says you."

"Yeah, says me. Get your ass a-haulin'."

Hoxie left the shade of the awning and wended his way down the boardwalk, passing stevedores carrying cargo on their shoulders, never hearing the gulls scream overhead as they dove at the fish in the carts. Beyond, nets dried in the sun along the curved shoreline as killdeer ran in and out, picking up scraps from the hundreds of broken clamshells littering the beach.

15

MARTIN COMPLETED THE deal with Jerome Winfield that evening in a Galveston tavern, the Ports O'Call. Anson had his first taste of beer and felt grown up. Juanito smoked his pipe and drank brandy sparingly. Anson's father drank rum with Winfield as they discussed the papers showing the boat's origin and ownership, its tonnage and the gear on board. Jerry gave Martin some money and they shook hands.

The tavern was crowded and the tables full of hearty drinkers and eaters. Anson's gaze swept the room. Never had he seen so many different people together in one place. Many of the conversations were in languages he did not know: Portuguese, French, German and even a different kind of Spanish that was alien to his ears. The talk flowed around them and he felt a oneness with the men and women, even though he knew none of them. Serving girls carried tankards of ale on wooden trays and brought food to the table—chicken, pork, sausage, duck, goose, shrimp, red snapper, crayfish, mussels, and clams. The smell of rum and whiskey was strong in air blue with cigar and cigarette smoke.

Two men at the bar kept looking at him and Anson felt uncomfortable. He poked Juanito in the side and whispered into his ear. "Who are those men standing up at the bar?"

Juanito looked over in the direction Anson was nodding. His gaze swept the men and he shook his head. "I do not know."

Jerry Winfield looked up, saw Anson and Juanito huddled together. He turned around, looked at the two men at the bar. "Uh-oh," he said.

"What is it?" Martin asked.

"Trouble, maybe. That big man smoking the cheroot is Sam Cullers. I got into a deal with him and we lost money. He blames me and has been trying to make me pay him. But it was an equal partnership, with equal risks."

"Don't know him," Martin said. "Who's the feller next to him?"

"Hoxie. I don't know his first name. Mean sonofabitch, though. I saw him stick a man in a fight over at Port Aransas one night. Laughed about it."

"Have I reason to worry with all this money in my pocket?" Martin asked.

"No. I don't know why they're here. I put Sam in his place a long time ago. They wouldn't be after you, anyway. Just me."

As Jerry finished talking, Sam Cullers walked over from the bar, stood over Jerry. Jerry looked up. "Sam."

"Are you forgetting you still owe me money over that catch you and me made?"

"Sam, I don't owe you a fart or a farthing. We both lost. That was it."

"Wasn't my fault you couldn't get the catch to port and it spoiled."

"An act of God," Jerry said.

"Your dumb luck, you mean."

"Look, Cullers, I'm not going to argue with you. Make your own money back, same as me, and quit your damned bellyaching."

"I ain't forgetting, Jerry. You'll pay, damn you, or else."

"What's that supposed to mean?"

"It means what I say. You'll pay me what you owe me, one way or another."

Jerry started to rise. Martin put his hand on Jerry's shoulder. "Let it go. We don't want any trouble in here, Jerry."

"Good thing you've got yourself a pal, Jerry," Cullers said. "I'll be seeing you."

"In hell," Jerry said.

"Maybe so," Cullers replied, and turned on his heel. He finished his drink at the bar, then left with his companion.

"There's a man carrying a big grudge, Jerry," Martin said.

"He doesn't worry me none. Sour grapes."

"Just the same, watch yourself."

"Don't worry, Marty. I will."

Martin signed the boat's papers and handed them over to Jerry, along with a bill of sale.

"The *Mary E*'s all yours, Jerry. And I've got something else for you."

"What's that?"

Martin looked at Juanito and winked. "You can pick up a load of goods dockside tonight for transport to New Orleans in the morning. There'll be a man with Jones Shipping waiting for you. You can earn back some of the money you paid me for my boat."

Jerry grinned. "Why, how did you do that so quick?"

"The man, his name is Dan Jones, nabbed me when we came in this morning. I told him I was going to sell the boat, but would see to it that his load was picked up tonight. Fruit and vegetables. He's pretty desperate."

"That's fine news, Marty. I'm obliged."

Martin slapped his friend on the back. "Think nothing of it."

"I was going to sail you boys back to Matagorda."

"Oh, we'll stay over the night. I'm going to look at horses tomorrow and buy some new stock. We'll ride back to the Box B overland. We need to get back home quick."

"Well, I'm still mighty obligated to you."

"Take care of the *Mary E*, Jerry."

Jerry ordered a round of drinks, but Martin could see that he was anxious to get to his new boat. Jerry sat in his chair as if he was sitting on a hot stove lid, then finally bade them all good night and left the Ports O'Call. "I guess I'd better see Jones and get his cargo loaded. Good night, boys."

"There goes a happy man," Martin said.

"But you'll miss the boat, won't you, Daddy?"

"I miss it already," Martin said.

16

M ARTIN OBTAINED HOTEL rooms for himself and Anson, and another for Juanito. He went to bed right after supper. Anson and Juanito walked down to the docks and found a place to sit while Juanito smoked his pipe. It was a cool evening with a fresh shore breeze. Lights from the lanterns along the bay striped the waters with orange banners. Bullbats flew over them, darting acrobatically as they devoured flying insects.

"Do you miss sailing, Juanito?" Anson asked.

"I miss the sea."

"Why did you leave it?"

"I grew up with the cattle. I missed the cattle. And while I left the sea, it never left me."

"I don't think it will ever leave me, either. There is something about it that I like."

Juanito laughed softly. "The sea casts a spell. It is like a home we left a long time ago."

"A home?"

"All creatures came from the sea, I think. We might have come from there, too."

"But how could we breathe?"

"I do not know. Perhaps we had gills like the fish."

"Aw, you're kidding me, Juanito."

The Argentine puffed on his pipe. The aroma of the burning tobacco wafted to Anson's nostrils. He liked the smell of it. He thought that one day he might get a pipe and try and smoke it. Once he had asked his father about smoking and Martin had told him he was too young. He was always too young, according to his father.

"Maybe I am kidding, maybe I am not," Juanito said reflectively. "Who knows where we really came from? That is a question we will always ask. And someday we will know."

Juanito saw something out of the corner of his eye. Then he and Anson heard the ringing of cables against the mast, the singing of sheets on the boom. They both looked at the *Mary E* as her mainsail went up the mast. They could see the lanterns shivering and trembling as the vessel got underway.

"Well, there goes Jerry," Anson said.

"He got that load on quick." Juanito drew deeply on the pipe. He had thought Jerry would set sail in the morning, when it would be easier for him to familiarize himself with the *Mary E.*

A rifle cracked and they heard a man scream. Then it was quiet for a moment.

There was a commotion on the dock. Anson and Juanito heard a man yelling. "Hey, where are you going? Come back, come back."

They saw a man waving his arms and jumping up and down on the dock.

"Let us go and see what is happening," Juanito said.

"That looks like the man Daddy was talking to this morning."

"Jones?"

"Yes," Anson replied. "I wonder what's the matter."

Anson and Juanito ran toward the man on the dock. Jones turned and saw them, looked at them for a long moment. "You there," he called. Then he started walking briskly toward them. "You two," he said.

"Yes, we are coming," Juanito answered.

The corpulent man broke into a ragged trot. "Do you see?" he shouted. "All those vegetables on the dock, ready to load."

Jones stopped running at the same time he ran out of breath. When Anson and Juanito got to him, he was puffing on scarce air, swaying back and forth, his lungs wheezing like a bellows.

"Ain't you two the ones that came in on that boat yonder?"

"Yes," Juanito said. "Martin Baron sold it to the man who's sailing it."

"But—but he was supposed to load my vegetables on tonight. He said he'd put into the dock. I've got men standing by to load."

Jones stopped rocking back and forth on his heels and his breathing seemed to be getting better, his breaths more even.

"He may be just trying the boat out," Juanito said. "He'll probably turn her back in."

"He looks like he's going out to sea," Jones said. He was a short man, rotund, his face tanned by the sun, his thick fingers cobbled with cracks and scars. "Did you hear a rifle shot? I heard a shot."

"Yes, we heard it," Anson said. "It was out in the harbor, I think."

"Damned right it was," Jones said. "And I didn't hear no ball hit the water. I heard a man scream."

"So did we," Anson said.

The three men watched as the *Mary E* cleared the harbor and caught the wind in its sails. It showed no signs of jibing or returning to port. Soon its sails disappeared into the blackness of the Gulf.

"Well, I'll be damned," Jones said. "I was sure as hell counting on getting these vegetables to New Orleans before they spoil. Don't that beat all?"

"He—he might come back," Anson said.

"There is something not right about this," Juanito said to Jones. "Did you see Jerry go aboard?"

"Yes, I talked to him. He said he would take on my cargo."

It was then that they saw the empty rowboat bobbing in the bay. As the *Mary E* cleared the harbor, the boat became clearly visible. It had been on the other side of the sailing vessel where they could not see it.

"Who does that rowboat belong to?" Juanito asked.

"Oh, that one. Cullers. I think he and some men rowed out to help your friend Winfield."

"Cullers?" Juanito asked.

"That's the man. I've heard nothing good about that one."

"Well, he was not going out to the *Mary E* to help Jerry Winfield, I can tell you that," Juanito said.

"He wasn't?" Jones seemed bewildered.

Anson gritted his teeth as the realization of what had happened blossomed in his mind. He felt an anger rise up in him as he stared at the abandoned rowboat bobbing in the bay, its oars shipped.

"I will bet money that there is someone in that rowboat," Juanito said.

"I don't see anybody," Anson said.

"No. If there is somebody in the boat, he is dead. Murdered."

"Who?" Anson asked.

"Jerry Winfield, I think," Juanito replied.

Anson let out a breath, shook his head in disbelief. "It—it can't be," he whispered. But he knew Juanito was right. Those men in the tavern had killed Jerry Winfield and stolen the *Mary E.* The thought of it sent shivers rippling down his backbone.

17

JUANITO WAS SOAKING wet as he rowed the Cullers boat up to the dock. He had swum out to retrieve the rowboat with its grisly cargo. He threw a line to Anson, who caught it and pulled him up snug against the pilings. He looked down into the boat. Dan Jones held a lantern high above Anson's head.

"Lordamercy," Jones breathed.

The man Anson had known as Jerry Winfield stared up at him with wide open sightless eyes. There was a bullet hole in his temple. Blood covered the dead man's clothing like flung barn paint. The front of his shirt was black with the coagulated gore. The pockets of his trousers had been turned inside out and his boots were gone, as well as his socks and belt. There were gash marks on his bloodless face, and one cheekbone was swollen so badly that the symmetry of Jerry's face was forever askew. The lantern swayed back and forth in Jones's hand as he began to tremble, casting an eerie orange light over the corpse.

"He was shot in the head," Anson said. "He must have tried to get away in Cullers's boat."

"Jerry put up a good fight," Juanito said.

"He was outnumbered," Anson said. "I wish we could have been there to help him."

"Anson, go and awaken your father," Juanito said.

"Oh, God," Anson said and his stomach turned over and bile rose in his throat.

"Go quick," Juanito said.

Anson turned away from the lurid sight of the dead body and ran up the dock, the boards clattering beneath his feet. Up a cobblestone street to the hotel he raced, flying through the front door past a startled desk clerk and on up to the door of his father's room.

"Daddy, open up. Come quick."

The door opened and Martin stood there in his nightshirt, barefooted, hair tousled, eyes bloodshot. "What in hell's all the racket about?"

"Daddy, they done killed Jerry. They shot him in the head."

"Huh? Who?"

"I don't know. Cullers, I guess. That's what Juanito thinks. He said to come and get you."

"What about the *Mary E?*"

"Gone," Anson said. "We saw it sail out of the harbor slick as anything."

"Goddamn. Give me a minute. I'll meet you down at the dock."

"It—he looks real dead, Daddy," Anson blurted. "I never saw anything so awful."

"Well, don't look at him. Damn it."

Martin closed the door. Anson stood there a moment, uncertain about what he should do. For a long moment he thought he had been shut off from the world of reality. A strange feeling came over him as he stood there in the dark of the hall. He heard what he thought might be whispers at the other end of the corridor. A board creaked and he turned his head suddenly to see if someone had come up behind him, but there was no one there. In the silence, he suddenly thought of Jerry Winfield, the way he had been savagely murdered. He could not erase that dead face from his mind, and the finality, the suddenness of it overwhelmed him. One minute Jerry had been laughing and talking and drinking with him, his father and Juanito, and the next he was dead forever. How could such a thing happen? he wondered.

He hated going back through those dark streets alone. He felt that Death was so close to him it could reach out and touch him almost anywhere, especially in a dark place.

"I'm not afraid," he said aloud to himself and walked slowly down the stairs and through the lobby of the hotel. The clerk stood there blinking. You could be dead, too, Anson thought, and hated himself for thinking such a thing, even if it was not out loud. When he got outside, he began to run back to the docks. He could feel Death right behind him, stalking him, breathing down the back of his neck. He tried to shake off the fear that gripped him and made it hard for him to breathe, but he kept looking over his shoulder, expecting something or someone to jump out and grab him.

Anson wished now that he had waited and walked back to the dock with his father, but he wouldn't have dared to admit that he was scared. He had to prove to his father that he was a man now and could handle grown-up situations. Or maybe he had to prove it to himself.

When he reached the dock, he took a deep breath, relieved to be back with Juanito, glad that the lantern Jones held up gave off as much light as it did. Two burly men who had been waiting to help load Jones's vegetables on the *Mary E* stood off to the side. One of them carried another lantern.

Anson tried not to look at Jerry Winfield's lifeless, blood-covered body, but he couldn't help but stare down at the grotesque sight. It was Winfield's unseeing, glazed-over eyes that gave Anson goose bumps. Even though he knew that the killers had gotten away, he felt an uneasiness creep back into his mind. An unknown fear that he couldn't explain.

Martin ran down to the dock a few minutes later. He had dressed and put on his boots, but hadn't bothered to comb his hair.

"Gawdamighty," he said. He stared down at the gruesome sight as Jones held the lantern above the bobbing rowboat, then shook his head. "Oh, God, Jerry, I'm sorry."

"It ain't your fault, Daddy," Anson said. He glanced at the grisly corpse, then turned away.

"Cullers did this?" Martin asked Juanito.

"I think so, from what he tells me," Juanito said, nodding toward Dan Jones. "He says the rowboat belongs to Cullers. And those thieving bastards sailed away in the *Mary E*, smooth as can be."

"That's right," Jones said as he lowered the lantern some. "I seen Cullers and a couple other fellers rowin' out there to the *Mary E*, and then we heard a shot. I thought they was goin' out to help Winfield, but I guess that ain't what they had in mind."

"No, I guess not," Martin said.

"Now, I'll never get these damned vegetables to market," Jones complained.

Martin ignored him and turned to Juanito. "I knew Cullers was trouble when we saw him at the tavern earlier, but I didn't think things would end this way for poor Jerry."

"He was happy with the boat," Juanito said. "Too bad he did not have a chance to enjoy it."

"What're you going to do now, Daddy?" Anson asked.

"I'm not sure yet, son."

"I mean, we'll be going home now, won't we?"

"No," Martin snapped. "We're going after Cullers."

"Well, you came here to sell the boat and you did that. You got the money for it and you sure can't do nothing to bring Mr. Winfield back to life."

"No, I can't, but I can do right by him by going after his killers and getting the *Mary E* back. You're just too young to understand, Anson."

"But—but Mother needs you."

"Your ma don't need me. She's got folks there to help her. If you want to go back to the ranch to be with your ma, then ride on back. I got things I need to do."

"But she wants us there, both of us, I know she does," Anson pleaded.

"Anson, I'm not going back home," Martin said sharply. "Someday, when you grow up, you'll understand such things."

Anson felt like he'd been slapped across the face. "I am grown up," he muttered, then turned and walked a few steps away, staying well within the dim light of the lantern. He barely listened to his father and Juanito discussing their plans. He was trying to deal with the conflicts in his mind. He desperately wanted to go home, where he'd be safe, and yet he knew his father was right in his decision to go after Winfield's killers and to try to get the *Mary E* back, and Anson wanted to be a part of it. He wanted to show his father that he was not a boy anymore.

He heard his father tell Juanito that he would arrange for a proper burial for Jerry, and then his father turned and headed back to the hotel.

"You okay?" Juanito asked Anson.

"Yes."

"Your father must do what he feels is right in his heart."

"I understand. He couldn't live with himself if he let Cullers get away with what he's done."

"I think you do understand."

"Juanito, my father really doesn't want to go home to my mother, does he?"

"Not right now. You know there has been trouble between him and your mother. It has been going on for a long time."

"Why?"

"She is carrying his child and sometimes that makes a woman lose her footing. She wants your father's shoulder to lean on."

"Well, he can't be there all the time. She should understand that."

"I am sure that she does, Anson. That is the way it is with women.

They do not want to feel abandoned, especially when they are with child."

"Carlos and the other women are there."

"I think your father wants me to act as an emissary."

"What's that?"

"A messenger of goodwill. He will want me to smooth things over between them before he returns."

"Oh, I see. I think," Anson said.

"Do not worry about it. Your father will see to your safety. If there is killing to do, he will do it."

"I thought he wasn't going to kill anybody," Anson said.

Juanito looked pensive. "Maybe he will not."

"But you think he will."

"I do not know. That is between him and what we call his conscience."

"You don't think it's the right thing to do."

"Who can say?" Juanito said. "If Cullers does not want to fight, perhaps it will end that way."

"Cullers looked pretty mean to me when I saw him."

"It is one thing to look mean in a crowded place with friends around you. What will he look like when he is facing death all alone?" Juanito looked very intensely into Anson's eyes. Anson got the queer feeling that Juanito was talking about him, not Cullers.

18

JUANITO RODE WITH Martin and Anson as far as Freeport. Martin checked at the port to see if Cullers had put in there. No one had seen him, nor the *Mary E.*

"It's best we part company here, Juanito," Martin said. "You ride overland to Baronsville. Stop there before you go on to the ranch. Tell Ken Richman to bring fresh horses and half a dozen men to the Matagorda. Plenty of powder and ball, too."

"It is not much farther to the Matagorda," Juanito said. "I could ride with you that far and then on to Baronsville."

"No, I want you to make time. I may need Ken. Tell him to bring the barber."

It was a chilling order to Juanito. Ken Richman had practically built the town of Baronsville by himself. He had attracted the merchants, the townsmen, and had laid out the city. He had become mayor with Martin's blessing. The barber, a man named Jim Shepherd, was also the surgeon.

"It is a long ride from Baronsville to the Matagorda," Juanito said. "Not so far from here to the Matagorda."

"I don't want you to ride along the coast. Don't go into Corpus Christi. Right straight to Baronsville, then to the ranch. *Claro?*" Martin's tone of voice left no doubt that he wanted no argument from Juanito.

"*Claro,*" Juanito said. "*Vaya con Dios.*"

Anson watched Juanito ride away from the small town on the coast. "There he goes, Daddy."

"I know it. Damn it. Juanito always thinks he knows what's best."

"But he doesn't?"

"No, he damn well doesn't. Come on. Cullers may be in Matagorda now and we might catch him before he leaves port."

"How long does it take to sail down there from Galveston?" Anson asked.

"Less than a day with a good wind. Cullers left port last night. He would have made it there by the dawn's light."

"And what do you think he will do?"

"If he's a pirate, he'll stock up on munitions and grub and take to the sea again, probably work up around New Orleans. If he's just a thief, he'll probably try and sell the boat there."

"Can he do that?"

"He's got the damned papers. He can fix them up so it looks like he bought the boat, not Jerry."

"What if he doesn't sell the boat and you catch him?"

"I guess I'll have my boat back."

"Will you try to sell it again?"

"I don't know, Anson. I just don't know."

Anson saw a shadow cross his father's face and knew that he had touched on a delicate and uncomfortable subject. Martin had sold the boat to Jerry Winfield and now there was blood on it. He was beginning to understand why his father wanted to get Cullers. It was more than the murder, it was the theft of the *Mary E.* He had not known how much his father loved the boat until they had sailed out from Matagorda and he saw the loving care he took of the *Mary E.*

As they rode away from Freeport, over the coastal plain, Anson thought about the *Mary E* almost constantly and the boat grew bigger in his mind until it was all out of proportion to its true size. He hoped they would see it again, anchored off Matagorda or somewhere along the beautiful peninsula that floated like an island in the sun.

They passed Mexicans, their burros pulling little carts along the road, heading for Galveston, and some going the other way, toward Corpus Christi. Martin stopped each one coming from the southwest and inquired about the *Mary E,* asking if they had seen it sail into the Matagorda. None of the Mexicans had seen such a ship, they assured him.

They did not stop until they reached Matagorda, and it was dark when they rode into the little settlement. There was no sign of the *Mary E* and Martin said it was too late to ride out to the peninsula. They bought tortillas, carne and *frijoles* off of one of the street vendors and made camp atop a small hill at the edge of the village.

"How's the food?" Martin asked his son after eating several bites of his own.

"Good. Full of sand, though," Anson replied.

"Less chewing."

Anson laughed. The wind was blowing sand at their campsite, the moon was rising through scattered white clouds in the sky. It felt good to get out of the saddle and he was glad his father had decided to wait until morning before returning to the search for Sam Cullers. The horses were ground-tied a few yards away, feeding on corn in their morrals.

When they had finished eating, Martin took out his pipe, filled it with tobacco and lit it. He sat back against his saddle and smoked.

"Daddy, what will you do when you find Cullers?" Anson asked. "Will you shoot him?"

"I don't know, son. Give him a chance to surrender peaceably, I reckon."

"What if he wants to fight?"

"Well, we'll just have to cross that bridge when we come to it."

"Will you try to kill him?"

"That's up to him. Why?"

"I just don't want anything to happen to you, that's all."

"There's always that chance." Martin thought back to the time when his family was attacked by Shawnees. His mother was killed in the first attack. His father, badly wounded, took a long time to die. After he buried his parents, Martin set out after the marauding Indians. He caught up to them and killed them. But there was little satisfaction in taking another's life in revenge. "I hope it won't come to that, Anson," he said. "It is not easy to kill a man. And if you do, you have to live with it the rest of your life."

"I hope you don't have to kill anybody, Daddy," Anson said.

"Better get some sleep, Anson. I want to get an early start in the morning."

"I ain't sleepy."

"I'm *not* sleepy."

"I'm not sleepy."

"Go to sleep anyway. I'll keep watch and wake you up to take over."

"You think somebody'll come way up here?"

"There's always that chance. A lot of people down there saw us ride up."

"I'll go to sleep," Anson said, and spread out his blankets. He lay down and looked up at the stars until they began swimming around in small circles. When he closed his eyes, he fell fast asleep.

19

—■—

WHEN HIS FATHER awakened him, Anson thought it was time for him to take over the watch, but it was already getting light out.
"Did you stay up all night, Daddy?"
"Most of it. I dozed."
"You should have got me up."
"It might be a big day. You need more sleep than I do."
"Did you see anything?" Anson asked.
"An armadillo, an owl and seagulls. Hungry?"
"I could eat a horse."
"We'd better save the horses. We might need them."
Anson laughed.
"Let's saddle up and get something to eat," Martin said.
A few moments later, they rode into the settlement which was just barely waking up. A few lanterns shone in the shanties. They found a small cafe, hitched the horses to the rings anchored to small cement mounds out front. The weathered sign over the shanty read: LA FONDA DEL MAR.
The two men sat at a table near the front window. There was a small counter where some fishermen sat. The room was full of the smell of cooking meat and beans, the aroma of hot tortillas and seafood. The counter and kitchen was manned by a short, heavyset Mex-

ican, who waddled out to their table and handed them a single slate scrawled with Spanish words chalked on it.

Martin ordered in Spanish for both of them: *huevos*, tortillas, *café* and *biftec*. He also asked the cook his name.

"I am called Gonzalo," the man said in Spanish.

In a low voice, Martin asked him, "Do you know a man named Cullers? Sam Cullers?"

"He does not come in here no more," Gonzalo said in English. "I throw him out."

"Have you seen him? Yesterday, perhaps?"

"I have not seen him," Gonzalo said, and his tone turned surly. "I will bring you the coffee and cook for you the breakfast."

One of the men at the counter turned and looked over at Martin. He was a swarthy Mexican, wearing a tattered straw hat, sandals, loose trousers and a dirty white shirt. He studied Martin for a long moment, then pushed away from the counter and walked over.

"I know you, señor," he said. "I have seen you in port many times. You keep your boat here. It is the *Mary E.*"

"I sold the boat two nights ago in Galveston."

"Ah, I was thinking about that when I saw the *Mary E* sail in yesterday. In the morning."

"Sit down," Martin said. "I am Martin Baron and this is my son, Anson."

"I know your name. I do not know your son. I have not seen him before. I am called Pedro the Pescador. It is a name that identifies me. I am a fisherman."

"I have seen you before, too," Martin said. "You have a small boat and you fish with bare line in the deep water."

Pedro laughed. "That is me. I catch many kilos of fish."

"You say you saw my boat come in. Did you see who was on it?"

"Oh, yes. I know the men who were on it, but I did not think you would sell to such a man as Sam Cullers."

"I didn't sell it to him. He stole it."

"Ah, then, that explains."

"Explains what?" Martin asked.

"Last night Cullers, Hoxie and another man, Lars Swenson, brought the little boat to the docks and tried to sell the *Mary E*. But nobody would buy it because they do not trust Cullers. Cullers and his friends got very drunk and killed a man in Rosa's Cantina. The others who live here got angry and chased Cullers and his friends out and smashed up their little boat."

"The *Mary E* or the dinghy?" Martin asked.

"The little boat, the dinghy. Cullers stole three horses and they rode away with men chasing them with knives and clubs."

"Where did Cullers and his men go?" Martin asked tightly.

Pedro shrugged. "They rode toward Corpus Christi on the road. Some men got horses and rode after them, but they lost them."

"So they are not going to Corpus Christi?" Martin asked.

"I do not think so. They took the road to San Antonio de Bexar."

"Now tell me what the horses that Cullers stole looked like and what brands they were wearing."

"They all carry the Circle B brand," Pedro said. "One gray gelding, two black geldings, one with a blaze face, the other with four white stockings. There is a reward for them. They belong to J. B. Bowers, who has a rancho in Nueces. They were brought in by a man I do not know, who said Bowers wanted to sell them."

"That all?" Martin asked.

"This man with the Circle B horses. He is just a kid. And he rode after Cullers."

"Alone?"

"Yes. But he had two pistols and a rifle with him. He was riding a tall black horse, much too big for him."

"And you do not know his name?"

"It is a funny name. I do not remember it. But he was a gringo."

"How old was he, Pedro?"

"I think he said he was but fifteen. He brought five horses for auction and three of them were stolen before that happened."

Martin let out a sigh. He looked at his son. "Are you real hungry, Anson? I'd like to get after them."

"No. We've got jerky and hardtack. We can eat on the ride."

"Good," Martin said, relieved. "Pedro, do you want to make a little money?"

"I always like to make the money. How little?"

"I'll pay you to watch after the *Mary E.* If a man comes here by the name of Ken Richman, you tell him what happened. Tell him I'm going after the man who killed a friend of mine."

"The man who was killed last night was a friend of mine, too," Pedro said. "His name was Carlos Gemelo. I will do this thing for you, Señor Baron. Will you pay me before you go?"

Martin laughed and gave Pedro some bills. The fisherman looked at them and smiled. "I will watch your boat and clean it for this much money."

"I'm much obliged, Pedro, but do not clean anything. Leave the boat just like it is." Martin left money on the table for Gonzalo and called to the man as they left. "Give the breakfasts to any man who's hungry, Gonzalo. We're leaving."

Gonzalo smiled and waved at them as they went out the door.

Martin rode down to the bay with Anson. "I just want to see if she's there before we go after Cullers," he said.

They saw the smashed dinghy still tied to the dock, holes in its hull. It floated just beneath the water, sadly ruptured. Martin and Anson looked out into the harbor of Matagorda and there was the *Mary E* at anchor, as they had last seen it in Galveston.

Anson thought the boat looked so peaceful floating there, anchored fore and aft, with no sign of the horror that had happened aboard not so long ago.

20

—■—

M ICKEY BONE RODE through the desolate wasteland of Mexico, a harsh desert country strewn with rocks and cactus and rattlesnakes. He followed no tracks, rode no trail but dim memory. Small rocky buttes jutted from the featureless plain like cairns erected by some mysterious nomadic people. He rode by memory and into memory as the sun blazed down on him. He rode past dry water holes and alkali bowls, cracked and scarred lake beds that had not held water for many lifetimes.

He remembered his people, the Lipan Apache, wanderers, doomed to skulk in regions where no others dared live, outcasts from places even the elders could not recall, living on lizards and snakes and cacti and the roots of plants.

He had crossed these plains before, but it seemed he had been in a delirium, a small child strapped to his mother's back, a hood of rabbit hide over his forehead to keep the sun from blinding him. He had sucked on cactus for moisture and fed on small, shapeless creatures, cracked their little succulent eyes for their juices. He had counted his ribs on both sides for a pastime on the endless journeys through the boiling hell of Mexico.

He rode through the little nameless towns and asked the old ones where his people might be. They pointed in all directions, but mostly

toward the mountains of his childhood, where his people had retreated
from death at the hands of Spaniards, Mexicans, others of their tribe,
redskinned men from the north, Comanches and others. So Bone kept
riding toward the distant mountains until he passed no more towns.
He had to find water in *tinajes* and dig for it in dry creek beds and
slash for it with his machete in the barrel cactus, and his food supplies
dwindled, and once again he could count his ribs like a man plucking
an outsized guitar, only there was no music, just the sad echoes in his
memory of his people singing plaintive songs of heartbreak and lost
battles, lost wars, lost tribespeople.

He followed the old trails, though they were no longer visible to
the eye, and the mountains drew close and his memory sharpened in
response to his hunger and his need, and he remembered the jagged
black sierra rising above the land, recalled the pictographs of beasts
and the tales told by the old ones when the fire threw shadows on a
cave wall in the blackness of night, and Bone found his way through
memory when the thirst was burning his throat and his stomach had
shriveled like a dry, twisted gourd collapsing from its own inner decay.

And then he was at the edge of the mountain range the Mexicans
called the Sierra del Tlahualilo, and Bone looked up and saw the signal
mirrors flashing silver from the dark recesses of rocks, and he looked
into the dark face of the sierra and knew that he was coming home,
home to a place where he had been before, and he could smell the
blood and hear the screams of his mother and sisters, could see his
brother fall to the lead bullet, as lifeless as a doll made of hide and
sinew and stuffed with quails' nests, and the drunken, laughing, rau-
cous Mexicans riding black horses through the camp and snatching
up young girls and throwing them to the ground and raping them and
then cutting their throats and scalping their private parts and their
heads and he could smell still the burning gunpowder, see the white
smoke like little clouds of death and hear the women keening until
explosions tore their throats open and their blood ran like rivers on
the earth.

Mexican men grabbed him and other boys his same age and they
asked them questions. They beat the young ones when they faltered
in their Spanish and then they asked the older braves questions in the
Spanish tongue.

"What are you called?"

Mickey did not understand and a Mexican drove a fist into his face.

And one of the old men answered. "He is called Counts His
Bones."

The Mexicans laughed and called him Cuenta Sus Huesos and another said that he looked like a boy he knew who was called Miguel.

The Mexicans called him Miguel Hueso and took him and the others back to their town and made slaves and servants of them. But first they slaughtered all the grown male Lipan Apaches and the old ones, both men and women, and smashed babies against rocks and cut off testicles and scalps until there was only an abattoir where the camp had once been. The ants and the worms were at the corpses before the sun stood straight over a man's head. Mickey never could erase those images from his mind of once-living people reduced to meat and bones, and he still heard the young girls screaming as they were kicked and struck and raped and murdered for no reason that he could ever determine.

As he rode into the sierra, the talking mirrors danced all around in front of him and he looked hard to see the people using them, but he never saw a face or a hand and did not understand the messages the mirrors flashed and rode on in ignorance, his throat tight from thirst and fear and his belly drawn up and burning with a pain he had never known.

The mountains swallowed him and the silence grew around him until it filled his heart and mind and the mirrors no longer flashed. He heard quail piping in the long draws and other birds that did not sound right. But there was a path, a narrow trail, and his horse took to it naturally and carried him up the spine of a ridge and then he saw the talking mirrors again.

The trail narrowed and took him into a bewildering maze of ravines and ridges and towering mountains. Then a man stepped out onto the trail and drew his bow with an arrow nocked to the string. Then others joined him, springing up out of the rocks and from the little ravines. They all had bows drawn except for those who carried pocked and rusted rifles with stocks bound in rawhide and dull tacks embedded in the wood.

Bone halted his horse and held up his right hand to show that it was empty. He looked at the men blocking his path. They were filthy and he could smell their musk. Some had scabs on their bare chests and arms, and one of them had a fleshy pock on his face where one of his eyes had once been. Their clothing was tattered and torn, old and patched. They looked worse than the beggars he had seen in the Mexican towns, and dirtier.

"I come in peace," Bone said in Spanish. He wanted to bite his tongue and pull the words back into his mouth and swallow them.

"Who are you?" one man asked in the Apache tongue.

"I was called Counts His Bones. When I was a baby. I am Querecho. Lipan." The Apache words sounded like baby talk to his ears. He was surprised that he remembered the language.

The men all seemed to speak at once. Bone could not understand very much of what they were saying, but the intonation, the aspirates of his own tongue were music to his ears. He had not heard that Lipan dialect in many years and more memories flooded his brain as he listened to the men talking. And then he picked up snatches of conversation that he could understand.

"I have not heard that name in many years."

"It is a dead man's name and should not be spoken."

"Why would this man use a dead man's name?"

"There was a baby a long time ago called Counts His Bones. The Mexicans took him away. This one is dressed like a Mexican vaquero."

"Maybe the Mexicans killed him. Maybe this is a Mexican who wants to kill some of us."

"Did he come alone? Do you see any Mexicans? Are there soldiers hiding?"

It seemed to Bone that he sat there on his horse for hours while the men spoke as if he was not there. Some looked at him from time to time and others studied him intently. He could smell the stink of their unwashed bodies and almost feel the lice crawling in their straight black dirty hair. He waited and wondered if he had done the right thing in coming to this place, this place so far from the life he had lived since being taken away by the Mexicans.

Finally, when the chattering got louder and the arguments more heated, Bone spoke, and his voice boomed over the men and silenced them.

"I am the one who was taken away. I am Counts His Bones and I have come here looking for my people."

One of the older men stepped forward. He carried an old trade gun that looked as if it had been thrown from a mountain and dragged by horses over rocks and cactus.

"Why do you look for your people?" the old man asked, in the Lipan dialect. "Maybe they are all dead."

"I have lost my way," Bone said. "My heart is on the ground. It is so heavy I cannot lift it. I have had dreams and visions that my people are here. I have dreamed that they can help me find my way back to the Great Spirit that is in all things. For this I come."

"Ah," voiced several of the men.

"He is lost," said another.

The old man stepped closer to Bone, but he kept a safe distance and held his rifle at the ready. "Do you know who I am?" he asked.

Bone looked at the man closely. There were old scars on his face, and part of his scalp was missing, grown over in a hideous blotch of flesh. No hair grew on that part of his head.

"I do not know who you are," Bond said. "But there was a man in my village who was called Big Rat. I saw him killed by the Mexicans."

Big Rat had been only a year or two older than Bone when the Mexicans had come to the encampment. He had fought bravely. He had tried to protect his sisters from being raped. Bone remembered that one of the Mexicans had shot Big Rat and had scalped him. He recalled that there was much blood on Big Rat's face, and after another Mexican struck him very hard with the butt of his rifle, Big Rat had made no sound. The visions of that day swam in Bone's mind, pieces that floated to the top and then sank below the surface, fragments of the terrifying things that had happened that day.

Some of the men gasped and others uttered oaths and they looked at one another in wonder and surprise. They seemed dumbstruck and confused.

"I am called Big Rat," said the old man.

"Then you did not die," Bone said. "Your face was red with much blood and you made no sound."

"I was dead," Big Rat said. "I died and the Great Spirit came to me and breathed the breath back into my chest. I have killed many Mexicans. I hate them."

"Do you remember me?" Bone asked.

"The Mexicans took you away. They made you into a Mexican."

"No. They called me Miguel Hueso, but I am an Apache. I am a human being."

The men all grunted and signed to one another in the old way, but they did not speak. They all looked at Big Rat to see what he would say.

"Give me your guns," Big Rat said. "Give us your horse."

"I will give them to you," Bone said.

"Then you can walk with us through these holy mountains and we will smoke and make talk. Do you have tobacco?"

Bone nodded.

"Good. You will give me the tobacco, too. Now step to the ground from your horse and give up all your things."

Bone dismounted and held out his rifle. Big Rat stepped forward warily and snatched the rifle from Bone's hands. Another man dashed forward and took the reins of the horse. Another took Bone's pistol, while still another rummaged through his saddlebags. A man held up Bones's sleeping blanket and wrapped it around him like a giant shawl.

Bone stood there as the Apaches swarmed around him. But as he looked at them more closely, he realized that they were not all Lipan. Some were Kickapoo, and he recognized another as being of the Yaqui tribe. He wondered then if they were going to kill him, and he began chanting a song he had heard long ago, a song some of his people had sung the day the Mexicans came to their camp. All time seemed to stand still as he stood there, singing in a very low voice.

The others looked at Bone and none said a word, for they knew he was singing his death song.

21

URSULA SIGHED DEEPLY as Jack slid from her and sank into the bed. She touched the raspberry flush on her face, felt the warmth of her blood. She basked in the passing rapture of the lovemaking, still felt Jack's fingers on her arms and shoulders. The heat of his body still lingered on her breasts. Her lips still tasted his mouth and tingled from his hungry kisses.

Jack was still breathing heavily when he reached over and touched Ursula's breast, cupped it tenderly. He tweezered the nipple with his thumb and forefinger, then tweaked it gently until it swelled with her blood once again.

"That was good, hon," he said.

"It was beautiful, Jack."

"Been a long time for me."

Ursula said nothing. She floated somewhere above herself in a roseate haze. She wanted never to come down from that high place where the air was thin and sweet, scarce enough to keep her in a giddy state, her body light as down.

She opened her eyes as she floated down from the heights. Moonlight pewtered the room with a delicate incandescence, softening the walls and the chest of drawers, divining the geometry of the room and defining the shadows as the moon rose, moving them slowly over shifting objects that seemed to float as she floated, in and out of focus. The room seemed different with Jack in it, more intimate, not so familiar. Changed. She sighed and closed her eyes again and began to hover once again, her body somewhere below, basking in the heat of the afterglow. She sighed with contentment and sorrow. She knew Jack was leaving in the morning and taking their son Roy with him.

"My heart," she said.

Jack grunted. "What?"

"You are my heart, Jack."

"Oh. Well, it was good, hon."

"Do you love me, Jack?"

"Sure. You know I do, sugar."

"Sleep tight," she said as Jack turned over on his side, away from her.

"Urs, I got to ask you something."

"Well, go ahead, Jack, and ask."

"Them soldier boys. The ones you talked about. Like the one who came here this afternoon to get his laundry."

"Yes, what about them?"

"Did you? Do you, I mean?"

"Did I? Do I? Do I what?"

"Don't keep me on the dangle, Urs. I got to know."

"Know what, Jack?"

"Dammit, Urs. Are they sparking you?"

"Why, Jack. I haven't been sparked since you started courting me."

"I mean, way outside of flirting. Did you ever take any of them boys to your bed?"

Ursula smiled in the darkness, in the dull rime of the moon's faint glow. "Jack, that's a crude thing to say."

"I got to know, Urs. Did you do it with any of 'em?"

"Would it make any difference?"

The silence lasted several seconds. "It might," Jack said finally.

"You wouldn't love me anymore?"

Another silence. Then Jack turned over, cocked himself up on his elbow and looked at her. She could not see his eyes. Just shadows and the pale glint of his tousled hair. She looked at the wall of his massive chest, felt the strength of him surge through her. She wanted him again, right at that moment.

"Well, sure, I'd still love you, I think. But I wouldn't feel good about it. I mean—knowin' you was with another man while I was gone, you know."

"Have you been with other women, Jack?"

"Shit," he said.

"That's quite an answer," Ursula said.

"I mean, what's that got to do with it?"

"Same with a man as with a woman. I don't like to think of you with other women. But I know you do. I know a man needs it more."

"Aw, Ursula."

"It's true."

"Just answer my question, will you, Urs?"

Ursula touched his chest, twirled a finger through the wiry red hairs. When she had a lock twisted firmly, she pulled on it.

"Ouch," Jack exclaimed.

Ursula laughed. Then she put her hands on his neck and pulled him close. "Jack, there haven't been any other men. Not that I haven't had the chance. But there's just no other man for me. Just you."

She could hear Jack swallowing. She pushed him away playfully.

"Are you just sayin' that to make me feel good?" he asked.

"Well, what do you think? Don't you believe me?"

She could feel his gaze on her, probing. But he could not see her, she knew. He could not see inside her. Could not see the deep parts of her, the secret places of a woman, the places where her love pulsed like a beating heart, where it always waited for just a single touch of his hand.

"I guess I believe you," he said lamely.

"Well, that sure gives me a boost up the ladder," she said.

"I mean, I want to believe you, I guess."

"Well, if you don't, Jack, then you'll never know. I'm not that kind of woman and you should know that. Without asking."

"Jesus, Urs, I had to ask."

"Then you don't know. And you'll never know. I think of us as one person. You see us as two people."

"That ain't true."

"Mmm. No? Well, it might be, Jack. You got to settle that with yourself. No answer of mine's goin' to change your mind. If you think the worst of me, then that's how I'm going to look to you."

"You make it hard, Ursula. You take a simple thing and just tangle it all up like brier brush."

"Do I? Well, you asked the question. And I gave you an answer. That should be enough to satisfy you."

"Damn, Urs. You make it sound like I just want to be satisfied. And that ain't true."

"Whatever you say, Jack. I love you and you are my heart. My only heart."

"Aw, Urs."

"Happy?" she asked.

Peabody Public Library
Columbia City, IN

She waited an eternal silence for his answer.

"Real happy, Urs."

"Good. Now, get to sleep if you want. I'll be here when you wake up."

"I am some tired," he said, dropping back onto the bed, on his back. He was like a giant, she thought, resting after a battle with a dragon. She leaned over and kissed him on the cheek. Then she withdrew to her side of the bed, glad that it was over, glad, very glad, that Jack had asked her. It showed her that he still cared about her, even if he couldn't say it straight out. That was enough for her.

She was content. She rose up again to tell him that, but she saw that he had fallen asleep. His mouth was open and he was breathing through his nose. It sounded like some mighty river at rest, its energy contained for the moment, but ready to burst into flood and roar like a lion.

"Good night, love," she whispered and lay back down. It was funny, she thought, how it was to make love. A Mexican woman had told her once that they called it the little death. There was that one starburst of rapture and then the little death. Sleep, she supposed, only sleep, and in the morning, Jack would awaken and they could die again in each other's arms.

22

THE TRACKS WERE not hard to follow. They were still fresh, as there
had been no rain overnight. Four horses, Martin figured, the
fourth fresher than the other three, by the better part of an hour, at
least.

"Can you read 'em, Anson?"

"Pretty much. You have to look at them a long time, figure out
which is which. Juanito taught me some, Mickey Bone taught me
more."

"Good. They may dim out on us, but we know where they're
headed."

"San Antonio?"

"Looks that way," Martin said. "But they could be headed any
damn where."

"What about that kid following Cullers?"

"What about him?"

"What if he catches up to them before we do?"

"Oh, I 'spect he will. Maybe he'll slow 'em down. Or get himself
shot in the brisket."

They had picked up the tracks outside of Matagorda, tracks leading
in a northwesterly direction. Apparently there had not been any trav-
elers behind the men. From Martin's reading of the sign, he thought

that Cullers, Swenson and Hoxie had ridden pretty fast getting away from the settlement, but then had slowed their pace.

They had left the crude road that circled the outlying houses around Matagorda and set off away from any heavily traveled route. Although Martin did not know if there was such a road to San Antonio, he supposed there was some way to get there, somewhere along the small road they had left behind. He had a rough idea where San Antonio lay by dead reckoning, and he supposed Cullers did, too. It would be the place a man would go if he wanted to lose himself or pick up supplies before venturing into the vastness of the Texas plain that stretched in every direction from that town.

The going was rough at first until they left the sandy ground behind. Then they crossed through rougher country, but with more solid footing. Martin found places where Cullers and the others had tried to brush away their tracks, but the fourth horseman, who evidently was a fair tracker, left his horse's hoofprints as visual as road signs.

"That little feller knows his stuff," Martin said to Anson at the end of that long first day. "Looks to me like he could track an ant in a windstorm."

"There was places when I could see only that one track. Looks like Cullers drug brush behind the horses."

"Yep, and he's been going over hardpan when he could. Smart."

"Do you think we'll catch him, Daddy?"

"If that little chunk shows us the way, we'll make better time than he is."

"How far ahead of us do you think they are?" Anson asked.

"Better'n a day now, I reckon. They likely rode all night and we've been slowed looking for tracks. Might be two, three days before we catch sight of 'em."

"And how long before they get to San Antonio?"

"Rough country here. They don't have no grain, probably. They'll have to find water and let their horses graze. A week or so. Maybe longer."

Anson let out a breath. He was used to riding, but not for days on end. He was already sore and stiff. He wished he could jump in a creek and just let the heat seep from his body and limber his muscles some. He hoped his father would find a place to bed down for the night. The sun was like a furnace full of dry logs, burning him even through his shirt and trousers.

Still, they rode on, Martin in the lead, Anson following, trying to see what his father saw, trying to think the way his father thought. They crossed streams and let their horses drink. They rode into bewildering hills that ran in every direction, down into steep ravines, and up onto wooded hilltops so thick with trees they could not see more than twenty feet in any direction. They jumped quail and deer and heard the beating wings of wild turkey they could not see, and the horses began to spook at every sound, shy at every enigmatic shape of tree and rock.

The sun crawled across the sky and burned into their eyes, though they pulled their hat brims down to shadow their faces, and they chewed on hardtack and jerky and drank sparingly from wooden canteens. Anson felt as if his body were bruised from his neck to the sole of his foot, and wondered if his daddy was not made of iron, for Martin never seemed to tire. Soon Anson's eyes stung so much from dripping sweat that he was no longer able to see the track of a horse or an overturned pebble, and he wondered if his father was as lost as he felt.

They rode over flat ground dotted with trees and wandered in and out of mesquite groves that seemed an impenetrable maze. Anson wiped the sweat from his brow and fought off the tiredness, glad to see that they were indeed once again following horse tracks and were not lost.

Martin stopped at a place where two creeks joined and rode up and down one, then up and down the other. He crossed both streams, rode a little ways looking at the ground, then rode back. He rode straight out from the forks and then back again. He stopped, rubbed his face with one hand. Then he took off his hat and scratched his head as Anson sat his horse and watched his father's curious behavior. Finally Martin rode back to where they had stopped. Anson scanned the ground. He could see nothing wrong. All four sets of horse tracks led into the creek and he imagined they all came out on the other side.

"What's wrong?" Anson asked.

"This has got me puzzled," Martin said. "For some reason, two men rode up one creek and another man rode across the other."

"So they split up," Anson said.

"Looks that way. But that ain't all."

"That isn't all," Anson said, correcting his father. Martin ignored him.

"Right. That little feller crossed straight over and rode on. He didn't follow either set of tracks. Just rode on as if he had lost the trail."

"And did he?"

"I don't think so. The tracks are all clear. Not wet anymore, but you can see the pocks left by the splashes of drops where the riders came out of the creeks. They didn't ride very far either, as if they might know they were being followed and didn't give a hoot nor a holler."

"So what do you think, Daddy? I can't figure it out."

"Well, if that little feller ain't careful, it looks like he's going to get flanked on both sides, maybe. Or else he might be a little smarter than Cullers."

"How so?" Anson asked in his best grown-up voice.

"Maybe he figured Cullers broke up his bunch just to throw him off the track and is going to meet up with his cronies somewhere up ahead. So the little guy is just saving himself some time."

"He'll jump 'em when they come back together?"

"Or lie in wait for 'em, maybe."

"A lot of maybes to this," Anson observed.

"Well, you can't read a man's mind. You can't read four minds, neither."

"So what are we going to do? Do we follow one of the Cullers bunch, or two of 'em, or do we follow the little feller?"

Martin laughed. "Good question," he said.

"And do you have an answer?"

"Well, we could split up, you and me, or we could toss a coin and decide which way to go."

"Split up?"

"That may be what they want us to do. If they know we're behind 'em."

"And they'd have easy pickin's, huh, Daddy?"

"They might."

Anson waited as his father pondered the situation. The horses switched their tails and pawed the ground. Anson let his horse drink. He listened to its slurping sounds as it sucked water into its mouth and squeezed it past the bit. Martin's horse whinnied and he rode it to the creek bank. It bowed its neck and drank even more noisily than the other horse.

"Don't give 'em too much water now," Martin said, hauling in on the reins. "We've got a ways to go and I don't want them logy."

"Okay," Anson said, then jerked his horse's head away from the water. The horse fought the bit until Anson dug his spurs into its flanks and backed the animal away from the creek. "Stubborn son of a bit," he said.

"They'd drink until they'd drown themselves if you let 'em," Martin said. He pulled his horse back, looked up at the sky. "Be dark soon. We'd better get a move on."

Anson said nothing, wondering what his father was going to do. The sun stood in the western sky above the treetops. He figured they had maybe an hour of light left, at best. He squeezed his fingers together and held them up between him and the horizon and the sun, the top finger just under the sun. He knew that you could time the sunset that way, fifteen minutes to a finger. But the trees took up a couple of fingers, he figured. Maybe an hour and a half at most. He sighed and put his hand back down.

"Two hours of riding," Martin said as if reading his son's mind.

"An hour and a half."

"We can go a ways after the sun sets," Martin said stubbornly.

"We won't go anywheres if we don't set out."

"Don't you go getting smart now, sonny."

Anson winced. He didn't like to be called that. It made him feel small and dumb.

"I was just prodding you, Daddy. We been here a good ten minutes."

"More like five."

"Five, ten. And them others are still ridin', likely."

"Well, we're fixin' to go," Martin said. He drew in a breath as if he had finally made up his mind. He clucked to his horse, put spurs to its flanks. The horse splashed through the creek.

"Finally," Anson muttered, and spurred his own horse, following after his father.

His father did not veer right nor left, but followed the big horse with the small man atop it. Anson shrugged, hoping his father knew what he was doing.

Anson caught up with his father, rode alongside him. "How far ahead do you figure they are by now?" he asked.

"A day, at least."

"Will we ever catch up to them?"

"Tomorrow, maybe. If they go to San Antonio, we might find them there."

"Well, I hope we find them before then."

"Why?" Martin asked.

"If they get all the way to San Antonio, they might get away."

"They might at that."

They rode in silence, Martin reading tracks, for about thirty-five minutes; then Martin suddenly pressed his horse to a gallop, leaving Anson behind. Anson slapped his horse's rump and spurred him. He looked at the ground and saw the reason his father was galloping ahead. The rider they were following had done the same thing. The length between the hoofprints and the deepness of the tracks showed him that the young man had gotten in a hurry all of a sudden.

23

────

STRIPPED OF ALL his weapons and his horse, Bone followed Big Rat deep into the sierra. He was surrounded by the other men who had challenged him when he first rode up. The way seemed familiar to him somehow, although he could not recall if the path they were taking was the actual one he had trod as a boy. He looked up at the peaks of the mountains and studied their broad faces. He felt strangely at peace, although he knew that for the moment, at least, he was a prisoner.

They walked for an hour, and that hour stretched to two, and yet Bone did not feel tired. He looked at each bend of the trail with wonder and he felt at home the deeper they went into the mountains. He marked time by the sun, and when they had walked a little over two hours, climbing ever higher, ever deeper, into the sierra, they crossed over a saddleback ridge and descended into a long, narrow valley. He looked around to see if this was the Apache encampment, but he saw no people, no signs that anyone lived there.

No one had spoken to Bone on the entire trek into the mountains, nor did anyone explain to him why they had come into this valley. He saw no smoke, heard no noise as the procession moved across the edge of the valley toward the southern end of it, where shadows deepened in a wooded place.

As they neared the woods, Bone saw a mirror flash in the sun, and he saw one of the Kickapoo tilting his tin mirror. Soon a man stepped from the shelter of the trees and held up a single hand, palm out. Big Rat signed back to him and the man disappeared back into the woods.

Bone felt the circle of men around him tighten, so that he was walled away from escape. He knew he would be shot if he started to run. But he did not want to run. He was curious, and he wanted to see if his people would accept him after all his years away, living with the Mexicans and the gringos.

Bone's guards moved even closer to him as they entered the woods, where the shadows were deep under the scrub pine and juniper. Still, he saw no one ahead of them. The trail was narrow and very difficult to see—a game path, he decided, ancient and smoothed down now from moccasin feet.

To Bone's surprise, the trail led to a clearing surrounded by rugged mountains rising high above it, throwing it into shade from the falling afternoon sun. There, like some forgotten image, stood the camp, with tents and lean-tos built against the mountain. He saw a path leading to higher elevations directly behind the camp—an escape route, he imagined—and atop a huge boulder stood an armed Apache, looking down upon the camp.

"Come," Big Rat said, and broke away from the others, headed for one of the small tents at the edge of the clearing. One man followed behind Big Rat and Bone, carrying Bone's rifle and pistol and his saddlebags.

The other men halted and split up, each going in a different way. Bone followed Big Rat to a tent where two men squatted by a spread-out blanket. They grunted to Big Rat and motioned for him to squat down. He turned to Bone and signaled for him to do the same. The man behind them stepped forward and placed Bone's possessions on the blanket. Then he turned and walked back through the meadow.

Bone squatted with the three other men. None said a word for several moments.

"This man," Big Rat said, "was once called Counts His Bones. He was captured by the Mexicans who came to our village many seasons ago, and he has lived with them as a slave."

"He looks very clean," said one man.

"He does not look like an Apache," said the other.

Big Rat addressed the first squatting man. "Red Leg, you are right. He is very clean." To the other, he said, "Drum, you too speak true. He does not look like an Apache. But he has the heart of an Apache and he seeks the spirit of his people. He has been lost to them for many seasons and now he wishes to come home. He wishes to eat with us and live with us and find his spirit."

Red Leg regarded Bone with an expression of deep contempt. He was a man in his forties, but his skin was wrinkled from the sun and from fasting, so that he looked very old. Drum, for his part, appeared to take no interest in Bone, but looked up and away at the clouds that floated overhead like the heads of thick dandelions.

"We hear your words, Big Rat," Red Leg said. "Do you want us to kill him and cut his head off? He may be a Mexican spy."

"I do not want this. I remember Counts His Bones. He fought the Mexicans. His mother and father were killed and their scalps taken away and sold for pesos. I would like to adopt him as my own son."

"What if this man is a Mexican spy?" Drum asked. "He will only sneak away and tell the scalp hunters where we live."

"Are you a Mexican spy?" Big Rat asked Bone in the tongue of the Lipan.

"No," said Bone and he made the sign the Apaches used sometimes to talk with other tribes who did not speak their language. "I have lived with the Mexicans, it is true. I was a slave. I have lived with the white men, too. But I am not a Mexican. I am not a white man. I am Querecho. I am Apache."

"He speaks well," Drum said, finally looking at Bone directly. "You speak well, Counts His Bones."

"I speak what is true," Bone said.

"You have fat on your bones. Why do you come to this place where the people starve?"

"I come to seek the spirit of my people. I do not know who I really am. I am not a white man. I am not a Mexican. I am Lipan. But I do not know what this means. I want to find what is lost. I want to find what was taken away from me when I was a boy."

Red Leg grunted. Drum was in his thirties, but he too looked older than his years. He had scars on his face and a deep booming voice that was like thunder rumbling from his chest.

"Big Rat, you may adopt this man as your son. But if he is a Mexican spy, we will kill you both."

"That is good," Big Rat said. "I will take him to my lodge and show him to my wife and my two daughters. My daughters will not remember him, but my wife knew his mother and father, Chanting Woman and Hopping Crow."

"Ah." Red Leg nodded as if he had known the parents of Bone. "Take him to your lodge. We will eat the meat of a young deer we killed this morning." He turned to Drum. "Call the women out and let them cook the deer."

"I will do that," Drum said and stood up. He walked out into the meadow and called to the women, who suddenly appeared from all the lodges, the visible ones and the unseen. He told them about Bone and Big Rat's adoption and the women and children all made strange sounds that Bone did not remember and many came to look at him when he stood up with Big Rat.

"I will keep your weapons," Red Leg said. "Until you prove yourself an Apache."

"Keep them," Bone grunted absentmindedly. For he saw a young woman walk over with the others. She was very beautiful. She had the eyes of a doe and long lashes that quivered like the wings of the butterfly, and she looked at him boldly as she walked by.

"Come," Big Rat said, "or do you want to be gawked at all day by women and children?"

"Who is that one?" Bone asked when he had found his speech.

"That one? She is a slave girl. A Yaqui. Too young. Too stupid. Nobody wants her. She has a bad heart, a flapping tongue. She would drive a man crazy with her constant talk."

"I want her," Bone said.

"What?" Big Rat asked. "Did you come here to find your spirit or a stupid woman?"

"Does not the spirit dwell in the heart of all?"

"So it is said. But she is a Yaqui, child of very bad people."

"Who owns her?" Bone asked.

"We all own her. She lives with two old women in the lodge next to mine. They beat her and she cooks for them."

Bone looked at the girl as she walked away. He was sure everyone in camp could hear his heart pounding. The girl looked back at him and he saw no meanness in her. And she did not look stupid. He was sure that she liked him, too.

"What is her name?" Bone asked, still in a stupor.

"Her name? The old women call her all kinds of names."

"But she must have a name. Her own name." He struggled with the unfamiliar words in the Apache tongue. "Her Yaqui name."

"She was called Starling by her people. We call her Magpie. She has only fifteen or sixteen summers. She says bad words to the old women who keep her."

"I wonder," Bone said, "if she would say bad words to me."

"Put her out of your mind," Big Rat said. "Come, I want you to meet your new family."

But Bone could not keep Starling out of his mind. He knew then for certain that she would be his wife, and he did not care that she was a Yaqui. She was the most beautiful woman he had ever seen.

And he knew that Starling was the reason he had come back to his people. She was the thing that was missing in his heart. She was the one who would give him back his spirit.

24

IT WAS ALMOST dusk when Martin and Anson came upon the hanging man. The shadows had thickened in the trees and clumps of cactus, and the glow in the sky was fading like embers in a dying campfire. It was almost too dark to see, but the hanged man stood out in bold silhouette against the pale sky, dangling from a tree in the center of a small clearing. He turned slowly in the slight breeze and it was that movement that had caught Martin's eye.

"What is it?" Anson asked when he rode up. Martin had reined in his horse and was looking at the dead man. But as Anson looked closely, he knew what it was. He gulped down a swallow of air and grew light-headed even as his stomach wrenched in his belly. "Gawda-mighty," he breathed.

"Looks like someone done did him a cottonwood blossom," Martin said.

"What do you mean?"

"That's an expression I heard once. When they hang a man, they usually do it from a cottonwood tree. That there's just a mesquite."

"Is—is he dead?"

"I reckon he's dead."

"Who is he?"

"Let's see if we can find out. It ain't no little guy, though."

"Look, Daddy," Anson exclaimed as they rode closer to the mesquite tree. "There's something white on his shirt, like a piece of paper."

"It *is* a piece of paper, I reckon," Martin said. The horses balked at riding up to the dead man, whose hands were tied behind his back with a short piece of rope. Martin and his son brought their mounts under control and rode warily up to the hanging man. Martin reached up and pulled off the note stuck to the man's shirt by a stick whittled at both ends until it was like a crude darning needle.

"What does it say?" Anson asked.

"Take a look," Martin said, handing the note to his son.

Anson read it quickly. The note read: KILT FOR STEELING HORSES. A chill ran up his spine. The way it prickled, he felt as if he had rolled in cholla. He looked at the dead man as his father pulled one of his trouser legs up and felt the leg.

"Still warm," Martin said. "Not stiff yet." He let the pants leg back down. One of the man's feet gave a little kick.

Anson jumped back in his saddle. "Gawdamighty, Daddy, he's still alive," he said.

"No, he's deader'n a stump," Martin said. "Just a dead man's kick, that's all. He might twitch like that for a long time until he's stiffened up."

Anson forced himself to look up at the dead man's face. It hung at a grotesque angle. A huge knot, wound tight, nestled at the corpse's ear. His face was purple, with a large swollen lump on one cheek, and his nose appeared to have been broken, the eyes battered and closed—almost peacefully, he thought. Anson smelled the stench of the man.

"He's gone in his pants," Anson said.

"There's a muscle that loosens up when a man dies," Martin said. "Makes him void what he's got in his innards."

"God, it's awful," Anson said.

"I reckon this to be Swenson. He's big, bigger than Cullers. Could be Hoxie, I guess. But he's got blond hair and looks like he might be a Swede."

"What's a Swede?" Anson asked.

"From Sweden. It don't make no difference. That little feller caught up with him and made him dance at the end of that rope. Something curious, too."

"What?" Anson asked in a slightly tremulous voice.

"Look how that rope's cut off. He used a long rope and after Swenson died, he reached up and cut it off."

"What does that mean?" Anson asked.

"I reckon he means to hang them others when he catches up to them."

"Can he do that?"

"That's the law, son. If you catch a horse thief, you hang him."

"But . . ."

Martin rode away from the dangling man, began looking at the ground for tracks as the dusk deepened. They heard the cry of a whippoorwill and the frogs started croaking.

Anson took one last look at the dead man and fought off the chill. He looked around at the light from the gathering dusk.

"It's awful spooky here, Daddy," Anson said.

"Look at these tracks, Anson. Looks like the little feller got ahead of Swenson and waited for him. He knocked him off his horse and fought him, man to man. Look at all those scuff marks. You can see where the little man on the big horse waited for Swenson. He didn't shoot him, which could mean a couple of things."

"Like what?" Anson asked.

"Maybe Cullers and Hoxie were nearby."

"What else?"

"The little feller might have wanted Swenson to suffer some."

Anson thought about that. He wondered what Swenson's last minutes of life were like for him. What was it like to hang? To strangle slowly, unable to breathe and fighting to get air inside his lungs? Did he look at the man who hanged him and hate him? Did he kick a lot before he died? Anson touched his neck with his right hand, wondered how it would feel to have a rope around it. He could not imagine anything more horrible. He felt very uncomfortable thinking about such a way of dying and quickly took his hand away from his throat.

"Did it take a long time for Swenson to die?" he asked his father.

"Probably went real quick."

"But if he choked to death . . ."

"Likely his neck broke once he fell off his horse. He probably kicked and danced some and then . . ." Martin made a sound in his throat and drew a finger across his throat like a knife.

Anson winced at the image of Swenson kicking and the knot under his ear getting tighter and tighter until his wheezing for breath stopped. It must have been a grotesque sight, he thought. And the little guy watching him the whole time, maybe smiling. It gave him the shivers inside.

"It's getting down to dark," Martin said. "We'd best sort out these tracks, see what we're facing."

He rode in a small circle, widened it, again and again until he had covered the entire clearing.

"Well?" Anson asked.

"No sign of Cullers and Hoxie coming here yet. Let's get the hell away from here."

"Good idea," Anson said, his voice quavering. The place gave him the chilblains.

The two men rode off into the dark, following the tracks of the small rider on the tall horse. They rode until they could see no more and the dark was upon them like black coal dust. Martin rode off the trail a hundred yards and found them a place to bed down for the night.

"We'll make no fire," Martin said to his son. "And as little noise as possible. Keep the horses saddled and tethered. We'll put on their feed bags and hope they'll whinny if they hear anyone coming up on us."

It was then that Anson realized how tired his father really was. He had not said a word all day, nor had he shown any sign of fatigue. But now it was in his voice and the slow way he got off his horse. It was the first time, too, that Anson realized his father was getting on in years. Not real old, maybe, but not too young anymore, either.

"I'll take care of the horses, Daddy."

"Good. I swear I'm plumb tuckered out."

Anson wondered if the dead man had affected his father as much as it had him. He wondered if he would see the dead, swollen face of Swenson in his dreams, see him gasping for breath and turning purple as he kicked and kicked, trying to get the rope from around his neck.

25

―■―

JUANITO FORDED THE Guadalupe River at a place he had never been before. He had found it necessary to ride much further north because the river was running high after a cloudburst that morning. Finally he found a fairly shallow ford where the water was not so swift. He surmised that the rains had passed the upper part by and had struck only at his usual crossing.

He had never seen that part of the country before and rode through it with a strong sense of curiosity. It looked much the same as the deeper part of the Rio Grande Valley, but was somehow different. There was not as much mesquite, for one thing, and the plain was more open. But there were many sand hills and grasses tough as wire. Here the wind blew free and blasted everything in its path, and the small trees were bent like old men.

The land seemed half seashore and half desert, and the sky was filled with phalanxes of fluffy white clouds that seemed to have been puffed out of some far-off funnel, for they diminished in size as they fell away in the distance. They lay in perfect rows as if the sky had been plowed and the dust that came up was white as flour and shaped like cauliflowers.

At times it seemed to Juanito that the clouds stood still and he was floating, and he drifted off into one of his meditative states where he detached himself from the world outside and sank deep into the world within. He felt a kind of rapture settle over him, so he gave the horse its head and let it drift through the dunes and nibble at the tough grasses and he let his mind roam above the earth and drift through the clouds, creating no thought of his own nor nurturing any that passed through, just letting himself become part of the sky, the universe, until a great peace grew within him and he knew that he was spirit-brother to all that he saw and all that was earth and sky and beyond, far beyond, the drifting clouds.

He came upon the small village—some would say by accident, but Juanito would say by design—and it seemed a perfectly natural place to find on his journey back to the Box B. But to his surprise, beyond the village, on a grassy plain, surrounded on three sides by mesquite trees, he saw a rope corral and about a dozen cattle milling around, six bulls and six cows, with a pair of vaqueros keeping them company. The vaqueros strolled around the enclosure, speaking in soft voices and singing to the cattle.

The village was no more than a few adobes scattered along a small creek, but Juanito saw flowers growing outside each one, anchored in baked clay pots, bursting with color. Two or three dogs, their ribs showing, lay basking in the shade. They did not bark when he rode up, but a few children emerged from some of the adobe huts and walked out toward the stranger.

"Are you the curandero?" one small boy asked in Spanish.

"He is the curandero," said a little Mexican girl with a clean, scrubbed face, her hair in curls, a pretty red bow atop her head.

"Does someone have sickness?" Juanito asked the boy who had spoken first.

"My sister," he said. He turned and pointed to one of the adobes.

"Watch my horse," Juanito said and dismounted. A small boy ran up and took the reins from Juanito's outstretched hand. "Let me watch him," the boy said. "She's my sister, too."

The older boy turned and walked toward one of the adobes. Juanito followed. Just then a man stepped from another of the adobes. He looked at Juanito, then stepped back in surprise.

Juanito caught the movement from the corner of his eye. He stopped and looked at the man. "Benito," he said softly. "Those must be your cattle."

Benito Aguilar blinked and stepped out of the doorway. His shirttail was out and he tucked it back in.

"Juanito," Aguilar said. "What brings you to this little village?"

"I rode out of my way to cross the Guadalupe. It was running full to the south."

"That is how that I am here. I bought these cattle from a man who lives on the Trinity. Breeding stock."

"They look to be fine cattle. Crossbreeds?"

"Yes, they have the Hereford blood and another that I will not mention."

"I understand," Juanito said. He had not really looked at the cattle closely. They appeared to be of good hardy stock with large frames. He might be able to figure out the other breed if he examined the cattle carefully. "You are heading home to the Rocking A."

"I am going home," Benito said. "But I have friends here as well."

"Have you seen the sick girl?"

"No. It is said that someone sent for a curandero who lives near San Antonio."

Juanito saw movement behind Benito in the adobe. Aguilar stepped outside a little way and a young woman appeared in the doorway, smiling. She was grooming her long tresses with a large tortoiseshell comb. She wore only a thin dress with nothing on beneath it. Her face was painted garishly, her cheeks smeared with rouge, her lips daubed with red. She leaned against the doorway and slid her skirt up high on one leg. Then she batted her eyelashes at Juanito.

"I will look at the sick girl," the Argentine said.

"Where have you been, my friend?" Benito asked.

Juanito told him only that he had been to Galveston with Martin Baron and his son Anson. He did not tell him why.

"Ah, you left them behind?"

"They are returning by a different way. Martin had business to do on the Gulf Coast."

"I will be leaving in the morning," Benito said. "Will you take a cup with me tonight?"

"I am just passing through. I will look at the sick girl and then be on my way, Benito."

"A man must take the rest sometimes."

"I rest where I am," Juanito said. The boy, growing impatient, beckoned to the Argentine. "I will talk to you again before I leave."

"Well, I do not know anything about the sickness of the girl. I am about to take my siesta."

"Well then, Benito, until I see you again."

"*Hasta la vista*, Juanito."

He walked past the adobe where the girl was, following the boy. He saw Benito go back inside and then he heard a loud slap and someone whimpering for a moment.

"*Puta!*" Benito yelled, and she screamed. Juanito heard a crashing sound and then all was quiet.

"This is my house," the boy told Juanito as they came upon another small adobe.

"What are you called?" Juanito asked.

"I am called Domingo. I was born on a Sunday."

Domingo led Juanito inside the casita. It was dark and cool. There were only two rooms, one larger than the other. The girl lay on a mat in the front room, a woman sitting next to her with a clay olla. She dipped a cloth into the olla and dabbed the cool water on the girl's brow. Juanito thought she might be twelve or thirteen. She was very thin and wore only a light dress that did not reach her knees. Her breasts were very small.

"You are the curandero?" the woman asked.

"No. I am just a stranger, passing through," Juanito replied.

"*Ay, Dios mío,*" the woman exclaimed. Then she looked at the boy. "Why did you bring him here? He is not the curandero."

"He said he wanted to help," Domingo said lamely.

"How can he help? Teresa is dying."

The boy shrugged and left the house.

"He is worthless," the woman said. "My husband is dead and I have only Domingo and his little brother, Julio, and Teresa. She burns up with the fever. Go away. You can not help."

Juanito stood there, looking at the girl and at the woman. Then he looked around the dim-lit room, only a pale shaft of sunlight filtering through the gauze-covered glassless windows, one at the front of the room, the other at the side opposite where the girl lay in a dark corner. There were *bultos* recessed into the adobe walls, a crucifix nailed in the center of one wall. The woman picked up a rosary and pressed the tiny crucifix to the girl's lips.

"How long has she had the fever?" Juanito asked.

"Last night and all of this day."

"Why do you call for a curandero?"

"He can heal my daughter."

"Your daughter can heal herself," Juanito said quietly. "The fever is burning up the poison. Have you prayed for her?"

"What do you mean, have I prayed for her? I pray for her now."

"Who do you pray to?" Juanito asked. He looked at a small statue standing on a wooden shelf recessed into the wall.

"The Virgin Mary, *por cierto.*"

"Do you pray to God?"

"*Claro que sí,*" she declared.

"You pray to the statues in this house," Juanito said.

"The statues, yes. I pray to them, too."

"Do you also pray to Jesus?"

"Of course. Why do you ask these things? It is none of your business."

"You should pray to your daughter," Juanito said.

Teresa's eyes opened and she looked up at the stranger. Her mother's mouth opened and then she glared at Juanito.

"Sacrilege!" she exclaimed.

"Listen," Juanito said. "Jesus said look to the kingdom within. It is here. In you, in your daughter. She can heal herself if she has faith. If she believes she is well, then she is well."

"That is nonsense," said the woman.

"Look at your daughter," Juanito said. "Already she is becoming well again."

The woman turned to her daughter. Teresa's eyes sparkled suddenly even though there was little light in the dark corner of the room where she lay. Her eyes were fixed on Juanito. He put a hand on the girl's forehead. Her eyes fluttered, brightened. "How do you feel?" he asked.

"I am feeling better," Teresa said softly, her voice husky with the fever.

"You have the same spirit in you that is God's spirit," Juanito said. "You have the power to heal yourself. If you see yourself well, you will be well. You can make the fever subside. Close your eyes and listen to your heart. You want to be well, Teresa, so you are well."

The mother gasped at this sacrilege. She touched a hand to Teresa's forehead. "She is still hot with the fever," she said.

"That is because you still believe she has the sickness. You must believe she is well and that her flesh is cool."

"Who are you to say these things to me?" the woman asked. "You are not a curandero."

"No, I am not a healer in your eyes," Juanito said. "I look to the Father of All to heal, and so should you. He is here, in this room, and your daughter is becoming well. Truly, I see only wellness here in this house."

"Get out, get out," the woman said. "You are the devil."

Juanito stood there. He smiled at Teresa. She smiled back at him.

"No, he is not the devil," Teresa said. "I believe him. I can feel the fever going away. I feel cool inside."

"There are no devils," Juanito said quietly, "unless you create them. Teresa is perfect as you are perfect, and she is well as you are well. There is no sickness here except your belief that there is, little mother."

The woman clasped hands to her ears and shook her head.

Juanito smiled at Teresa again and nodded. "Teresa believes. She knows what is true."

"Get out of my house," the woman said. "Now."

"I will go," Juanito said. "I will pray for you both."

"And to whom will you pray?" asked the woman.

"I will pray to the Father, to God, to His spirit which is in every living thing. So I will pray to you and Teresa."

The woman spat and motioned for Juanito to leave. Her daughter reached out and grabbed one of her mother's arms, drew it back so that her mother's hand rested on her forehead. Juanito smiled at both of them again and turned to go. He heard the woman gasp and then she was sobbing. He looked back and Teresa had drawn her mother down into her arms and was giving her comfort. He walked outside into the sunlight.

Domingo was waiting for him. He had an anxious look on his face. "How is my sister?" he asked.

"She is well," Juanito said. "Have your brother bring my horse. I will ride on."

"I will get your horse myself," Domingo said.

"What do you call this place?" Juanito asked.

"It does not have a name, but we call it Victoria. I do not know why."

"Maybe it will become a town then. If you have given it a name, it exists."

The boy looked bewildered. Juanito smiled broadly at him.

"I will get your horse," the boy said.

Domingo appeared a few moment later, leading Juanito's horse. Juanito gave him some coins and Domingo grinned. "Thank you," he said.

Juanito mounted his horse and rode from the tiny settlement. As he headed southwest for the Box B and Baronsville, he saw an old man riding a donkey. They passed on the wagon-rutted road that wound through the sage and cactus.

"Have you come from Victoria?" the old man asked. He wore a small straw hat tied under his chin with string. His face was leathery, furrowed with the channels of age. He looked at Juanito with watery brown eyes, the whites streaked with brownish veins.

"I have. It is not far."

"There is a sick girl there. I am a curandero."

"You are mistaken, *viejo*," Juanito said. "There is no sick girl there."

"And how do you know this?"

"I have seen her. She is well."

"I will see for myself," said the curandero.

"Yes. It will be good for you to see her. It is easy to believe what you can see with your own eyes. Just be sure that you cause no harm."

The curandero snorted and clapped heels to the burro, and switching him with a length of leather. The burro tottered off toward the village.

Juanito waved good-bye to the old man, but the curandero did not respond. Instead, he stuck his nose up in the air and switched the burro even harder than before. The burro galloped away while the curandero posted up and down on its back like a mechanical toy.

But the old man turned and shouted *"Vaya con Dios"* at Juanito before he rode out of sight.

"*Siempre,*" Juanito shouted back. Always.

26

———

A NSON MOVED THROUGH cobwebs of dream in a forest of shadowy trees and columns of nightmare, a maze that he struggled through with a broken pistol that he could not put together. Ropes scaly as snakes dangled from the trees, each looped and tied with a hangman's knot, each writhing and coiling, casting out for him as he passed.

He spoke to people during his journey and he saw the faces of men dead and living and he fired at some of them with his broken pistol and nothing emerged from the barrel but a soupy substance that had no existence in the waking world. The yodels of a pack of coyotes threaded through the fabric of the dream, and it seemed to him that he could see their cries in color as they floated like bright ribbons through the artificial forest. He cried out as the men chased him and he fled upward through the watery depths of nightmare and floundered in the cobwebs of sleep, fighting for every breath, gasping and choking on the smoky webs until his arms were tangled and he felt as if he were drowning and falling at the same time.

"Ho, Anson, wake up," Martin said in a gravelly voice. "You're all tangled up in your bedroll."

Anson awoke with a start, still gasping for air, the dream fast slipping away from his consciousness, but some of the nightmare still holding him fast. He rubbed his eyes and blinked. He kicked at his blanket and grabbed a corner that had wrapped around his shoulder.

"Bad dreams?" Martin asked.

"Sort of."

"Well, it's time to go."

"It's still dark," Anson said.

"It'll be light enough to see once we get going."

Anson's bladder was full. He was fully dressed, even to his boots. He fought out of the tangled bedding and rose to his feet. He staggered into a grove of mesquite and relieved himself. He heard the horses nicker as his father put on the morrals. He walked back to their camp, shaking the stiffness out of his joints. He was still sleepy. He felt as if he had struggled all night in some fading dream. He could remember only the ropes that were like snakes and the face of the Swede, Lars Swenson. He remembered him, all right, but he now wondered if he had even dreamed that.

"We got hardtack and jerky for breakfast," Martin said. "We can eat as we ride."

Anson laughed. "I wish we had some of Mother's flapjacks and eggs, maybe some fatback."

"You'll tangle your stomach worse'n that bedroll of yours you keep talking about food like that."

"I know."

"Catch up your horse. They can eat out of the bags for a ways while we pick out the tracks. At least it didn't rain."

"Did you think it would, Daddy?"

"I can feel it in the air. Can't you?"

Anson sniffed the air. It was cool and dark and the night birds had gone silent. It was very quiet except for the munching of the horses on oats and corn, the clacking of their teeth. But it did feel like rain for some reason. He looked up and saw no stars, but it was hard to see the clouds, too.

"It feels some like rain. It's pretty early."

"The sun comes up sudden out here," Martin said, and mounted his horse. Anson caught up his mount, removed the hobbles and stuffed them in his saddlebags. He checked his rifle and pistol. He put fresh powder in the pan after wiping it clean, rammed the wiping stick down the barrel to make sure the ball was still seated tightly.

Martin rode his horse around in the clearing as if on parade to see how his legs were holding up. Anson mounted his horse. From his seat in the saddle he saw that the trees were gradually coming into focus. The dawn was already breaking on the eastern horizon.

"Can you see well enough to track, Daddy?"

"I think so. I think we might be gaining on Cullers."

"You mean on that little feller, don't you?"

Martin laughed dryly. "Whichever comes first," he said.

They rode out of the clearing as the sunrise lightened the land. Anson smelled the fresh scents of trees and flowers, the earth itself. He was no longer sleepy because he could see the horse tracks himself. He wondered how long it would take them to catch up to the little feller. He was very curious about him. He still wondered how such a small man could beat up a bigger man like Swenson and put a rope around his neck and pull him high up on a tree limb.

The tracks got fresher as they rode and Martin found a place where the small man had bedded down.

"He didn't stay long. Less than an hour from the looks of it. How in hell can he track at night?"

"He must have good eyes," Anson said.

"He's not tracking with his eyes at night. His are the only tracks."

"Which means he hasn't caught up with Cullers yet."

"No, but I think the little feller sure as hell knows where Cullers is going."

"How can he? We don't even know that ourselves."

"He knows," Martin said grimly, and he put his horse to a gallop as the sun rose over the trees and burned through the clouds spreading across the sky before it was swallowed up again and the land turned gray and somber and it did feel like rain.

27

THERE WAS STILL only that lone track. One horse, one man, and the horse had walked and galloped and the man had stopped and rolled a smoke and ground the butt into the ground before mounting up and riding away at a good clip.

"Where in hell is he going?" Martin asked for the tenth time that morning.

"West," Anson said before he realized his father did not want to hear a logical answer.

"He knows where he's going. But how?"

This time Anson said nothing. But he could see that his father was puzzled and frustrated, if not downright angry.

"The tracks are plain. He's going somewhere and he's not far off now."

"We'll catch up to him, Daddy."

"I wonder if he knows we're trailing him."

An hour later, Martin knew. The tracks turned off and looped back and crossed theirs, and the rider had then gone on to make a complete circle and they were following him again.

"He knows now, doesn't he, Daddy?"

"Yep. He knows now."

And on they rode, father and son, into the afternoon and they did not stop to rest, but ate jerky and hardtack out of their saddlebags and drank water from their canteens. Anson could feel his saddle turn to iron and his legs to wood. He lost all feeling in his toes and his butt felt dead no matter which way he shifted his weight and he grew drowsy and his eyes closed and snapped open again and again, each time that he felt himself falling out of the saddle. He slapped his face and peeled his eyelids back one at a time and drank water and pissed standing up in the saddle as he had seen his father do and he wanted to do more, but he knew his father would be mad if he stopped and probably wouldn't wait for him, but would press on through the deep heat of the day under clouds that had turned black and ponderous and looked as if they would rain at any minute.

And finally it did rain and they were blinded by it and the wind tore at them and they had no slickers to put on, so grew wet and heavy and rode on blindly with the rain stinging their eyes and faces and the wind tearing at their soggy clothes and confusing the horses, who plodded on like animals gone blind from living in caves for thousands of years.

"Daddy, we got to stop," Anson shouted above the roar of the cloudburst. He heard his words get snatched away by the wind and disappear in curtains of steel rain.

"He ain't stopped, so we don't stop," Martin yelled back and to Anson his father sounded far away when in reality he could reach out and touch him, so close was he, a dark and faceless man.

And they rode on like riders plowing through quicksand, bent over their saddle horns like men beaten and taken prisoner. The decision to ride on in the driving rain was soon taken away from them as they came up on a high knoll and heard the roar of rushing waters only yards ahead of them and Anson looked up and saw the tall horse with another one next to it, and the small man hunkered on the ground underneath both horses, holding on to the reins with one hand and his big, wide-brimmed hat with the other.

Anson thought he was seeing some apparition created by the rain, so he stopped his horse. Then he realized his father had already reined his mount in and was dismounting in the brunt of the wind and walking toward the man, using his horse for shelter.

"Bunch your horses next to mine," the little man said in a deep, booming voice, "and get under them."

"That a flash flood I hear?" Martin asked.

"The worst, I swear," said the man under the horse.

"Jesus," Martin said as he pulled his horse next to the tall one and Anson slid out of his rain-slick saddle and pulled his horse around behind the other three, using him like a cross-brace. He ducked down and squatted with his father and the little man, surprised at the shelter the horses gave them.

"You Baron?" the little man asked.

"Yes. How did you know?"

"I heard them bastards stole your boat."

"They murdered a friend of mine, the man I sold the boat to," Martin explained.

"Damned shame."

"This is my son, Anson. Who are you?"

"I'm Peebo Elves. Cullers and Hoxie stole my horses."

"You know where they are?" Martin asked.

"They're just on the other side of that creek yonder, the one you hear roaring like a pack of lions."

"How do you know?"

"I saw 'em cross just before the flood up and come. They barely escaped with their thieving asses."

"How did you know they'd be here?" Martin was almost pleading for answers to the questions he'd been asking himself for two days. "I mean, your tracks were the onliest ones we saw for miles."

Peebo erupted with a curt laugh, shut it off as quick as it had started. "After the bunch split up, I already knew why and what them other two would do. So I followed the Swede, who was slow and stupid as a sackful of sash weights."

"But how'd you know where Cullers and Hoxie would go?" Anson asked before his father could form the question.

"Cullers is follering a line," Peebo said. "He's got him a sailor's compass or something. But he'd go off the line and double back to check his back trail every so often, then come back to the line. I marked it out in my head. After I strung up the Swede, I just took a ride alongside Cullers's main route and aimed it so's I'd catch up to him, and that's what I just about done."

"I still don't know how you beat him here," Martin said.

"I knew Cullers was doubling back. Him and Hoxie took turns. They been doin' that all along. I just rode faster and made twice the time. I was waiting for 'em, but that flood come up and they beat me across the creek."

"Well, I'll be damned," Martin said. "Now that I think back, Cullers was checking his back trail, but I didn't notice it."

"No, you probably didn't because he was slick about it. He made Hoxie wait for him and dusted off his tracks. When he come back, he just took up where he left off."

"Slick is right," exclaimed Anson.

Peebo looked at the young man and laughed low in his throat.

"Once you get on to what a man does, you can figure him pretty good to stick to what he knows how to do best. That Hoxie's been run to hounds before, I reckon."

"I reckon he has," Martin said.

"Well, he'll change his pattern now," Peebo said. "But I'll catch him just the same."

"What do you figure his next move is?" Martin asked.

"I figure he'll make a beeline for San Antonio. But he'll be counting the minutes, all the time wondering how long that flood will keep us stuck up on high ground. Then he'll find another way to throw us off."

"But you don't know what?" Martin asked.

Peebo grinned and water dripped from his lips so that it seemed his teeth were moving when they were really standing still.

"I don't know what exactly, but whatever he does he'll give himself away and I'll figure him out same as before."

"You've tracked men before."

"I was a guard over to Huntsville and I ran a chain gang down in Georgia, and I've hunted game from the Florida swamps clear up to Montana. Man or beast, they lay down a track that suits 'em and I can track 'em."

"Ever work cattle?" Martin asked.

"Whatever men work at, I've done it," Peebo said. "I'm workin' on a ranch right now, in fact. These horses ain't mine, but they was in my keep and I aim to see they get back where they belong, come hell or that damned high water out there."

Martin and Anson laughed. Peebo couldn't have been much over five feet tall, but he had the rounded shoulders of a man used to hard, heavy work, and his boyish face—he seemed a man in his mid to late twenties—only contrasted with his powerful build. Even squatting he looked as if he could lift a ton of iron and walk off with it.

"Well, if you're ever looking for a job with good pay and plenty of hard work, you come over to the Box B in the Rio Grande Valley and I'll put you on."

Martin stuck out a hand. Peebo looked at it for a minute, then stuck his out, and the two men shook over the offer. "I'll surely keep you in mind, Mr. Baron."

"Call me Martin."

"Martin, you just might have yourself a hand one of these days. But I got business to take care of first."

"Understood," Martin said.

"Ever fight Apaches?" Anson asked.

"Nope, that's one thing I ain't done," Peebo said. "But I've waded into Seminoles, Tuscarorys, Shawnee, Paiute, Crow, Sioux, Utes, 'Rappyhoes, and every other kind of red nigger 'twixt here and the Atlantic Ocean. Apaches any different?''

"I don't know," Anson said.

"They're different," Martin said.

"Different how?" Peebo asked.

"For one thing," Martin said, "there's so blamed many of 'em. All different tribes and all mean as hornets. They're good on horseback, like the Sioux and the Crow, but they don't fight like 'em. You can't see 'em until it's too late, and when you think there's only two or three of them, you're ass-deep in a dozen or more."

"Same as the Plains tribes, it sounds like to me," Peebo said. "Crow and Cheyenne are part horse and plenty smart. The Sioux, too. They come out of nowhere on a man and you can't count 'em until it's too late."

Martin and Peebo laughed together. Anson envied them. They had found a common bond and he'd hardly seen more than half a dozen Apaches in his whole life. They were like ants. You didn't see them until they had already stung you and then you might find you had been sitting on an anthill all along without ever knowing it.

"Well, if you get tired of fighting Apaches," Martin said, "we've got Comanches, too. And it's hard to tell who's meaner."

"I guess it don't make no difference long as you've got one in your sights," Peebo said. "A lead ball don't care what it hits and it does the same to mean or kindly."

Again the two men laughed, and Anson wished they would talk about something else. The only thing he'd ever fought was a bull with the pinkeye, and once he got it down, he ran away as fast as he could before it got up again.

The rain drove down harder than before, and the flood roared past them just over the knoll. It was almost pitch-black and Anson couldn't see more than five yards in any direction. The horses gave them some shelter from the downpour, but he was getting cold and starting to itch where his clothes clung to his skin.

"Reckon Cullers is lighting a shuck?" Martin asked Peebo sometime later when the rain and the wind subsided for a moment.

"He's likely holed up same as us," Peebo said. "He knows as long as it's raining, we're not going nowhere."

28

―――

K EN RICHMAN WORKED the horse through its paces in the circular corral. He used a small whip to get the sorrel's attention, but he never touched the horse with the leather. The horse wore a halter and Ken held on to the rope looped through one of the D-rings. This was a morning exercise he dearly loved, just the horse and him—the big Texas sky and Baronsville, the town he was building, forgotten for an hour or so.

"Ruddy, you can get to that next gait, boy," Ken said to the gelding. "It's in your nature."

Ruddy whickered softly as if in response to Richman's conversational tone. He had three gaits down pat, but Ken wanted to bring him up to five gaits. He snapped the whip and it cracked crisply. Ruddy went into the fourth gait, a canter, and Ken beamed.

"That's it, boy," he said. "You can run that one all day long."

Ruddy's ears stiffened to rigid cones and his eyes broke open in a wild fixation on some object in the distance. Ken turned and saw the lone rider through the shimmer of the morning dew alight in the rising sun.

"Ho, boy, that's enough. Slow 'er down." Ken clucked to Ruddy and the horse slipped out of the canter and slowed to a walk. Out of the corner of his eye, Ken saw a rider appear on the horizon. "I wonder who that is," he said to Ruddy as he stepped up and rubbed its delicate nose. The horse bowed its neck and pawed a territorial crease in the dirt.

Ken walked the horse over to one of the posts in the corral and snubbed the bitter end of the rope around it. He climbed over a pole and stepped outside of the corral. He pulled his hat brim down to shade his eyes from the sun. His florid face seemed to flare in the glow of morning and his square jaw tightened as he squinted to make out who the rider might be. He didn't recognize the horse.

He waited as the rider drew closer and soon he saw who it was. His jawline softened and his blue-green eyes sparkled.

"What brings you all the way out to Wolf Ridge, Juanito?" Ken asked when the man on the horse was within earshot. "I thought you were up the coast with Marty and Anson."

"I was," Juanito said. He made no move to dismount. "Martin wants you to do something for him."

"Glad to. He back?"

"No. It is a long story."

"Tell it," Ken said.

Juanito recounted the events that had brought him back to Baronsville with a request that Ken get some men and ride to the Matagorda as soon as possible.

"I know Cullers," Ken said. "Who he is. A cutthroat."

"Yes, that is true."

"I'll put Ruddy away and saddle my riding horse and round up some men. You think Marty will be in the Matagorda?"

"I do not know."

"Where are you headed now, Juanito?"

"Back to the Box B. Martin wants me to look after Caroline. Have you seen her?"

"Nope. I rode out once to check on her, but she was asleep. The *criada* said she was fine. Lonely."

"Yes. Get down to the Matagorda fast, will you, Ken? I think Martin is going to need some help with those *cabrones*. There is only Martin and the boy to go against them. They are very dangerous men, those three."

"Yes, I expect so. Swenson I don't know. Hoxie is never very far away from Sam Cullers. Cullers is a backshooter and knifer."

"Hasta la vista," Juanito said, and turned his horse toward the Box B. Ken watched him go and then walked back to the corral, opened the gate. He hadn't told Juanito, but he had known Jerry Winfield, too. They had once helped Jim Bowie and his brothers smuggle some slaves into New Orleans. Neither of them had liked the job much, and

Jerry had wanted to let the Negroes go. But they were broke and needed the money. Jerry had worried about it for a long time, though, and now it was hard to believe he was dead.

Tears came unbidden to Ken's eyes as he led Ruddy out of the corral and toward the stables. "Damn that Cullers," he muttered.

29

THE RAIN SLACKENED and the roar of the runaway creek gradually subsided.

"Maybe we can get across now," Peebo said, pushing the horses out of his way as he stood up.

"Worth a try," Martin said.

The three men mounted their horses and rode over the top of the knoll. Below, the floodwaters were subsiding. They had made a wide pool and were now receding fast.

Anson looked across the creek at the empty land beyond. But then he saw something. "There's somebody on horseback," he said. "Straight out yonder."

"I see him," Peebo said. "Duck."

Martin and Anson ducked, but Peebo just sat there, looking at the man. A second later, they saw a puff of smoke, then heard the crack of the rifle. A lead ball whistled overhead.

"High and wide," Peebo said.

"That Cullers?" Martin asked.

"No, I figure that to be Hoxie." He paused as the rider turned his horse. The horse galloped away and disappeared over the horizon. "And there he goes," Peebo said.

"Can we cross that flooded creek?" Martin asked.

"We're damned sure going to try," Peebo said, and rode down the slope of the knoll, leading the way.

Martin and Anson followed.

The three men picked their way across the creek, and after some close calls, with the horses struggling against the current, they made the other side, high and dry.

"We can catch Cullers now," Peebo said. "I figure he left Hoxie behind to try and shoot me down. But Hoxie got rattled when he saw there was three of us."

"You read a man pretty good, Peebo," Martin said.

"I try."

"By the way, is that your real name? Peebo?"

Peebo laughed. "My first name's Peabody, but I never could pronounce it when I was a kid. So, everybody started calling me Peebo and I figure it's a hell of a lot better than Peabody. The name sounds too British for a Yankee."

"Yeah," Martin said. "I like Peebo a hell of a lot better."

Anson snorted. He didn't like Peebo, either as a name or as a man. He didn't like the way his father took to him so quick. He felt shut out. He watched as the two rode away together. He jabbed spurs into his horse's flanks, but he didn't care if he caught up with them.

"They wouldn't notice, no way," Anson said aloud. As he rode, he tried to squelch the resentment he bore toward Peebo Elves. But he had a hurt somewhere inside that wouldn't go away. "Who in hell does he think he is, anyway? Peebo, my ass. He ought call himself Short Britches."

Anson was surprised when his father finally turned around in the saddle and motioned for him to catch up. He grinned and slapped his horse on the rump. He galloped into the wind just as a last spatter of rain dashed against his face.

30

SAM CULLERS HEARD only a single shot, a faint crack from faraway, the sound of it dulled by the lumbering dove-gray clouds overhead. He barely heard it, since he had put distance between him and that persistent little bastard who was following them like his own shadow. Still, he did not slow his pace. He rode on, thinking to himself how lucky they were to have crossed that dry creek bed before the sudden flood. But then the rains had been so relentless they hadn't been able to see two feet in front of them, so they'd had to wait out the storm. He had left Hoxie within two hundred yards of the last place he had spotted that little bastard on that seventeen-hand horse.

"Either Hoxie got the bastard, he missed, or that short stuff changed him out of the saddle," Cullers said to himself. But he kept looking back over his shoulder, and when he saw a rider coming, he knew it was Hoxie, hell-bent for leather, wearing out a good horse.

Sam didn't wait for Hoxie to catch up with him, but eventually Hoxie did. His horse was well lathered with the yellow foam of sweat, breathing hard.

"You dumb bastard," Cullers said. "What the hell happened?"

"Soon's I catch my damned breath, I'll tell you," Hoxie puffed.

"Likely your horse'll founder before you get your breath."

"I ain't partial to ridin' bareback noway, 'specially when the hide's slicker'n greased owl shit, but it ain't just one no more, Sam. We shoulda stole us some saddles while we were at it, goddamn.''

"Quit your grumblin'. You mean you got the little bastard?"

"No, I mean they's three of 'em a-doggin' our trail. And the little bastard's pullin' the horse the Swede stole."

"Who are the other two?"

"Looks like them fellers we seen in Galveston at the grog shop."

"Shit," Cullers said. "Baron and his brat, you mean. Is that gaucho sonofabitch with 'em?"

"I don't reckon. Just Martin and the boy. They must have got Lars and done somethin' to him, Sam."

"Like what?" Cullers snapped.

"Hell, I don't know. Shot his ass to pieces, I reckon."

"Maybe Lars just run off and gave back the damned horse. How far behind do you figure?"

"They crossed where that creek bed was. Half a mile at most."

Cullers looked back over his shoulder. He could see half a mile. The land was flat. Ahead, it looked much the same. If they continued on their course, they'd be caught out in the open, outnumbered, shot down like a couple of dogs. He searched to the north and the land appeared to get hilly, broken up. He turned his horse, put it to a gallop.

"Hold on, Sam. I—I can't keep up with you. My horse needs rest."

"Tough luck, Hoxie. Maybe you can hold 'em off or down 'em."

"You bastard. We're in this together, ain't we?" Hoxie tried to get his horse to break out of a walk, but the bottom had gone out of him. He would be lucky to ride another mile. The sound of the horse's lungs working gave him the shivers.

"Not no more, we ain't," Cullers said and slapped the tips of his reins against his horse's rump.

"You sonofabitch!" Hoxie yelled, but he heard his words die in the empty air.

But despite what Cullers had said, Hoxie was not stupid. He knew he had little chance against three men. Not out in the open like that. He dismounted and walked to the front of the horse. He grabbed the animal by the ears and pulled downward with all his strength. The horse stumbled and tried to stand up, but Hoxie's weight was too great for him. Finally the horse went to its knees and Hoxie climbed onto its neck and forced it to lie flat. He lay on the horse's neck until it quieted and then slid back beside it, one hand putting pressure on the neck to keep the horse down.

He wished he had a saddle to use to stop a bullet, but all the horses had on when they stole them were halters. He lay against the horse's back, listened to its labored breathing, felt its backbone undulate like a bellows against his belly.

Hoxie pulled out his knife, a big-bladed bowie, sharp on both sides of the blade.

"I'll shut you up, you mangy sonofabitch," he said, and plunged the knife into the horse's throat, drew it back toward him quickly, leaving a huge gash that poured blood out as the horse kicked and thrashed, sucked blood into its lungs. "They might get me," Hoxie said, holding the horse down so it didn't roll over and crush him, "but they ain't gettin' you back."

The horse twitched spasmodically for a few more seconds, then expelled air from its anus and was still. A putrid smell hung in the close air and Hoxie pinched his nose. He lay his reloaded rifle across the dead horse's side and waited for what he was sure would be certain death.

31

P EEBO PUT UP his hand as a sign for Martin and Anson to halt.
"What's up?" Martin asked. "We can catch that bastard easily. He
can't be more than a quarter mile away by now."

"Just a minute, Martin," Peebo said. "First, some figuring. We
know a couple of things about Cullers and Hoxie. Might be important."

"What's that?"

"They left the Matagorda in a big hurry. We know they have one
rifle. Hoxie probably has a pistol and I know Cullers does. They don't
have any food or water. No saddles to carry anything."

"So?"

"So even with a rifle and two pistols, they could stand us off awhile.
And they're probably waiting up ahead for us to ride right into them."

"That could be," Martin admitted.

Anson stood his horse a dozen yards from the two men, listening
to them talk. He wondered how his father could be so subservient to
a little man like Peebo. So trusting. It galled him to think that his
father would let a complete stranger tell him what to do. Surely his
father was a lot smarter than Peebo Elves, who couldn't be more than
a few years past twenty, if he was that old.

"Now," Peebo said, "we can sure as hell chase them jaspers and we might get lucky. Or we could buy the farm. But I think we have a good chance, with the three of us, if we come at them from a different angle."

"Flank 'em?" Martin asked.

"Something like that. Now, the most dangerous path is to follow Hoxie's and Cullers's tracks. I'll do that. You and Anson can come up on their flanks and we'll have them boxed in."

"Might work," Martin said. He looked over at Anson. "Better get in on this, son."

"I can hear you," Anson said, his tone sullen as the shift in a cat's purr from soft to growl.

Peebo looked at the two men, his cyan eyes aflare with light. "Or I can go on alone," he said. "You two can foller like you done."

"We have a stake in catching Cullers, too," Martin said. "We'll back your play."

"Good. We've wasted enough time as it is. You two ride a wide half circle on either side of me. I'll follow the tracks right to the end."

Martin looked sharply at his son. "Anson, you take the right flank. Keep Peebo in sight if you can, but don't sit up too straight. You don't want to give either Hoxie or Cullers a good target. Keep your rifle ready."

"All right," Anson said, and wheeled his horse off the track.

Martin took the left flank and Peebo rode on, following the fresh tracks of Hoxie and Cullers. He put his horse to a gallop and drew his rifle, lay it across the pommel.

Anson drew his rifle from its scabbard and checked the priming. "Damn," he said. The powder was wet, had turned to paste. He dug a finger into the pan and wiped the goo out, buffed it clean with his thumb. Then he took a dry patch and wiped the pan dry. He bit the wooden stopper out of his small horn and poured fresh powder in the pan. He blew away the excess and pulled down the frizzen. He heard Peebo's horse galloping away and spurred his horse up to the same gait, which was not smooth, but rough and ungainly.

His side began to ache, and the rifle took on weight, was difficult to handle with the horse's rough gait making him bounce like a sack of spuds on the saddle. He ranged well to the right but he could still see Peebo on his left, riding slightly ahead of him. He found himself hoping that Peebo would come upon Cullers and Hoxie first and shoot them both dead. And he almost wished all three would die in a hail of gunfire, but he knew that it was not good to think that way. Peebo had done nothing to him. He just didn't like the way his father had taken to him so quick.

He wrestled the horse, trying to break it into a gait that was less jiggling, but the animal wouldn't respond. Apparently it had but two gaits, a walk and a gallop. His side was shot through with a piercing pain that almost doubled him over with the intensity of it.

How much farther do we have to go? Anson asked silently.

The ground was rough, dotted with sage and cactus, sand and dirt and wildflowers that blurred past. Anson could not distinguish any particular thing anymore as his eyes teared up from the pain in his side. He wondered if there was going to be an ambush and whether he would hear the sound of the rifle and hear the ball whistle before it struck him in the face. He knew these thoughts were morbid, but they took his mind off his unbearably painful side ache. He remembered he was supposed to hunker low over his horse's neck, and when he did that, the pain only got worse, and still he kept waiting for that rifle report, which could come from Peebo or his father or from Hoxie or Cullers.

He wanted to turn his horse and run away because it seemed to him he was riding into an unknown situation, a place where death waited, and he was too young to die and didn't know how to kill a man or if he could even throw down on a man and shoot him and what it would feel like if he did and if he'd be proud or sad or sick to his stomach or just numb and empty inside, and then there was the Swede's dead face floating up in his head and he felt his throat constrict as if Swenson had his hands around his neck and was shaking and choking him like a chicken. God, I don't want to die and I don't want nobody to die, just let this ride end with nobody out there, Cullers long gone and Hoxie with him. How much is a couple of horses worth, anyway? and I keep forgetting about Jerry Winfield and his dead face. Oh God, just let it end, all of it, end quick and let the sun come out and dry me off and burn the eyes out of my head that keep seeing dead men's faces and me about to die just like them, Jesus.

Anson's horse came to a sudden halt and almost threw him out of the saddle. He looked to his side and no longer saw Peebo, but he heard his voice shouting. "Anson, look out, boy."

Anson saw the horse lying just ahead, and way off he heard hoofbeats pounding and Peebo was two hundred yards away. Then he saw the rifle barrel and it rose in the air and there was a man behind it, holding it and leveling it at him and nothing but empty ground between them and his horse standing stock-still and quivering all over so that his wet sleek hide shook and rippled like water in a pond.

In that lucid particle of an instant where a man faces a life-and-death decision, Anson saw that Peebo was not going to ride down the man with the rifle. And the rifle was coming to bear on him. In another fraction of that same instant, Anson brought his rifle to his hip and cocked the hammer, thumbed down the frizzen so that it was tight next to the pan. He turned his horse in what seemed to him like a slow crawl and headed it straight at the man with the rifle and charged like some chivalrous knight jousting with a mortal enemy. He got so close he could see the man's face, see his eyes widen, and the horse ate up the distance between them.

With one hand holding the reins tight, Anson veered the horse at the last minute so that his rifle was pointed straight at the man's chest. He squeezed the trigger and heard the sparks ignite the powder in the pan. The rifle bucked as the powder in the ignition chamber exploded, and he felt a sharp pain in his forearm as it took the brunt of the powerful recoil. A cloud of white smoke blossomed from the barrel of his rifle and blotted out the man standing not three yards away.

The horse charged past the puff of smoke and Anson could smell the acrid aroma of burnt black powder. Behind him, he heard a rifle crack and ducked as if expecting a ball to come whizzing at his back. Then he realized that the man with the rifle must have fired as he fell. Anson reined up the horse and put him into a tight 180-degree turn.

The white smoke wafted away like a gauzy fog and Anson saw the man lying on his back, staring up at the sky. He didn't know if the man was dead or alive, but Peebo was the first to reach him and Anson never saw a man get down from a saddle so fast. Peebo seemed to be in two places at once, first in the saddle and then standing over the fallen man with the muzzle of his rifle nestled up under the man's chin.

"That was one hell of a shot, Anson," Peebo said. "Right square in the brisket."

"I—is he dead?"

"He may not be all the way dead, but he ain't breathin' none."

Anson halted his horse over the body of the man he had shot. He looked down at him as if from a great height, feeling dizzy all of a sudden.

"It—it's Hoxie, ain't it?" Anson said.

"Him or his twin, I reckon." Peebo took his rifle away from the dead man's chin.

Anson looked at Hoxie's eyes. They were fixed on a point in space, but they seemed to be staring straight at Anson. Hoxie's eyes didn't move, seemed to be frozen solid on something beyond the earth. There was a hole in his chest and more blood than Anson had ever seen on a man before. His upper torso was bathed in blood. His right hand still gripped the trigger and a tiny plume of smoke seeped from the muzzle. Anson closed his eyes for a moment. It seemed to him he was swaying in the saddle and might fall off his horse at any moment.

"He's really dead?" Anson said when he opened his eyes.

Peebo nudged the man's side with his boot. "He's already turning stiff."

A moment or two later, which seemed like hours to Anson, his father rode up, his face lit with the splash-light of surprise.

"You got him, eh, Peebo? That's Hoxie you shot."

Anson felt a tug of resentment when he heard his father's words. Did he think that Peebo was the only one who could have shot Hoxie? Why did he jump to such a conclusion? It was almost as if he, Anson, did not exist. He felt his neck and face go hot with the anger building up inside him.

"That's Hoxie all right, Martin. But I damned sure didn't shoot him."

"I heard two shots," Martin said.

"Yep. First one come from your son's rifle, and the second one was from Hoxie's gun, what you call a dead man's trigger. All Hoxie shot was a hole in the sky as he was fallin'. Anson there put out his lights."

"Anson?" Martin looked at his son, the surprise on his face shifting to a look of bewilderment.

Anson didn't say anything. He felt the anger in him subside and his face felt cool again.

"He rode straight at Hoxie before I could get here," Peebo said. "Shot him from his horse at a gallop, from no more'n five yards away. And Hoxie had the boy in his sights. It could've gone either way."

"Anson," Martin said, "you really surprise me."

Still Anson said nothing, but he began to feel a sense of pride swell up inside him.

"It was a close call," Peebo said, as if he sensed there was something thick and dark between father and son. "Your boy done real fine." He stood over the dead man as if the body were game for the table, boasting of the hunter's prowess.

"I'll be damned," Martin said. "I'm real proud of you, son."

"Aw," Anson said.

"No, I mean it. I'm right proud of you."

"For killing a man?" Anson said, a challenge in his voice.

"It was him or you," Martin said.

"I—it just happened," Anson said. "I didn't really mean to kill him. It's just that the ball hit him right."

"Well, it was a good shot and you deserve credit," Martin said.

"I don't want none," Anson said and turned his horse away from the dead man.

"Now, what the hell's eatin' him?" Martin asked.

"He's just got a little buck fever, that's all," Peebo said. "He'll get over the shakes once he gets off by himself. He's a brave boy."

Anson wheeled his horse in a tight turn and rode right up on Peebo, looked down at him. "Listen here, Peebo," Anson said, "that's the third time today I've heard you call me boy. I'm no boy no more and you better quit callin' me that or I'll damned sure give you a larrupin', you hear?"

"Sorry," Peebo said quickly. "I didn't mean no harm."

"Well, I ain't no boy," Anson said.

"No, I reckon you sure as hell aren't."

Martin said nothing, but he looked at his son as if he had never seen him before. He lifted his hat and scratched the back of his head.

Anson stopped glaring at Peebo and swung his gaze to meet his father's stare. "And that goes for you, too, Dad."

With that, Anson reined his horse into a turn and rode away from the dead man, stopped, and calmly began to reload his rifle, never looking at Peebo or his father.

That was when his hands started shaking. He spilled more powder than he poured down the muzzle of his rifle. He took a deep breath and held it a long time, trying to regain control of his senses and his palsied hands. He didn't know if he was shaking because he was angry at Peebo and his father or because he had just killed a man. Maybe both, he decided. He let the air out of his lungs and took in another deep breath. He looked down at his hands. They were still trembling slightly.

He closed his eyes, hoping Peebo and his father were not looking at him. He did not feel very much a man at that moment. He was scared inside, but he didn't know what he was scared of. Hoxie was on his mind. It had all happened so quickly, he didn't know exactly how he had managed to shoot Hoxie dead. He didn't mean to, or did he? He damned sure aimed his rifle at him and pulled the trigger. But now it was different. He was different. Something had happened to him at that moment that he could not understand or explain to himself.

Anson felt as if he had stepped across some imaginary line. One minute he was just riding along, following Peebo's orders, and the next he was on his own with a man's life in his hands. It was as if he had walked into a room and the floor had fallen out from under him. And then he was no longer in that room, but down in a cave somewhere underneath with the wind blowing through the empty room, blowing through his mind like some keening death wind.

And now he felt empty inside, as if something had gone out of him, had been taken away from him. But he didn't know what it was.

Just a gnawing emptiness that made him feel all hollow. He opened his eyes and looked up at the sky. It was the same, pure blue and serene and calm and steady.

He thought of something Juanito had told him: All things are one; sky, earth, sea, air, the beings in the whole world, the universe, are all one. If a man is afraid or worried, all he need do is look to the sky, lift up his eyes, Juanito had said, and feel the eternal peace that is in all things. Get to your center, Juanito had said, that secret place inside you where you are pure spirit and invisible. No one can see your soul, your spirit, and it is always calm. Go there, Juanito had said, and you will find your way back from whatever dangerous place you find yourself in. To your center. To the place where the spirit that is in all things dwells.

Anson looked up at the sky and felt himself being drawn up into it. He let himself go and wondered where his center was and if he could find it and if what Juanito had said was really so or just some crazy Argentine jungle stuff. But his hands stopped trembling and he felt a calmness inside. He began to breathe easily as he poured powder down the barrel. He placed a patch and ball a top the muzzle and rammed them down partway with the short starter, then pulled his wiping stick and seated the ball firmly. He tapped the stock just below the lock and then primed the pan with the fine powder. When he finished, he turned his horse to see if his father and Peebo were looking at him.

They were not.

The two men were piling brush and stones and dirt over the body of Hoxie.

Anson smiled. Everything was back to normal.

Maybe Juanito wasn't crazy after all. Maybe he knew things that other men had never even imagined.

32

—■—

CAROLINE GRIPPED THE bedpost until her knuckles drained of blood. Sweat oiled her forehead and face and the bedsheets were damp with her perspiration. She gasped for breath and swung her legs to the side of the bed. Then, she groaned as she tried to sit up. Her belly was swollen even more than it had been when Martin, Anson and Juanito had left for the Gulf Coast to sell the Mary E. It seemed to her that she would never be able to bear such a baby to term.

She heard noises from another part of the house and when she groaned again, she heard a knock on her bedroom door.

"Who is it?" she gasped.

"It is Luisa."

"Come in."

"Is the *Señora* well?" Luisa Buenjoven asked as she opened the door.

"The goddamned *Señora* is not well. Where is Carla?"

"She has gone to town. To Baronsville. She buys the flour and the coffee. She thought you would sleep through the afternoon."

"Help me get out of bed, Luisa. The baby has been kicking me to death all afternoon."

"Too soon, too soon," crooned Luisa, as she stepped carefully into the room.

"I'm sick," Caroline said, as if to confirm her suspicions, as well as to elicit sympathy. "Get the chamberpot from under the bed."

"The *Señora* is going to vomit?"

"Stop calling me that. My name is Caroline. And Caroline is going to vomit if you don't drag out that pot."

Quickly, Luisa, who was but eighteen, bent down and pulled the chamberpot from under the bed. She held it gingerly over Caroline's lap. Caroline scooted forward, still gripping the bedpost and leaned over the porcelain pan. She waited for the telltale contractions of her stomach.

"Was it something the, something your grace ate for lunch?"

"I don't know. I feel awful. My stomach feels like it's full of grease." She knew Luisa wouldn't understand half of what was said in English, but Caroline had been speaking Spanish ever since Martin had left and she was tired of the language. Carla could at least understand her, if she spoke English, but Carla did not speak it very well. It was sometimes exasperating, trying to communicate.

"Do you want me to get you some salts?" Luisa asked. She still held the bedpan just above Caroline's lap. "Some unguents?"

"Ugh," Caroline said. She had no idea what was in the various pastes and oils and purgatives Carla had been giving her, but her stomach rebelled at the very idea of any substance introduced into it by this young Mexican girl. One time she had been on the chamberpot for a week from something Carla had dosed her with one night when she had been feeling terribly ill.

"Here, give me the chamberpot," Caroline said in Spanish, snatching it from Luisa's hands. "Let me die alone."

"I have fear, *Señora.* Do not talk of dying this way."

"Go away, Luisa. *Por favor.*"

"Yes, of course."

Luisa left the room and Caroline sat there with the chamberpot in her hands. She looked down at it. So clean, so white, so empty. A shame to disturb its porcelain beauty. But, she stuck her finger down her throat and bent over. She retched, but nothing came up. Only a little gastric gas, she thought, and then remembered that she'd had only tea and toast for breakfast and nothing for lunch. The tea had been a gift from Ken Richman who had come to see her recently. But, she had been asleep. He had left some groceries for her, tea, fruit from the tropics. Ken was always able to bring them delicacies that were out of reach for most people in that part of the country.

Caroline threw the chamberpot on the bed and forced herself to touch the floor with her bare feet. She felt so stuffed, so full of the baby that it was almost suffocating. Perhaps if she moved around she would feel better. She waddled to the wardrobe and opened it. She picked out a housecoat that she'd had to let out three times in recent months, adding material ingeniously so that it looked as if the stripes of colored cloth had been planned. The coat also made her look slightly slimmer.

She put it on and then bent down slowly to slide out a pair of slippers one of the Mexicans, Carlos, had made for her. He had called them *huaraches*, and they were sandals made of woven leather attached to smooth leather soles. They were very comfortable. She slipped her swollen feet into them. Carlos had made them so the leather could expand as her feet got larger from all the fluids she retained. She couldn't look at her ankles anymore. They were almost nonexistent, anyway, just little lumps in her skin and veiny, besides. Ugly, like the rest of her.

She stepped to the dressing table and picked up a kerchief and dipped it into the bowl of water. She washed her face free of perspiration, then dabbed herself dry with another kerchief from the stack she had placed there. She dried between her breasts and touched up her hair as she looked in the mirror. She hated to look at her face anymore. She looked so haggard lately. The work was so hard.

Two days before, some of the cattle had gotten out of the pasture near the house, broken through the fence Martin and Juanito had built of mesquite and timbers hauled in from Houston. The big longhorns, led by a rangy bull named Tonto, had trampled her garden and knocked down some young fruit trees. She and Carla, after cutting Tonto out of the herd and penning him in the barn, had finally gotten the cattle back in the pasture and mended the fence, but it had been dark before they finished. The next day, she and Carla had taken Tonto to a corral where he could not get out. She could still hear his mournful bellowing that had lasted for two long nights.

It had been one thing after another since Martin had left. The Mexican women had complained when they had run out of dried corn and Caroline had had to send Carlos to town to buy more from the mercantile. Then, they had run out of flour and again, she'd had to send Carlos into Baronsville in the wagon for flour and salt. She had berated the women for waiting until they were all out of staples before coming to her. And it had rained and rained and the wind had blown some of the shutters off the house and one of the adobes was washed away in a flash flood and a family had become homeless. She had put them up in the barn until another casita could be built for them.

She sighed as she remembered all these things and wondered when Martin would be back and when they would have money again. She had not heard from her parents in weeks and worried about them.

But, she had not written, either, so she realized she could not fault them for their neglect in corresponding with her.

She got up from the dressing table and put a fresh kerchief inside her sleeve. She turned away from the mirror, shaking her head at the image she was leaving behind.

She heard the noise of footsteps in another part of the house as she waddled toward the door.

"That damned Luisa," she said. "What is she doing? Playing with the children in my house?"

Then, she heard voices, too low to understand. She walked out of her bedroom, curious now, and started for the front room where the noises were coming from, her sandals making soft sliding sounds as she shuffled on the hardwood flooring.

Two people were speaking in rapid Spanish. It sounded like quarreling to Caroline, but she could not hear the words plainly. She was already out of breath and had not reached the front room yet.

"She is not well. She will not see anyone."

"Well, I must see her. Please tell her that I am here."

"She will be very angry if I go in there again."

"Juanito, is that you?" Caroline called.

"Yes, Caroline. I am here."

"I'll be right there."

A moment later she stepped into the living room. Luisa stood at the door, inside. Juanito stood on the porch, his way barred by the diminutive *Mexicana.*

"*Abre la puerta,*" Caroline ordered. Luisa opened the door.

"*Vete,*" Caroline snapped and the girl quickly left the room, headed for the kitchen.

"Please come in, Juanito. Where's Martin?"

"Perhaps we had better sit down, Caroline. There is much to tell you." He took off his hat and held it in front of him with both hands.

She looked at him closely. He was still dusty from the ride, so he had not gone to his house and cleaned up. She wondered inanely what he was doing here in her house. He should have been away with Martin.

"Is something wrong, Juanito?"

"Please," he said, "will you not take a seat?" Juanito stepped up to her and took her arm. He led her to the divan and helped her get settled on the seat. Then, he sat in a chair nearby and set his hat on the floor.

"What's happened, Juanito?" Caroline asked, her voice rising in the early stages of hysteria.

"There is nothing to worry about. Martin and Anson are delayed, that is all. I will tell you what happened."

"Oh, God," she said.

"It is not what you think," Juanito said and proceeded to tell her about selling the boat, the murder of Jerry Winfield and when he had last seen her husband and son.

Caroline sat there, trying to control her emotions, but there was a tightness in her face and her lips were compressed until Juanito finished.

"So, they will be here soon and we will find out the rest of the story," Juanito concluded. "Already, Ken Richman is on his way to the Matagorda to lend assistance."

"I told him not to go, Juanito. I begged him. But, no, he wouldn't listen. And now he and my son are chasing after cutthroats. Murderers. I knew it. I just knew something terrible would happen."

"Calm yourself, Caroline. Calm yourself. Everything will be all right, I assure you. Martin sent me back to look after you. He cares about you."

"No, he doesn't," she said and started to sniffle.

Juanito searched in his pockets for a clean handkerchief. Caroline unfurled the kerchief she drew out of her sleeve, dabbed at her eyes.

"You know that is not true, Caroline."

"Well, he doesn't act like it. He knows I'm with child and still he leaves me here to run the ranch. I've had to deal with so many problems since you left, Juanito. I'm worried about the baby. It's kicking all the time now like it wants to jump out."

"The baby will come when it is ready."

"That's what the doctor said."

"He has been to see you?"

"He comes out every week. Carla knows more than he does about babies."

"Most of the Mexican women on the ranch will be able to help you. They are very wise about babies and childbirth."

"How is Anson?"

"He is well," Juanito said.

"His father does not treat him very nice."

"That is the way with a father and a son. The son is a rival."

"What?"

"There will be some competition and then one day Martin will see a man where his son once stood."

"I hope so. I don't like to see them fight."

"Anson does not like to see you and Martin fight."

"Oh? How would he know?"

"Children see everything," Juanito said. "They hear everything."

Caroline closed her eyes for a moment, trying to remember what Anson might have seen and heard. Then, the fear she harbored rose up in her and she wondered whether or not Juanito could read her mind. He was so wise about people, so intuitive.

"Well, I'm sure Anson hasn't seen much. Martin and I quarrel, but it's nothing serious."

"It passes," Juanito said.

"Passes?" Caroline took a deep breath. "I hope so."

"What doesn't pass is what you keep in your mind, Caroline."

"Memories, you mean."

"Resentments. Hurts. Little things that are of the past."

"Why, everyone does that," she said quickly.

"Those bad things you keep in memory, the hurts, the resentments, they can make you unhappy. They can eat at you like a poison."

"I'm not like that, Juanito."

"I hope not. You can do nothing about the past. It has already gone. And you cannot do anything about the future, either. It is not here yet. The happy person is the one who lives in the present, like a child. That is the one moment of life and it is eternal."

"I'm afraid I don't understand you, Juanito. So much that you say is beyond my learning."

"See life as a child sees it. Just the single moment. You can take care of that much, no? Only a single moment. Be happy. Do not look down the dark corridor of the past, nor try to see into the future. Just look at this one moment and see how happy you are. Nothing has ever happened to you, nothing ever will. You are alive, you have life inside you. That is enough. Just that one single eternal moment. God's moment."

"You make it sound so simple. Just forget the past and don't worry about the future. Just be glad that I'm alive now."

"And safe," Juanito said. "That is the secret. Now. Only now."

"I will try and remember that," she said, and they both laughed.

"Well, you are fine, I see," Juanito said. "I have not yet unsaddled my horse nor opened the door to my casita. I will do these things and if you need me, send Luisa or Carla and I will come."

Juanito stood up. Caroline started to rise, but he waved a hand at her.

"I—I'm glad you came back," she said. "I wish Martin were with you. And Anson."

"They will be here soon. The future, remember?"

Caroline laughed.

"You're right. I can't bring them back, can I?"

"Not in the way you think," he said and was gone from the room before she could ask him what he meant. Juanito was such a strange men, but Martin trusted him and he knew a lot about cattle and horses. And life, she thought, and sighed.

She had never seen such a strong friendship that existed between the two men. Sometimes she envied Juanito, for he was privy to things about Martin that she would never know. Men things. The things that men did that women were not allowed to do. Fighting, using their muscles to conquer man and beast, racing their horses just for the sport of it, competing in rough games and speaking the private scatology that women were not supposed to hear, swearing in a language forbidden among women of breeding, doing things that were theirs alone to do, things that made them bond with each other as no woman could bond with a man.

Caroline did not resent that bonding, but she envied it. At times, she had tried to enter Martin's world, and Juanito's, but she had been quickly shut out, made to feel an outsider. Men, she decided, did not like tomboys if they had a romantic interest in the woman. But a real tomboy was accepted as long as she didn't ever grow up and become a woman. She had been such a girl when she was still at home with her parents. Until she had met Martin, in fact. Then, it seemed important to show him her feminine side, but there were times that she wanted to sit with him in the bunkhouse and talk with the hands, the vaqueros, and be accepted as one of them. But, that was a forbidden world to her, she knew.

And only once in her marriage had she crossed that line and suddenly knew that she had gone too far into a man's world. It was a dangerous place for a woman, for a woman as vulnerable as she. She had gone into that dark cave where men were still savages under the veneer of civilization and she had come out less a woman than when she had entered, and even more shut out than she had been before.

Caroline arose from the divan and walked to the kitchen where Luisa was banging pots and pans, setting out dishes for the evening meal. Caroline ignored her and walked to the back door and looked out through the glass. She looked at the trampled garden and recoiled inwardly at the sight. The small fence, to keep the rabbits out, was torn down, even the scarecrow she had put up to frighten the birds was in tattered rags, and the bent cornstalks drooped disconsolately, rattling as they brushed together in the slight breeze.

She looked at Juanito's casita and saw the front door open. His horse was gone. She saw him emerge from the stables a few moments later, pause at the corral where she and Carla had penned up the rebellious Tonto. He stood looking at the huge longhorn bull for several moments, then continued walking back toward his casita.

Caroline turned away from the door and walked back into the kitchen.

"When will Carla return?" she asked Luisa in Spanish.

"At four hours," Luisa replied. "In a little moment. It is almost four hours now."

"What are you doing?"

"Carla asked me to set the pots out for the supper she will prepare."

"Set another place at the table for Juanito, please."

"*Por cierto.*"

"And see that there is a good wine on the table."

"Yes, *Señora,* I will do that."

"I want to dine at sundown."

"Yes, at sundown, most certainly."

Caroline walked back to the back door, opened it, hesitated a moment, then stepped outside. She let the door shut behind her, then walked down the porch steps toward Juanito's casita. She walked slowly, her weight shifting from side to side, so that she appeared duck-like in her housecoat and sandals.

Juanito stepped outside his door, apparently having seen Caroline approaching. When she drew near, he spoke to her.

"You have come to see me, Caroline?"

"I just wanted some fresh air. And, I want to invite you to supper. At sundown."

"Ah, sundown. A fine time to eat a meal."

"You are settled in then?"

"I have not much to do. I do not dust."

Caroline laughed.

"You bachelors," she said. "Don't you want a wife, Juanito?"

"Ah, a wife," he said. "Some men think a woman is a necessity. I would think it a luxury."

"And?"

"And, I have no time for luxury. My work is my life."

"But if you found a woman to share your life, wouldn't that be nice?"

"She would have to be a very special woman. Like you, Caroline."

Caroline blushed.

"I am not so special." She looked away from him, toward the corral where Tonto ranged like a caged lion, cracking each post with the tip of his long horns. The sound of those horn-tips striking the posts and the fence rails rattled Caroline's tautened nerves.

"Yes, you are," Juanito said. "Martin is a very lucky man."

"I wonder if he knows that."

"He does."

"Does he say so?"

"Not in those words, perhaps, but he says them."

"You are a very considerate man, Juanito."

"And truthful."

"Of course," she said, laughing as well. She started walking toward the corral. "Come with me a moment, will you?"

"Gladly," Juanito said.

"Didn't you wonder why Tonto was in that corral?" she asked.

"I saw the garden and the patched fence when I rode in. Tonto is a very strong-willed bull. He has sired some very good stock. He will sire many more. Martin and I caught him in the brasada two years ago. He was very smart and he crippled two of the vaqueros' horses before we caught him."

"He is wild," Caroline said. "And mean."

They stopped at the corral. Tonto stopped pacing and glared at them, his head lowered as if to charge them if they came any closer. He pawed the ground with a cloven hoof and snorted.

"He was very wild, yes, but he has domesticated well."

"He destroyed my garden," Caroline said.

"That was an unfortunate accident, yes."

"I think he did it deliberately. He didn't eat any of the vegetables."

"Some say the intelligence of a longhorn is that of a deer or a horse. I would think that Tonto was going somewhere that he remembered, perhaps to the brasada where we caught him and that your garden was just in his path."

"I don't believe that. Not for a moment."

"Who is to say?" Juanito said, shrugging. "You can replant the garden."

She turned and looked at Juanito. The look was flat and iron and seething with an undercurrent of anger that seemed to flash in her eyes.

"I want you to castrate Tonto," she said coldly. "Tomorrow."

"That would be a shame," Juanito said.

"I was going to do it myself when Carlos returned."

"Tonto is a very fine bull. Very fine for breeding."

"Juanito, I'm not asking you. I'm telling you. I want Tonto's nuts cut off. Now, will you do that for me, or must I wait until Carlos returns?"

"I will do it," Juanito said, "but with sadness. He is a perfect sire for my Argentine cows. He will give us a strong breed of cattle for market."

"Oh, pshaw! What market? You are a dreamer like Martin is."

"Caroline, are you sure it is the bull you want castrated?"

"What do you mean by that?" she snapped.

"I think you ought to think very long and deeply about doing this thing to Tonto. It is a punishment he does not deserve. But, perhaps he is only a substitute for someone who does need castration."

"Do it," she said. "I won't have you talking to me like that, do you hear?" She glared one last time at Juanito then turned on her heel and duck-waddled back toward the house. Before she got there, she turned and called out quite pleasantly: "Don't forget. Supper at sundown."

"I will be there," Juanito called back. To himself, he said, "Women. There is no understanding them." Then he looked at Tonto. The bull stood there, no longer pawing the ground, but looking sadly at Juanito. He spoke to the bull in Spanish.

"I wonder who you really are in Caroline's mind," he said. "I wonder who she wants to castrate, eh? Do you know, big bull? Do you know the answer?"

The bull shook its head, raking the air with its massive horns.

Juanito laughed. "They call you Tonto, which means 'stupid' in Spanish. But, perhaps you really are intelligent," he said. "Now if you could only speak."

Tonto snorted and rammed his boss into the corral pole where Juanito stood. Juanito did not move, but listened to the wood shudder and tremble as if it had been set in motion by an earthquake of terrible proportions.

33

—■—

PEEBO ELVES STRADDLED the tracks on the ground, slicing them in two symbolically with a guillotine downslash from his arm. When his hand stopped in midair, perpendicular to his body, it pointed northwest through a maze of low hills and rolling land.

"That's where Cullers headed and he's a-whoopin' his horse," Peebo said.

"He's going into hiding," Martin said.

"No, he's going to kick up some dust puttin' distance 'tween us, but he's a-goin' to cut him some trails through them hills and find hard rock when he can. He's a wily one, all right."

Anson watched the two men from several yards back. They had tracked Cullers on foot for the past five minutes after Peebo made a big circle to pick up his trail. Whatever else he was, Anson decided, Peebo was a good tracker. He could read tracks like other men read books. He could almost tell what a man was thinking by the trail he cut. Or maybe Peebo could tell what Cullers was thinking, for all Anson knew. His father was equally mesmerized by the diminutive man's tracking ability.

"Can you figure where Cullers is headed?" Martin asked.

Peebo turned around, took off his large-brimmed hat and scratched the back of his head. Anson wondered if that was an act.

Peebo didn't seem to him to have to stop and think very much. He had called all the shots right so far, tracking three men, figuring out where Swenson would be and Hoxie, too. Anson wondered whether Peebo would scratch his head if he was by himself. He seemed to be as good an actor as he was a tracker.

"Well, sir," Peebo said, putting his hat back on, "he don't have no money, no friends, no food and just one stolen horse and no papers for it and no running brand with him, so I guess he'll just run it on out like a mountain cat until he's treed."

"You think he'll fight or give up?" Martin asked.

"I think he'll do one or the other, dependin' on how much breath he feels hot on his neck."

"So?"

"So we press him. Keep him awake. Run him down like we was hounds. 'Course that means we don't get no rest neither, and the horses will pay a price."

"How far ahead of us is he?"

"Less than an hour, I'd say."

"Then let's get to it, Peebo. You lead the way."

"One good thing," Peebo said as he mounted his horse.

"What's that?" Martin asked.

"He don't have no more men to lay down false trails. I reckon we'll see just how wily Mr. Cullers is." Peebo clucked to his horse and touched spurs to its flanks. The horse had to be seventeen hands high, Anson figured. Peebo looked like a child in the big Santa Fe saddle. A child wearing an oversized ten-gallon hat.

The hoofprints of the horse Cullers was riding revealed that he was eating up ground, following a more or less straight line. However, once into the low hills, Cullers apparently had to slow down, rest his horse. The tracks began to look fresher and the three trackers knew that they were closing the distance between them and their quarry.

The clouds began to thicken and the sky grew darker. Peebo stepped up the pace, looking up every so often.

"If it rains again, we might lose Cullers," Peebo told Martin.

"He can't be far ahead of us now."

"No. Fifteen, twenty minutes, maybe."

"Then let's get him."

"Easier said than done," Peebo said.

The hoof tracks led them into rougher country, country thick with thorny brush and brambly undergrowth. For a time Cullers followed a small stream, emerged in a dry wash and climbed to a narrow ridge. Then he plunged downward again and rode through a small ravine, went again to higher ground and rode across a rocky ridge, where he left few tracks. But Peebo noticed every overturned stone, every broken twig and bent or crushed blade of grass.

"He's tricky," Peebo said sometime later as the tracks got fresher and the route more serpentine and circuitous. "Cullers ain't tryin' to gain ground no more. 'Stead, he's hopin' to botch us up."

"Botch us up?" Martin said.

"Confuse us. Maybe hopin' we make a mistake and lose him."

"Any likelihood of that?"

"Nope. But I wouldn't put nothin' past him from now on. He's pretty desperate, I reckon."

The track switched back and forth through a series of ravines and gullies, and then over open ground the hoofprints stretched out. Cullers had run the horse hard to gain some time and distance.

Peebo put his horse to a gallop. Martin and Anson followed suit and caught up with him at the edge of a dropoff. Below, the land was once again rolling, with many small hills and ridges, ravines and stream beds broken only by sandy hillocks and thick brush and mesquite.

"He ain't far off now," Peebo said, pausing for a moment to get a line on where Cullers might have gone. "He could be anywhere down there."

"Hard to follow him down there."

"Well, if he makes it easy for us, look out," Peebo said.

"What do you mean?" Martin asked.

"I mean he might have another trick or two up his thievin' sleeve."

Peebo headed his horse down into the maze of ravines and hills. From what Anson could see of him, Peebo was having no trouble in following Cullers. They rode steeply down a ravine, over another hill and then, abruptly, it seemed, Cullers started riding in the opposite way, up a deep ravine. Even Anson could see the tracks, the rolled-over stones, the broken brush. Cullers was having a hard time making it up the ravine, just as they were doing.

They heard a sound up ahead and Peebo raised his hand to halt the small column of three. Martin rode up just behind Peebo's horse, since the ravine was too narrow for him to come up alongside.

"What was that?" Martin whispered.

Peebo shook his head, then seemed to ponder for a moment. Then he gestured with his right hand toward his horse's rump. Martin nodded in understanding.

Peebo rode on, Martin and Anson following.

The ravine was a tangle of cedars and juniper, a few scrub mesquite and thick tangles of black chaparral that slowed the horses. Anson saw that some of the brush was trampled and broken. They continued to climb and finally emerged at the crest. Peebo kept following the spoor past the top of the ridge and down into another ravine on the other side.

Martin crested the ravine and plunged down into the next one, following Peebo. Anson came up last in line and hesitated for a moment. He looked around, but could not say why. Some slight sound, the scrape of a boot on stone, the rattle of a tree branch, the hoarse whisper of a man's heavy breathing.

He watched as Peebo disappeared from sight, then his father rounded a bend in the ravine and he too was gone. He heard brush break ahead of the two men and he started down the same path.

Then from the side a blur, a shadow, and he twisted in the saddle too late and felt something hard strike him in the side. His feet left the stirrups and another blow from an unseen assailant knocked him out of the saddle.

He tumbled downward and struck the ground hard. Sparks and fireflies danced in his brain and the darkness spun in his head like a whirlwind.

34

U RSULA LAY ON her bed watching the pale light of morning seep
through the windows. She looked over at the dark hulk of her
husband, Jack, sleeping on his side. Had she dreamed it all? She
thought he had made love to her three times during the night, but it
might have been only twice. No, three times, and each time better
than the time before.

She sighed deeply, trying to remember the last time. It couldn't
have been more than a few moments ago, yet Jack was sound asleep,
the expression on his face one of innocence. No, she had gone to
sleep after that and dreamed. But she couldn't remember the dream.
It was like gauze in her mind, wispy fragments she could not connect.
She sighed again and slid from the bed. Let him sleep, she told herself.
I'm content. Very happy.

The room reeked of their twin sweats, but the scent of Jack was
overpowering. She let the aroma of him linger in her nostrils for a
long time, thinking of the massive weight of him on top of her, but
strangely light, not crushing, but clinging in a gentle way. For all his
roughness, she thought, Jack was a gentle man, at least with her. She
had thought about the scents of him for a long time after he had gone
away, and for a long time his musk lingered in their bedroom, like
some heady perfume from a dark flower.

And she had been sad when Jack's scent had faded away and only her own clung cloyingly to the bedding, the dainty powder, the flowery perfume that seemed so tawdry now in the strong bouquet that was Jack.

She heard footsteps and then the back door slammed and she knew Roy was up tending to his chores before breakfast. It was her signal to rise and prepare the morning meal, put on the coffee. And this was a special morning, a bittersweet morning, for her men would leave her and she would be alone. She sat up and turned, dangling her bare legs over the edge of the bed. She was naked, and in the soft light of dawn her body was comely, soft, like a young girl's. She smiled and stepped to the floor.

She groped for her gown on the chair near the bed and pulled it over her head. Then she found the wrapper at the foot of the bed and put her arms inside the sleeves so that she would be decent in front of her son.

She tiptoed from the room carrying her old slippers, the ones she had brought from Saint Louis years before. She wore them only once in a while. They were pink, but the pink had faded, and there were tiny blue bows at the toes. She felt like a ballerina when she was wearing them.

She opened the lid on the firebox of the woodburning stove carefully so that she made no sound. She stuffed splints of kindling wood in the box and reached up and brought down a small tin box. She removed the contents and stuffed a wad under the wood. Then she struck a match to the excelsior she kept in that tin box on top of the stove.

The excelsior burst into flame and the kindling caught fire. She set the lid back down gently, then walked to the counter. She dipped coffee from the can of Arbuckle's and put it in the blackened coffeepot, then filled it with water from a wooden bucket set beside the counter. Roy had filled it the night before, as he always did.

Ursula began humming to herself as she prepared breakfast: cured ham, potatoes, eggs, biscuits and red-eye gravy. She smiled when Jack, rubbing sleep dust from his eyes, appeared in the kitchen doorway half dressed.

"Umm, I could smell it," he said. "Hungry as a bear."

Ursula laughed. "Why don't you get dressed and go out and fetch Roy? He should be about through with the milking by now."

"I'll help him finish up. God, that ham smells good. Coffee ready?"

"It will be by the time you two get back in here."

The men, washed up and ravenous, sat down at the kitchen table.

Ursula piled food on their plates, filled their tin cups with steaming coffee.

"There's milk, too, if you want, cool from the springhouse."

"Yes," Jack declared and began to burrow into the food on his plate. He washed the eggs down with coffee and smeared a biscuit with fresh-churned butter. He dragged the biscuit through the red-eye gravy and smacked his lips after he bit into it.

Ursula sat down and proudly watched her two men as she sipped coffee and dabbled at her food. The mood was dampened only by a touch of sadness at their leaving.

"You both eat like you've never seen food before," she said.

"It's the best, Mother," Roy said.

"Better'n that." Jack cut a large chunk of ham and impaled it with his fork. "Sweetest pork I ever tasted."

"It was . . ." Roy started to say. But Ursula gave him a sharp look.

"What's that?" Jack asked.

"It was a good buy," Ursula said quickly.

"Well, it's mighty fine-tasting," Jack said.

When Roy and Jack were finished eating, Ursula suggested they go outside for a smoke while she cleaned up the dishes.

"I reckon we'll saddle up," Jack said, a bit awkwardly, Ursula thought.

"I kind of hoped we could talk a little before you leave, Jack," she said.

"Sure, we'll talk. Come on, Roy, let's have a smoke. You all packed?"

"You bet," Roy said, and a moment later, Ursula was alone in the kitchen. She felt lonesome for them already, even though they had not left yet. She drew in a deep breath and began to clear the table.

35

ROY STOOD IMPATIENTLY beside his new horse, his new pistol strapped on, his bedroll tied tightly behind the cantle of the saddle. He fidgeted with the reins while his parents talked quietly on the porch, just beyond earshot of the boy. The sun had just cleared the eastern horizon and had begun to burnish the high, thin rolls of clouds.

"I want Roy to go with you and I don't want him to go with you, Jack," Ursula said.

"I know. We'll be back."

"When?"

"Eventually. I figure three or four months at the outside."

"I can stand it for that long, I suppose."

"Sure you can," Jack said.

"It's just that, well, seeing you go away again like this. Breaking up our little family."

"Aw, it ain't like that, sugar."

"It is, Jack," she said, a stubborn tone in her voice.

"Why, we'll be back before you know it."

"The nights get long, Jack. The moments stretch into years."

"Don't make me feel any worse than I do, Urs. I need the boy. He needs to become a man."

"What if something happens?"

"To me or to Roy?"

"Either of you," she said.

"Ain't nothin' goin' to happen. It's just a cattle drive, up into New Mexico."

"Indians."

"Why, we'll be travelin' with a regular army—wranglers, drovers, a cookie, the cattle. With men who can shoot and aren't afeared of Injuns."

"It just won't seem like a family no more, Jack. Me all alone. You and Roy out God knows where."

"You just keep the home fires burnin', sugar."

"I'll be waiting," she said. "And worrying."

"Now, now, don't you worry none," Jack said. He leaned close to her and pecked her on the cheek.

"Is that all I get?" she asked.

"Aw, not in front of the boy," he said.

"Jack, you give me a hug and a proper husbandly kiss or I won't let either of you ride off."

"Dammit, Urs. You got to make a fuss?"

"Yes, I do. I have to remember this last kiss a long time."

Jack cursed soundlessly and took Ursula in his arms. He kissed her quickly as her fingers dug hard into his back. Then he tried to break away, but she held him fast.

"Now, don't go cryin' on me now."

"I—I won't," she said.

"And let me go. We got to make tracks."

"Good-bye, Jack."

"Good-bye, hon."

"I love you."

"Yeah, me too," he said, and turned from her, took the porch steps without touching a one.

"Better go give your ma a last hug, Roy," Jack said when he reached his horse.

"Aw, do I have to?"

"You better," Jack said.

Roy gangled over to the porch. "Good-bye, Mother," he said.

"You come up here right now, Roy Killian, and give me a good-bye kiss."

"I already give you one," he said.

"It ain't the same."

Reluctantly Roy climbed the steps and embraced his mother.

"You take care, you hear?"

"I will, Mother."

"Mind your father."

"Yes'm."

"There now. Hurry back and bring me something pretty."

"Yes'm, I will. I promise. Good-bye, Mother."

Roy dashed down the steps and trotted to his horse. He climbed up into the saddle, glad that he had cinched it tight. It didn't slip as he pulled on the horn and his weight concentrated on the left stirrup.

"I'm ready, Pa."

"Wave good-bye to your ma," Jack said.

Roy turned and flung a hand into the air. His mother looked so small there on the porch he couldn't bear to look at her but for just a moment.

"Good-bye, Mother," Roy yelled.

"So long, Urs," Jack said, and touched the brim of his hat in a casual salute.

"Good-bye, boys," Ursula called out and her hand hung in the air until her husband and son began to get smaller and smaller and she knew they could no longer see her. She sniffled and turned away, her eyes already watering with the strain of trying to see them. Just before she walked back inside the house, she turned for one more look, but they were gone and the horizon, flat and featureless, looked desolate and empty.

Two hours later, with three apple pies baking in the oven, she heard the sound of hoofbeats. Ursula's heart quickened, and she went to the front door, hoping against hope that Roy and Jack had returned.

Her heart fell when she saw the familiar horse, the blue-clad soldier with three chevrons on his sleeves. He rode up to the hitch-rail and stepped down from his big-boned army horse, a bay mare. As usual, his boots gleamed from polish and his uniform was well pressed.

Ursula opened the door, waited for the man to climb the steps.

"Top o' the mornin' to you, Ursula."

"What brings you out here so early, Dave?"

"Why, I could smell your pies clear to Fort Worth."

"Liar," she said.

"Are you goin' to invite me in? Isn't that some of the ham I gave you that I smell?"

"You might as well come in, Dave. Yes, we had ham for breakfast."

She felt the slight tension between them. She had not expected Dave Riley to come out so soon, so early. He took off his hat as he entered the house.

"Umm, it sure smells good in here. Them pies."

"You didn't come out here for pie, did you, Dave?"

"Why, I surely come out to see my best gal."

Dave was a large, beefy man, a sergeant with twelve years of service. He was not married, she was almost certain, and he saved his money, but was often helpful to her and Roy. He helped with the chores and brought them things from the commissary. She knew his saddlebags were full of tins containing cookies, sweetmeats, perhaps some coffee, and other delicacies.

"Is that all?" Ursula teased.

"Well, I admit I saw your boys ride by and thought to myself that you might need sparkin', seein' as your men was gone and all."

"You saw Jack, then?"

"I saw him buyin' that horse for Roy and I figured he was comin' out here. Didn't expect he'd stay long."

"Why not?"

"Man leaves a good-lookin' woman alone for ten years, he can't be too rooted in family."

"I won't hear any bad talk about Jack, now."

"No'm, I didn't mean no harm. It's just that you and me have been pretty good with each other while he was gone. I hope that won't change none."

Ursula felt a sudden giddiness. It was too soon, she thought. Although she had made the bed, Jack's scent was all over the room, like the scent of wisteria, only stronger, like rich red wine.

"No," Ursula said. "I guess not. It's just that. . . ."

"I know, I shoulda waited a day or so. But. . . ."

"No need to explain, Dave. You been good to me and Roy."

"Now, now, no need to lather me up with all that. I'd just like a little kiss to know I'm still welcome."

She looked at him, tried to shut him out of her mind. But Dave Riley was a presence in the room, tall and sturdy, with broad, heavy shoulders, graceful sideburns shining with pomade, a handlebar moustache without a hair out of place. He smelled of horse and liniment and bath oil, all at once. She breathed of him and closed her eyes.

Dave took her in his arms and held her so tightly she could barely breathe. His kiss was long and vigorous and she almost swooned with the thrill of it. But she pushed him away, the kiss suddenly sour on her lips.

"No, not now," she breathed when Dave broke the kiss. "I—I want you to leave. I just can't do this."

"You're tellin' me you don't want it?"

"That's what I'm saying, Dave. I want you to go. Now. And don't come around no more."

Dave's shoulders sagged. He frowned and stepped away to look at Ursula. "You don't still like that feller, do you?"

"Jack? I—I love him, Dave."

"I'll go. But you'll beg me to come back."

She turned away from him, heard him clump out of the house.

Later, when it was quiet, she sat down and wept.

36

PEEBO STOOD UP in the stirrups to make himself taller. He was trying to see over a clump of brier at the bottom of the ravine. He heard something thrashing around just beyond the patch of brush, but could not see what was making the noise.

"I don't like this," he said.

"I hear something in there," Martin said.

"Don't sound natural."

"Sounds like a big animal of some sort."

"Like a horse, you mean?"

"Horse, bear, a man," Martin said.

"You wait here. I'm gettin' off my horse and goin' in on foot." Peebo drew his rifle from its scabbard, checked the pan and slipped out of the saddle, landed lightly on his feet after the long drop down from the horse.

Martin pulled his rifle from its sheath and lay it across his pommel, visually checking to see that the pan was primed. He turned and looked back over his shoulder just as Peebo entered the brier patch.

"Anson?" he whispered.

There was no answer.

"Anson, don't be funny now," Martin said. His voice sounded hollow in his ears. It was like talking to an empty room. He listened intently for a sound that would tell him Anson was still following them. But he heard nothing. The silence rose up around him until he thought he was going deaf. He no longer heard the thrashing ahead of them, nor Peebo stalking through the briers. Instead, he heard only the sound of his own breathing.

And he felt absolutely alone.

A sense of panic rose up in Martin to the point that he felt as if he were suffocating. For a moment he thought he might not be breathing. He gulped for air and called out again. "Anson, are you back there?"

Still no answer.

"Peebo?" Martin's voice was a squeak in his throat.

Now the silence was eerie. Martin felt as if someone was playing a trick on him. He looked around wildly to see if either Peebo or Anson would suddenly appear. But there was no one there, anywhere.

"This isn't a goddamned bit funny," Martin muttered and turned his horse to go back up the ravine. Then Peebo called out to him.

"Hold up, Martin." Peebo's loud whisper sounded like the backdraft of an arrow slicing through the still air.

Martin turned in the saddle and saw Peebo emerge from the brush. He was leading a horse Martin didn't recognize. "What you got there?" he asked.

Peebo held a single finger to his lips. He tied the horse to his own saddle, walked over to Martin. He leaned close to him. "That's the horse Cullers stole," he said. "But no Cullers."

"Anson's not here," Martin whispered.

"Then Cullers has him."

"Christ," swore Martin.

Peebo gestured for Martin to climb off his horse. "We'll have to backtrack on foot. Be real quiet."

Martin nodded. He checked his rifle again, the pistol in his belt. Then he followed Peebo along the back trail, climbing back up through the ravine with a heavy heart.

37

A NSON STRUGGLED TO find his way out of the sudden darkness. Lights danced in his throbbing skull like shooting stars across a velvet-black sky. Pain shot through his right shoulder and his right elbow hurt. Then he felt rough hands on his neck, pulling at him. He was jerked upright, then dragged somewhere. He tried to keep up but his feet wouldn't obey. One of the hands released his shoulder and clamped around his mouth. He tried to open his eyes, but his lids seemed to be made of iron.

"One word out of you and I'll cut your throat," someone said to him, and through the fog in his brain he recognized the voice as Cullers's.

Anson felt the fingers over his lips relax and drop away. Then he went down as Cullers pushed him to the ground. He wondered where his rifle was, wondered what had happened to him. Slowly the clouds of darkness parted and he regained consciousness, moved into the full-blown pain of an aching head. He opened his eyes.

Cullers stood over him carrying Anson's rifle. It must have dropped out of his hands when he fell, Anson thought. He reached down with his hand. His pistol was gone too, but he still had his knife. When Cullers turned around, Anson saw the pistol jammed behind Cullers's belt, the butt jutting out within easy reach.

"Come to your senses, did you?" Cullers said in a hoarse whisper. "Not a word out of you, hear?"

Anson nodded.

"I'll blow your brains out if you make a sound."

Again Anson nodded. But his mind scrambled for a way out of this. He had no doubt that Cullers would kill him if he tried anything. There had to be something he could do, though. His father and Peebo might come looking for him and Cullers could easily kill them both. He figured that Cullers had taken him hostage for that very purpose.

Cullers was breathing hard after the tussle and watching the trail, which Anson saw was only a few yards away. He saw his own horse standing there, hipshot, his reins tied to a scrub oak. From where Cullers stood he had a clear shot at anyone who came up to get Anson's horse.

Anson touched a hand to the side of his head where he had struck it when he fell. This brought an instant reaction from Cullers, who whirled on him, Anson's rifle aimed at his chest.

"Don't you move," Cullers ordered in a thick whisper.

Anson quickly brought his hand down, but he had felt the lump, the stickiness of his own blood. But as he sat there, helpless for the moment, he mentally assessed his injuries. Not crippled. No broken bones. A headache and a pain in his right elbow, that was all.

Cullers moved a foot away for a clearer shot through the brush at the place where Anson's horse stood. He made no sound. Anson watched him closely, holding his breath whenever he could, drawing it into him as if to give himself strength in case there was an opportunity to make a lunge at Cullers before he shot anyone, either Peebo or his father.

He wondered where they were. They should have discovered Cullers's trick by now. Perhaps Peebo was coming back for him. But if he did, he would have no chance against Cullers. And what if his father came back first? Anson shut his eyes. Cullers would put a bullet into him for sure.

"Where in hell are those sonsofbitches?" Cullers muttered under his breath. But Anson heard him clearly and hoped his father or Peebo could hear him too.

The quiet stretched into agonizing moments for Anson. He listened for any sound that might indicate Peebo and his father were coming for him, but it was deathly still. Cullers was breathing more easily now and Anson cursed his luck. His own breathing had returned to normal, but his head began to throb with a fresh pain that seemed timed to his heartbeat.

He looked at Cullers and realized his vision was blurred. Cullers swam around in a misty double image that Anson could not bring into sharp focus. Then, as suddenly, the throbbing diminished and his vision cleared.

38

PEEBO STUCK OUT a hand behind him. Martin stopped in his tracks. He wanted to ask Peebo why they had stopped. They had walked to the top of the ravine and a little beyond, some yards from where the other ravine peaked.

Peebo gestured to his right, then stepped off the trail, careful to make no sound. He beckoned for Martin to follow him. They walked for what seemed a long time to Martin, well away from their back trail. Then Peebo stopped and squatted. He motioned for Martin to do the same.

"Why are we going this way?" Martin asked, still in a whisper.

"Because I saw Anson's horse, the ass-end of it anyways. Just a-standin' there in the open."

"So? Did you see Anson?"

"No sign of him. I figger that horse was left there for a reason."

"What reason?"

"I think Cullers jumped Anson. But not to steal his horse and ride off in the opposite direction."

Martin thought about it for a moment. "You think Cullers has Anson and is just waiting for us to come up and look for him."

Peebo nodded. "That's just what I think. If we walk up to that horse, Cullers will be waiting for us. And he'll shoot us both dead.

He's probably got Anson's rifle and pistol aimed smack-dab at that horse."

"What'll we do?" Martin asked, a quaver in his voice. He tried to push images of his son's dead body out of his mind, but the thoughts kept surfacing and turning concrete, sticking there in the whirlwind of his fears for his son's safety. He thought of bearing Anson's body back to the Box B and explaining to Caroline how he had taken his son into a dangerous situation and gotten him killed. His throat constricted and went dry, and deep inside him there was a trembling that made his heart stutter and his hands tremble and turn cold.

Then Peebo did a strange thing. He smiled a crooked little smile like that of a conspirator or someone about to play a prank on someone. "Listen," he said. "Do you hear that?"

Martin jumped up, looked all around. "Rattlesnake, Peebo. Get up." Then he looked at Peebo, who had a strange expression on his face. He realized then that Peebo was making the sound of a rattler. It sounded very authentic to Martin.

"Holy jumpin' shit, was that you?"

For an answer, Peebo made the sound of a quail calling. A bobwhite. He did the female call, then the male. Martin looked at him, dumbfounded.

"What do you intend to do with that talent, Peebo?"

"Maybe it will give us an advantage, Martin. Look, Cullers is probably up there holding a gun on Anson, or he's knocked him cold and is standing over him watching that horse. What we're going to do is outflank him, and I want you to be quieter than you've ever been when we do it."

"All right."

"I want you to circle to the left of the trail. Real wide. The horse is about thirty yards from the crest of that other ravine, right at the top. You've got to be on the mark, so get it all set in your mind where you're going to wind up. I'm going to make a circle on the right and then I'm going to become a rattlesnake. If either your son or Cullers hollers, we'll know where they are."

"Then?"

"Then we move in and shoot the shit out of Cullers before he shoots us."

"What if he shoots Anson first? Or if we miss and hit Anson?"

"That's why you've got to sneak up behind Cullers. To the right of the horse. Where we are now, it's thick brush, but I noticed a little opening where we come up, and my hunch is that's where Cullers is waiting right now. He'll have a clear shot at anyone comes up on that horse."

"Question is, will Cullers hear us going through that brush?"

"Ever stalk a deer? You watch each step and set your foot down so that it don't make no noise. You take an hour to go ten yards if you have to."

"I'll step careful. And make damned sure you do the same."

"We can do it, Baron. Just takes some concentration, that's all."

"I hope to hell you're right, Peebo."

"Me, too," Peebo said, and grinned that sly little prankster smile of his.

Martin set out as Peebo went in the other direction. If Peebo's plan works, he thought, they'd have Cullers in a cross fire. If it didn't work, Anson might be shot and killed, and how would he ever explain such a thing to Caroline?

39

A NSON WATCHED CULLERS, trying to figure out what was going through the man's mind. His vision kept blurring and Cullers would waver and develop shadows of himself, sometimes two or three of them, until he came back into focus. Cullers never said a word, just waited, watching Anson's horse, his finger inside the trigger guard of the rifle. Anson wished now he had not been so careful to keep the rifle primed, the powder dry. Too late for second guesses, though, he reasoned. He wondered if he could get the jump on Cullers and over-power him before he had a chance to kill anyone else.

Cullers was bigger and stronger than Anson, he knew, but several times while he sat there, he thought he might have the advantage. He cursed himself silently for submitting to the outlaw's threats, for just sitting there and doing nothing. But he knew that if he made a mistake, Cullers would kill him and his efforts would have been for nothing.

Anson mulled over what Juanito might do in such a situation. Juanito was not a violent man, but he was a man of action. And Anson knew that Juanito would not hesitate to defend himself. And then he remembered some things Juanito had told him in one of their talks. He wondered if Juanito would try and jump Cullers if he found himself in the same situation. There was the knife he wore, Anson thought. He wasn't unarmed.

How do you kill a man with a knife? Did he stick it in his back? Or cut his throat? Anson shuddered as an image of bloodletting filled his mind. What if the knife hit a bone and didn't go in? If he didn't kill Cullers right away, Cullers would turn on him and shoot him or stab him to death.

He looked at Cullers. So close, yet so far away. He would have to draw his knife and jump those few feet and have the knife ready to plunge into Cullers. Where? In the back, that was the closest, but would that kill him right away? Where in the back? If he tried to stick the knife in his ribs, the blade might slide off. Sure, Cullers would be hurt, but if he didn't fall down and bleed to death, he would be mad. He would still be ready to kill.

Anson thought that he would not be able to kill Cullers like that, with a knife. He had shot Hoxie, but that was almost an accident. He had not been close, but far away. He hadn't smelled the breath of the man or got any of his blood on him. If he had a gun, he was sure he could shoot Cullers. But a knife? It sounded so easy. Cullers could probably do it that way. Kill a man with a knife in cold blood.

I'm not a killer, Anson thought to himself. Yet he had killed Hoxie. But it didn't seem real to him. Not when he did it. A gun was not so personal as a knife blade. A knife meant you had to touch someone and mean to kill. "I couldn't do that unless my life depended on it," Anson almost said aloud, so deep was he in his thoughts.

What had Juanito said about life and death? So much. So many times. Anson tried to clear his head, but he was still slipping in and out of consciousness for brief moments, probably for no more than a second or two. There was something he had to know, something that was just beyond his grasp. Something Juanito had said that might help him in this situation.

"Life is a journey," Juanito had told Anson one day. "A hero's journey. And every so often there are other little journeys to take."

"You mean we are going somewhere?" Anson had asked.

"Even if we do not know where, we are going somewhere."

"Where?"

Juanito had shrugged and smiled. "Who knows? That is part of the journey, too. Wondering, looking, searching."

"You don't made sense, Juanito. Ever."

Juanito had laughed.

"Do you not wonder what is around the next bend of the road? Do you not wonder where you will be in ten years, twenty, thirty? Forty?"

"I think about it now and then. Don't do no good, though."

"No, because we cannot see into the future. But we take the path nevertheless. The journey. And the little journeys that teach us things."

"Teach us what?"

Juanito had smiled wisely and looked off into the distance. As if he was seeing something that was invisible to everyone else. "Maybe nothing, Anson. Maybe everything."

"There you go again, Juanito. Speaking in riddles. Tell me something I can understand."

"All stories, all of the old stories are the same. All are myths, smoke to hide the truth. But you can look through the smoke and see beyond the shadows."

"I don't know any old stories, Juanito. Only those I've heard from you."

"The hero is always on a quest. He leaves his world to enter another. There is great danger waiting for him. But he is on a journey, a hero's journey, and he must keep his wits about him. He must fight and sometimes kill to gain what he seeks."

"Are you saying life is like that?"

"In many ways. You will face many perils in your life. Sometimes they will seem small and of no importance, but once in a while you will have to make a difficult decision."

"Like what?" Anson had asked.

"Oh, I think you might have to kill another human being to save yourself or someone you love."

"I hope that never happens to me."

"I hope so too, Anson."

"What if it did? I mean, what would I do and how would I know it was right?"

"Ah, very good questions. In the old stories the hero must always enter the deep and dark place of the journey. It may not be a real place, but it will seem real to him. And there is where he faces the greatest danger. And that is also where the object of the hero's quest is to be had for the taking."

"It all sounds like a fairy tale to me, Juanito."

"Many fairy tales are myths, true stories in disguise. But they mask the struggles of people like you and me. Sometimes because in their very truth they are too horrible, and sometimes because to reveal the true story would cause great harm."

"Would I know if I was in a dark place?"

"You would know. You would know because you must complete the journey and your life would be in peril. When you enter the dark place, the cave where the evil one, the monster, the bad man lives, then you must be on your guard, and perhaps you might have to kill this man to get what you want."

"That doesn't seem right to me."

"It will seem right if what you seek is your own life."

Anson had not understood all of what Juanito had told him that day, but now his words began to make sense. He and his father had been on a journey. And they had faced many dangers. He had killed a man and saved his own life. But not in a dark place. Not in a cave. Was this what Juanito had been talking about? Was this the dark place where he must act to save himself? His father? Peebo? Perhaps all of their lives?

Anson looked again at Cullers. The man was getting fidgety. He would walk away a few steps and then return to his hiding place. The cave? It certainly did look dark for him and for Peebo and his father. Maybe Cullers was the monster in the cave, waiting to kill them all.

He wished Juanito were with them so he could ask him what to do. It was one thing to wish a man dead and try to be a hero. It was another to actually do such a thing.

Suddenly everything seemed unreal to him. Cullers blurred in and out of focus. Darkness all around him as he slipped away from reality. In and out of darkness. Cullers a shadow, a creature that faded in and out of reality. A bad man. A killer. He had cut Jerry Winfield's throat and mutilated him.

"Don't forget that," Anson said, without realizing that he had spoken aloud.

"Shut up," Cullers said.

"I—I didn't say anything."

"You keep your damned mouth shut or I'll shut it permanent."

"Sorry."

"I'll sorry you, you young whelp. One more sound out of you and I'll put your goddamned lights out."

That was the trigger. Suddenly Juanito's words made perfect sense to Anson. He knew what he must do. He knew he would not come out alive if he didn't do what Juanito was trying to tell him. He was in the cave, the deepest, darkest cave he had ever been in, and Cullers was the evil one who held Anson's life in his bloody killing hands. Cullers was the monster he, Anson, had to destroy.

Anson's hand slid to the handle of his knife. He looked at Cullers with a slit-eyed hatred that fueled his loathing for the man who had so brutally murdered Jerry Winfield.

"You sonofabitch," Anson muttered as he drew his knife from its sheath. His head was clear, he could see Cullers, could see his mouth drop open in surprise, could see him swinging the rifle around, could hear the click and scrape of the lock as Cullers pulled the hammer back.

And then they both heard another sound that froze them for a moment when all time seemed to stand still and nothing so much as a heartbeat could be heard for that split second of eternity when the two men faced each other and looked across a vast chasm at Death, an empty, desolate place, dark as a cave, darker than a night shrouded in the blackest of clouds.

40

MICKEY BONE LISTENED to the old man, who spoke slowly in the Lipan dialect so that Bone would understand his words. The two sat in the shade of a large boulder high above the camp where they could talk privately. The Old One had his pipe and his tambour with him and was wearing his medicine pouch beaded in the sacred pattern of the Thunderbird and the Four Directions and the First Woman.

"I am called Dream Speaker," the old man said. "I knew your family. I saw you grow to be a young boy who had been taught the Way of the Eagle. Do you remember that?"

"Yes," Bone said. "I remember. It was a long time ago."

"It was the time before the Mexicans came and spilled our blood upon the ground."

"It is said that you can tell me what my dreams mean."

"I listen to the spirits. They tell me what the dreams mean."

"I dream of a maiden in this place. She is Yaqui. Of the tribe of Yaqui."

"And of what tribe are you?"

"You know, Dream Speaker, of what tribe I am. Lipan."

"Who says that this is so?"

"It was always so."

"Are you, then, Apache?" Dream Speaker spat the last word out as if it was filth in his mouth.

"That is what the white eyes call us."

"Ah, then you are what the white eyes call you. You are not a human being as I am."

"I do not understand, old man."

"Apache is a bad word given to many of us by the frog eaters, the French, and it is not what we call ourselves. We are human beings created by the Great Spirit that blows through all life, even to the stars and beyond."

"I know this," Bone said. "Is not Lipan my tribe?"

"They call you a Querecho too, do they not?"

"I have heard that some of us are called by that name. It is a Spanish word."

"Then you are not Querecho?"

"I do not know," Bone said.

"You are not Lipan, either, my son."

"And what am I, then?"

"You are a human being. As long as there are tribes with separate names, they will fight one another. It is only when people know who they are, of one spirit, that they will fight no more. They will know that they breathe the same air, bleed the same blood and are of the same tribe. Then they will fight no more."

"But this can never be," Bone said. "My father said we are fighters, that we always have been fighters and always will be."

Dream Speaker sighed and shook his head. A look of sadness came into his eyes. "That is so. But we no longer raid the pueblos and bring back slaves and take scalps and fight our enemies. Instead, we run and hide and are hunted ourselves, like rabbits. And now we must talk of the girl, the human being you want for your woman."

"I dream of her with my heart and with my eyes open and I dream of her when my eyes are closed and my heart sings a song of sadness," Bone said.

"Yes. It is said that you look at her with longing in your heart. It is said that you undress her with your eyes."

"That is true," Bone said.

"Then you dream of being with her, of lying on top of her while the blanket grows hot with the warmth of your coupling."

"I want her as my woman."

Dream Speaker opened a leather pouch that was attached to his sash by a pair of draw-thongs. He took out some bones and feathers and painted stones, some dried bugs, beetles and dragonflies and horseflies and some pieces of metal hammered into strange shapes. He held these objects in his hands and lifted his arms. Then he let fall the sacred things and they struck the ground and made a pattern that only he could decipher. The old man bent over and looked at the jumble of objects very carefully, his eyes scanning them for meaning.

"You must give this woman a new name before you can have her."

"A new name?" Bone asked.

"A human name that you know from your boyhood. You must tell this woman her new name and then she will be yours to take. You must build a lodge for her and it must be purified as you have been purified since returning to the people."

"Who will purify such a lodge?" Bone asked.

"I will do this. And you will bring me a horse and kill a deer for me, and these I will take as my due for performing the ceremony."

"What if the girl does not want to be my woman?"

"I will cast a spell that will sing inside her head and she will look at you with a heart full of love."

"That is all?"

"That is how men and women find each other, my son. Their spirits sing the same song. They are in harmony like the doves that coo and the quail that hum through their noses and make the flute sounds. That is why you can take a bone from the wing of a bird and play music with it. Are you stupid?"

"No," Bone said. "I do not think so."

"Then listen, for I am going to give you a song that you must learn. It is an old song that must be passed down from the fathers to the sons or there will be no more life. You must make this song your own and you must teach it to your son before you die. Will you do this?"

"I will do this," Bone said, feeling the power of the Old One, the medicine that he was making for him.

"We will smoke and offer tobacco to the four directions and to the Great Spirit, and then I will sing the song for you. Remember it. Remember it always."

"I will do this," Bone said.

Dream Speaker picked up his pipe and brought out a small leather bag of tobacco from his medicine pouch. He offered the tobacco to the four directions and to the sky and the Great Spirit, then filled his pipe. He lit it with a small piece of glass that he held to the sun so that the sun's rays came through to the tobacco and ignited the dry leaves. He puffed on the pipe and then handed it to Bone.

Bone smoked while the old man chanted an ancient prayer, only part of which Bone could understand. He had been with the people of the mountains for nearly a month. He had gone through the purification ceremony and had heard the tongue spoken, but he had felt like a stranger until Dream Speaker had befriended him and helped him learn the words he had forgotten.

"I pray to the Great Spirit that blows like the wind through all things," Dream Speaker chanted, "and I give thanks for my life and for all life that I see around me. I pray that my friend, Counts His Bones, finds his own spirit and becomes a human being again."

It was a solemn moment for Bone. The old man's face was radiant as he looked up, eyes closed, directly at the sun beyond the rock shadow.

Dream Speaker put out his pipe and saved what had not been burned, putting the leaves back into the little leather bag and returning that to his medicine pouch. He picked up his tambour, which was beaded along the worn rim of leather and tied with the rattles of snakes that hung six centimeters apart. He began to shake the tambour with his left hand and then thrummed it with the bony fingers of his right hand in a staccato tattoo in counterpoint to the snake rattles.

"This song is the song of Counts His Bones," Dream Speaker sang, "and tells how as he sings, he flies through the air like an eagle to a holy place where Yusun gives him the power and the magic to do wonderful things. I, Counts His Bones, am surrounded by clouds decorated of spun and hammered gold. I am high away from the places of human beings and I fly like the great eagle with the snows of winter on his head. As I fly fast through the air I change and change until I am no longer a human being but am become spirit only, and then I am one with all things for all times to come."

When he was finished with the song, Dream Speaker sat with his eyes closed and Bone closed his own eyes and thought of the words he had heard and sang them over and over in his mind until it seemed to him that he was dreaming with the mind of an eagle and he was flying high above the earth, high above the mountains until he was in the clouds. Then he was very light, like the air, and he was no longer an eagle but a spirit being and he had no body but was only spirit, only air that one could not see but only feel against his face and in his hair. He knew the song was holy and would make him very powerful and let him do great things whenever he sang it.

The two men sat there through the long afternoon, their eyes closed. The sun went down and they were still sitting there hours later when Dream Speaker opened his eyes and tapped Bone on the shoulder. "Come. Let us go back to camp and sleep. This is a very good day. This is a holy day."

"Yes, Dream Speaker. I thank you for my song. I thank you for helping me find my way to my own spirit."

"It is Yusun you must thank, my son."

And together they made their way down the mountain to their village and Bone felt the lightness of being as he crawled into his shelter and onto his flea-ridden blankets. He had no hunger or thirst. He had only the peace he had sought for so long and the dreams of making the Yaqui girl his woman and bringing a son into the world, a son whom he would teach the old ways of the human beings and the sacred song that would become his own to pass down to his son someday as the song had been passed down to him on that holy day when he had flown like an eagle beyond the sun.

41

JUANITO SAT IN the shadows of his casita watching the main house. He had enjoyed the supper with Caroline, a fine meal after a long ride. But her ambivalent feelings toward Martin disturbed him. He also sensed a feeling of hysteria emanating from her whenever she spoke of the child she carried in her womb. She did not speak directly of either her husband or the baby, but obliquely, and he wondered if she had not been too long alone without her son and husband nearby.

He had offered to help with the dishes, since he had seen Martin do such a thing, but Caroline had shooed him away, extracting from him the promise that he would "take care of Tonto tomorrow." He had not lied to her. He said he would see that her wishes would be carried out, but as he was saying this, he was certain that she did not really know what her wishes were. Not truly, not in the deepest sense. She was a woman on the brink of either coming to understand her feelings and her situation, or destroying everything in her path. Not a mad woman, but a woman teetering on the edge of hysteria.

Juanito knew that the word came from the Greek word for womb, and he once again marveled at the brilliance of the ancient scholars, the physicians, the mystics.

When he saw the lights in the house go out one by one, he waited several more moments before rising from his chair. He put out his pipe, knocking the bowl on his boot heel to shake out the hot dottle. Then he walked slowly past the barn and down to the cluster of adobes that lay scattered out of sight of the main house, where the wranglers and their families lived. It was a pleasant summer evening and he did not hurry.

Well beyond the little village of adobes was one that stood alone, surrounded on three sides by mesquite and live-oak trees, a place he might have picked out for himself, since its wildness reminded him of the cordilleras of his home in Argentina.

"Chato," he called softly and heard a chair scrape inside the adobe. Not a chair, he knew, but a crate brought from Baronsville, suitable enough for a man who had grown up in Mexico without furniture of any kind.

"*Buenas*," Chato said as he opened the door.

"Do you want to do a little work?" Juanito asked. "It will not take long."

"*Serguro, jefe.* What is it that you want me to do?"

"Come with me. I will show you."

"Do I need the rifle?" Chato was both a vaquero and a hunter, not only of game, but of wolves and other predators on the Box B. He had come from the deepest reaches of Mexico, from a poor family who had lived desperately off the land. Chato was one of those men who could smell quail in the brush and see into the hearts of animals. All but Juanito thought him strange. It was Chato's ability to think like an animal, be it horse or cow or wolf or eagle, that made him a good hunter and a man of much patience.

"No, it will not be necessary. You have your boots on."

"Yes."

"Then walk with me and I will tell you a story."

Chato did not close his door, which was only two blankets folded together and nailed to the wood frame above the doorway. The blankets hung open on a sixteen-penny nail just inside the door. He had no lantern, only candles, and he seldom lit them. Chato could see in the dark better than an owl.

As they walked back toward the barn and corrals, Juanito told Chato of a woman in his country who raised sheep and rabbits.

"This woman was not married. Her father had beaten her and her mother. The father had beaten his wife to death and the daughter grew up hating him. Then her father was killed by a jaguar, a female jaguar, which was later tracked down and shot by hunters.

"The woman had fifty ewes and one ram among her flock. She had one buck and twenty does in her rabbit hutches. Over the years, she managed to make a good living selling her wool and her mutton, her rabbits. She was patronized by the mine owners and the miners in the little village where she lived, Plata.

"But many of the miners lusted after this woman, whose name was María. She would have nothing to do with them, so they began calling her La Virgen María and this was very cruel and hurt María deeply. The rich son of one of the mine owners lusted after María as well, and she rebuffed him and he grew angry. He boasted to everyone that he would be the one to deflower the virgin, and bets were made and money passed hands.

"One night this rich son of the mine owner came by Maria's little house to buy mutton. She was afraid of him, so she locked her door and did not come out. This made the mine owner's son very angry, so he broke into her house and raped her. Then he called in all the miners, waking them up, and brought them to her house and showed them the blood on her legs and on her loins and bragged that he had deflowered her.

"Then because he hated María, he let the others take her one by one until all of the miners had tasted María's blood and left their seed in her womb. After that, María became deranged and the miners stayed away from her. Some sent their wives to buy rabbits and wool and mutton from her, but she never saw any of the men except at a distance.

"Finally one day she took one of her kitchen knives and sharpened it, honing it on a leather strap until it would cut a hair in two, and she castrated the ram who serviced her flock of ewes, and she castrated the buck who serviced her does and she screamed into the night and became quite insane.

"But she sold her mutton and her wool and her rabbits until she had no more. She had no ram to impregnate her ewes and she had no buck to make babies with her does, and so she had nothing to sell but herself and none would buy her body for they all knew that she was crazy and they had all tasted her. So she starved to death and the mine owner tore down her house because all the women and the men of Plata were superstitious and the house reminded them of their shame. María was not buried, but left to rot in her house, and the rats and the worms and the jackals ate her up and carried away her bones.

"And to this day no one in Plata will eat rabbit meat, nor dine on mutton, and they do not want clothing made out of wool. It is a very strange village, and there were many riots against the cruel mine owners over the years. Finally the silver ran out and the mines closed and the town became a ghost and few go there, only hunters passing through. Even they do not linger, for they say at night they can hear María's screams when she was deflowered and when she castrated the ram and the buck and sealed her own doom."

"Is that the end of the story?" Chato asked.

"Yes, I think so," Juanito said.

"Why do you tell me this, Juanito? It is a very sad story."

"Yes, it is a sad story."

"Then why do you tell this story to me?"

"Ah, does it have the point, you mean?"

"Yes."

"Do you know the bull Tonto?"

"The big longhorn? Yes, I know this bull. He is a grand bull of sound Spanish stock and is very agile and graceful for his immense size."

"Yes, Tonto is a very good bull and he has sired many fine calves."

"What does Tonto have to do with the sad story you told me, Juanito?"

"Caroline has ordered me to castrate this grand bull. She wishes this to be done tomorrow, but we are going to the corral where Tonto is kept tonight."

Chato gasped loudly. "What? You are going to castrate Tonto? I can't believe you would do such a thing. Señor Baron would not like this."

"No, he would not. And neither do I, but Caroline made me promise that I would cut off the eggs of this big bull so that he can sire no more calves for the grand herd of Martin Baron."

"It is criminal," Chato said. "It is a thing that is savage."

"I agree."

"Then why will you do this thing?"

Juanito smiled in the darkness as a screech owl hooted in the mesquite thicket beyond the pasture. Bullbats knifed the air, scouring the insects from the dark sky, and cattle lowed in the distance. As they neared the house, they heard a guitar playing a mournful song and the clucks of children in their casitas as they played after supper.

The Baron house was very dark, the only light from a lantern in Juanito's casita shining bravely through the window, its pale golden glow no match for the blackness of the night. They walked to the corral where Tonto measured the distance between the corner poles with his endless pacing, and they could see the steam of his breath like silver cobwebs in the pale light of the moon just rising above the treetops.

Juanito and Chato stood just beyond reach of Tonto's horns and the bull stopped pacing and looked at them with dark eyes that they could not see. They felt his steamy breath and heard him paw the ground and sensed him exude power as if he were some bovine god caught in man's puny snare for only a moment.

"I would not like to see this bull lose his machismo," Chato said.

"This bull will not lose his maleness. He will carry seed in his bag for as long as he lives."

"But . . ."

"But you and I have much to do before the morning, Chato."

"You are not going to castrate this bull?"

"No. We are going to castrate another bull in the morning."

"Not this bull?"

"No."

"But la señora knows this bull."

"Yes, but there is another that resembles him."

"I do not know this bull, Juanito. Where is this bull?"

"Do you know the bull with the big horns that we caught down in El Rincon some weeks ago? He is a very large bull, not so fat as this one, but he has the calico hide and the very long horns."

"That is a skinny bull," Chato said.

"When a bull has his balls cut off, he fights and loses much weight, is this not so?"

"Not so much weight, but some, I think."

"But if you stand Tonto with this other bull, one would know which was which, would one not?"

"*Claro.* One would know which was Tonto and which was the lesser bull."

"But if Tonto did not have the big horns he would look smaller, would he not?"

"Yes, I think Tonto would look smaller if his horns were cut short."

"Then this is what we will do this night, Chato. We will take Tonto to the place where the lesser bull chews the grass and we will tie him up with ropes and snub him against a very large tree and we will saw off his horns so that he looks like a small bull. Then we will bring the lesser bull here and call him Tonto and in the morning we will tie him up and sit on him and slice his balls from his bag and show them to Caroline and she will be happy that I carried out her orders."

"That is much to do in one night."

"We will have little sleep this night, Chato."

"*Verdad.* And if Caroline discovers what we have done . . ."

Juanito slapped Chato soundly on the back. "I do not think she will castrate us, my friend."

Chato swallowed hard, the sound like a gurgle in a deep and swirling river.

"After all," Juanito said, "she is nothing like María of Plata. She would not do such a thing."

In the darkness, Chato crossed himself and murmured a small prayer to the Virgin Mary and Juanito laughed softly and walked toward the barn to get a saw that was used to dehorn the meanest of the longhorns on the Baron ranch.

42

A NSON LUNGED AT Cullers with a rattlesnake's brittle sound clattering in his ears. At the same time, he heard the bone-shivering
click of the cocking mechanism.

Cullers stiffened slightly at the sound of the rattlesnake's burr, but
continued to swing the rifle in Anson's direction. He cocked the hammer back as the barrel arced at his waist, wondering if he would have
time to shoot before Anson closed on him. He saw the knife in the
young man's hand, one of those split-second impressions that lodges
incongruously in a man's mind in the compressed instants of mortal
combat, and cursed himself for his stupidity in not taking the knife
away from the Baron boy.

Peebo brought his rifle up to his shoulder, cocked it and took dead
aim on Cullers. Then two things happened: he saw a blurred figure to
Culler's right, coming out of nowhere, and Martin's hand as it clamped
onto his rifle barrel, forcing it down, even as Peebo was squeezing the
trigger.

Anson reached up and grabbed the barrel of the rifle in Cullers's
hands as it swung toward him and felt a jolt as Cullers pulled the
trigger and powder exploded lead and fire through the muzzle. He
winced as hot powder peppered his side and the ball cut a furrow in
the flesh of his hip.

Peebo's rifle cracked a split second later and the ball dug harmlessly into the ground. But the sound startled both Anson and Cullers as Anson pulled the rifle from Cullers's hands and it fell to the ground. Off balance, the pain searing his hip, Anson slashed the air with his knife a few inches from Cullers's belly.

Cullers grunted and clawed for Anson's pistol, which he'd stuck in his own belt. He pulled it upward, but the front blade sight caught on his waistband and he was unable to snatch it up.

Anson regained his footing and crouched as he came toward Cullers, holding the knife away from his body, ready to slam it into Cullers's body.

Peebo quickly reloaded his rifle with powder and ball, then spun around and raised the weapon. He swung the rifle in a wide arc and Martin ducked. The barrel made a whooshing sound as it completed the arc. Martin reared up suddenly and rammed his head into Peebo's belly, knocking the wind from his lungs and sending his rifle sailing lazily through the air into the brush.

Both men fell to the ground, Peebo pinned there for a gasping moment by the weight and force of Martin's body. Peebo gulped for air as Martin's hands groped for his throat. The small man thrashed wildly, flailing with his arms to knock Martin off his belly and to keep those hands from strangling him to death.

Cullers cursed and grabbed the handle of his knife, jerked it from its scabbard. Anson grappled with the man, trying for an opening. Cullers slipped away from the younger man, agile as a cat and bent to a fighting crouch.

"Come on, you young pup, just come on," Cullers said, his words a breathy rush.

Anson said nothing. The two men circled each other, each looking for a chance to charge in and cut the other. They both heard the thrashing in the nearby brush, but neither would look over to see what was making the noise.

Cullers feinted with the knife and Anson danced sideways. Cullers feinted again from another direction, and again Anson bounced out of harm's way. He made a feint of his own, but Cullers did not react. Instead, the older man stalked closer, holding his knife waist-high and at an angle.

Anson backed away and jabbed with his knife as if to show Cullers he was ready for him.

Peebo and Martin rolled through the brush, neither gaining the advantage, and came to rest against a large tree. Peebo grabbed Martin's left arm and slammed it into the tree. A stinging pain shot up Martin's arm from the wrist to the elbow.

"Damn you, Baron," Peebo whispered, "what in hell are you tryin' to do?"

"You damned near shot my son."

"I had a clear shot at Cullers."

"Like hell you did."

"Like hell I didn't. He'd be wolf meat by now if you hadn't grabbed my damn rifle."

"I couldn't take that chance."

"Don't you never touch my rifle again, Martin."

"Let me go, Peebo. My boy needs help."

"Like as not you'll get him and the both of us killed."

But Peebo released his grip on Martin's arm. Martin grabbed his elbow and massaged it to lessen the pain shooting through his arm. The two men got up and dashed back to where their rifles lay, picked them up and ran to the place where Anson and Cullers were fighting.

They witnessed a grim scene, a dance of death played out in eerie silence in that small clearing near the trail where Anson's horse stood, no longer hipshot, but stiff and rigid, staring at the tableau with wide eyes and ears cocked forward, twitching like the tips of cats' tails.

Martin cocked his rifle. "You draw one drop of blood from my son, Cullers, and I'll blow you to kingdom come."

Cullers said nothing.

"Too risky to shoot," Peebo whispered.

"Damn it, I know it is," Martin said. He stood there with Peebo, watching as Anson and Cullers circled and feinted and changed position, both very close to each other now, both breathing so loud they could be heard, but neither winded.

"We should rush Cullers," Martin said under his breath.

"He'd cut you before you could lay a hand on him. Might cause Anson to make a mistake and get himself killed."

"I just can't stand by and watch him murder Anson."

"Anson's holding his own. You keep that rifle ready, and if you get a chance, shoot Cullers. I'll finish him off before he can do any serious harm to your son."

"Anson," Martin called, "just run away and we'll take care of Cullers."

"Can't," Anson said with a slight breathlessness. "Leave me be, Daddy."

"Damned if I will," Martin said, but there was no conviction in his tone.

But Martin saw no chance to shoot Cullers. Instead, he looked on in horror as his son kept circling, circling, Cullers a mirror image of him, round and round, both moving closer, each gazing hard into the other's eyes, looking for a sign of weakness, any hesitation, any doubt.

Anson dug deep inside himself for a way to outwit Cullers. Nothing in his experience had prepared him for such a life-and-death struggle. Fear rose up in him like a cloud, suppressing his normal senses, heightening others. He had never felt so alive, yet never been so close to death. Cullers seemed like some monster risen from the earth, bent on killing him. The knife Cullers held in his hand looked deadly, was deadly. And no doubt Cullers had used that same knife to murder Jerry Winfield. Perhaps others had fallen victim to that same killing knife.

Cullers seemed a towering figure, and he was so close now that Anson could smell his breath, the stink of his clothes. Still they circled, coming ever closer to each other in this macabre ritual that seemed so ancient and primitive. Anson fought the fear inside him and his senses quickened.

Could he kill Cullers? The question kept cropping up in Anson's mind. Could he stick his knife in him so deep the blood poured out onto the ground? Would Cullers kill him first, cut his throat so that his very life gushed like a fountain from the open wound?

Cullers swiped the air in front of Anson's face with his knife. Anson bent over backwards and Cullers moved in closer, switching the knife to his other hand. Back and forth, Cullers changed knife hands until it was like some hypnotic dance, puzzling, confusing. Anson knew he could not do such a thing. He was right-handed and that's where his knife would stay.

His eyes, Anson thought. Like a snake's eyes. Cold and black. Meanness in them. The eyes of Cullers were chilling, but Anson stared into them, looking for any warning flicker, any blinking.

"Look inward," Juanito had told him once. "Depend upon yourself. If you can do that, you will have no fear."

The words popped into Anson's mind as Cullers slowed down his circling, as each man got closer to striking distance of the other. All motion slowed. Anson was just barely aware of his father and Peebo standing a few yards away, watching, waiting.

"I am not afraid of you," Anson told himself silently. "I am not afraid."

Was that what Juanito meant by going within? Talking to himself? Building his courage with brave talk? Maybe not, but he kept saying it to himself and he felt stronger, slightly stronger, than he had before. Now he looked at Cullers as a stone in his path, not human, but just an obstacle. Maybe it was better that way. Cullers's eyes did not seem so threatening now. They were just holes in a rock.

And Anson saw himself strong and muscular, able to push the rock away and go beyond it. Push it away, he thought, and the cave opens. I can get out. I can get out alive.

Cullers suddenly stopped circling. Anson, surprised, stopped also, and then Cullers made a small jump, thrusting with his knife. Anson did not jump back this time, but crouched lower and watched Cullers's eyes for any shift of light, any flicker of intent. Cullers jumped again, like a wolf spider, a short hop that brought him almost within range of Anson's knife.

"Say your prayers, boy," Cullers said.

Anson glared at the man, rankled at his arrogance. The rock in the road. The obstacle. He saw that Cullers was steeling himself for a charge, that at any moment he would rush toward him, slashing with his knife.

"I'm not afraid of you, Cullers," Anson said aloud and the words put iron in his muscles, steel in his resolve to defeat this killer of men. He looked at places where he might strike with his knife and keep himself away from Cullers's own blade. He looked at the neck of the man; it was too small. The chest was too full of rib bones. The stomach seemed soft and vulnerable. His abdomen was the closest, the softest, the most reachable.

Anson turned his blade over in his hand so that the cutting edge was topside. He knew what he must do and how he must do it.

Cullers saw the shift of the blade in Anson's hand and then made his move. He hopped to one side and then charged in at an angle, his blade held throat-high close to his chest.

Anson drew in a quick breath, held it. He wanted to close his eyes, but resisted the impulse. Cullers came at him so fast he thought the man would run right into him, stick his knife deep in his throat.

Anson came out of his crouch and met the charge head-on. At the last moment he ducked and jabbed at Cullers's abdomen, exerting all the force he could muster, keeping his eyes on that one spot just below his attacker's gut.

Anson felt a searing burn in his right shoulder, a fire that traveled down his back and flooded his brain with the bright light of pain. At the same time he felt his knife sink into Cullers's abdomen, felt the flesh yield to the blade. He drove in deep and felt the tip of the knife strike bone. He twisted the knife and slashed away from the solid object he had struck and the knife broke free and bloody in his hand.

Cullers cried out in agony as his abdomen opened and coils of intestines bulged from the open wound.

Anson staggered away and whirled instinctively to meet a second charge from Cullers. His shoulder buckled and throbbed and he felt a wash of blood down his back. He saw Cullers reach down and try to stuff his intestines back inside his gut. The sight sickened him, made bile rise up in his throat, made his stomach wrench with the sudden sickness of revulsion. There was a look on Cullers's face of stark surprise, the contortion of disbelief.

"You got him," Peebo yelled. "You stuck him good, Anson."

"Holy Christ," Martin murmured.

Anson stood there shaking, his knife still at the ready. He looked at the pathetic sight of Cullers trying to stuff his intestines back inside his abdomen, the slippery gray coils writhing and twisting like snakes in his gory hands. The strands of intestines kept falling farther and farther, getting longer, and longer and blood and other things seemed to drop through the large gash in Culler's abdomen as if the man was emptying himself out all over the ground.

Cullers's face went from red to gray and he opened his mouth in a silent scream as he slipped to his knees, trying still to gather up his insides and put them back in order. He began to sob as none of his guts would stay inside him, and then he lifted up his head and screamed: "For God's sake, Baron, shoot me!"

Anson turned to his father.

"I'm not going to shoot him," Martin said.

"Me neither," Peebo said.

"Don't let me die like this," Cullers pleaded. "Not even a dog should die like this. Kid, shoot me quick."

Anson stood there, transfixed by the sight of the once-powerful man reduced to a kneeling mendicant, his gore-stained hands holding a pile of ruptured and stinking intestines, blood pouring out of his abdomen and pooling up on the ground.

Everyone froze as Cullers dropped the slithering intestines in his hands and reached for Anson's pistol, still stuck in his waistband. His crimson fingers closed around the butt and he pulled the pistol free, held it in both of his slick hands. He pointed the weapon straight at Anson and slid a finger inside the trigger guard.

"Anson, look out," Peebo shouted.

Martin's throat filled with a pulpy lump of phlegm and the sound he made did not come out of his mouth. His feet seemed rooted in quicksand and his arms froze as if he had been suddenly paralyzed.

Anson stared into the dark barrel of the pistol without fear. Whatever he had felt before Cullers had attacked him was gone now. He was shaking from emotion and physical exertion, not from temerity. Cullers was no longer a threat to him, despite the fact that the thief had a loaded pistol pointed at Anson's face.

"I'm not afraid of you, Cullers," Anson said.

"You . . . you . . . ." Cullers gasped, his voice very weak now.

"You got what you deserved."

"Ah . . . ah . . ." Cullers's hands began to shake and the barrel wavered like a shadow seen under moving water.

Anson knew Cullers was dying. The killer's legs were bathed in blood and his intestines kept sliding away, uncoiling like a nest of serpents, gray-blue lengths of his guts strewing the ground. The man's face was contorted with pain and his eyes were glazing over with the frost of impending death.

Martin stood there in a frozen state, staring at the pistol in Cullers's hand.

Cullers winced as if a sharp pain had cut him in another place and his torso swayed back and forth as if he was listening to some strange strand of hypnotic music. Then he pulled the pistol back toward him and turned it around in his hands. He removed his index finger from the trigger guard and put his thumb inside as the pistol was reversed. He stuck the barrel in his mouth at an angle, so that the muzzle pointed up through the back of his mouth and toward the skull.

Anson started toward Cullers, his left arm outstretched, as if to stop the man from taking his own life. Before he had taken two steps, Cullers depressed the trigger with his thumb. A percussion cap exploded and Cullers's head jerked with the force of the explosion. His forehead bulged for a split second before the top of his head flew apart, spewing blood and brains into the air in a roseate cloud. He slumped over to his right, the pistol barrel still jammed into his mouth and blood gushing from the exit wound in the back of his head.

"Jesus," Martin uttered.

Anson staggered backward, repulsed by the horror of what he had just witnessed. The sound of the shot reverberated in his brain and he heard its echo for a long time after Cullers was dead, like some ghostly reminder of the first shot ever fired in the eternity of time stretched across vast centuries.

The young man stood there, no longer shaking, but drained of all emotion and feeling, a scarecrow fallen victim to the wind and the weather, an empty shell with no thought, no judgment, no sorrow or compassion.

"He's dead," Anson said, his voice a flat monotone. He was aware of the pain in his shoulder and back, the slight burning in his hip where a lead ball had burned a small furrow. He thought he was no longer bleeding much. His back itched where Cullers' knife had grazed it and he knew his shirt was ripped. The wound there was not deep; he was grateful for that.

"Keeerist, yes," Peebo said. "God, I never saw nobody do that before. Your boy had a lot more nerve than I expected."

"Shut up, Peebo," Martin said, suddenly freed from his prison of paralysis. He stepped forward and put his hand on Anson's shoulder. "A terrible thing," he said flatly.

"I'm glad he's dead," Anson said softly.

Thoughts flooded his mind as he stood there staring at Cullers's grotesque heap in front of him, all his humanness gone, his visage twisted into featureless putty.

Anson knew that this death was like no other. Hoxie had been almost an accident, but this death had been up close and intimate. Cullers had not really died by his own hand, but by Anson's, for when Anson cut him with the knife, Cullers had begun to die. He had been doomed from the moment when his insides had come tumbling out like so much garbage. Cullers may have pulled the trigger and blown his head apart, but it was the act of a man already dead, the closing act of a savage.

I have gone into the cave, Anson thought, the deepest darkest cave, and I have come out alive. But what have I gained? I feel empty inside. Hollow. Empty as that man lying there dead as a stone. And there is nothing to bring back. It was not like Juanito had said. I have given nothing to mankind, only death, and now I feel dirty inside and out and I feel as if Cullers took something from me. Something that I can never ever get back.

And then the tears came and Anson's body shook with grief, and it was not grief for Cullers or Hoxie, but for himself, for what had been taken from him. He didn't know what it was, only that it was gone and he would never get it back because it was lost, lost in that world he had entered where he had met the beast and slain it and now stood over it a hollow man, a man empty of all decency and kindness and whatever manners his mother had taught him. He hated Cullers and his kind and wished he could kill him all over again and again and keep killing him until there was nothing left to lie there and stink in the sun and remind him of what death was and how slender the thread between life and nothingness was and how empty a man could be when he crossed the threshold and went into that dark place of the heart where it is always midnight and always lonesome and cold and grief-stricken.

There should have been something, Anson thought, something better than this, what I feel, what is hurting inside me. There should have been some satisfaction, some great knowing that what I've done was for the good and meant something. But there is nothing here but a dead man and my own emptiness, my own sorrow for something good in me that I lost.

"I hate you, Cullers," Anson said to himself. And then he spoke aloud, without realizing it. "I feel so bad. I hate this."

He felt a hand on his shoulder and turned to see his father standing there beside him, a look of understanding on his face.

"You're hurt," Martin said. "You've got a cut down your shoulder and back."

"My hip, too," Anson said. "It doesn't hurt much. Not like I hurt inside."

"Don't feel bad about this, son," Martin said. "You did what you had to do. Cullers was a bad man. It might have gone the other way."

"I'm sick about it," Anson said. "Sick in my heart. Sick all over."

"That's just a normal reaction. It's a terrible thing to see a man take his own life."

"No, I killed Cullers."

"In a way . . ."

"No, I wanted to kill him and I did, and it feels wrong. It just feels bad wrong."

"Son, I know it does. Cullers should have been caught and hanged. He should have been judged by a jury and sentenced. But he picked the way he died. You didn't."

"You mean Cullers should have gotten what you and Mother call justice?"

"That would have been better, I guess."

"This isn't justice, then."

"Son," Martin said, a grave tone in his voice, "in a place where there are no laws, there is no justice. And then it becomes a good man's duty to see that justice is done."

"So this is justice?"

"It's the only justice Cullers will ever get. You remember what I said, Anson. This is a hard old world and you don't get many chances to do what you done. Cullers meant to kill you and he got what he deserved. That's all there is to it."

His father's words sunk into Anson, but he was dazed by what he had done, what he had seen, and he could make no sense of any of it. He wiped the tears from his face and looked down at the knife in his hand. The blade was smeared with the blood of Cullers. At first he wanted to throw it away, throw it so far away he would never see it again, but he held it tightly and then wiped the blade on his trousers and stuck the knife back in its sheath.

"Let's get out of here, Daddy," Anson said. "I want to go home."

"Sure, son. No need to stay here no longer." Martin turned to Peebo. "You got all you need, Peebo?"

"I reckon."

"We'll be going on back to Matagorda now. Have to meet my friend Ken Richman, who's probably waiting for us."

"I'll ride with you if you like."

"You can come along."

"I'd feel right comfortable in your company," Peebo said. "You and Anson seem like pretty fine people."

"We do our best," Martin said.

The three men walked to where Anson's horse stood. Anson mounted up and looked down at his father and Peebo.

"I want to ride on alone for a while if that's all right," he said.

"Sure, son. We'll be right behind you," Martin said.

Peebo lifted his huge hat off his head. "I tip my hat to you, Anson. You're a brave boy."

"I ain't no boy," Anson said, and turned his horse.

"I'll buy you a man's drink in Matagorda," Peebo called after him. "Bein' it's all right with your pa."

Anson rode out of sight, down into the ravine they had come up earlier in the day.

Martin turned to Peebo. "Hell, I'll buy him one myself."

And the two men laughed, the tension between them gone like the mist of morning from the low places when the sun rises clean and golden over the earth from a place of darkness.

43

L UZ AGUILAR PEERED through the window at the man on horseback. He just sat there staring at the house, and he made her feel afraid. It was just after dawn, and the eastern sky glowed with a pale hue of saffron through a rent in the long, spear-shaped clouds, and none of the men had risen from sleep yet on the rancho. The man made no move to light down from his horse, nor did he hail the house. He just sat there on his scrawny horse, looking at the house, like a statue placed there by some unknown person during the night.

Quickly she ran back to the bedroom. Her husband was still asleep, naked, the thin blanket twisted at his feet. She leaned over the bed and grabbed his shoulder, shook him.

"Matteo, get up," she said. "Matteo. Do you hear me? Get up."

Matteo mumbled from somewhere in his dream and turned away from his wife. She shook him again, harder this time.

"You must get up, Matteo. Someone is here. A strange man. He looks like an *indio. Ándale, pues,* Matteo. *Levántate.*"

"Huh? What?"

"There is a man outside the house. He looks like an Indian. He is just sitting there watching us."

Matteo opened his eyes, rubbed the grit of sleep from his lids.

"Who is this man?"

"I do not know. It is not even light yet, and when I looked out the window, there he was. He is on a horse, a skinny horse, very skinny. I have fear, Matteo."

"Do not worry. I will see who this man is."

Matteo slipped on a pair of trousers and a shirt, slid his feet into a pair of huaraches. He grabbed the rifle leaning against the wall next to the bed.

"I will come with you," Luz said as Matteo left the bedroom.

"Walk behind me, then."

Luz, a small woman with sad dark eyes and long lashes, followed her husband nervously as he went to the front room. She had a beautiful face, reflective of her Spanish and Indian bloodlines. A true Mexican woman, who carried herself proudly as if she were born of royalty, yet with the furtiveness of a wild creature, she stepped cautiously behind her husband as though ready to pounce on any who might attack him.

"Our son is asleep," she whispered, "and I have seen none of the vaqueros."

"Good," said Matteo as he stepped to the window and peered out onto the small courtyard. Beyond the hitchrail he saw the horseman, still sitting his horse as if he was waiting for someone to call out to him.

"Do you know who that is?" Luz asked, her voice soft and liquid with the Spanish tongue.

"Yes."

"Who is he?"

"He is called Mickey Bone. I have not seen him for months."

"Is he dangerous?"

Matteo laughed. "I think that he is, my Luz. But I will talk to him."

"I have fear of such a one."

"He will not harm you. Go quick. Prepare the table, make the coffee."

"You would have this . . . this *indio* come into our hacienda?"

"Yes. He is a man I very much wish to see. Go quick, woman."

Matteo set the rifle down by the door as Luz scurried off to the kitchen. He opened the door, stood in the doorway.

"Mickey."

"Matteo."

"Welcome, my friend. Come and break the fast with my wife and me."

Mickey rode over to the hitchrail and dismounted. Matteo noted that he had no weapons showing. No rifle in a scabbard, no pistol on his belt. Not even a knife. That was very unusual, and very dangerous.

He waited in the doorway for Mickey to walk the few steps to the house. There was no porch; it was a simple dwelling, but it had four big rooms and was cool in the summer, warm in winters, with its thick adobe walls, painted on the inside.

"What passes, Mickey?"

"I have come to see you, Matteo. To ask you a favor."

"Come in, come in, and we will talk. Do you take coffee? Are you hungry?"

"I will take some coffee and I have not eaten in many days."

"Ah, how lamentable. Come, and you shall meet my wife and my son if he has arisen from his bed."

The two men walked into the kitchen. Luz had the firebox going in the woodstove and a pot of hot water on to boil. She was setting cups and plates on a table. A bowl of brown sugar and a small pitcher of fresh cream were already set at the center.

"This is my wife, Luz. Luz, this is Mickey Bone. He used to work for Benito and for Martin Baron."

"It is a pleasure meeting you," Luz said tightly, and she did not smile.

"My pleasure," Mickey said, and from then on he remained wary of Luz and was reluctant to talk.

"So where have you been?" Matteo asked.

"To the mountains."

"And did you find what you were seeking?" Matteo asked.

"Yes."

"So you are back, then. To civilization?"

"I am back to ask you for a favor."

"Ah, we will get to that. First, we drink the coffee, then we eat the tortillas and beans, some *carne*, eh? And there is rice. Luz will cook it. I am a happy man, Mickey. I have a wife and a son. Luz, awaken little Delberto and bring him to the kitchen, eh? I want to show Mickey what a fine son we have."

Obediently Luz left the kitchen and returned some minutes later with a very handsome boy, slender with good strong clean features, plenty of black hair and bright brown eyes.

"This is my Delberto. He will someday inherit the wealth of the Aguilar family."

"Yes, he looks to be a strong boy," Mickey said, and he felt a prickling sensation at the back of his neck. Delberto was no more than two years old and his father had already planned his future.

"That he is," Matteo said proudly.

"You have a fine ranch here, Matteo," Mickey said as Luz set warm steaming tortillas on the table. They were in a clay bowl, and she served beans and rice and strips of flavorful *carne asada*. "You have many cattle and horses."

"I will take them to the Rocking A one day," Matteo said, "all those that you see, and I will build a fine herd of cattle and breed the good horses."

"You will not stay here on this ranch?" Matteo asked.

"No, this is only something I dug out of the earth with my bare hands and my fingernails. I will take back the ranch that was stolen from me by that *puerco* Benito and his stupid wife."

"I do not know why you need to go back there," Mickey said. It was plain to Matteo that the Indian was trying to eat politely, but it was also clear that he was very hungry.

"Because I want what rightfully belongs to me," Matteo said. "Because it is a promise I made to myself."

"There is much blood on the ground at the Rocking A."

"There will be more."

Luz picked up little Delberto. "I will take the boy back to bed. You and your friend need to talk alone."

"Yes, that is good, Luz. I will see you in a little while."

"Do not forget that we are to leave for Juárez today."

"I do not forget," Matteo said, with impatience.

Luz and her son left the two men to talk alone.

"Eat, eat," Matteo said. "You have much hunger. What have you been eating?"

Mickey looked slightly sheepish. "Lizards, snakes, bugs, sometimes a rabbit. There is very little to eat in the mountains."

"Where is your rifle, your pistol? You do not even have a knife."

"I gave those things away when I went back to my people."

"It is very dangerous to ride in this country without arms to defend yourself."

"I walk with the Great Spirit," Matteo said.

"And there are plenty of your relatives who have gone to that Great Spirit because they were shot and killed."

"I am a very poor man now in your way of thinking, Matteo. But I have found a woman and I want to marry her."

"That is good. What is this favor you want of me, then? I can give you a rifle and a pistol and we have knives to spare."

"I want a horse. I will pay you back."

"You have a horse."

"I need one to buy my wife."

"Ah, so you came to borrow a horse to pay for your woman."

"Yes."

"And, how will you pay me back, Mickey?"

"I do not know. I have tried to catch the wild horses, but I have grown very weak. I have had no food."

"Eat much, then. I will give you a horse, Mickey, but you must pay for it."

"How will I pay for it?"

Matteo pushed away from the table and got up. He left the room and came back a few minutes later with some cigarros. He placed one next to Mickey's plate and put one in his mouth. He leaned back and opened the firebox. He withdrew a flaming faggot and lit his cigarro and blew the smoke out in a long blue trail, away from Mickey's face.

"After you have taken your woman for wife, and after you have done what you must do with your people, I want you to come back here and work for me. One year, Mickey, and I will pay you good wages and give you horses so that you will be a rich man among your people."

"I do not know about this, Matteo. You want me to come back to the white man's world."

"No, Mickey. You will be my shadow. You will work only for me. You may live as you wish as long as you are near me."

"I will work here, on this ranch?"

"When you return," Matteo said, "we will go to the Rocking A and I will take possession."

"What about Benito and Pilar?"

Matteo smiled.

"We will see what will happen to them when the time comes."

Bone watched the smoke from Matteo's cigarro rise in the air and fan out, dissipate. He thought long and hard for several moments before he spoke again.

"One thing leads to another," Bone said. "I need the horse to pay for my woman. I need my woman to make me a human being again, to bring a family into the world. An old wise man in the mountains told me that a man lives in his heart, not in the world. He said that we all live in two worlds, the one we see and the one we cannot see."

"Yes," Matteo said, " 'my kingdom for a horse,' said the king."

"Who is this king?"

"I do not know. But he was fighting a mighty battle and he could not win without a horse. So he was ready to trade his entire kingdom so that he could win the battle. He knew that he could trade his kingdom for a horse and reclaim it in victory."

"That, too, is a wise saying," Bone said.

"So what is your decision, Mickey?"

"I will take the horse and the arms you give me. I will work for you for one year and go where you go. But I will live my life in my heart."

Matteo smiled. He pointed to the cigarro next to Mickey's plate.

"Let us smoke on it, Mickey," Matteo said. "Pick up the cigarro and I will light it with mine. This will seal our agreement."

Bone looked at the cigarro for several seconds. Finally he picked it up, put it between his lips. He leaned over the table and Matteo held the burning end of his cigarro to the tip of Bone's. Bone drew air through the cigarro and the tobacco began to glow. He leaned back in his chair and exhaled smoke into the air.

"The Great Spirit leads us down many paths," Bone said to Matteo. "And we cannot see the end of our journey."

"That is true," Matteo said. "But we can still choose the path we will take. I have chosen mine."

"And I have chosen mine," Bone said, a somber cast to his tone. He looked at the smoke from the two cigarros mingling above the table and thought of the girl he would soon take for his wife. He thought about the new name he would give her and spoke to his heart for guidance.

He looked out the window and the Spanish word for dawn came unbidden into his mind. *La madrugada.* It was an unwieldy name, but it suited her. It was a name of beginning. In Lipan, it was a very beautiful name. In English, it was also beautiful. And he knew then, that he would call his bride Dawn and she would be his sunrise every day for the rest of his life.

44

B ENITO AGUILAR SAT on the top rail of the corral at the Rocking
A, watching the three riders move slowly toward the house from
the north. The riders wound their way through the small bunches of
cattle feeding on sorry summer grass. One of his vaqueros rode out to
see who was coming, but Benito already knew.

He sighed deeply and rubbed his tender, cracked hands. Sun and
sweat had created fissures in his flesh around the knuckles. Pilar had
put salve on them that morning, but already the salve was drying and
the pain had returned.

He climbed down and walked away from the corral.

"Basta," he said to Simón Carrasco, who had just finished shoeing
the fourth horse. "We will do the others later in the day when it is
cool."

"Sí, patrón," Simón said, wiping his hands on his leather apron. He
began picking up the shoes and the nails as Benito walked toward the
house.

Benito moved like a man grown old beyond his years. He seemed
to carry a great weight on his shoulders. His hair was laced with gray
streaks; his sideburns were peppered with the frost of aging. He
seemed stiff-jointed, slowing his pace when he was near the porch. He
pulled the brim of his battered old hat down over his eyes to shield

them from the sun, and the brim painted his chin and the right side
of his face with shadow.

The vaquero he had seen ride out to see who the riders were had
turned and was riding slowly back to the house. Benito recognized him
as Federico Ruiz, one of the few who still remained on the ranch,
although he had not been paid in anything but beans and flour for
several months. Cash was something Benito had not seen in some time,
though he had a deal pending on the horses he was shoeing, and the
new infusion of cattle had helped his breeding stock. But the grass was
poor that summer and he had been forced to feed his stock with winter
hay and mesquite cakes.

"The Barons, they come," Federico called out as he was riding up.

"I see them, 'Rico."

"Martin gave me tobacco. He asks about your health."

"That was good of him. Keep the tobacco. Give some to Simón, if
you can."

"I will do that, *patrón*." Federico rode off toward the barn, the ribs
of his horse stretching the animal's hide so that it looked like something made out of wood and brown paper.

"Who is coming?" Pilar called from the front door.

"Martin Baron," Benito said.

"Good. Maybe you sell him that whore you brought back from
Victoria."

"Be quiet, Pilar." There was patience and resignation in Benito's
voice.

"Where is your lazy whore, Benito? Why does she not show her
face?"

"Be quiet or I will slap you quiet."

"You and your filthy whore."

Benito did not stop at the porch as he had intended, but walked
on past the house to the other side where he could meet the riders.
He heard the front door slam. He should not have brought the woman
back to the ranch with him, but she was a solace, and he could beat
her if she was bad to him. But Pilar he could not bring himself to beat.
She was always with the blind boy, Lázaro, and she always inspired pity
in him, and sometimes even shame.

He kept the woman in one of the adobes that had been vacant
since two vaqueros, who were brothers, had moved out while he had
been gone to buy the cattle up north. He knew she had the sickness,
but so did Pilar, and Pilar had gotten it from his brother, Augustino.
The sickness that had blinded Lázaro in the womb and infected them
all, curse him.

The woman's name was Caridad, which was ironic, and he had

never mentioned her name to Pilar. Indeed, he had tried to keep Caridad a secret, but Pilar had found out, perhaps from one of the other women who knew about her.

He heard the back door of the house slam shut and knew that Pilar and Lázaro had gone out the back. They would probably go out in the field to play, or perhaps she would let him ride his pony and pretend he was a vaquero. Lázaro's name was ironic too, he thought. He would never see, never be able to rise from the dead.

"Benito," Martin called.

"Welcome," Benito said. "Do you want to go into the house? I can offer you cups."

"Whatever pleases you," Martin said. "I want to talk to you."

"I see you have brought your young son and Juanito. It is good to see you again."

"Benito, how goes it?" Juanito said.

"It passes," Benito said. "I am well."

"Mr. Aguilar," Anson said, not knowing what to say. Their saddlebags were bulging with things Martin had brought: tobacco, coffee, flour. Small gifts to give them something to talk about before they discussed business.

"Tie your horses up at the house," Benito said. "We can sit on the porch and talk. I do not know where Pilar is. She has gone with the blind boy somewhere."

"That's all right," Martin said. "It was you we came to see. I have some things for your wife and for you."

"You are very *simpático*, Martin," Benito said as he walked with them to the house. He waited while the three men dismounted and tied their horses to the hitchrail. Anson dug into the saddlebags and began laying the things they had brought on one step of the porch. Benito walked up the steps and motioned for Martin and Juanito to sit on one of the benches there. He set out two chairs for him and Anson.

"Caroline says to tell you hello," Martin said.

"Please give my good wishes to your wife as well. Those things you brought—Pilar will have gratitude for you, Martin."

"There is some tobacco for you and some aguardiente, a pair of spurs I hope will suit you. Some playthings and some *dulces* for Lázaro."

"I am most humbled," Benito said.

"Will you have a smoke now?" Martin asked.

"No. My throat is very dry."

"Some brandy, then?"

"I will wait and have the brandy tonight—unless you will take a cup?"

"No, we cannot stay long," Martin said.

"You have come to talk business."

"Yes. I sold my boat and have brought some money. I am hoping you will sell me more land," Martin said.

"You have a great deal of land now."

"Yes, but I am expanding my herd. I think that someday soon we will have a good market for beef."

"Yes, I am hoping that will be so. You have heard that the Rocking A is not doing so well."

"I have not heard that. That is not why I came. I sold my boat so that I could buy more land from you, Benito."

"Do you have a price in mind?" Benito asked.

"I will pay the same price as I paid Victoria."

"Perhaps the land is worth more now."

"It is empty land. It is doing you no good. It is doing me no good if I cannot call it my own and make use of it."

"That is true," Benito said. "How much land do you want to buy?"

"I have measured it and I have brought the surveyor's reports. It is roughly a half a million acres to the west of La Loma de Sombra and north of Bandera Creek. You hold title to it and I have brought the documents that tell of it and pass ownership to me."

"That is a lot of land. I might need it someday."

Martin took out his pipe, filled it with tobacco. He struck a match and lit it. He would wait Benito out if he had to. He knew Benito was cash poor and that he would not pass up the money, even though he was selling part of himself, part of his brother Jaime's dream. Jaime had obtained the Spanish land grants for millions of hectares in the Rio Grande Valley, but had been killed by Apaches before he had the chance to build his ranch as he had wished.

Juanito said nothing. He just looked at Benito, and Benito turned away from him in shame. He wondered if Juanito had told Martin about the woman in Victoria, the whore he had been with when the Argentine passed through.

Anson leaned his chair against the porch rail, sucking on a horehound candy, listening to the talk, wondering how long it would take to complete the deal. He had ridden over the half million acres with Juanito and liked the lay of the land. He could see it thriving with new grass and the new breed of cattle they were raising. The addition would give the Box B room to grow and make it one of the largest ranches in Texas.

"Let me see the papers you have brought," Benito said finally, and Martin reached inside his shirt and pulled out a sheaf of documents.

Benito studied them all carefully. He looked over at Juanito, whose face was impassive. He looked at Martin.

"The papers seem to be in order," Benito said.

"They are. I have the money with me—gold, silver and some currency." Martin nodded to Anson, who went to his father's horse and lifted a small satchel out of one of the saddlebags. He carried it to the porch and set it down beneath Benito's chair so that it was between his legs. His father had told him to do it that way.

"Open it," Martin told Anson. Anson opened the satchel's mouth and spread it wide.

Benito looked down into the satchel. The money was arranged so that the gold coins were on top, the silver beneath the gold and the currency forming a bed on the bottom.

"That is a lot of money," Benito said.

"Count it if you wish."

"No, I trust you, Martin."

"Sign the papers then, Benito." Martin said it so softly, Anson could barely hear him.

"Who will witness?" Benito asked.

"I will witness," Juanito said, and his words carried much weight. Benito looked at the Argentine for a long time, wondering if he should offer some explanation for the whore. He decided that it was not the time to bring up the subject.

Benito signed the documents, handed them to Juanito. Juanito signed them and handed them to Martin, who wrote out a receipt and gave it to Benito. These actions took only a few moments, but Anson thought that hours must have gone by.

"You will be a very rich man someday, Martin."

"And so will you, Benito. Perhaps the cash will help you keep the ranch going for a long time."

"Then you do know I am having trouble keeping vaqueros to work the ranch."

"I have been having the same trouble," Martin said. "Now we must return to the Box B." He stood up, walked over and shook Benito's hand as the Mexican rancher arose from his chair.

"Go with God, Martin."

"Take care, my friend."

Just then Pilar and Lázaro came around the corner of the house. She stopped at the bottom of the steps and stared at them all. She looked at the things Martin had brought.

"Did Benito tell you he has brought a whore to this place?" she asked.

"We are here on business," Juanito said. "We wish you a good day, Pilar."

"Why don't you take the whore with you, Martin? You have bought all of our land."

"Not all of it," Martin said. "There is plenty left for you all to make a good living."

"A curse on you, Martin Baron. A curse on you too, Juanito. You do not care what Benito does with this whore of his. You only want our land."

"I am sorry, gentlemen," Benito said. "Please forgive my wife. She is very upset and is not well."

Martin and Juanito joined Anson at the bottom of the steps. The three men tipped their hats to Pilar. Anson stuck a piece of candy in Lázaro's hand.

"Good-bye, Pilar," Martin said and walked to his horse.

"Go with the devil," she spat.

Martin, his son and Juanito mounted their horses and rode slowly away so as not to appear to be in a hurry.

"Daddy, you left the satchel there. Don't you want it back?"

"No, let Benito have it. We have the land. That's what I came for."

"I'm glad for that," Anson said.

Juanito looked back at the house as they rode away. Pilar was kicking all of the gifts off the porch steps. Lázaro stood there in darkness. Benito was picking up the satchel and closing it tightly.

"Yes, the land," Juanito said. "Men will kill for it and men will die for it."

"What was all that talk about some whore?" Martin asked.

"I do not know," Juanito said. "Something in Pilar's mind, perhaps. Something she carries with her, some real or imagined wound, like a soldier carries a scar or a limp from which to gather sympathy."

"I don't like family arguments," Martin said.

Anson looked at his father with a sudden shift of understanding. In that one sentence, Martin had said it all and the portent was chilling. He felt a gust of wind in the breezeless air and the hairs on the back of his neck stood on end. His father's words had been like a warning, Anson thought, and the bristling hairs, the chill made him think of the old saying that when such a thing happened, it was if someone had just walked over his grave.

45

MARTIN CUT THE last calf out of the herd and chased it into the rope corral. A vaquero named Mario Garcia closed the gate as the calf bawled, mingled with the other calves. The calf's mother lowed loudly, disturbing the air of a late spring morning on the spread at La Plata.

Martin was proud of his vaqueros. Juanito had taught them to ride and rope cattle so that it was now second nature to the Mexican cowboys. They were quick in the brush, had trained their mounts to cut and stop on a two-bit piece when the slack went out of the rope. It was damned hard work, and a lot of the men had no chaps, so their trousers were torn and ragged at the end of a day of rounding up cattle. The Mexicans seemed born to the saddle and made natural cowmen. There wasn't a one who could not work the cattle better than Martin himself. And Anson had taken to the vaquero life like a horse to sugar.

"That makes forty-two," Anson said, turning his horse to chase the mother away from the corral.

"Looks like a good bunch," his father said. "You want to try your hand at branding?"

"Sure," Anson replied without hesitation. His grin cracked wide in gratitude.

They had been beating the brush for a week and Anson had never felt happier. He was sore and tired after every day's work and his chaps weighed two hundred pounds when he took them off at night, but they slept under the stars on blankets and saddlebags and his father talked to him more than he ever had before. He wished Juanito were there so he could see how his father was treating him; like one of the regular hands instead of a wet-behind-the-ears boy.

"Light down and grab up an iron, then," Martin said to Anson. "I'll throw one down for you."

The branding fire was just outside the corral. Three branding irons jutted from the hot coals, all fashioned in the shape of a Box B. Anson swung down from the saddle of Matador and swaggered over to the corral. He climbed through the ropes and took his place near the fire. His father followed him a few seconds later and slipped through the ropes.

"Mario, you and Carlos get in here and keep those calves boxed in a corner. We'll take 'em one at a time, at first." The two Mexicans climbed into the corral and spread their arms, began moving the bunched calves into a corner. "Horky," Martin ordered another Mexican named Horcasitas, "you drag 'em out once they're branded. Minta, you and Leon, get ready to grab up them other two irons."

Arminta and León entered the arena. Another man, Chaco, stood by with a can of salve to daub on the fresh brands. Chaco was well prepared, having performed that task before. He was Carlos's eldest son, just a couple of years younger than Anson, at fifteen. Like the other vaqueros, he wore a straw hat, a cream-colored shirt made of cotton, loose-fitting trousers, and sturdy leather sandals. Martin looked at the bunch of calves he'd put together for the branding and grunted in approval. Then he walked to the bunch and cut one calf out, chased him around in circles, finally grabbing it around the neck and twisting its head as he put his weight on the animal, driving it to the ground near where Anson stood, ready to yank a branding iron from the coals.

"Right on that left hip, son," Martin said. "Do it quick and steady."

Anson grasped the handle of the branding iron and pulled it from the hot coals. His father knelt on the back legs of the calf, giving Anson a fairly motionless target. Anson stood over the calf, holding the hot iron in his gloved hand. But he could already feel the heat through the handle. He jabbed the iron straight down on the calf's hip. Tendrils of smoke arose from the burning flesh. He could smell the burning hairs, hear the hiss of the brand burning through the calf's hide.

"Whoa, that's enough," Martin said.

Anson took the iron off the calf and felt his stomach roil with a queasy sensation. "Ah," he said.

"Take a look at it, son. Pretty clean."

Anson forced himself to look at the fresh brand—a small capital letter B inside a tiny box. The flesh was whitish pink and the stench of burning hair still floated in the air.

"Is it good?" Anson asked.

"Perfect," Martin replied. He stood up and loosened his hold on the calf's neck. He motioned to one of the vaqueros to let the animal out of the corral. "I'll get us another one. Put that iron back on the coals and get ready to grab another one."

"Mmmmff," Anson said, slightly out of breath.

Martin let Anson brand three more calves, then called another two vaqueros into the corral. Soon the air was filled with smoke and the aroma of burning hair and flesh. They had half a dozen calves left to brand when Anson heard a rider coming fast from the direction of La Loma.

"Somebody's coming, Daddy," Anson said.

"I see him. Looks like old Paco Serra." Paco was in his forties, but looked to be at least eighty years old. He took care of the goats and helped Caroline with the garden, made sure the water troughs were clean and filled at the ranch headquarters. He rode a moth-eaten horse he called Carnicero because the animal had once torn a coyote to bits with its hooves and mashed most of it into the ground.

"Must be trouble," Martin said.

"He's riding pretty fast, Daddy."

"Yeah. Come on, let's go see what he has to say. Boys, you finish up the branding."

The vaqueros all assented in Spanish as Martin and Anson climbed out of the corral.

Paco was nearing them as the Barons mounted up and rode out to meet him. Paco reined in Carnicero and sat puffing like a worn-out bellows. His eyebrows were streaked with gray, as were his sideburns. He wore a battered straw hat full of holes and frayed around the brim.

"What passes?" Martin asked in Spanish.

"Aire," Paco gasped.

"Get your breath and then tell me why you're wearing out that horse."

"It is the woman, your wife, patrón. She is very bad, much sick, I think. You come quick. Juanito says you come quick."

"What's the matter with her?" Martin asked. The color drained from Anson's face until it looked covered with paste.

"Está enferma con el niño, creo."

"Jesus," Martin breathed. "Paco, you rest up, then go on back to the rancho. Anson and I will go there pronto."

Paco was too winded to speak anymore, so he lifted a hand and mouthed a silent farewell.

"Come on, Anson, let's go."

"But, Daddy, don't you want to—"

"No. I may need you. The boys will bring back our gear."

It struck Anson then how worried his father was. He understood what Paco had said. It had something to do with the baby his mother was carrying in her belly. But Paco didn't know what was wrong or how bad it was. Still, Juanito wouldn't have sent the old man unless there was something very wrong with his mother.

Father and son struck out across the grassy plain. Martin did not set a killing pace, but kept his horse moving. When the animal began to breathe hard, he slowed to a walk. The land seemed strange to Anson, as if he had never seen it before. He felt as if he and his father were riding through an unknown country, across a deserted plain where no living thing grew, where buzzards waited just out of sight, perched on skeletal trees that were invisible except in his mind. He swallowed and knew his throat was bone dry.

"Daddy, what do you think's wrong with Mother?"

"I don't know, son. Must be pretty sick, I guess."

"I hope she doesn't die."

"Don't say that."

"I mean, I hope it's not real serious."

"Serious enough, I reckon."

"Well, I hope the baby's all right."

"Why shouldn't it be? Your mother's healthy. I'm healthy."

"I don't know. It's just that she's been awful sick a lot of the time."

"I know, dammit."

Anson wondered if his father was taking out his anger at him again. Whenever there was trouble, like when the storm came and he couldn't make the drive to New Orleans, it seemed as if his father had taken his anger out on him. Anson said no more. He kept silent as they rode the long miles to La Loma. It seemed to him that his father was more angry than worried.

They left the grassy pastures of La Plata and rode across a somber and desolate stretch of land that had been ravaged by the flash floods. The rotting carcasses of longhorn cattle lay strewn along a gully floor and the scent assailed their nostrils and made them wince with the smell of death. Rattlesnakes buzzed as they passed, and as the sun went down, the air whistled with the dark flights of bullbats on the prowl, their shapes stark against the empty, half-lit sky.

They rode on the edge of sunset, their shadows drawn long and

grotesque toward the darkening east. Anson felt as if they were enter-
ing some dreamscape of the mind, floating through death's ageless
caverns of darkness into an eternal underworld of horror. He was terribly worried about his mother and his sense of dread grew until it
turned the landscape into a nightmare where no thoughts could pen-
etrate, no cry could be heard.

It was after dark when the Barons reached the ranch house. Lamps
blazed in every window There was a buggy outside, and horses tied to
the hitchrail, one of which belonged to Ken Richman. Martin slid off
his horse and hit the ground running. One of the vaqueros stood on
the porch, a rifle in his hands.

"Is the señora all right?" Martin asked.

"She lives," replied the vaquero, whom Anson didn't recognize.
Anson tied up their horses and ran into the house. Ken met him just
inside the door.

"Whoa there, Anson. Your mother's in her bedroom. Don't go in
there. She's pretty sick. I've got a barber with her and a couple of
Mexican midwives."

"I want to see her." Anson tried to push Ken aside.

"You can't. The baby's coming, I think. You'll just be in the way.
Like me."

"Jesus, Ken, I'm scared to death."

"She'll be all right. She's in good hands."

"What's wrong with her anyway?"

"Baby was turned wrong or something. Mighty painful, I reckon."

Just then Juanito came into the room. His face was dark and somber. He saw Anson and shook his head.

"Juanito, is my mother—is she . . ." Anson broke away from Ken's
grip and ran toward the Argentine.

"I—I do not know, Anson. I think the baby might not come out
by himself. He does not try."

Ken said nothing. He put a hand on Anson's shoulder and gave it
a squeeze.

Anson tried to breathe, but his chest was tight and he felt the walls
of the house closing in on him. His palms became slick with a clammy
sweat and he felt light-headed, giddy from a sudden hunger that over-
took him. Even though this was the house he grew up in, lived in, it
seemed suddenly alien, peopled with hostile strangers. He felt almost
as if he were living inside a bad dream, a dream of changing faces and
shapes, of warped walls and long dark corridors.

"Why can't I go in there?" Anson asked Juanito.

"Because you would be a distraction, I think."

"You mean I'd be in the way."

"Yes. Just wait. Be patient. You cannot change things that are to be. Not these things."

"Maybe I could help," Anson said weakly. He felt as if no one was listening to the screams he could hear inside himself. Shadows raced across the landscape of his mind, like hooded figures with only shadows for eyes that could not hear him, would not listen to his pleading cries.

Ken sighed. "It's in God's hands."

Juanito frowned, but said nothing.

Anson strained to hear what was going on in the back bedroom, but he heard only whispers, snatches of words, fragments of conversation. And then he heard his mother scream and felt his blood run cold. The scream tore through his mind like a bullwhip and cracked the air wide open as it snapped. He shuddered with the sound of it.

"Ken, for God's sake," Anson said. "What are they doing to her?"

"Kid, the baby's coming. It hurts."

Juanito started for the front door.

"Where are you going?" Anson asked.

"I am going to my house. I do not want to hear your mother cry out in pain."

"That's not the reason. You think she's dying." Anson's tone was accusatory.

"No. I have heard her pain too much. There is nothing I can do. I am going to rest and think."

Anson knew that Juanito often went off by himself to think. Once Juanito had told him that whenever he felt bad, he had to sit in silence and listen to his heart. "That is where the spirit lives," he'd told Anson. "That is where my center is, where there is only me and God."

Anson had brushed it off, not knowing what Juanito meant. But now he thought that Juanito must want to go to his center and be with his God. He hated Juanito for that. His mother needed help and nobody was doing anything.

Juanito walked outside and his footsteps faded on the porch. Anson's mother screamed again and he forgot about the Argentine. He saw Ken cringe when the scream reached its highest pitch. When the scream trailed off, it was like a lash across Anson's face. He felt her pain and wanted to be with her, to comfort her, to lay his head on her shoulder and speak soothing words to her.

"I'm going in there," Anson said. Ken did not try to stop him.

"This might be the time," Richman muttered under his breath. He drew a sack of makings out of his pocket and walked outside onto the porch. He built a smoke, struck a lucifer on his boot sole and lit the rolled cigarette. He wished he had a drink. Caroline had been in labor a long while and everyone's nerves were on edge. He wondered how Martin was handling his wife's pain. A lot of men couldn't take a woman screaming, but Martin was hard to rattle. That man had a lot of iron in him. Still, a man was helpless at such times and he'd seen some of them crack under the strain of a hard childbirth.

Ken walked out to the railing, straining to hear what was going on in the back bedroom. He heard Caroline moaning loudly, but at least she had stopped screaming. Maybe that was a good sign.

Anson slowed his run when he got to the bedroom. The door was only slightly open and he could see shadows moving around through the lamplight. He heard his mother groaning and sobbing and the sounds tore at him. He pushed the door open and went inside his parents' bedroom.

The barber, who was also the only surgeon in Baronsville, was holding something wet and bloody in his hand. Two Mexican women were holding down his mother's arms and another stood at her feet, her back to Anson. His father was staring openmouthed at the object in the barber's hands, his eyes wide in a fixed stare.

The barber turned the baby over and patted its back.

"Cut the cord," he told the Mexican woman at Caroline's feet and she held up a knife. Anson saw the cord then, a knotted, twisted mass of gray matter marbled with blood. It looked like an intestine, he thought. The Mexican woman cut the cord deftly, and it dropped onto her other hand. She pulled on the cut end of the cord and Anson's mother screamed again.

Anson slipped to one side of the door. No one had noticed him, and he hoped they never would. Everyone in the room seemed frozen for a moment and then the barber turned the baby over. It was black, Anson thought, and smeared with blood. It didn't move, nor did it make any cry.

The barber kneaded the baby's chest with his fingers, held it upside down, then right side up. He pressed a hand to its chest and dug in its mouth with his index finger. Anson felt something squeeze his heart. The baby was not breathing, did not respond to the barber's manipulations.

The barber held the baby up and pressed his ear to the center of its chest. He held it there for a long time, kneading its tiny throat with gentle fingers.

"The baby is dead," the surgeon said. "I'm sorry."

Anson's mother screamed again, and the two women bent down to comfort her. Martin stared at the baby for several seconds, then turned his head to look at his wife.

"Maybe it's just as well," he said. "You'll damn sure pay for your sins, Caroline."

Caroline sobbed violently and Anson could not look at her. He saw only the terrible look on his father's face as he turned back away from where his wife lay stricken with grief.

"Give me my baby," Caroline wailed and the surgeon handed it to her quickly.

Anson's mother took the child and held it to her breast. Then she began to cry, more softly this time, and rocked the child back and forth as if to give it life.

Martin charged past Anson, scarcely glancing at him, and stormed out the door. Anson hesitated for a moment, then followed his father, keeping a safe distance. He could almost feel his father's anger as Martin's boots pounded on the hardwood flooring.

Anson heard the front door slam and he ran across the front room. He waited until he no longer heard his father's footsteps on the ground, then went out onto the porch. Ken Richman tossed a cigarette over the porch railing.

"Where'd he go?" Anson asked.

"Toward where Juanito lives, I reckon," Ken replied. "What the hell's the matter?"

"The baby's dead," Anson said.

"Is that why he's mad?"

"I don't think so."

Ken said nothing. He just stood there.

Anson stepped to the edge of the porch. "I'm going after him," he said.

"You might want to wait until he's cooled down," Ken said.

"Why is he going to see Juanito?" Anson asked, and his heart squeezed again. He thought he knew. He had seen the baby. Its skin was very dark, unlike his own, his father's or his mother's. He didn't quite understand it, but he knew it must have something to do with Juanito. That thought filled Anson with a sense of dread. But he could not push himself to think the unthinkable. He only knew that he wanted to know what his father was going to say to Juanito.

The moon rode high on a thin strip of cloud gauze as Anson walked through the darkness to Juanito's casita. Shadows striped the ground and the wind threaded its way through the barn, whining in the rafters like a child keening for a lost pet. The sound made the hackles on Anson's neck rise and he shivered involuntarily.

When Anson was halfway to Juanito's, all sounds faded away except for the wind. There should have been shouting and screaming and arguing. Instead there was a deathly silence.

46

MARTIN WALKED INTO Juanito's casita without knocking. "Juanito," he growled.

"You are here," Juanito called from the main room, just off the small hallway at the entrance. "Do you have news?"

Martin strode into the room, his jaw set tight, his lips pursed in anger. "I want you to pack it up tonight and get out, Juanito."

"But why?" Juanito's eyes did not widen, nor did his eyebrows raise.

"Just get out, I said."

"Is that enough to say between friends?"

"We are no longer friends. I am sorry I ever met you."

"I do not understand, Martin. Have I done something to offend you?"

"You have violated my trust."

"How so?"

"You know."

"No, Martin. I do not know."

"I want you out of here before the sun comes up. I don't want you to ever set foot on Baron land again."

"But is some of this land not mine, too?"

"You send me your address and I will pay you what your share is worth."

Juanito walked over to Martin and stood close to him. His eyes bored into Martin's. Martin did not break his own stare.

"You are very angry, Martin. But I do not know why. Is something wrong with the baby? Is Caroline all right?"

"You sonofabitch, don't ever mention her name to me again. And the baby is stone dead, the black little bastard. Now get out, or I will come back here with my gun in the morning and shoot you dead."

Juanito sighed and shrugged. "Very well. If that is what you want. But I wish you would tell me why you are angry with me."

"You know damned well why."

"No, I do not."

"Well, you'll have a long time to think about it."

"And so will you, Martin. There are circles of life, my friend. Big circles and small ones. You have just stepped from a big circle into a very small one."

"I've said all I'm going to say, Juanito. Don't make me kill you."

With that, Martin turned and left the room. He did not close the door when he left. Juanito went to the door and watched his friend stride across the shadowed stretch of land between their houses. He shook his head sadly.

"Good-bye, my friend," he said softly. He saw Anson emerge from the shadows and pick up the step with his father. He heard Anson's voice, but could not make out the words. In a moment, the two disappeared into the darkness. All Juanito could hear was the keening of the wind in the barn and the lowing of cattle in the pasture.

47

MARTIN DID NOT sleep that night, but paced through the house like a caged lion. The barber, a man named Jim Shepherd, and Ken Richman had left hours ago. One of the midwives had taken the baby, promising to bury it, and two had stayed behind to comfort Caroline. Anson, angry that his father had sent Juanito away, had gone to his room. Martin supposed that he was sleeping.

Juanito had left two hours after Martin had told him to leave, taking only his horse and three others, the clothes on his back and some personal possessions. Martin had walked out to his casita and looked around, and a deep sadness began to grow in him.

Now he paced the front room, watching the dawn break over the eastern horizon. He thought of Juanito out there somewhere asleep, or riding into the sunrise. He had trusted Juanito all these years, and now he hated him for what he had done. He probably should have just killed him so he would not have to think about him anymore. But that would have been too good for him. Let him suffer. Let him think about what he had lost and know that if he ever set foot on the Box B, he would be shot down like the dog that he was.

Martin heard a sound. He turned from the window and saw Caroline standing at the edge of the room. She was in a nightgown, and the two women were holding her up. She looked pale and thin, her face a ghastly shade of white. "Martin, what did you do?"

"What are you talking about?" he asked curtly.

"Consuela and Raquel said that Juanito rode away during the night. They said you made him go."

"That's damned right."

"Why? Have you gone mad?"

"I saw the baby. It looks just like him."

"Juanito?"

"Same skin color, same face, same hair."

Caroline sagged and the two women had to prop her up. She started to walk toward Martin, but did not have the strength.

"You fool, Martin. Do you know what you've done? You've sent your best friend away, all for nothing."

"You bitch. You slept with that bastard behind my back and you had his baby. What did you want me to do? Welcome him into the household?"

"Didn't you ask him about it? Didn't you listen to him?"

"He didn't have a word to say," Martin replied.

"No, he wouldn't. It's true that the baby was not yours. But it wasn't Juanito's either."

Martin stared at Caroline in disbelief. "What are you saying?" he croaked.

"You were gone so much. I was so lonely. One day I made a big mistake. But not with Juanito."

"Then who in hell was it?" Martin suddenly felt giddy, light-headed. "One of the Mexican hands?"

"Didn't you ever wonder why Mickey Bone left in the middle of the night? Didn't you ever think about him being here all the time you and Juanito were in New Orleans or out on the range? Didn't you ever suspect that I might be lonely enough to ask Mickey to take me to bed? No, I suppose not. Well, it was Mickey Bone who fathered that poor dead child. Mickey Bone, damn you! Mickey Bone!"

Caroline collapsed in a faint and the two women grabbed her before she hit the floor. Her eyelids fluttered and her arms went limp. The two women quickly carried her away, back to the bedroom, leaving Martin standing there, his mouth open and his stomach all torn inside as if he had been stabbed a dozen times.

Martin swore and staggered to the window. He stared at the glowing ball of sun wrapped dark in haze. The eastern sky was all red, a broad smear of blood blazing like some hideous rash on the horizon.

"Red sky at morning," Martin muttered. "Sailor take warning."

Then he began to weep softly and curse himself for what he had done.

And suddenly he grew cold inside and longed for the merciless sea, where he could be swallowed up, out of time, where he could roam the vast deeps on a close reach and hear only the wind in the rigging, instead of the beat of his heart.

48

ANSON BARON LOOKED over the assembled vaqueros. They sat in a circle around him, just inside the shade from the barn, their stoic, leathery faces impassive as wooden carvings. Most of them were older than he was. Some of them he had known for a long time, others he had just hired a few days before.

For the past year he had been riding with many of them, learning to handle cattle with the best of them, learning their language. He had managed to drive a few head of cattle to New Orleans and to bring in some money to keep the ranch going without his father, who was at sea, carrying freight along the coast, fishing for a livelihood.

He crossed his father's path now and again, heard word of him in New Orleans, Galveston and Corpus Christi. But he had not seen his father in over a year, and his mother never asked after him, only cleaned the house and tended to the outside chores without complaint or comment, a shadow who sat silently at the supper table and scarcely touched her food.

"Friends," Anson said in perfect Spanish, "we are going to build up the herds on the Box B and make some money."

The vaqueros let out a huge cheer.

"It is going to be hard work, but I know you will help me."

A chorus of *sí*'s.

"We are going to beat the brush in the brasada and drive the longhorns onto the fenced pastures with the good grass. We are going to breed these cattle with the Argentine bulls and the cows. Then we are going to drive these cattle to a market up north, where we will sell them for much money. Are you ready to go to work?"

"*Sí, sí*," the vaqueros yelled and leaped to their feet.

For months the Mexicans had been digging wells, building fences, fighting off Comanches and Apaches. Many of them were like brothers to Anson. But they had not replenished the herds and the good stock was thinned down. Anson knew that there was now competition and that he must bring the biggest and fattest cattle to market if he was to survive.

The Mexicans crowded around Anson and he gave them orders. Some were to stay behind and see to the cattle on La Golondrina, the huge grassland that Anson had nurtured until it was lush and ripe for grazing. Some were to ride south with him to the brasada, where they would gather as many longhorns as they could and drive them back to the breeding pens. It was a vision Anson had sustained for months.

"We will leave in two hours," Anson said. "We will drive ten head of our most docile domestic cows down there to tease the longhorns out of the brush. We will cut the nuts off every bull and make them tame as housecats before we drive them back. We'll gather all the calves, yearlings and full grown, and brand every head we take out of the brush. Say good-bye to your wives and children and tell them you will be gone at least two months. I hope all of you men were stallions last night because it will be a long time before you dip your poles in those warm wells again." The Mexicans laughed uneasily before Anson continued. "Bring your bedrolls and the hard biscuits, the beans. We will live like rabbits and hunt like wolves."

The men scattered and Anson strode back to the house, the big empty house that still echoed with his father's footsteps. He knew his mother would be churning in the kitchen that afternoon. He wanted to say good-bye.

"Mother," Anson called when he entered the back door.

She looked up from the churn between her legs, but said nothing. She continued to work the butter, her hair swept back away from her face and tied at the back. Her apron dropped between her legs. Anson did not speak to her much. There was still something between them, although he had tried to put it out of his mind. He could not forget that she had let Mickey Bone into her bed, that she had been unfaithful to his father and had driven him away. Still, he loved her, but he no longer saw her in the same way. He did not understand this thing between man and woman yet, but he knew that his father had been hurt deep, like a man gored by a bull, and that his mother had some-how betrayed both father and son.

"I am leaving with some of the men. I will be gone for a couple of months. Carlos will be here and several of the women will look in on you. Consuela, Luisa, Carmen, and some others."

"Where are you going?" She tried to make eye contact with her son, but he avoided her gaze as he had on every occasion since his father had left their home.

"To get some longhorns up to La Golondrina."

"Oh, Anson, why?"

"We need to breed stock for market." He still could not look his mother in the eye. He was afraid of what he might see there, afraid he would see that ugly thing that made her do what she had done. Afraid that he might see something forbidden and shameful.

"What market?"

"There are some new ones up north, I think. I met a man named Charlie Goodnight a couple of months ago."

"Who is this Charlie Goodnight? I never heard of him." She con-tinued to stare at her son, who would not look at her. Anson was aware of her eyes fixed on him, but he could not bring himself to look at her face unless she was looking away.

"He rode out here about two months ago, wanting to look at some land. I rode around with him, showed him the ranches we own. Ken Richman brought him over from Baronsville."

Caroline stopped churning and brushed sweat-sogged hair off her forehead.

"Why, I haven't seen Ken in months. When did he come here?"

"Mother," Anson said, looking at the churn, but not at her, "I haven't got time to explain everything to you. Ken just rode out here with Charlie one day and then he went back to town."

"I haven't been to town in a long time."

"I've asked you, Mother. You never want to go."

"I don't know any of those people. They are all your father's friends."

"No, they're not. He would hardly know any of them."

"Still, I don't feel comfortable in Baronsville. People stare, and there is so much talk."

Anson bit his lip. He did not want to argue with his mother. She lived in a world of her own and he penetrated it only on the shallowest level. It was as if she had been frozen at a particular moment in time. Her mind did not go back into the past very far. Ever since that night when her baby had been born dead, she had been confused and subdued, the life gone out of her, a woman whose complexion had lost its bloom, whose eyes had dulled over, whose hair had started turning gray. Her parents had come to the ranch once and left without speaking to him at all. They had left with angry expressions on their faces and since then had not so much as written a letter to their daughter. She had not written them or anyone else. And she never asked about Anson's father. But he knew that people did stare at her. He had heard some talk, but it died out when he drew near. It angered him that people spoke of his mother in derogatory terms, but he couldn't help it. He couldn't help her, either.

"Well, I would like to have spoken with Ken. He's a nice man and I like him."

"He said to give you his best, Mother." That was true. Ken was about the only one who asked how his mother was doing. Nobody else even mentioned her name.

"What about this Charlie Goodright?"

"Goodnight, Mother. He came here and I rode him around the Box B. Charlie's plenty smart, was my impression, and he wants to make a good living in the cattle business."

"What's he poking around here for?"

"He just wanted to know how we were doing with our cattle."

Caroline started churning again, cranking the stick in a circular motion, struggling against the thickening cream inside the small barrel.

"So is he going to build a ranch out here?"

"I don't think so. He thought this country was about as bad as it gets, no more'n a yard from the gates of hell itself. But he said he would see me again sometime."

"Is that all?"

"Well, no, Mother." Anson was becoming irritated. He really didn't want to talk to his mother about things she didn't understand. It was as if she had lost part of her mind. Sometimes, he thought, she acted like a child or an idiot. "He told me I ought to build up my stock and be ready for some good markets up north. He said he was going to look into that for all of us. He said beef was going to be the king crop some day and he said I had a pretty good start on being one of the lucky ones to cash in on it."

"Talk, Anson. Just talk."

"Mother, I have to go, damn it. I just wanted to say good-bye and let you know that you'll be looked after."

"Why, I'm just fine, Anson. You shouldn't swear, though. You're still just a boy. Did you see the garden? It's going to be the best one ever, with squash and pumpkin, string beans and corn and cabbage. I'm growing chamomile and pansies too, and violets and morning glories. And look at the milk the cows are giving.''

"Good-bye, Mother." Anson glowered, but his mother did not see his face because he had already turned away. He didn't want to insult her, but when she questioned him too closely, he felt as if she was invading his privacy. No, it was something more than that. Something impure, something he did not want to face because it was too horrible to imagine. He just felt that she was—was violating him in some way. He could not explain it, did not want to explain it—not to himself, nor to anyone else. She was so cloying at times, and made him feel as if he had done something wrong when he had done nothing at all.

Caroline did not look up as Anson swept past her to his room. A while later she heard the front door slam, but did not connect it with her son. She kept waiting for someone to come into the kitchen and talk to her. When she could no longer swirl the cream, she sighed and removed the churning stick and set the small barrel up on the counter.

She glanced out the window and saw the ashes of Juanito's casita. Martin had burned it down the night Juanito had left, and she had always wondered why he would do such a thing. It had been a perfectly good house and someone might have wanted to live in it. The following day Martin had left and she had not seen him since. But she knew he had been angry at her. Now she could no longer remember what he had been mad about.

Caroline looked into the churn and thought of the small grave out in back between two box elders. A wooden marker bore the legend BABY BOY BONE. That was all. No date of birth, no date of death. Both the same, and etched eternally in her own mind.

"Whatever am I going to do with all this butter?" she asked no one, and then she looked out the window again at the burned remains of Juanito's house. A tear flowed from one eye and ran down her cheek, leaving a lone track like a tiny scar.

49

DREAM SPEAKER OFFERED tobacco to the four directions, and then he lit the pipe and smoked, blowing the smoke to the four winds. He then handed the pipe to Bone, who sat opposite him on the mountain where the sun turned the stones to sepia and puddled shadows under the stones.

"So you have taken the Yaqui woman for your wife," Dream Speaker said, "and you have given her a new name."

"I call her Dawn," Bone said.

"That is a good name. I can see that you gave it much thought."

"I did, Dream Speaker."

"You have new weapons as well."

"Yes. They were given to me by a friend."

"And the horse you traded for your wife."

"Yes."

"It would have been better if you had taken these things from an enemy."

"I do not have an enemy," Bone said. He blew the smoke from the pipe to the four winds and waited to hear what Dream Speaker had to say. He had brought gifts to the people in the mountains, gifts Matteo had given him, gifts of food and tobacco and knives, blankets.

"You will have enemies wherever you go," Dream Speaker said. "You have enemies in the camp."

"I did not know that."

"Your gifts caused much jealousy. When you give things to the poor, you also give the gift of hate."

"I meant to help them."

"You are a stranger to them. They are suspicious of you. You have taken a Yaqui slave as your wife."

"I do not understand them."

"You will understand them when you understand yourself."

"I am going away, Dream Speaker." Bone handed the pipe back to the old man.

"Yes."

"You know this?"

"I know that you had to pay something for the horse and the gifts."

"Yes."

"You must go down into the white man's world again."

"Yes. For a time. A season."

"The season will stretch into many years, my son. If you can remember that you are a human being, maybe you will live through it."

"I will remember."

"Do you know the story of the Deathless One and the wine?"

"No," Bone said.

"Do you know why I offer tobacco and smoke to the four directions, to the four winds?"

"No, I do not. I remember my father told us some story, but I have forgotten it."

"Ah, so you have forgotten one of the things you need to know. One of the things you must teach your son if you have such a one."

"Yes, I have forgotten."

"Feel the wind on your face, Counts His Bones. See how it flows from the four corners of the world. Listen to my story, which is a very old story and was not a dream story."

"I listen," Bone said.

"This is the story of the Deathless One and his wife. The Deathless One is the son of God and he has much power. One day he went out to cut the nopal while it was young and tender. When he was gone the Hot Wind saw his wife all alone and he swept her up in his warm arms and flew away with her. In those times there was only one wind and it was the Hot Wind.

"When the Deathless One returned he saw Hot Wind's tracks and knew that Hot Wind had stolen his wife. So he went to see his grandmother, First Woman, and told her: 'I have seen the tracks of Wind and I am going to follow his trail.' First Woman told him to go and to be careful.

"So Deathless One followed the Wind's tracks. He came upon some people who lived beyond the sunset and asked them if they had seen Wind pass by. The people told him they had seen Wind pass by and he was carrying a beautiful woman in his arms. They also told him another thing. They said: 'Wind is a mighty pole and ring player. He has bested everyone here and has won all the people who waged themselves against him.'

"The people asked Deathless One to stay awhile so they could recount to him how good a pole and ring player Wind was. So he stayed and listened as they told him how they had lost to Wind. 'If you let him play with the pole he carries, he will always beat you, and when he beats you he will take you with him and the other people he has won. He has won men, women and children.'

"So Deathless One asked them what he should do. They told him they would make him two poles for him to take with him, and a ring. 'With these,' they said, 'you might be able to beat Wind and return our people to us and get back your wife.' So they made very good poles for him and a good ring of a willow branch and Deathless One left and took up Wind's trail where he had left off.

"Finally Deathless One came to Wind's lodge, which was made from the snowy wool of the cottonwood tree, and he looked inside and saw his wife there with Wind. 'Ho there, young man,' Wind called. 'Will you play pole and ring with me?'

"And Deathless One said that he would, for that was why he had come.

"And Deathless One looked at Wind's pole and saw that it was made from the thighbone of a man's skeleton. He did not want to play pole and ring with that dead man's thighbone. So he said to Wind, 'Let me see your ring,' and Wind gave his ring to Deathless One, who saw that the ring was made of a living rattlesnake. He could see the gleam in the snake's eyes. Deathless One used the small thorns in his hand to pierce the snake's eyes and make it blind. Then he gave the ring back to Wind.

"When Wind tried to throw the ring, it fell to the ground dead. He tried again and again to throw the ring, but it just dropped to the ground because it was a dead snake. Wind saw that the snake was dead and asked Deathless One, 'How did you do this?'

"Deathless One said: 'I do not like your ring and I do not like your pole. I have a good ring to play with and two strong poles.' The Son of God threw away Wind's snake-ring and his pole and offered Wind a new pole.

"Then Wind said, 'Where did you get these poles and the ring? They are very good poles and that is a good ring. I will play with you.'

"And Deathless One said: 'What will you wager?'

"And Wind said: 'I will wager half these people here with me.'

"They played the game and the ring bounced off Wind's pole and ringed Deathless One's pole and so Deathless One won the game and half the stolen people. They played another game and Deathless One won the other half of the people.

"Wind was angry that he had been beaten, so he challenged Deathless One to a race. 'I will race you,' Deathless One said.

"So Wind said, 'Let us start at the south of the earth and race all around it back to the starting point. If I win, I will kill you. If you win, you may kill me.'

"So the two went to the south of the earth and raced around the earth. Deathless One reached the starting point first and waited for Wind to come. When Wind ran up he said to Deathless One: 'You have won the race. Now you may kill me.'

"The Deathless One picked up a stick and struck at Wind, but every time he struck, Wind ducked and dodged and Deathless One could not strike him. Wind laughed at Deathless One and a little fly heard Wind laughing and flew up to Deathless One and hid inside his ear.

"The little fly said to Deathless One: 'Aim for Wind's head, but strike his shadow on the ground.'

"So Deathless One aimed at Wind's head and Wind sprang to the side, but Deathless One struck Wind's shadow and killed him. Wind fell dead and Deathless One looked at him and said: 'I have never seen a man as strong and wily as this one. So I will take away his manliness and make him wind, only wind.'

"So Deathless One took out his knife and cut Wind into four quarters and threw the parts to the east, west, north and south, to the four quarters of the earth. That is why the wind blows from four directions, but no longer lives on earth as a man.

"After he had done this, Deathless One went back to Wind's home and rescued his wife. He destroyed the snowy house and hung the cotton in trees to remind people that Wind had once lived on earth as a man, but now lived as wind in the four corners of the earth and had no special home. Then Deathless One returned with his wife to the place where they lived. You can still hear Wind howl and cry out to be a man again, but he will always be only wind."

"That is a good story, Dream Speaker," Bone said. "I will remember it."

"Good," Dream Speaker said. "Whenever you hear the wind whispering to you, do not answer him, for he might come inside you and live in your body and be a man again."

"Why do you tell me this story?" Bone asked.

Dream Speaker puffed on the pipe again and handed it to Bone. "Because I think you are going to go after the wind and follow him to the four corners of the earth and you will never find him, for he is no longer a man."

"I am not going to chase the wind," Bone said. And he let out the smoke in his lungs and watched it float away and disappear on the wind that came up suddenly. He handed the pipe back to Dream Speaker.

"I think you will chase the wind, Counts His Bones, or the wind will chase you and blow you to places that will be very dangerous."

At that, Dream Speaker put away his pipe and got up and leaned on his stick-cane and started back down the mountain. Bone stayed where he was for several moments and then started to follow Dream Speaker. The wind blew very strong into Bone's face, making a sound like water rushing over rocks, and he could not move until it died down.

Dream Speaker looked back up the trail at Bone and smiled.

50

────

THEY RODE OUT of the dawn mist, through a path beaten through the brasada, the scent of sweetbrier strong in their nostrils. They made little noise at their slow, purposeful pace. Though in no hurry, they seemed to know where they were going. The horses did not snort or whinny, but plodded forward through the curly mesquite, munching on grass and leaves as they went.

Matteo Miguelito Aguilar rode up to El Llano, the main section of the Aguilar rancho, where Benito and Pilar lived, wearing two pistols on his hips and packing two rifles in his saddle scabbards. He carried a sheaf of documents in his saddlebags. Behind him in a covered wagon rode his wife, Luz, and his son Delberto. Four men rode alongside the wagon, rifles jutting from their hands, their large sombreros shadowing their faces. They were ugly men, with scars on their faces and chests, large mustaches and long sideburns. They all carried large knives and wore big pistols tucked in their waistbands.

At the rear of the small caravan, there was another wagon, this one open. Sitting on the seat were a woman and a young boy, and riding alongside, dressed more like an Apache than a Mexican, was a dark-eyed man, his face hairless, his black hair long and straight. He too was heavily armed.

Matteo waved his arms and the four men rode to the front of the big house and stationed themselves at intervals along a half circle facing the porch. They drew their rifles but did not cock them. Then Aguilar turned in the saddle and motioned to the man in back of the caravan. He drew his rifle from its scabbard and checked the pan, adjusted the flint.

"Benito," Matteo called, "come outside. I want to talk to you." As he spoke, he rode to the far end of the porch so that he was positioned between two of the riflemen and at an angle to the others, so that he was not in the line of fire from the house.

"*Quién me llama?*" yelled a man from inside the hacienda.

"*Yo*, Matteo Miguelito."

"Ah, Matteo. You have come back home. What do you want?"

"Come outside. I will talk with you, Benito."

A curtain moved at a window and a man's face peered out. Then the curtain closed quickly and shook for a moment or two.

"So many men, Matteo. So many rifles. Do you want to talk or to shoot?"

"We will talk, Benito."

"Tell your men to put down their rifles and I will come out. Or you can come inside the house. It is so early. Are you not hungry? Are you not tired from the long ride?"

"I will stay out here, Benito. You come out." Matteo nodded at the men with the rifles. They put them down across their pommels, their fingers inside the trigger guards.

There was a long silence. Matteo waited. He drew a cigarro from his shirt, struck a *fósforo* on his pommel, lit the cigarro. He puffed and let out a plume of smoke. A rooster crowed from somewhere in back of the house. A horse in the stables whickered.

"I do not see the men with the rifles go away, Matteo. Until they do, I will not come out."

"I just want to talk to you, Benito. I have some papers I want to show you."

"Papers? What papers?"

"They are Spanish land grants and official documents. Deeds to my property."

The front door opened slightly, but no one came out. The men with the rifles shifted uneasily in their saddles. Matteo Aguilar continued to smoke the cigarro.

"Why would I want to see the deeds to your property?" Benito said after a time.

"Because you are living on it," Matteo said.

"I do not think so, Matteo."

"That is why I want you to see the papers. I want you to leave this place. *Inmediatamente.*"

There was another long silence.

"You leave this place, Matteo. It is not yours."

"Benito, do not fight with me. Come outside and we will talk."

The door moved slightly, and Matteo turned in his saddle. He nodded to the man who had been waiting well behind the others. The man slipped out of the saddle, hunched down and began to move toward the side of the house. When he reached it, he stayed low so that he could not be seen from the house or porch. He went to the right side of the porch, where he had an angle on the partially opened door.

"I am not coming outside," Benito called. "Leave the papers on the porch and I will look at them later. You go away. All of you."

Matteo smiled. He got down from his horse and reached into a saddlebag. He withdrew a small sheaf of papers wrapped in oilcloth. He walked to the edge of the porch and set the papers down on the top step.

"Here are the papers, Benito."

"I will get them after you leave."

Matteo turned his back to the house and walked back to his horse. He climbed back in the saddle and nodded to the man at the side of the house. A rifle barrel appeared on the edge of the porch. It moved so slowly, it might have been a snail.

Matteo turned his horse. The other riders did the same. The wagons turned as well. But they did not go far. As Matteo and his companions appeared to leave, Benito stepped out of the doorway. He held a rifle in his hands. He was looking at Matteo's back and did not see the rifle rise up from the porch and come to bear on his chest.

Mickey Bone dropped the barrel of the rifle slightly. He took aim on Benito's abdomen. He held his breath and squeezed the trigger. Benito took the ball in his lower abdomen. He doubled over and fell to his knees. Blood squirted from the wound and pooled up on the boards of the porch.

A half second later, Pilar stepped out and knelt over her husband.

Matteo and his men turned their horses. One of the riders shot Pilar in the hip and she cried out as she spun sideways. Matteo galloped to the porch, jerking his rifle free of its scabbard. He hit the ground on the run as Mickey Bone calmly reloaded his own rifle and walked around the side of the porch.

"Benito, you son of a whore," screamed Matteo. "Do you see your blood on the porch? Pilar, you bitch, can you see the blood? Just like the blood you spilled when you killed my mother."

Pilar moaned and tried to stop the bleeding in her hip. A white shard of bone jutted from the wound where the bone had shattered. *"Ay de mí,"* she wailed.

Matteo stood over Benito. Benito rolled over and looked up at him. The wounded man clasped his abdomen with both hands. Tears streamed from his narrowed, pain-filled eyes.

"You would do this, Matteo? You have shot your own mother."

"That bitch is not my mother."

"Your mother was barren. Jaime put his seed in my wife's womb. Pilar is your mother."

Matteo's face contorted with a deep hatred he had carried in his heart for many years. He stepped away from Benito, put the muzzle of his rifle an inch away from Pilar's temple. "I will show you what I think of this bitch," he said, and squeezed the trigger.

Benito winced as he saw Pilar's head explode, jerk away from the muzzle blast. A rosy spray from the other side of her head spattered against the wall of the house and chunks of skull and wads of brain matter flew in all directions.

"You killed my mother, Benito. Now I have killed your wife."

"You bastard," Benito said. "Pilar *was* your mother, *estúpido.*"

Matteo drew one of his pistols and knelt down beside his uncle. His lips curled back against his teeth as he rammed the pistol barrel under Benito's chin.

"I have waited a long time to see you squirm, Benito," Matteo hissed. "You spineless son of a whore. You murdered your own brother, and now I murder you."

"Do what you would do, Matteo. But Victoria was not your mother. Pilar was."

"What difference does it make? Victoria was a lady. Pilar was a whore. You killed the only mother I had. Well, I have the papers now to prove I own the Aguilar rancho and you have nothing."

"You are a stupid man, Matteo."

"I would like to see you die slow, Benito, but I want to clean up the mess and move my family into the house. Where is the little blind one? Lázaro?"

"He died of the yellow fever," Benito lied.

"That is good. I was going to kill him, too. I want nothing here that reminds me of you and your whore wife."

"Besides being stupid, Matteo, you are cruel, too. I never hurt you."

"You killed my mother. I carry that wound in my heart."

"I did not want to kill her. She and my brother were—"

"I do not want to hear any more words from your filthy mouth, Benito," Matteo said, interrupting his uncle. "I am going to blow you to hell, damn you."

With that, Matteo Miguelito Aguilar squeezed the trigger. The top of Benito's head came apart like a cracked melon as the ball shot through his skull. His eyes glazed over with the frost of death as his head jerked backward with the force of the blast. Blood spewed onto Matteo's face, freckling him with crimson spots.

Matteo stood up as Bone climbed the steps to stand beside the new owner of the Aguilar ranch. They both looked down at the lifeless body of Benito. "*Peste. Mentiroso.* I hated him." Matteo said.

Bone said nothing, but he was thinking that he had always liked Benito. The Mexican was a fair and honest man. He wondered if Matteo would be as wise as his uncle. He would not tell Matteo that he had seen a boy run around the house in back and cross his line of sight as he dashed for cover. The boy had seemed to be blind the way he stumbled and held out his hands to keep from running into a tree or structure. Perhaps, he thought, the blind boy had some purpose as yet unfulfilled and was meant to escape death at Matteo's hands.

"Where do you want us to bury them?" Bone asked.

"I want no graves of these dogs here," Matteo said. "Burn them. Burn them until there is nothing left but ashes and then scatter their ashes to the wind."

"I will do this," Bone said.

"You will always have a place here, Mickey. You and your family and your grandchildren to come. This will be your home."

Bone said nothing. He had not worked off his debt to Matteo yet. He still had part of a year to pay him for the horse he had used to buy his wife, Dawn. For he knew he was still an outcast, not only from his own tribe, but from all others, Mexicans and whites. He had married a Yaqui woman, a slave who had been rescued from Mexican bandits, and she too was an outcast from her own tribe.

And so was Matteo, for he had no family, except the one he brought with him from Mexico. All of his ancestors were dead. All of his roots had withered up and he stood alone on trembling, blood-soaked ground.

51

MARTIN BARON TIED the dinghy to the wharf and stepped ashore, his duffel bag slung over his shoulder. The western sky stood like some burning canvas frozen in midflame, the clouds etched in fire and gold like ingots snatched from a furnace.

The *Mary E* lay at anchor in the harbor with other boats that had been blown there by the previous night's storm. Some had not fared well in the blow. The wreckage of sail and spar and mast lay atop their decks like broken matchsticks and shredded paper. There were boats in the harbor and along the coast he had never seen before, and several had been smashed against the shore and lay battered and so broken up they would never sail again. One, a single-masted forty-foot double-ender bearing the name *Whippoorwill*, lay in four or five pieces, its cargo innards spilling out into the water and waders scrambling to salvage what foodstuffs and gear that they could. He felt sorry for the owner, for what had obviously once been a fine sailing ship was now only detritus, sea debris that would be better off six fathoms under, out of sight.

A terrible storm, he thought, to cause so much damage. But he had weathered it well, considering. He was tired, though, as tired as he had ever been, and he wondered if he would ever be able to weather such a storm again.

He approached some small boys playing near the docks. He spoke to them in Spanish. "Watch my little boat and I'll pay you five pesos," he told the oldest Mexican boy.

"Yes, sir."

"I will pay you when I return."

"Pay now," said one of the other boys.

"Later," Martin said and he gave the older boy a peso. "More later."

"I will watch your little boat," the boy said.

Matamoros was a dirty little border town, full of carretas and burros and stray dogs, thieves and bandits and American outlaws. Martin had been there before and didn't like the town much, but he knew where to go to get a drink and where he could buy supplies: cheap rum and cheaper tequila and mescal, beans, rice, bread, perhaps some coffee.

He passed the little shanties and aged adobes with their lanterns still dark and the smells of fish and clams and lobster permeating the air, the flies boiling about the open stalls, the burros switching their tails and flicking their ears. People strolled the streets, the women with woven baskets bulging with vegetables and fish, the men wary-eyed and sullen, the white cloth of their trousers and shirts oddly incongruous with the mud of adobes, the gray of wind-blasted stalls and sheds.

He harbored a powerful thirst after the night's ordeal, hove to at sea with swells big enough to swamp the *Mary E* and rain so sharp and hard his flesh still stung from its needles. The roll and pitch of the boat had made him sick and he had lost all the food inside him. Now the emptiness was replaced with a gnawing hunger and thirst and his body begged for rest, for a sleep not jarred by the creak of wood and the crack of the rigging snapping like bullwhips in the darkness of the storm.

Martin found the cantina he was looking for, near the center of the small village, relieved that it was still there. Miraculously, the storm had not hammered Matamoros, but had it done so, it would not have taken more than a few days to repair the damage, for the village seemed made of scrap lumber and earth and there was plenty of that all along the coast.

The sign on the false front read CANTINA GRANDE, but it was not a large place. Yet, compared with the other buildings in town, it was the largest. Most were only adobes with dirt floors, a bar made of old lumber stretched across a couple of barrels. Cantina Grande had a real bar, crude, but made of whipsawed lumber and lacquered with mescal and tequila to a kind of wistful shine. The flooring was made of wood and at least three inches of sodden sawdust, so that it felt as if one were walking on rubber.

Martin entered the cantina, ducking to keep from knocking his head on the doorway. The place was crowded with sailors and fishermen, men he knew from New Orleans, Galveston, and the Matagorda, and many he had never seen before. They crowded around tables and sat in corners on the floor and milled around the bar with cups and bottles in their hands. Some nodded at him and he nodded back. Others eyed him grimly as if he had just emerged from the sea that robbed them of all their possessions.

Candles and coal-oil lamps glowed in strategic niches and corners and beams, giving little more than definition to the interior. The drinkers sat in complex patterns of shadows that continually shifted as men moved to and from under the lamps. The air was laced with the smells of alcohol and burning tobacco and hazy from the fumes of cigars, cigarillos, cigarros and pipes.

At the center of the room, a large man sat like some decadent king at his throne, a bottle of mescal in one fist, a cigar in the other. He wore a torn shirt with horizontal stripes. His beard and moustache were trimmed neatly, in contrast to the thinning hair on his high-domed head. His laughter rippled through the room as he told story after story to the great entertainment of those seated around him. From the pile of money on the table in front of the man, Martin figured he was also paying for the drinks.

Baron made his way to the crowded bar, where two Mexicans wearing grimy aprons were pouring drinks.

"*Qué quiere?*" a bartender asked of him.

"Tequila, *una copa*," Martin replied.

"*Dos pesos.*"

Martin reached in his left pocket where he carried Mexican currency and pulled out a handful of pesos. He tossed two onto the bar. The barkeep snatched them up before they stopped rattling and handed Martin a cup of tequila. Martin stepped away from the bar, seeking a quiet corner somewhere in the crowded room.

He leaned against a wall and turned his attention to the big man at the center table.

"So here it was pitch-dark and I've got me this big fish on me line and I'm thinking it'll bring me enough money to pay for the trip and give me a tidy profit besides. So I lands the fish and it turns out to be a dolphin and he breaks me line and he proceeds to tear up the deck and he's got me tangled in the line and he throws the hook and it catches me in the shoulder and I'm ass over teakettle tryin' with all me might to throw this dolphin back into the sea."

The others laughed and then the big man continued his story.

"And that dolphin, he takes out me boom and tangles up the rig-

ging and rips down me sail and breaks all the hatches open and I'm
slitherin' after him and every time I get close he leaps in the air and
whips his tail and smashes the gunwales to splinters and I'm lookin'
for a gaff in the dark and wishin' I had a harpoon or a belayin' pin in
me grasp and meanwhile this dolphin is reducin' my boat to kindling
wood with every bloomin' flip of his tail and me lungs a-burnin' and
now sails droppin' on me like shrouds and besides not bein' able to
see jackshit in the dark, I'm blind from bein' draped in torn canvas
and the boat pitchin' and creakin' and I fight me way out of the sail
and dive at the dolphin as he skitters by me and I grab him by the
tail. The next thing I know, I'm over the side and in the black water
and not a heavin' line to be had and me bein' able to swim like a
rock.''

The speaker paused and took a swallow of mescal, then wiped his
corpulent lips on his half sleeve and took a puff from his cigar.

"What happened then?" one of the listeners asked.

"Well, sir," the big man said, "I was caught with the hook and the
line tangled 'round the dolphin and he come overboard to join me in
the water, like he was wantin' to play and wrestle some more, and here
he splashes next to me and starts beatin' me sides with his tail and I'm
flayin' the water like a coot tryin' to lift off with me wings and then
the dolphin dives and I go right with him down to Davy Jones's
locker.''

The big fellow paused again and took another swig of the mescal.
He sucked on the cigar and blew a cloud of smoke into the lamplight,
where it spread like an umbrella over the table.

"How did you get away?" asked another at the table.

And the speaker looked each man in the eye and cocked one of
his own and leaned forward to speak confidentially. "To tell you the
truth, me hearties, I didn't get loose. I drowned.''

There was a shocked pause and then the listeners broke into laughter, slapping their knees and doubling over with mirth.

The storyteller's eyes locked on Martin's gaze. The man beckoned
to him and Martin walked over to the table.

"That was a pretty good story," Martin said.

"And all of it true, except for the drownin'. Rob Coogan's me
name, cap'n of the *Whippoorwill.*''

"Was that your sloop I saw scattered along the shoreline?"

"Aye, that was me home, alas and alack.''

"Too bad, Coogan.''

"Well, I've got me life and I can always get another boat so long
as I can fish. And I'm the best fisherman in the Gulf, I don't mind
sayin'.''

"So happens I could use a hand," Martin said. "I've a small sloop. Be tight quarters for a man your size."

"I've slept in barrels and Mexican kips. I've slept on decks no bigger'n a widow's hassock. If you'll take me on, I'll fill your lockers with the biggest fish in the sea. By the way, sir, I didn't catch your name."

"Martin Baron."

"Martin Baron. Now, where have I heard that name before?"

"I have no idea," Martin said.

"You the *Mary E*?"

"That's my boat, yes."

"Know an Argentine by the name of Juanito Salazar?"

"Yes. He used to be a friend of mine."

"Used to be?"

"We had a falling-out. My fault. I haven't seen Juanito in some time."

"Well, he's been lookin' for you. Met him in New Orleans. He raises beef, I think. Likeable sort."

"How long ago was this?"

"A month or two ago. He said if I run into you to ask you to come by the ranch. Can't remember the name of it."

"The Box B."

"Yes, sir, that was it. He said some funny thing I'm tryin' to recollect." Coogan scratched his head with the hand that held the cigar. "Oh, I know what it was now. He said to tell you that he hoped you still had the dream. I didn't know what he was talkin' about, but he seemed some serious that I tell you that."

"Juanito said that?"

"That's what he said, right enough. Sit down now and I'll buy you a drink."

"I'll sit with you. Hungry? I'm starved."

"Well, now, eatin's an entirely different matter, one that takes concentration. I'll have me a few more sips of the cup, I think, and then I'll break bread with you."

"Fair enough."

"Well, do you, Martin?"

"Do I what?"

"Still have the dream."

Martin looked at Coogan, into his blue eyes. He thought he saw understanding and compassion there. The truth was, he couldn't answer him. He did not know if he still had the dream or not. He often thought about the ranch and what a fool he had made of himself. But he couldn't get the thought of Caroline's betrayal out of his mind. Did he still have the dream?

"I don't know, Coogan. Maybe it wasn't my dream at all. Maybe it was Juanito's dream all the time and I was just riding on it."

"Well, now, Martin, you talk every bit as puzzlin' as Juanito. That man is a river with plumb deep waters."

"Yes, I know," Martin said, and when he thought about Juanito there was an ache in his heart, the kind of ache one feels for a lost friendship. He wondered if he would ever go back to the Box B and how he would look at Caroline when he saw her again. And he thought too of Anson, and the ache was there as well. Different, but an ache just the same.

He finished his cup and Coogan filled it again from his bottle of tequila.

"Here's to the storm and the sea," Coogan said, clinking the bottle against Martin's cup. "They giveth and they taketh it away."

And then Coogan laughed his hearty laugh and Martin smiled, glad to have some company at last. He had been a long time at sea, looking for something that was just out of his reach, something that was just beyond the horizon, just beyond the next sunset, the next port of call.

52

JACK KILLIAN WAS dying, and he was doing it the hard way. He took another swallow of mescal and pulled on the Comanche arrow that was rammed into his abdomen just below his rib cage. The arrow moved a half inch, and then Jack's fingers slipped from the shaft and the barb sank in again, more firmly than before.

Jack tried to scream, but all he could do was make a throat sound that was just a gargled rasp.

"Pa, you've got to let me ride back and get someone to help."

"Ain't nothin' nobody can do, boy. That arrer got into my lung for sure."

"Then let me try and pull that arrow out."

"Hell, son, you'd pull out half my lung. It's rammed up in there under my damned rib."

The Comanche had been on the ground and shot upward, piercing Jack's abdomen, the arrow tip just ticking the left lung. Another Comanche, on the opposite side of Jack, had driven an arrow into Jack's horse, dropping it out from under him. Jack hit the ground hard, sliding on his back down a slope and landing in a nest of ropy cholla. He had drawn his pistol and Roy had shot at the Comanches, but missed. It had been a brief fight. He and his son had been lucky to get away alive. As near as Jack could figure, there were only two Comanches lying in wait for them. But now they were stuck in a damned arroyo with no water, no food, and the trail herd a good three or four miles back, already smelling the Concho and maybe Comanches waiting just ahead, all hid out in the brush like a pack of rattlesnakes.

Jack coughed again and little tiny specks of blood flecked the rag he held to his mouth. Roy winced. He did not like the rattling sound in his father's chest, the blood coming up with the phlegm.

"I got cholla needles in my backside," Jack said. "Burns like fire. That's the least of my troubles, for damned sure."

"Maybe I could push the arrow on through, Pa. Bend it some and. . . ."

"God, you would kill me, Roy. Don't you have no brains?"

"I got as much as you. I didn't ride over no rattlesnake."

"Damned red bastard should have been dead."

"Well, he wasn't when he shot that arrow into you."

"You think you're one smart kid, don't you?"

"No, Pa, I—I just don't like to see you suffer none."

"Kid, I got to tell you something. Something important. So you just set still and listen, you hear?"

"Pa, go on ahead. I'm listenin'."

"Once't I was on a big ranch down in Texas. I seen land like I never seen before, and seen grass so green it hurt you to look at it in broad daylight. Grass where no grass grew before. And I seen rangy longhorns changed into fat beef cattle by breedin' 'em with big-framed Argentine beeves. And I met men with a glint in their eyes and iron in their bones, and they had them a mighty dream."

Jack stopped talking and began to cough up blood and choke on it. Roy's eyes filled with tears and his stomach knotted up like wet hemp. Jack wiped his sleeve across his mouth and smeared the blood so that the lower part of his face looked as if he'd been eating blackberries.

Jack drank down another swallow of whiskey and gagged, sputtered, gasped as he fought to keep it down. His face turned purple for a few moments and Roy's eyes glazed over with a shadowy film as he blinked back fresh tears.

"Pa, let me ride for help. I—I don't want you to die."

"Roy, you stay here, damn you. I don't want to give it up alone."

"But you won't let me help you."

"Just—just listen, while I get this all out. I 'member that country down in South Texas where Baron and Aguilar got so much land they don't know what to do with it, and I didn't have sense enough to stay with it. I had me a cocklebur under my saddle and I bucked everything what was good for me. You know?"

Roy winced. "Well, you left me and Ma in Fort Worth and rode off after Uncle Hardy and we never thought you was comin' back. We didn't know if you was dead or what. I guess you had to go, but me and Ma felt awful bad about it."

"And Hardy got himself killed down there, but it was his own damned fault. I thought it would be sweet medicine to kill them that killed him. But I was wrong, Roy. Dead wrong."

"Pa, it don't make no difference. You don't have to tell me about all that. It's all in the past."

"No it ain't. I seen something. I sure did. And Hardy was wrong. He went to the wrong place. And maybe I was guided there myself. Maybe . . . maybe I was supposed to go there too. Only I was supposed to make something right, not keep on doing wrong, like Hardy."

"Pa, I don't understand."

"Listen, there's a man down there you got to see. Not Martin Baron. He bought all his land from the Aguilar family. And that's what you got to do, who you got to see, one of the Aguilar family. His name's Benito Aguilar. He's got him a lot of land and he's gone begging. He needs cash money and you might be able to buy yourself some of that land and make a good life for yourself."

"Aw, Pa, I don't want no land, honest."

"That land is dirt cheap now. But someday you and your sons will be rich. You do what I say, hear? You go see Aguilar and work for him or steal for him and you get yourself some land."

"I will if you want me to, Pa."

"Good. You do it. Never forget your promise to me, Roy."

"I won't, Pa."

Roy sat down next to his father, but he looked back in the direction from where they had ridden, hoping some others on the drive would ride up and help save his father from an agonizing death.

Jack was breathing with difficulty and he swallowed more of the whiskey, choking it down, belching blood back up. The blood was thin and milky, frothy, and now Roy could hear the wheezing in his father's chest. He closed his eyes and prayed to a dim and uncertain god for his father's life.

They had driven the herd out of the Palo Duro Canyon, two thousand head. Jack had been the main scout through dangerous country and Mr. Goodnight had let Roy go with his father, against his better judgment. All of the men who rode for Mr. Goodnight were heavily armed, but Jack knew the country better and had told Charlie Goodnight that he had fought many an Indian.

Roy had thought his father was dead, gone those long years from Fort Worth and nobody knowing what had happened to him. Word had come back from riders along the trails out west that both Hardy and Jack had been killed by Apaches or Mexicans, so Roy and his mother, Ursula, had thought Jack was dead.

Then one day Jack had showed up out of nowhere, patched things up with Ursula and taken Roy with him. It had all happened so fast, Roy wondered now if he had done the right thing, leaving his mother all alone like that. But she had acted as if she had wanted him to go with his father, so he guessed it must have been all right.

That had been six months ago, and they had worked the herds on the Palo Duro until Charlie Goodnight said the grass was high enough to make a drive to Fort Sumner in New Mexico. But he didn't know of any trail and they hired Jack on to help them break one through dangerous country.

Roy worshiped Charles Goodnight. He had never met a man like him before. And he knew his father liked him a lot, too. Goodnight had been grateful to Jack for telling him about Martin Baron, even though he knew there had been some trouble between Baron and his father.

Roy had gotten all this in bits and pieces, but once he put it all together, he knew some of it. He knew that his uncle Hardy had been hanged for a horse thief by the Aguilars, and he thought that his father had tried to kill Benito, but something had happened. And now his father was telling him to go and buy land from a man he had tried to kill. Maybe, Roy thought, his father was so sick with the arrow in him that he was out of his head. But he didn't know, and he wasn't about to argue with his father while he was dying.

The long shadows of afternoon painted stripes on the shallow walls of the arroyo, and Gamble's quail piped somewhere amid the ocotillo and nopal that dotted the landscape. A lizard blinked at the two men from its perch on a rock embedded halfway up the right slope of the arroyo. A pair of doves whistled overhead, their shadows racing across the arroyo bed like swatches of cloth whipped by the wind.

But Jack was hanging on, staying alive somehow, with that arrow feeding on him, drawing his blood out drop by drop, and pushing into his lung with every breath. Roy wanted to ride away as fast as he could and fetch help, but he knew his father wanted him to stay to the end, which seemed close now.

"I'll last until the herd catches up," Jack said, as if reading his son's thoughts. "But if I don't make it, you tell Charlie that they got Comanches lyin' in wait for them yonder this side of the Concho."

"I will, Pa."

"God, the whiskey ain't doin' me no good," Jack said, and managed to swallow a few drops of the liquor. This time he didn't choke and held it down. But his face was changing color like the clouds at sunset and Roy's nerves sang like maddened crickets in a swamp. He jumped at every sound his father made and strained to hear the sounds of the oncoming herd.

"Pa, I think I hear somebody comin'," Roy said.

Jack could not move, but he listened hard. He heard the hoofbeats, too.

"Might be another damned Comanche," Jack said. "You get that caplock pistol out and be ready to shoot." Then his head swam and he passed out for a few seconds. When he came to, the hoofbeats were louder, but he could not, in his stupor, determine which direction the sounds were coming from.

Jack bit down hard and grabbed the arrow by its shaft. He took a deep breath and closed his eyes. Suddenly, it was silent. Then he felt a hand on his wrist.

"Better not try it, Jack," said a voice and Killian opened his eyes.

"That you, Long Joe?"

"Mr. Goodnight got worried he hadn't seen you, so he sent me up. Caught you an arrer, did you?"

"Seems like. I got to get it out, Long Joe. Damned thing's burrowin' into my lung."

"Ah nah, Jack. Too risky. You wait. We'll see can Mr. Goodnight pull that arrer fer you."

"I wanted to get help for him, Long Joe," Roy said, "but Pa wouldn't let me leave him."

"You did right. That's a Comanche arrer, 'thout a doubt."

"I reckon," said Roy. "He just shot Pa out of the saddle and run off toward the Concho."

"Likely they'll be a passel of 'em waitin' on us to cross," Long Joe said. He was one of the eighteen wranglers Goodnight had hired for the drive to the government post at Fort Sumner. He was a pretty good Indian fighter and had the scars to prove it.

"This'un was a scout," Jack said, his voice raspy with blood coagulating in his throat. "We ain't heard a sound since, but you can bet they seen the herd."

"I been smellin' 'em for five, six mile," Long Joe said. "Hair on the back of my neck's been standin' on end for the last two."

"How soon will Mr. Goodnight be here?" Roy asked, a quaver in his voice.

"Directly, directly," Long Joe said. "Get your hand off that arrer, Jack, and let me take a look-see."

Jack released his grip, realizing he no longer had the strength to pull the arrow out, even if he had wanted to. He felt a numbness in his toes that was creeping up to his feet and Long Joe's head was spinning slowly above him, like a child's balloon on a string.

"Um," said Long Joe as he bent down to look at the Comanche arrow sticking out of Jack's side.

"What the hell's *um* mean?" asked Killian.

"Means you got stuck for fair. About a third of the arrer's in your gut. Could be a damn sight worse."

Jack didn't know Long Joe's last name. He doubted anyone did. Nor did he know what it meant that Long Joe had never said his last name. Some of Goodnight's hands thought it meant Joe had been an outlaw. Others thought it meant Joe could stay in the saddle a long time. They all agreed that was true, at least. Joe was a tireless soul, steady and quiet, never saying much unless it had to be said. Long Joe was a good enough name for the man. He didn't need no handle on it, Jack thought.

"You got enough cholla stuck in you to make a porkypine jealous," Long Joe said.

"It tickles," Jack said, his mouth curved in just the trace of a smile.

"Least you didn't get your sense of humor shot out, Jack."

"This ain't funny," Roy said.

"Well, we could just sit around bawlin' about it, I guess," said Long Joe.

"Aw, Long Joe. You know what I mean," Roy said.

"Charlie will be along directly. Cows done smelt the Concho and Charlie wants to cross before dark."

"Can Mr. Goodnight help my pa?" Roy asked.

"He's the boss and he can sure enough tell us what he thinks we ought to do. I been studyin' that arrer and it's sure enough in a bad place."

Jack reached for the whiskey bottle, took another swig. He coughed and he felt the arrow moving against his lung. He held his side to hold his chest steady and drank again.

53

C HARLES GOODNIGHT WAS the first to spot the downed horse.
"Why, that looks like Jack Killian's mount," he said to Pete Wiley,
one of the wranglers.

"If so, it has a Comanche arrow stuck in its heart," Pete said. His
face showed the effects of wind and weather. His arms were brown
from wrist to sleeve. He rode his horse like a man born to the saddle.

"Damn. If we could have made it to the Concho, we've got help
coming."

"You think that man you hired will meet up with us?"

"Pete, I'd bet my life on Juanito Salazar."

"Well, it looks like he didn't make it across."

"Wasn't supposed to. He'll be riding out from Fort Sumner, and
I'll bet dollars to bear claws he'll have a good price from the army."

"I've never met the man," Pete said.

"He was partners with Martin Baron, the man I told you about.
Knows cattle. Raised them in the Argentine and had stock shipped to
the Box B."

"I know, I know. I'll believe it when I see him."

"Well, we'll know soon enough. Can't be more than a mile or two
before we hit the Concho." Goodnight clicked his teeth, a habit that

made men in open country jump the first time they heard it. "I'm going to ride up to that arroyo and take a look."

"Keep your eyes peeled," Pete said. He did not slow the herd as Goodnight rode away, but kept them moving. They had already scented water and the two thousand head were now a moving force, their eyes pitching wildly in their sockets, nostrils flared, bosses low to the ground as if they were set in a slow charge. Only the outriders kept the herd in check or the cattle would have broken for the river a long time back.

Goodnight rode cautiously up to the arroyo, halted his horse at the rim and looked down.

"Long Joe," he called.

"Better come down and take a look, Mr. Goodnight. Jack's caught him one in the lung."

"I'll be right down." Goodnight dismounted and ground-tied his grulla to a creosote bush so that Loving and the others would spot it easily. He walked down into the arroyo on properly bowed legs, his high boot heels making him wobble slightly. His ruddy face was slightly ruddier when he reached the three men.

"Roy, what happened?" Goodnight asked.

Roy Killian told him. Goodnight hunkered down next to Jack and observed the arrow jutting from under Jack's rib cage. Jack's eyes were reddened from drink and pain. He just stared at Goodnight without blinking, like a man ready to die.

"Long Joe, you and Roy go up top of this arroyo and keep a lookout for Pete and the herd. And if you see any Comanches sneaking around, you holler real loud."

"Yes, sir, Mr. Goodnight," Long Joe said. He motioned for Roy to follow him. They led their horses out of the arroyo and waited by Goodnight's grulla. Long Joe pulled out a blade and snapped it open, cut off a chunk of nopal and began to chew it after he raked the spines off with his pocket knife.

Roy looked down into the arroyo, watching Mr. Goodnight and his pa, his pulse pounding in his eardrum. He watched as Goodnight bent over his father. He seemed to be speaking to him, or listening.

"Jack, what do you think I ought to do?" asked Goodnight.

"Don't know what you can do, Mr. Goodnight."

"Hurts pretty bad, does it?"

"Hard to breathe. Seems like the arrowhead is pushing on into my lung."

"It looks that way to me, too."

"I don't hold out much hope. That was why I was drinking some whiskey."

Goodnight patted Killian very gently on the shoulder as if to reassure him. "That's all right." He paused and touched the arrow. He saw Jack draw back instinctively.

"Might tender, I reckon, huh, Jack?"

"Some."

"I can push it on through, but I think it would tear you up bad. Or I can jerk it out real quick. Get it out and maybe we can do something about the bleeding."

"I seen a man or two die from a Comanche arrow, Mr. Goodnight. Warn't pretty."

"No. I want to try and help you, Jack. But it's going to be a powerful hurt. And you might die quicker or slower. Your choice."

"I reckon I ain't got a whole hell of a lot to lose."

"I'm going to grab this arrow, Jack, and give it a real hard pull. Do you want a stick to chew on?" Goodnight stroked his immaculate, closely cropped beard flecked with gray. His sweeping moustache curled slightly upward at the ends, like the horns of a Mexican steer.

Jack put the whiskey bottle up to his mouth. He took a small swallow, then a bigger one. His throat felt raw inside, but numb. This time he didn't choke. The whiskey burned down to his stomach and he felt a tingle in his veins. Then he gagged as blood rose up in his throat. He gasped for breath and spit out a spray of his own blood. The blood had air bubbles in it.

"I better have that stick, Mr. Goodnight, or I'll scream and scare you away."

Goodnight smiled slightly, then looked around for a stick to put between Killian's teeth. He found a thin one close by, handed it to Jack.

"You watch over my boy, will you, Charlie?"

"I'll look out for Roy, Jack. Don't you worry about that."

"Thanks." Jack put the stick in his mouth, bit down hard. He closed his eyes and held his breath.

Goodnight didn't hesitate. He grabbed the shaft of the Comanche arrow and gave it a hard jerk straight downward.

Jack felt the pain immediately. It shot through him like a bolt of lightning. Sparks danced in the blackness of his mind as the pain lanced every nerve in his body. He could feel his flesh ripping, and it seemed to him that he had been plunged into a fiery bath. The pain was sudden and simultaneously gripped his entire body.

Goodnight felt the arrow pull free, but it brought an enormous amount of flesh with it as it slid from the entrance wound. Blood gushed from Jack's side as the arrow cleared the passageway. Goodnight wrenched his bandanna from his throat and thrust it into the hole to stop the bleeding.

Jack bit the stick in half and his scream broke loose and ran up the scale to a high pitch. Blood bubbled up in his throat and choked him. He gasped to pull in air and writhed with the pain. Goodnight held him down, kneeling on one of Jack's knees and pressing downward on his chest. The bandanna fell away and more blood gushed from Jack's open wound.

"Hold still, Jack," Goodnight said tightly, "or for dadgummit sure you're going to bleed to death."

Jack stiffened, and Goodnight stuffed the soaked bandanna back into the opening the arrow had made.

Just then Goodnight heard the sound of the herd breaking for water, the deafening pound of hoofbeats drowning out the sounds of Jack's labored breathing.

A moment later, he heard gunfire from the direction of the Concho and men shouting. He looked up at the rim of the arroyo, but Roy was no longer there. Dust crept over the rim and rose to the sky as the herd pounded past in a rush to get to the river.

Goodnight steadied Jack and checked the bleeding wound. The bandanna seemed to be soaking up the blood, but Jack's face was pale beneath its week-old beard, and his eyes were fluttering. Not a good sign.

"Do you want more whiskey, Jack?"

No answer.

Goodnight turned Jack over so that he lay flat on his back. And then he waited.

The sounds of the herd subsided and the shouts in the distance faded as Goodnight hunkered over the dying Jack Killian. He put a finger to Jack's neck. The pulse was weak, thready. He waited some more.

Then he heard hoofbeats again, coming from the direction of the Concho. He looked up, dreading what he would see.

Two men rode down into the arroyo. One of them was Roy Killian. The other was a man he had come to know well and to respect.

"Do you need some help, Mr. Goodnight?" Juanito Salazar asked.

"How's my pa?" asked Roy.

Goodnight looked down at Jack. Killian's eyes were closed. He seemed to be sleeping. Goodnight bent over and listened for Jack's breathing. He raised his head and looked at Roy.

"I'm afraid he's gone, son."

Roy's lips flattened as he pressed them together tightly. "God," he said.

Juanito stepped out of the saddle and walked toward Goodnight. He took off his sombrero and held it at his side.

Roy sat astride his horse, staring blankly at the man who had been his father.

"I am sorry," Juanito said.

"He just lost too much blood," Goodnight said. "I think a lot of it was already broke loose inside him. I couldn't save him."

"You did your best."

"What was all the shooting about?"

"We cleaned out some Comanches on the other side of the Concho when the herd came up. The cattle all crossed safely, all but two or three, I reckon."

"Good. The army ready for the herd?"

"They'll pay you eight cents the pound when you get to Fort Sumner."

Goodnight grinned. "A pretty fair price."

"I wish I could have seen Jack again," Juanito said. "I am sure his life changed much."

"Well, just look back yonder at his son," Goodnight said solemnly.

Juanito turned his head to look at Roy Killian.

"Good-bye, Pa," Roy said softly. And then he began to cry.

54

CAROLINE NO LONGER grieved for her lost child. For she had found another to take her dead son's place in her heart. But he was her secret, and one other's, the woman who had brought the blind boy to the Box B one night when the stars were hidden by somber clouds and the moon shed no light on the trail between the Rocking A and the Baron ranch.

The woman who brought the boy to Caroline was Esperanza Cuevas, an old widow who had helped raise the boy and teach him to speak Spanish and a little English. She had feared for the boy's life when she found him wandering alone and weeping a few yards from her casita on the Aguilar ranch. At least he had known where to come, and God had brought him near so that she could help him. She knew he would never be safe as long as Matteo Miguelito Aguilar was alive, so she had come to the only place she knew where she and the boy might find a home.

Caroline carried a basket on her arm, the warm food inside covered by a checkered cloth. She walked from the house to the little adobe on the other side of the barn where one of the Baron hands had once lived. It was a warm, pleasant evening, with the aroma of wisteria and daffodils wafting lightly on the spring air, the stars just beginning to spark silver sprays in the aquamarine sky, the first few lightning bugs winking on and off in the fields of alfalfa and clover behind the Baron house.

Anson was off to La Golondrina, branding the last of the spring calves, before going on his first big drive to Fort Sumner in New Mexico. But Caroline was still circumspect as she walked through the broad square shadows of the barn and around to the back, where the twilight lingered in a faint pewter afterglow. She looked both ways before crossing the broad expanse to the little adobe house where Esperanza and the boy waited in semidarkness for her to come. She knocked softly on the door.

"*Entra,*" said a woman in a familiar voice.

Caroline opened the door and slipped inside, slightly breathless. "*Abre la luz,*" she whispered, and Esperanza struck a match and lit the lantern hanging from a beam. The room gradually lightened as the Mexican woman turned up the wick, bringing a soft golden glow to the small Spartan room.

"Mama," crooned a boy sitting at the table next to Esperanza.

"Lázaro," said Caroline and rushed to him, placing the basket on the table and taking the blind boy in her arms.

55

—■—

T HE SOUNDS OF hammering and the flat-toned slap of whipsawed
boards came through the open window in Ken Richman's office
in the main section of Baronsville. His desk was a clutter of documents, deeds, bills of sale, promissory notes, rental agreements, and
letters of intent. He seemed a busy but happy man. He grinned as
Anson Baron came through the open door, a tall, lean man of nine-
teen with curly black hair, an engaging, mystical half smile seemingly
permanent on his face. Anson had to duck to keep from hitting the
top of the doorway.

"Good morning," Ken said. "I was hoping you'd stop by before
you made the gather."

"A few more days," Anson said. "We 'bout got all the calves
branded."

"Rest your bones."

"Naw. I won't be but a minute, Ken. I need a favor and I need it
fast."

"Favor, yes. Fast, I don't know. Maybe."

"I want you to find Juanito Salazar. Wherever he is. I need him. I
want him on this drive."

"So happens, I know where Juanito is. I think."

"Where is he? Can you get him out to the Box B right away?"

"In a few days, yes. He's been dealing with that Capitol Company over in Austin, but he'd probably be back up in the Palo Duro by now. I think they hired him to look over land they had surveyed up there. Might be A. C. Babcock wants to raise cattle there. Heard of him?"

"I've heard of Capitol. And Babcock, from Charlie Goodnight. Will you get word to Juanito? I want him bad."

"Sure. But I want a favor, too."

"Oh?"

Ken kicked his boot off the table and stood up. "I want to go on the drive for Fort Sumner with you."

"I could use you, but from what I hear from Charlie Goodnight, it's no supper on the grass. 'Sides, I heard you were sweet on a gal that works in the mercantile."

"Jean? Well, yeah."

"Jean Gates, isn't it?"

"That's her name. Lives with her widowed mother. Come out from Missouri a month ago. Wagon full of clothes and no man to look after them."

"So are you looking after them?"

Ken grinned. "I sure am."

"Well, you'd have to leave them both behind to fend for themselves."

"They can do that. After working on a hardscrabble farm in the Ozarks, they can pretty much take care of themselves, I reckon."

"Be gone a long time. Over a hard road."

"I know," Ken said. "Rattlesnakes, Comanches, drought, wind, rain, scorpions, sand fleas, cactus, you name it."

"Goodnight made it. I'm going to do the same."

"How many cattle are you driving up?"

"Pert near four thousand head," answered Anson.

Ken blew a long low whistle. "God, I can't wait, Anson. Ever since Charlie told me how it was when he drove cattle north, I got the hankering."

"You don't sit a saddle much, do you, Ken?"

"Not lately. But I rode out here from New Orleans and I still have a couple of horses I keep."

Anson smiled. "If you can get Juanito for me, we'll have it a lot easier."

"You feel bad about what your daddy did to him, don't you?"

"My daddy was wrong. But that's not the reason. Goodnight told me that he might have lost more cattle if Juanito hadn't helped him cross the Concho. And Charlie rode away with plenty of cash. That's what I need. Cash."

"You've been holding your own."

"I want to make the Box B the biggest ranch in Texas. I need more land and I aim to buy it."

Ken walked around to the front of the desk and slapped Anson lightly on the shoulders. "And by God you will, Anson Baron. You're a chip off the old block."

"With one exception," Anson said. "Unlike my daddy, I ain't no quitter."

Ken sucked in a breath, cocked his head. "No, Anson, you're not a quitter."

56

JUANITO SALAZAR LOOKED at the burnt-down remains of his casita, grown over now with grass and tumbleweeds blown against the collapsing fence. He smiled wryly and turned his horse. He rode to the hitchrail in front of the Baron house and lit down. He wrapped his reins over the rail and walked up the steps, knocked on the door.

"Come in." He remembered the sound of Caroline's voice and smiled. He opened the door and walked inside. The house was cool, breezy from windows being open, and yet there was a melancholy hush to it that bordered on being eerie. "I'm in the kitchen," Caroline called.

When Juanito saw her, he almost didn't recognize Caroline Baron. She stood at the long counter, her faded dress just touching the tops of her button-down shoes, her hair caught up in a bun, with strands of it falling over her face. There was some gray in it, silver where the sun streaming through the window burnished it. Not much color in her face, but that same proud look and those pretty blue eyes that had made Martin's heart turn somersaults.

"Caroline," Juanito said. "How are you?" He took off his battered and dusty hat. His clothes were rumpled and dirty from days in the saddle and he knew he reeked of sweat. But politeness did not care what a man wore, but what he was.

"Is that you, Juanito?"

"Truly."

"Why, land's sakes. You don't look a day older than—"

"Than the night I left. Well, I have a couple of years inside of me."

"Pshaw," Caroline said. "Why, sit down there and I'll fetch you some sweet milk from the well house."

"I came to see Anson. Ken Richman told me he wanted me on the drive to Fort Sumner."

Caroline glided gracefully over to where Juanito stood and looked at him for a long moment. Something flickered in her eyes, a fragment of regret, a flash of something that had flown by her once in her life a long time ago, a spark that flared and died. Her look stabbed at Juanito's heart, for he recognized that she was still a young woman, still in love with Martin, and the sadness in her could not silence her cry of remorse for the things that might have been.

"You haven't seen Martin, have you, Juanito? I feel bad that I was the cause of the misunderstanding between you and him."

"No, I have not seen him. I do not think he can face me or you just yet. Martin sails the sea like a man just burning up his days."

"Will he ever come back home? Will he ever forgive?" She could not finish the sentence.

"I do not know, Caroline. I hear about him from time to time. He goes to Biloxi, to New Orleans, to Cuba."

"But he does not sail to Matagorda." It was a flat statement, devoid of bitterness, but rich with the resignation that only a woman of wisdom could summon from the depths of her despair.

"No."

For a moment Juanito thought she was going to embrace him and cry on his shoulder, but she clamped her lips together when the lower one started quivering and sighed. He wished he could give her some comfort, but Martin was driving himself beyond endurance, a loner with few friends, an anger in him that he could not quench with strong drink so that it only turned against him, leaving him bitter and disconsolate. He had heard many stories about Martin Baron, but none that he wished to repeat to Caroline. He saw Martin as Ulysses, following his own adventure, homeless, but perhaps not homesick, and Caroline as Penelope, weaving her tapestry at night and tearing it apart each dawn.

Abruptly Caroline turned away from Juanito and returned to the counter and her vegetables. "I don't know where Anson is," she said. "He might be at La Golondrina. He does not stay home much."

"I will find him. I just thought he might be here."

"He doesn't talk to me very much anymore and he's almost never home. I don't know who does his washing."

Juanito sensed the desperation in Caroline's voice. Now she felt abandoned not only by her husband but also by her son.

"He has the ranch to run. It cannot be easy for him."

"I think he wants to stay away from me. I think he has condemned me as his father has. To Anson, I'm a disgrace."

"What about yourself? Do you think you are a disgrace?"

"Yes," she said.

"Then, that is what you have created for yourself. This is how you will live, Caroline."

"What are you saying, Juanito?"

"We make our own lives, weave our own webs. You have paid for your indiscretion many times over, and it is time to put the past behind you. It is not something you can change. And you cannot see into the future or live in it."

"I know that," Caroline said without rancor.

"There is only this moment, Caroline. This single, solitary moment, and it is eternal."

"What?"

"I mean that we live only in the present, in the now, and the way we see ourselves is the way we are. Live now and the past and future will not harm you."

"You've always talked strangely, Juanito. Martin told me he often could not understand what you were saying."

"It does not matter," Juanito said. "Your heart knows what I am saying. Do not punish yourself. Do not look back down the long tunnel to the past. Look at what you have and perhaps it will seem that you are rich. If you do not have Martin here with you, he had you with him wherever he goes, for he has wronged you as much as you have wronged him."

"He's wronged you, too, Juanito."

"Has he? Who is to say that I did not sin with you in my mind?"

"Juanito! Don't you dare say such a thing."

Juanito smiled. "It is possible, Caroline."

She blushed and Juanito thought she looked quite fetching at that moment. But he had never thought of her as a woman he might take as a lover, for she was married to a man who had once been his best friend.

"You're teasing me, I think."

"No, I do not tease you, Caroline. It is just that you must not blame yourself for what has happened. What you did was one thing. What Martin did was quite another. Revenge is not sweet. It is a mean and bitter root that one must chew on all his life until its poison kills him."

"I wish Martin thought that way."

"Perhaps he will come to think that way."

Juanito looked at Caroline more closely now that the blush was fading from her cheeks. Beneath her eyes there were creases under puffed and swollen skin. It appeared to him that she slept little.

"You're very kind, Juanito. Quite the kindest man I've ever met, I think."

"You look tired, Caroline. You do not sleep well?"

"I—I sleep when I can. I'm not tired. Really."

"Well, it is nothing," Juanito said, but he knew there was something Caroline was not telling him. She had a secret, he guessed, but he did not know what it was. A lover, perhaps, but possibly something more complicated than that. "I must go now, but it has been very good to have seen you again."

"Please tell Anson to come home when he can."

"I shall. And, I am sure he will."

"Good-bye, Juanito. Thank you for stopping by."

"It was a pleasure to see you again, Caroline."

Juanito put on his hat and turned to leave, when Caroline's voice stopped him.

"If you see Marty . . ."

He turned to look at her. "Yes?"

"Tell him . . . tell him I want him to come back home."

"I will do that, Caroline," Juanito said softly. "That is very brave of you."

"Yes, it is, isn't it? I never knew how to be brave before. But I miss him and I love him and I want to ask his forgiveness."

"Surely, you are entitled to it," Juanito said.

"Thank you. I hope to see you again soon. I want you to come back home, too."

"I am sure we will meet again bye and bye." Juanito left the house, leaving its empty echoes behind him, and the sadness he felt at seeing Caroline again, a widow with a living husband, a woman who had been punished so much for such a momentary indiscretion.

He was disappointed in Martin. Not just for what he had done to his wife and son, but for what he had done to himself. He had thought Martin's ambition was a pure thing, a good thing, but it had faded at the first sign of trouble. He had never thought Martin would let anything get in the way of his dream to build a cattle empire in Southwest Texas, but the man had turned on himself over a woman's mistake and was now committing slow suicide. It was a tragedy, Juanito thought.

And now he worried that the sins of the father would be inherited by the son, for he had not seen Anson Baron in two years and did not know if he was soft inside like his father or made of the iron that he thought Martin had once possessed for a backbone.

57

C AROLINE WENT TO the front room and peered out the window. She watched Juanito unwrap his horse's reins from the hitchrail and mount up. He rode away toward La Golondrina and she felt suddenly sad and lonely. When he had disappeared, she went out the back door and walked straight over to Esperanza's adobe, her heart racing, her head held high. Somehow Juanito had given her the courage to see Lázaro in the daylight. She did not want to hide him anymore.

"I am here," Caroline said as she tapped lightly on the door.

"*Entra, señora.*"

Lázaro rose from his cot and ran to Caroline, his arms open wide. "Mama, mama."

Caroline took the boy in her arms. He was growing tall and strong. She played with him at night, sometimes let him go out in the daytime.

"What do you want to do today, Lázaro?"

"I want to play on the cannon again."

"It is not a toy," Caroline said.

"I know. It is a gun. A big gun. I want to ride it and shoot it. I like to feel it."

Caroline smiled. She had let him play with the cannon and had taught him how to shoot it. He was surprisingly adept at learning the shapes of things through touch. His favorite game was pretending to shoot the cannon. And he loved to climb on it and run his hands over the smooth brass barrel.

Caroline stood up, tousled the boy's head with her hand.

"Esperanza, I want you and Lázaro to move into the main house today."

"But are you not afraid someone will see Lázaro?"

"I am no longer afraid and you should not be either. I want him to be a normal boy, to sleep at night and play in the daytime."

"Oh, señora, you make me so happy. Lázaro, do you want to live in a big house?"

"Oh, yes, Esperanza. That would be fun."

"Let us go to the barn and play with the cannon," Caroline said. "Esperanza can begin moving your things into the house. Put Lázaro's cot in my bedroom, Esperanza. You can pick out a bedroom for yourself."

"Good-bye, Esperanza," Lazaro said and put his hand in his mother's. Together they went out to the barn, with Lázaro skipping along, chattering to his adopted mother about everything he heard and smelled along the way.

"It is cool inside the barn," Lázaro said when they had entered. "Where is the cannon?"

"In the center, where it always is," Caroline replied.

Lázaro ran straight to the cannon, as surefooted as any sighted boy. He found the cloths in the box and began to rub the brass. He checked the breech and the muzzle. "Is it loaded?" he asked.

"It is always loaded," Caroline said.

"Can I shoot it?"

"Not today, Lázaro. Maybe someday."

"I want to kill the men who killed my real mother and father," he said.

Caroline felt a chill strike her. She was surprised that the boy knew so much about the world around him. He had told her that some man shot his mother and father. He knew the name of the man who now lived in his father's house. Esperanza had told him everything that had happened to Benito and Pilar Aguilar, something Caroline would not have done.

The boy didn't hate Matteo Aguilar, but in his simple dark world, he thought it was proper to kill him. Esperanza had told him about "an eye for an eye," and so revenge lived in the boy's heart. The cannon represented a chance to kill his parents' assassins.

"It is wrong to kill," Caroline said tonelessly, as she had so many times before.

"But Matteo killed my real mother and father. I could shoot him with this cannon. Look, I know how to do everything."

As Caroline watched, Lázaro went through all the motions of firing the cannon, reloading it with powder and ball, inserting a fuse in the hole, lighting a fire and touching a flaming faggot to the fuse.

"Boom," Lázaro said, grinning and holding both hands to his ears.

Caroline shuddered. She was sorry now that she had told the boy so much about the cannon. For as blind as he was, he could sight the weapon by sound and he knew how to arm it and fire it.

"Don't you ever come out here and play with the cannon if I'm not with you, Lázaro. Do you understand?"

"Yes, Mama. I will not. I promise."

But Caroline knew, even as he spoke the words, that he was just saying them for her satisfaction. Someday, she knew, he would shoot the cannon. She just hoped that no human would be in its line of fire.

Lázaro pushed down on the barrel of the cannon, then pushed up. He made the barrel swing from left to right. And each time the barrel stopped moving, he said "Boom."

"I am going to make you some toys to play with," she told Lázaro.

But she knew he never heard her. He was too busy making believe that he was shooting at Matteo Aguilar.

58

THE HERD OF longhorn and mixed-breed cattle moved slowly out of the pastures of La Golondrina, strung out for a count before reaching the trail Juanito had marked out. In the lead was a rangy longhorn steer with wide, formidable horns that measured better than six feet. The vaqueros called this one Jefe, which meant "Chief" in Spanish. His calico hide was plain to see at the head of the column of darker cows and steers, and his horns served as a kind of front gate to the herd, for he was as good a cutter as some of the Mexican horses. If any cow tried to get in front of him, Jefe would swing his wide horns and the gate would close.

Anson counted from one side, Ken Richman from the other, each marking down the tally by fives, four straight vertical lines, the fifth line slanted across the "fence."

Juanito rode up and down the procession of cattle, turning back the potential strays, talking to the riders in low tones. The cook wagon stood off to one side, waiting to fall in behind the herd after it passed. He waved to Alonzo Guzman, the cook whom Anson had nicknamed "Lonnie," and his helper, a young Mexican named Joselito Delgado. The pair on the wagon waved back, grinning through the light dust that began to rise in the hot still air of morning.

Riding point for the start of the drive was Roy Killian. Juanito had

brought him down from the Palo Duro after he got Ken Richman's
message. When Anson asked him to join the drive, he said that he
would on one condition. That Anson hire Roy as well.

"I don't know him," Anson said. "But his name's familiar."

"His father once lived on the Box B."

"Jack Killian?"

"Roy's father."

"But my daddy run Jack off."

"He did. But this one is of good character. Jack died on the drive
to Fort Sumner with Goodnight. I took Roy under my wing."

"On your say-so, I'll take him along. Does he know cattle?"

"He is wise beyond his years."

"About cattle?"

"About cattle. And men."

"How do you know all this, Juanito?"

"Roy watched his father die. That makes a boy grow into a man
very quickly. Just as your father grew into a man when he watched his
father and his best friend, Cackle Jack, die. I have worked alongside
Roy Killian and he does not complain. When he is given a job, he does
it. And as a boy, he drew all the short sticks."

Anson laughed. "I know something about that."

"Indeed you do," said Juanito.

"Well, I've got just the job for young Roy Killian," Anson had said.
"And we'll see just what kind of man he has become."

Juanito still did not know what job Anson had in mind for Roy, but
when he made the introductions, Anson had made no reference to
Jack Killian, nor had he singled the boy out for some of the more
distasteful jobs. He figured he would find out soon enough what Anson
would ask Roy to do. Juanito and Roy had worked together and stayed
up late over many a campfire, talking. Juanito thought Roy was intelligent and of good character. In short, Juanito liked being with young
Killian and found him good soil for the seeds of his own philosophy,
just as it had been with Anson.

"I count twenty-five hundred head," Anson called out.

"I make it twenty-five hundred and two," yelled Ken as the last of
the herd passed by.

"Close enough," said Anson. "But you're dead wrong."

"I'm an optimist," Ken shouted, and Anson laughed as they fell in
behind the herd to ride drag for a time. The chuck wagon pulled in
behind them, and they listened to the rattle of iron pots and pans and
tin cups and the creak of yokes and leather. "Besides, you forgot to
count the two head pulling the cook wagon," he added.

Anson looked around at the two steers under yoke and shook his head. "You're a damned good man, Ken Richman. At least you can count better'n I can."

"I'll bet I get more saddle sores than you do before this drive is over, too."

"I couldn't cover it," said Anson, already feeling the butterflies swarm in his stomach and ropes knot up in his abdomen as they left La Golondrina behind and headed into an unknown world, toward places he had never been. "And I wouldn't bet against you if I could."

Ken grinned and pulled his hat brim down to shade his eyes from the blazing sun climbing above the eastern horizon. He pulled his bandanna up over his mouth as he had seen Anson do, to try and keep some of the trail dust from blowing into his lungs.

The solid, muscular feel of the horse under him and the sight of the long line of cattle made Ken's pulse beat faster. Mist arose from the grass as the sun drew the moisture from the land. This had been a dream of his ever since he was a boy, and when his father had given him his first horse, he knew that he was born to the saddle.

"Ken, you ride drag. It'll give you a good feel for the drive."

"You mean I'll eat dust all day."

Anson laughed dryly. "Good for the digestion."

"Sure."

"I'll ride up and give Roy his instructions. We'll do good to make ten miles today. And a lot of it will depend on Roy Killian."

"Okay, boss," Ken said. Anson touched a finger to the brim of his hat and rode slowly up the line of cattle at a canter. Ken saw him disappear into the scrim of dust that now hovered over the trail.

Anson drew Juanito aside before he rode on ahead of the column of cattle.

"I'm going to ride up and see how Roy's doing, Juanito," Anson said.

"Good idea."

"Ken and I counted twenty-five hundred head, nearabouts."

"I notice the cattle all carry the Box B brand," said Juanito.

"That's right," replied Anson.

"Didn't Benito want to join you?"

"I wouldn't know. Benito is apparently dead."

"Dead?"

"My mother has adopted the blind boy, Lázaro, Pilar's son. He told her that his father and mother were murdered."

"By whom?"

"Matteo Miguelito."

"The son who went away," Juanito said.

"And came back and murdered Benito and Pilar."

"For sure?"

"No proof, but my mother believes the blind boy. I didn't ask Matteo to come along."

"Because of that?"

"No, because I want to buy more land from him. He doesn't have enough help to make a drive—too busy fighting off Apaches."

"Maybe he will not like you for not inviting him."

"He's cash poor. It won't make any difference. When we get back, I'm buying more of his land for the Box B."

"I think you are going to be a very good man with business, Anson. You have the killer instinct."

Anson laughed. "I wouldn't know about that. I do know that the Box B is going to grow. And to grow, we need more land."

"Your father would be proud," Juanito said.

"My father has nothing to do with it. I've already filed on all the land he bought. Put it all in my name."

"You had a bill of sale from him?"

"I have my mother," said Anson. "She gave me a bill of sale."

59

ANSON FOUND ROY Killian about two miles ahead of the herd, head-ing north. Anson hailed him and Roy reined in his horse. The air was clear and sweet and the empty land stretched for miles, with no visible landmarks in between.

"Do you know what you're looking for?" asked Anson.

"No, sir, I reckon I don't."

"Are you just out for a ride, then?"

"Well, sir, I thought I was heading generally in the direction of the Nueces River, north of us. And I was generally keeping my eyes out for Indian savages, sir."

"That's good, Roy. But what I want you to do is ride about ten, twelve miles ahead as hard as you can without foundering your horse and find a water hole big enough to wet this herd. And then I want you to ride back and tell us where it is exactly. Can you do that?"

"Well, yes, sir, I reckon I can."

"And after you've found that watering hole and come back and told us where it is, I want you to ride back beyond that hole and find us another, fifteen, twenty miles ahead. And then come back and tell us where that'n is. Okay?"

"Yes, sir, Mr. Baron, I can surely do all that."

"You might have to sleep some nights all by your lonesome."

"I reckon I can do that, too."

"Do you know the way to Fort Sumner, Roy?"

"Yes, sir, I've got the way pretty much fixed in my mind."

"That's good. 'Cause you're going to be doing this all the way there unless I find someone to spell you."

"Yes, sir."

"And, while you're looking for these watering holes, you'll also be on the scout for hostile Indians, right?"

"Right, sir."

"It's a big job. Think you can handle it?"

"I know I can, sir."

"Good. Now, light out and find us that water."

Roy turned his horse and rode away at a brisk trot. Anson watched him until he became a tiny dot and then was swallowed up by the distance. He waited at that spot until Juanito rode up a few minutes later, the herd about a half mile behind him.

"Where is Roy?" Juanito asked.

"I told you I had a job for him. Well, he's working at it right now."

"You sent him ahead to look for water."

"How'd you know?"

"Because that is what I would have done. I did not know you would rely on Roy."

"He seems capable of the job."

"I am sure that he is," Juanito said.

"We'll damned sure find out, won't we?"

"Did you have any special reason for sending Roy up ahead by himself?"

"What do you mean?" Anson asked.

"I thought perhaps you might have a dislike for him."

"Because of his father?"

"Yes."

"No. I didn't really know Jack, except as a boy looking at a grown-up. And I don't know Roy at all yet."

"That is a good job you gave to him," Juanito said.

"Yes, I thought so. It will give him the chance to show me what he can do, and it will give him a chance to think about whether he wants to be in the cattle business."

"That is good, Anson. A man needs time to think about such a thing."

"Do you believe Roy can do his job, Juanito?"

"Find water? Yes."

"And Indians, if there be any?"

"Yes, his father was killed by one."

"Let's hope he doesn't inherit that from his father," Anson said, with the thinnest smile a man could make.

60

R OY FOUND A watering place for the herd that first day, and then
found another for the next day. When they crossed the Nueces,
they lost six head of cattle, but the herd was soon making fifteen miles
a day and sometimes more. They grazed at night, listening to the vaqueros playing their guitars and singing sad songs of lost love and
wrongful imprisonment.

Anson came to love the weeping minor chords his vaqueros played
on their instruments, with leathered fingers as delicate as a woman's
flying over the frets.

Counting Anson, Roy, Ken, and Juanito, there were only nine of
them to look after the herd, so they were all very tired at the end of
each day.

Some days they bucked the stiff headwinds that blew across the
Texas plains and the cattle and horses seemed to stand still more often
than they moved. The men's hats blew away and were never found. A
man yelling would often eat his own words, literally, as the wind blew
his voice back down his throat.

After they crossed the Nueces, water became more difficult to find
and the men's tempers sharpened as their nerves stretched to the snapping point. The cooks served stew peppered with sand and at supper-
time the sound of teeth grinding grit in the tortillas was the only noise.

Roy found the water holes that he had seen when he and his father rode with Goodnight. There too grew provender for the drovers, thanks to the cook who rode with those two men.

"Charlie Goodnight's cook planted garlic, onions and other herbs and tubers under the chaparral," Roy explained to Anson. "You tell Lonnie he can find stuff to make his meals taste less like dried horseshit."

Alonzo soon began to look for the garlic, onions, potatoes and cilantro underneath the spiny chaparral, and he mixed them with the dough for hardtack, in the corn and wheat flour, and in the pinto and black beans, and he used them with the dried chilies he carried in the cook wagon. He even spiced up the coffee with thyme and cilantro.

"A man can smell Lonnie's cooking five miles away," remarked Ken.

"And taste if for five days after he's eaten," Anson said.

The days grew long, and too often Roy rode back to camp, saying that he was unable to find water. But before they reached the Concho, a thunderstorm descended upon them and watered the land. During the lightning and thunder, the cattle fought to turn their backs to the wind and the vaqueros had to bunch them and turn them into the wind to keep from losing ground.

Between the Concho and the Pecos, they lost three hundred head of cattle to Comanche raiders that they hardly ever saw. It took the drovers three days and three nights without sleep or rest to cross that desert. They had to keep the cattle moving so that they could get them to the Pecos before they died of thirst.

Anson rode the same horse for those three days and nights, and the only sleep he got was in the saddle. As the cattle got nearer to the water, they became senseless beasts. When they struck the Pecos, the cattle stampeded, swam straight across and then doubled back before they stopped to drink from the river.

"Crazy," Ken said, his body dripping with sweat. "I've never seen such a sight."

"We probably lost a half hundred head when they spooked," Anson said. "We'll be lucky to make the government post with any herd at all."

"We will get there," Juanito said.

And so they did. Fort Sumner served as a supply depot for the Apaches at Bosque Redondo. There Anson received from the quartermaster eight cents a pound for the 2,176 head of beef.

"That's nearly ten thousand dollars," he told Juanito. "All in silver and gold."

"That was the easy part," Juanito said. "Now you have to get the money back to the Box B."

"What do you mean?" Anson asked.

"Every Mexican bandit, gringo renegade, Apache, Comanche, Kiowa and coyote between here and the Rio Grande knows that you have all that shining metal," Juanito said. "And they will be sniffing your trail and following you and waiting for you at every step of the way."

"What do you think I should do with the money? Bury it?"

Juanito laughed. "No. They would dig it up very soon, I think."

"Then what?"

"Try and fool the bandits."

"And just how do I do that?" Anson asked.

61

—■—

THE NIGHT AFTER the sale of the cattle to the government was completed, Anson paid off all of the vaqueros in silver. He paid off Alonzo Guzman and Joselito, too. He gave Ken Richman some of the money to put in the bank at Galveston.

"Juanito is going to lead you back to the ranch," Anson told them. "You have plenty of guns to fight off any bandits."

"Aren't you coming with us?" Ken asked.

"I'll be along in a few days," Anson replied. "Roy and I will stay behind. Roy, put your horse in the remuda along with mine. We'll buy fresh mounts."

Puzzled, Ken shook his head. Juanito had thought it better that the fewer who knew about the plan, the better.

The next morning, Juanito led the men out of Fort Sumner, riding back the way they had come. Anson and Roy waved good-bye to the men. When they were gone, Roy turned to Anson. "You didn't pay me, Mr. Baron. And now I don't even have a horse to ride."

"I can pay you now and you can catch up with them, but I hope you will decide to ride with me."

"Why?"

"I'm betting that any bandits will think the money is with the guns.

You and I are going to take another route and act like the poorest sonsofbitches in the country.''

"I—I guess I don't understand, Mr. Baron."

"Roy, you can call me Anson. That's my name. Come on, we're going to buy us a couple of nags and some pack mules."

"I hope you know what you're doing," Roy said.

"Me, too," Anson said.

62

ANSON AND ROY slipped away from Fort Sumner in the deep hours of the night when almost all the lamps were turned off and it was pitch-black outside the confines of the outpost. They used the stars to guide them well away from the trail the others had taken. Pulling the pack mules behind them, the panniers loaded with water, food, lean-to canvas tarps, guns and ammunition, they rode through the eerie, moon-dusted landscape like wanderers from some other time and place, nomads who had no roots, no homes and no destination.

In the frail pewter glow of moon and starlight, Anson glimpsed the mysterious shapes of living things gone dead with the dusk, and some were terrifying monsters, demons with rigid outstretched arms like the shadows lurking in a nightmare, like the horrors populating the landscape of a man going mad.

Roy too was uncomfortable in the dimly seen cosmos of phantasms, his horse jumpy beneath him, shying at every unknown shape that loomed on the darkened skyline. The men rode through the desolate nocturnal world of shades and visions, heading southeast on trackless waste, each with his own soft prayers voiceless in the silver-spattered shroud of night, sojourners in a strange land, the boy in each of them aghast with wonder and fright.

Coyotes spooled their chromatic ribbons of laughter across the forsaken spirit trails. An occasional distant howl of a wolf pierced the stillness. Bullbats streaked overhead like wraiths with silver dollars on their wings.

Before the sun rose, Roy took their bearings and double-checked them with Anson.

"We'll sleep by day and ride at night," Anson said. "Find us a shady spot if you can."

"I fear there ain't much shade in this desert," Roy said. "But maybe we can bunch the horses and mules so that they'll shadow us some."

They stopped that morning in a shallow draw and hobbled their mounts and tied the mules to each horse. They put the feed bags on the animals and hoped that eating would keep the stock occupied.

"Shouldn't we set a lookout?" Anson asked. "One sleep, one stay awake?"

"The horses will sound a warning," Roy said, and Anson felt stupid. There was so much he didn't know, and so much he had to learn.

The two men slept fitfully in the harsh light of day, their flesh dried and parched by the wind, the fluid in their bodies sucked out of their pores by the blistering heat of the sun. They awoke in the early afternoon, their bellies empty, the mules braying for water and the horses fidgety and fighting the hobbles.

The men swallowed hardtack and dried beef, washing the arid food down with water. Anson gave the mules water from one of the large canvas bags hanging from the pannier while Roy watered the horses with cupped hands for water bowls.

"Guess we'd better move on," Anson said. "If there's anybody out there, we'll see them coming."

"Don't bet on it," Roy said. "Comanches is kin to lizards, I swear."

"I ain't seen no lizards even," Anson said.

"That's what I mean," said Roy.

63

THEY STOPPED AND gathered nopal and scraped the spines from their leaves and fed them to the animals like green cakes and pierced their fingers and hands in the process, while the heat bore down on them and sweated them dry.

And they saw no one in the shimmering oceans of heat that made the land dance and lakes appear before them like magic mirrors flashing in the dazzling sunlight. The sun fell away in the long blue sky and the breeze lifted up out of some far-off place and dried their sweat as if they had ridden into a blast furnace somewhere on the edges of hell.

"We should have gone on back with Juanito and them," Roy said as the sun sank toward the western sea.

"Do you remember those Apaches we saw when we crossed out of Texas into New Mexico?"

"Yeah, they were miles away."

"Just a-watchin' us. And now they're waiting for Juanito and the others."

"I only saw three or four."

"Well, you can bet there were half a dozen more for every Apache we saw," Anson said.

"But they would have had the two of us to help fight 'em off."

"And we might have lost our money in the fight," Anson said.

"We could do the same out here."

"We could, but I'm counting on the Apaches and the Mexican bandits to stay on the trail. There were a lot of big eyes back at that fort."

"Maybe some of them saw us leave," Roy said.

"I've been watching our back trail ever since we left Fort Sumner. The only thing I've seen is a jackrabbit."

"Well, I don't much like riding at night," Roy said. "No telling what's up ahead."

"Like it or not, Roy, if we can't see them, they can't see us in the dark."

"I wouldn't bet on that, neither," Roy said.

The night shapes of saguaro and chaparral spooked the mules and the two men tussled with them until moonrise, when the animals could see better.

Sometime after midnight, the two men had their hands full when a wolf howled close by. The mules bolted so quickly, they jerked the ropes out of Roy's and Anson's hands. Then the horses squealed in terror and started to bucking.

"I'm going down," yelled Roy.

Anson saw him slide over the cantle and fall to the ground. He tried to catch Roy's horse, racing after him in the darkness. His own horse stumbled and pitched him out of the saddle, and he landed in a prickly pear plant that speared him in a dozen places.

He heard the hoofbeats of the galloping horses and the squealing bray of the mules. Then there was only a deep silence as he picked himself up out of the cactus plant and began to search for Roy.

Anson called out to Roy Killian several times, but there was no answer. He stood there picking cactus spines out of his arms and chest, and the only sound he heard was of his own breathing.

"Roy, where are you?" he called.

The wolf howled again, closer than before. Anson touched a hand to his pistol, prepared to draw if he heard the wolf coming after him.

He listened for the sound of the horses coming back, but he knew they were gone and that he and Roy, if Roy was still alive, were all alone in the desert, on foot, at the mercy of whatever peril came their way.

"Royyyyyyyy!" Anson yelled, cupping his hands together on his mouth.

The silence closed around him once again and Anson felt his throat constrict. When he looked up at the sky, the stars swam in a bleak mist and the moon seemed to mock him in the cold stillness of the eternal night.

64

KEN RICHMAN SAW his horse's ears quicken to cones and twist from side to side. He turned the horse's head with gentle pressure on the reins and saw the fear in the animal's eyes, the flared nostrils. He felt the bunched muscles beneath the saddle and knew something was wrong.

"Ho there," he said, reining up, the hairs on the back of his neck prickling as if he had been stung by a swarm of insects. He stood up in the stirrups to see what was making the horse nervous, but he saw no movement. They were following the Pecos down from Fort Sumner on the east bank, staying close enough so that the stock did not want for water, and perhaps the horse had smelled water. But even as he thought it, he knew he was dead wrong. The horse was not thirsty. The gelding was scared. Scared of something it could not see. Just ahead, beyond a wide bend in the trail.

He started backing the horse slowly, pulling gently on the reins in his left hand, sliding his hand toward his rifle stock sticking out of its scabbard.

"Easy, boy," he said to the gelding. "Just back it on down."

The horse was still quirky and Ken kept the spurs off the gelding's flanks, but close enough that he could ram them into the tender flesh if he had to ride away from there in a hurry.

It was then that Ken realized he hadn't heard a sound in the past several seconds. Before, quail had been piping, a Mexican dove had been calling from a nearby perch. Again, the hackles rose on the back of his neck.

He turned the gelding and started back to where Juanito and the rest of the vaqueros were following him. What was it? he thought. A mile, two miles? He really hadn't been paying much attention. It was a glorious day, bright and sunny, not a cloud in the sky and they'd had a hearty breakfast fixed by Lonnie and Joselito—fresh biscuits, bacon and some kind of adobo or mole gravy and quail Ken had shot the evening before. Guzman had cleaned them, packed mud around them and baked them beneath the coffee coals so that they were cooked in time for breakfast.

Ken spurred the gelding lightly and the horse broke into a loose, wandering gallop. "Too much noise," Ken said to himself and looked over his shoulder. He saw nothing suspicious. But he had the distinct feeling that he was being followed—or watched.

Ken rounded a bend in the trail and saw Juanito and the vaqueros, followed by Lonnie and the cook wagon all riding at a leisurely pace, as if none had a care in the world.

"What passes, Ken?" Juanito asked.

"I—I don't know. Something spooked my horse, Dom, and I got a funny feeling that somebody's waiting for us just down the trail."

"That is good to trust your feelings," Juanito said. "Could have saved your life." He spoke to the vaqueros, who pulled their rifles from their scabbards and checked them. Some took pistols from the saddle-bags and stuck them in their sashes. Lonnie and Joselito brought rifles out of the wagon and checked the caps on the nipples. "Spread out and stay about ten or twelve meters apart," Juanito ordered.

Ken jerked his rifle from his scabbard. He wore a gun belt with a new Colt Navy .44 loaded with powder and ball in five of its six cylinders. He tapped the butt of the Colt. "I'm ready," he said.

"Let's ride ahead and you show me the place where Dom spooked."

"You remember that little bend in the trail? There was a draw just before it, kind of a gully?"

"I remember the place," Juanito said. He remembered a lot more about it. At the bottom of the draw was a dry wash, a place where flash floods had run their course. Where the trail took a bend, the flood-waters had left a lot of deadfall. The cattle had spooked and refused to go past until the vaqueros whipped them, and Juanito had had to rope Jefe by the horns and practically drag him past the pile of brush and dead cactus. It was a perfect place for an ambush.

On both sides of the draw men could wait on high ground and men could hide behind the brush and catch any oncoming riders in a deadly pocket. If men closed in behind them, they would all be trapped in deadly cross fire.

When they came to the place where Dom had heard or smelled something, Juanito stopped.

"Is this the place?" he asked.

"Near 'bout," replied Ken.

Juanito looked behind him. The vaqueros were spread out and riding cautiously. Jefe and the other steer pulling the cook wagon lumbered on, unsuspecting of any trouble. The horses, however, all had their ears perked taut.

"If we go down in there, we might not come out," Juanito said. A cloud shadow passed through his mind and for a moment he felt as if time had stopped. He looked up at the sky and there was no cloud across the sun. He closed his eyes for a moment and went to that deep place within where all was calm and where he could listen. Whispers, only whispers, and a faint pinpoint of light in the darkness. When he opened his eyes again, he looked around him. All was serene, but again that quick cloud shadow flitted across his mind and he knew it was a premonition of some kind. But he knew that was part of the grand mystery of life. Man could not see around corners, except in rare cases, and he must trust his own spirit to give guidance.

"We could ride around it, wide as it is," Ken said.

"Maybe. Let us think it through." It would be easy, of course, Juanito reasoned, to do what Ken had suggested, but would that be tampering with the steady rhythms of the universe? Who was he to change the course of journeys that had perhaps been arranged long before he was born into this world? Still, man had choices. He did not have to follow every path blindly. "Perhaps we should check it out," he said finally.

"You don't like it," Ken said.

"I have a funny feeling about it. In my gut. I can almost smell an ambush. Someone is waiting for us to come through that dry wash."

"How do you know that?" Ken asked.

"Sometimes a man can tell if he is not going to live much longer," Juanito said cryptically. "There is an emptiness in the mind, as if a sky full of clouds had cleared suddenly. As if a shadow had fallen across his face with no shade nearby."

"I don't understand what you mean," Ken said, but there was an edge to his voice that had not been there before. "Like a hunch?"

"Much stronger than a hunch. I have always known that I would die on foreign land. That I would never see Argentina again. And when we started on this drive, I thought that I would not come back."

"You give a man the willies, Juanito. You hadn't ought to talk like that."

"In my saddlebags, there is a letter. I want you to give it to either Anson or Martin Baron. I wrote it the last day we were at the fort. I thought maybe that I might not . . ."

Before Juanito could finish the sentence, the stillness broke with the crack of a single rifle shot. The echoes seemed to reverberate for an eternity. One of the vaqueros had ventured close to the gully, probably out of curiosity.

Then out of the draw, men on foot came charging forward, their rifles blazing orange flame, yelling at the top of their voices.

Ken raised his rifle and tracked a target. He heard the vaquero's rifles spit lead and crack like bullwhips behind him.

He heard a sound and turned to see Juanito's face drain of color. A stain appeared in his side. He looked at Ken and smiled.

Ken found his target again and squeezed off a shot, but his mind was on Juanito Salazar, who was still sitting his horse, but twisted in the saddle as if in the grip of a terrible pain. A split second later, Juanito fired his rifle, and Ken saw a bandit go down, writhing in agony, his arm nearly torn off at the shoulder.

And then Ken was drawing his pistol and firing at close range, firing at men he knew, men he had seen before, and wondering why they were there and why they were shooting at him.

65

ANSON HEARD ROY groan in the darkness.

"Roy?"

"Here."

Anson stumbled through the darkness, trying to find Killian. He floundered through sage and chaparral and stepped in prickly pear, trying to follow the sound he had heard. He fought against the tug of cactus spines and the brush that grabbed his boots with invisible fingers.

"That you, Roy?"

"Down here," came the reply.

Anson saw a dark shape a few yards away, like a shadow on the ground. He stepped toward it, saw that it was Roy.

"You all right?"

"I—I don't know. Head feels like it's full of lead and everything's spinning around. Jesus, what happened?"

"Your horse ran out from under you. Mine, too. Mules and horses are gone."

"Give me a hand up, will you?"

Anson extended his arm. He felt Roy's hands grasp his wrist. He pulled the man to his feet. Roy swayed and Anson put his arm around him to steady him.

"Dizzy," Roy said.

"I reckon."

"Good thing I fell on my head. Hit anywheres else and I might have gotten kilt."

"At least you didn't lose your sense of humor."

"No, but I feel bad about losing my horse and all that money."

Anson laughed harshly. Roy started to buckle and he lifted him up until he stood straight.

"Something funny?" Roy asked.

"I've got some of the money."

"All that gold and silver? Where?"

"In my boots, under my shirt, stuffed in my trousers. I must weigh two hundred pounds."

Roy laughed and then winced with the pain in his head. He put a hand gingerly to his neck and rubbed slowly upward.

"I got me a good-sized knot up on top," he said.

"We've got to find those mules at least," Anson said. "When you feel up to it."

"In the dark?"

"First light, at least. They got all our water. Unless they dropped a water bag on their way out of the country."

"Where do you figure they went?"

"I haven't the least pip of an idea," Anson replied. "I just hope they left some tracks for us to follow."

"Listen," Roy said.

"Damn," said Anson.

As they stood there in the dark and the stillness, both men heard the sound of the rising wind. In moments they became engulfed in a sandstorm that stung their faces and whipped their clothes. They pulled bandannas over their mouths and struggled to suck breath through the sand. They leaned into the wind and held on to each other like men sinking through some great black sea to the bottom of the ocean.

The wind lasted for the better part of an hour, but to both young men, it seemed like an eternity as they huddled together, trying to protect their eyes from the blowing sand.

When the wind finally died with the surging of the yellow dawn, Roy and Anson stood in the center of a deserted world, a world swept clean by the sandstorm.

"Not a track," Anson said.

"Do you know which way the mules and horses went?" Roy asked.

Anson shook his head. "No, but I know where we have to go."

"Where?"

"Unless we find the Pecos, we're dead men."

"Well, we know where to find it," Roy said.

The two men started walking toward the southwest, the blazing sun at their backs, their stomachs roiling with hunger, their thirst almost unbearable after the blowing winds had left their throats parched, their mouths desiccated as dried corn husks.

66

KEN STEADIED HIS rifle, curled his finger around the trigger. He had reloaded after the vaqueros had shot two of the bandits and the others had thrown up their hands. A man knelt before him, his hands folded over his head. The other bandits were also on their knees, surrounded by vaqueros with reloaded rifles and pistols. Juanito lay on a stack of saddle blankets, bleeding from a hole in his side.

"How do you call yourself?" he asked the Mexican.

"I call myself Julio Herrera."

"You work for Aguilar."

"Yes."

"Tell me why you are here."

"Matteo Miguelito Aguilar told us to come here. He said that you would have much gold and he told us to take it and bring it back to him."

"Where is Matteo?"

"He is at the ranch, I think."

"I ought to shoot you dead right now," Ken said.

"Please. I have a family. We did not want to do this. Matteo said he would kill us if we did not rob you."

Ken turned away from the man in disgust. He gave orders to the vaqueros to tie all of the bandits up. "They can walk behind the chuck wagon," he said. "Rope them around their necks. We'll see what Anson wants to do with them when we get back to the Box B."

"Let them go," Juanito said, his voice weak and raspy. "It is not their fault."

"But they killed one of us and would have killed us all if they could have."

"They will not go back to the Aguilar ranch," Juanito said. "Let them go."

Ken hesitated. He respected Juanito, but it was clear to him that the man was dying and did not know what he was saying.

"I will let them go if you pull through, Juanito. Otherwise, I'm takin' 'em back."

"I will not survive the journey back to the Box B," Juanito said.

Ken spoke to Lonnie. "You and Joselito get some men to help you lay Juanito in the wagon. We are leaving this place."

Juanito lifted a hand, beckoned to Ken. Ken walked over to the dying man, knelt down.

"There is a letter, the one I told you about, in my saddlebags. When I die, you give it to Anson."

"You're not going to die, Juanito. It's not your time to die."

"Time? What is time to God? What is time to man? To man it is both abstract and concrete. Our time is artificial, made by man to record his days, the seasons, the cycles of life. Eternal time, God's time, is no time at all."

"If you say so," Ken said, beginning to feel very uneasy.

"I do not say so, Ken. The ancients say so—and they knew. They knew all the secrets of life. And of death."

"Old men. Dead men," Ken said.

"No. Living men. Living in words, in knowledge they passed on to us."

"I guess maybe," Ken said awkwardly. He knew he was listening to the mindless babble of a dying man, and it made him feel sad. "You've lost some blood, but we'll make your ride easy and you'll get it back."

Even as he said the words, Ken knew that Juanito would not survive the ride back to Texas. They had bandaged his wound, but he was torn up inside and still bleeding. His face was very pale and his eyes were glazed with pain.

"It has been a good life," Juanito said. "When we get back, will you ask Anson to bury me where my little house once stood?"

"I will do that," Ken said tightly. "If it comes to that."

"Thank you, my friend."

Lonnie, Joselito and two of the vaqueros lifted Juanito gently and carried him to the cook wagon. Lonnie had already prepared a bed for him. They laid him inside. Joselito crawled in and stayed with him. Juanito's eyes were closed, but he was still breathing. Joselito did not like the sound of the breathing. It was very shallow and threaded with death.

67

ANSON PLODDED A few yards ahead of Roy, forcing each step with a will that overcame the lethargy of muscles starved for moisture.

The trackless desert stretched out endlessly, maddeningly, a sameness to it all, a monotony to the slow hours that passed under a cruel, heartless sun. His parched lips were cracked and sore, but no longer bled. His mind filled with mouthwatering images. Watermelon and cantaloupes, plump milky figs and juicy persimmons, overripe tomatoes that squirted when he bit into them, icy spring water bursting from cool blue clay and pears from the storm cellar full of a sweet and wet nectar that trickled down his throat smooth as golden honey.

"Anson," Roy croaked from a few yards behind. "Wait a minute. We've got to stop."

"Go to hell," Anson said, his mind going back to that night when Roy had lost his mount, plunging them into this predicament.

"Listen. We've got to have water."

"You bastard."

"There is water," Roy said, his voice rasped dry by the boiling heat.

Anson stopped in his tracks, swayed there, his eyes squinted to slits to shade them from the burning sun.

"Are you trying to be funny, Roy?"

"No, I seen a dry stream bed a minute ago. Might be water underneath. We could dig into it."

"I never saw no creek bed, dry or otherwise."

"Just a few steps back. Looks like water run through it real recent."

Anson suppressed his skepticism. "If you're lyin' to me, Roy, so help me, I'll kill you with my bare hands."

Roy stumbled back the way they had come. He had gone only a few yards when he turned and drifted off to his left. "There," he said, pointing to a dry wash that looked as if it had recently been ravaged by a flash flood. It was on ground that sloped slightly downward, running off in the distance before it disappeared behind a bend in the terrain.

"I missed it," Anson said. "God, do you really think there's water underneath?"

"Might be," Roy replied.

The two men stumbled down the embankment into the dry stream bed. Anson knew that water often went underground in hot weather. There could be moisture a few inches or a few feet underneath the creek bed. Or there might be just sand.

"Find us a place to dig," Anson said, licking his swollen and ragged lips.

Roy walked along the bed, finally stopped. "This looks like a good low spot. It's soft here."

"We'll try it," Anson said.

The men hunkered down opposite each other and drew their knives. They began digging in the sand, chopping away, scooping it out with their hands. They widened the hold and deepened it. The sand began to come up damp, and then wetter and wetter, until finally a dirty little pool of water appeared.

"Water!" exclaimed Anson.

"Easy now. Just dip your fingers in and wet your lips. I'll do the same and then we'll dig deeper."

Anson forced himself to just wet his lips, but he yearned for a deep drink. He waited impatiently while Roy wet his lips. Then the two men began to dig frantically, spurred on by the thought of finding enough water to drink, to turn their dry insides into an ocean.

"Apaches drink all the water they can," Anson said. "Make themselves sick with it. And then they can go for days without water. A white man drinks a little at a time and then dies of thirst."

"I never knew that," Roy said. They dipped into the water with their hands and chewed on it, let it slink down their throats like wine and then scooped up more. The water was hot and brackish, but they didn't care. It was the first wetness they had tasted in days.

"I hate to leave this water," Anson said. "Little as it is, it saved our lives."

"We could follow this stream bed. It ought to take us right to the Pecos."

"Yeah, but how far? How long can we last without water?"

"Not long," Roy said. "When I was riding with Juanito, he told me some things."

"Like what?"

"He said to expect what you want and you'll have it."

"Yeah, he told me something like that, too," Anson said.

There was a long silence between the two men.

"So do we leave this water hole and go on?" Roy asked finally.

"We'll drink as much as we can and go tonight," Anson said.

"We won't be able to see this dry bed at night."

"I guess I'm not thinking straight, Roy. You're right. We have to go on. The sun will suck this water up faster than we can drink it."

Roy drew in a breath. "I wish Juanito was here with us right now."

"Yeah, me, too. How come you to ride with him, anyway?"

"Do you want the truth?"

"Sure."

"I didn't until he said he used to ride for the Box B. My pa told me about your pa and about the land there. He said I should buy some of it someday, so I went with Juanito."

"You want to buy land in the valley?"

"Yes. I want a ranch of my own, a wife, a home. Like everybody."

"You and I get back to the Box B, I'll see to it you get some land."

"Shake on it?"

"Shake on it," Anson said, and held out his hand.

68

SAM MAVERICK PAID Martin Baron off in cash after the freight on Baron's boat was unloaded at Matagorda. He counted out the bills and placed them in Martin's hands. "You can count it again if you wish," Sam said.

"Your count is good with me, Sam. You know that. How's your health?" Martin knew that Maverick had almost been executed as a spy at the Presidio de San Antonio de Bexar in 1835, which at that time was under Mexican rule. He had come as close to a firing squad as a man could get without dying.

"Damned fine since I got out of the goddamned cattle business."

Martin laughed. Maverick had never owned more than a few hundred head of cattle in his entire life, but he was a builder of empires, a smart businessman whose name would live longer than anyone's in that part of Texas. He had gotten cattle in lieu of a debt owed to him, and the herd had multiplied so much without any help from Sam that every stray cow came to be known as "Maverick's cow," or just a "maverick." People still called any wild cow a maverick. Cowmen branded such strays, which might have been Sam's, and laughed when they counted up the mavericks they had put their brands to.

"You were damned smart to get out when you did, too."

"Oh?"

Peabody Public Library
Columbia City, IN

"Haven't you heard? The Apaches are on a rampage. Some buck named Cuchillo and his son Culebra are torching every blamed homestead from the Rio Grande to the Nueces. Stealing cattle right and left, murdering people. A damned menace if you ask me."

Martin's face paled. "Where did you hear this?"

"Why, just this morning. They murdered your wife's folks, Larry and Polly Darnell, and they were headed north, with a few murderous stops in between."

"The hell you say."

"A damned fact, Baron. Those ranchers in there had better pack up and give the land back to the savages. That's what I think. But I also heard that Matteo Aguilar made some kind of deal with Culebra, the Apache chief. If so, he's a mighty dangerous man and a scoundrel to boot."

Martin had heard that Matteo Miguelito Aguilar was running the Rocking A, but if he was in cahoots with the Apaches, that could only mean that he wanted the Baron ranch to go under. He had heard rumors that Aguilar was desperate for money to keep his spread going and regretted the land that had been sold off.

"You believe that Aguilar is behind the Apache raids?"

"I do. But whoever's behind this latest outbreak of Apaches on the warpath, it means big trouble in the Rio Grande Valley."

With that, Maverick stalked off the pier, giving orders to his men waiting by a wagon to haul off his supplies shipped in from New Orleans. Martin watched him go, stuffed the bills in his pocket, and then clenched his fists. He thought of Caroline and Anson, all alone on the Box B, unaware of the raiding Apaches. He wondered if he could find a horse to ride and how fast he could get there.

He walked back aboard his boat, the *Mary E,* and yelled at his mate, Rob Coogan, a giant of a man who could cook and fight and drink. He could also wrestle cargo like Mike Fink could clear a tavern at the drop of a hat or the uttering of a fighting word.

"Rob, get up here on deck."

Coogan had already started his port leave in the galley, swigging down West Indies rum and squirting lime juice down his gullet.

Coogan's balding head appeared first at the hatch and then his face emerged, an engaging smile on it.

"What's up, Marty?"

"I've got to go to my ranch quick. You stay here and take on cargo for New Orleans. Hire a helper if you need one."

"I thought you was never goin' back to that old ranch of your'n," Coogan said, now fully on deck and towering several inches above Baron.

"There's trouble. Get my rifle and possibles and pack me some grub. I'll be back within the hour. Get my pistols, too. You know where I keep 'em."

"Sure, Marty, sure, and I'll do that. I just wish you weren't in such a dither so's we could talk and have a drink together. We made a bit of money this trip, eh?"

"Yes, I'll give you money before I leave. Just take care of business, will you? Don't get too drunk."

"Me, get drunk? Why, I can drink with the best of them, I can, and still hold me liquor."

"Okay, Rob, whatever you say. Now pack me some grub and get the rifles and pistols, will you?"

"In a twinklin', Marty." The big man disappeared below and Martin ran up the gangplank like a man on fire.

All he could think about was Caroline and Anson facing Cuchillo and his Apaches. He had been away too long and for the past few months had been screwing up the courage to go back and apologize to them for his desertion. He had been too critical of Caroline, he knew. Had branded her for life over something that he'd seen happen time and time again in other places he had been. It still hurt to think about it, but he wasn't entirely blameless. He had left her alone too much, and many times had neglected his husbandly duties because he was too tired, too worried or too caught up in the cattle business.

He'd had time to think over the years and now it was time to go back. On the way to the stables, he thought about what he would do. He would sell the *Mary E* and ask Caroline to take him back. If only he could get there in time. If only he could get there before Cuchillo did and help his family fight off the Apaches.

He ran to the stables and started thinking about how long it would take him to ride to the Box B.

The stableman was out back, throwing hay to several horses in a corral.

"I need two horses quick," Martin told the man. "Also a saddle, saddlebags, and a bridle."

"Rent or buy?"

"Buy."

"You by yourself?"

"Yes, what's that got to do with it?"

"Nothing, I guess. I just wondered what you were going to do with two horses and only one saddle. You going to pack the second one?"

"No, I'm going to ride both of them."

"At once't?"

"No. But I'm going to kill one of them riding him into the ground. Now, get me two fast ones. I haven't got time to argue with you."

"Cost you."

"I don't give a damn what it costs."

"Hundred apiece."

Martin fished in his pocket, took out the wad of bills Sam Maverick had given him. The stableman's eyes widened.

"That'll do," he said. "I'll pick you out two good 'uns."

"Make it quick," Martin said to the stableman.

"Sure, mister," the stableman said and continued to pitch hay into the feed bin inside the corral. Martin wanted to wrench the pitchfork out of the man's hands.

"Hurry, hurry," he said to himself. And then, "God protect my family."

And he realized that he hadn't prayed in a long, long time.

69

E SPERANZA CUEVAS SAT outside on a little stool in the shade of a
tree at a little table she had made by placing two boards across
two small barrels. Four twenty-five-pound flour sacks filled with dirt
and sand, placed on top of the boards at either end, steadied the
makeshift table. She ground the corn in a metate with a pestle made
of stone.

Lázaro was playing nearby, a little game he had made up involving
small pebbles in deep-cut circles in the earth. The pebbles were of two
nearly uniform sizes, big and small. He rolled the little pebbles into
the big ones, knocking them toward the inside perimeter of the circle.
Then he would feel the big marble to see how close to the line it was.
He did this until he had all the large stones near the line without going
outside of the circle.

"Ptooey," Lázaro said, flicking a small stone into the circle. He
heard the click as the stone struck another. "Ay!" he exclaimed. Then
he thumbed another one at a large pebble and heard nothing.
"Missed," he said in Spanish.

Esperanza listened to the sound of the stones clicking together and
only half heard Lázaro's exclamations. She ground the corn into fine
meal, pushing hard on the pestle and swirling it around in the bowl.

That sound, too, was soothing to her, for it represented good work for a good purpose.

Then she heard something else, something that made her skin prickle. She didn't know what it was, but she stopped grinding the corn and lifted her head. She turned to determine the direction from which the sound had come. What was it? she asked herself. A whisper? A small wooden mallet striking a dowel? A horse lightly kicking one of the poles in the corral?

She looked all around her, but saw nothing. Not at first. Then as she started to bend her head and go back to the grinding of the corn, she saw a shadow, a flicker or something just at the edge of her vision. She turned quickly, wondering what it was. She saw only the barn and the corrals out back, the gently undulating grasses in the fields, the vegetables in the garden in back of the house.

"What is it, Esperanza?" Lázaro asked suddenly, and she realized he had stopped playing with the stones.

"Did you hear something, Lázaro?"

"I heard something. Somebody running."

"Running?" The boy's hearing was very keen, she knew. "Running? Where?"

"By the barn. I heard something else, too. Something buzzing through the air."

"Buzzing?"

"Like a whirring some birds make with their wings."

Esperanza felt a cold chill creep over her. She looked back at the barn, but saw nothing. She looked at Lázaro, who was looking at her, even though she knew he could not see her.

"Where did you hear these things?" she asked.

Lázaro pointed. "Over behind the barn."

"Was it Carlos?"

"I do not think so," said Lázaro. "But it was a man I heard running. After I heard the other sound."

"Carlos would not be running in the heat of the day. Unless something was wrong. Even then I do not think he would run."

"No. I have never heard Carlos run. He walks very slowly, too."

"*Ay de mi*." she whispered. "Quick, let us go into the house and tell the señora."

"Tell her what?"

"I think there is something wrong. Quick, quick. Hurry, hurry."

She stood up and walked to the boy, grabbed his hand, dragged him toward the house. She wanted to scream, but she willed herself to silence until she reached the safety of the house. Then just before they reached the back porch, Esperanza saw something that made her heart skip a beat. On the hill beyond the front of the house, she saw a horse and rider. The rider held a lance over his head and waved it back and forth. Then the Apache wheeled his horse and disappeared beyond the crest of the hill.

Esperanza was out of breath by the time she reached the back porch and clambered up the steps. She flung open the door after pulling down the latchkey and stumbled into the kitchen.

"Carolina, Carolina," she called. From somewhere in the house, Caroline answered.

"I am in the sewing room."

"Apaches, Apaches," Esperanza blurted out as she released Lázaro's hand and raced to the little room Caroline had made into a place for sewing and crocheting.

"What do you mean?"

"Here. Up on the hill. I saw one." Esperanza entered the room. Caroline had a piece of thread in her mouth and a needle in her hands. On her lap was the cutout piece of cloth for a shirt she was making for Lázaro.

Caroline stuck the needle into a pincushion shaped and colored like a tomato and set her sewing aside. She arose from her chair and swept past Lázaro and Esperanza. "You two stay here. I'm going out to the barn."

"I want to go," Lázaro said.

"No," Caroline said emphatically. And then she was gone. She did not hear the tug-of-war going on between Esperanza and Lázaro as he tried to break free to follow his adoptive mother.

On the way out of the house, Caroline took a rifle out of the gun cabinet in the front room, slung a pouch of ball and a powder horn over her shoulder. She checked the pan and flint, made sure the rifle was loaded. She walked out the back door, moving swiftly toward the back of the barn and checking the hillside for any sign of Apaches.

Carlos had been butchering a calf that morning, she knew. It was so quiet, she wondered if he was still alive or had run away at the sight of the Apache that Esperanza had seen.

The back doors of the barn were slightly open. She waited before going in, listening for any sound. When she heard nothing, she slipped through the doors and stood to one side, holding the rifle, a Maryland-made rifle in .60 caliber that Martin had taught her to shoot. It was heavy, but she had confidence in it.

"Who's there?" she asked loudly.

There was no answer.

"Carlos?" Again no one replied.

Her eyes adjusted to the light. In the nearest corner stall, she saw the carcass of the calf. It had been gutted and partially skinned. She walked over to it and then jumped backward when she saw Carlos's body lying in the shadows. She fought down the bile that rose up in her throat and stepped closer.

"Oh, my god," she shrieked. Carlos lay dead, his shirt gory with blood, his throat slashed hideously from ear to ear. And his head was bloody as well, the scalp snatched from it, leaving a small circle of exposed skull. She brought a fist to her mouth to keep from screaming. "You bastards," she breathed.

She thought of the Apaches out there beyond the hill. They always came from that way to attack La Loma de Sombra. The high ground, Martin had called it. Well, the cannon, its brass gleaming like gold, he had bought so long ago was still there, aimed at the flat ground beyond the barn. Aimed precisely at the place where they would come off the hill and start their charge. The cannon was loaded with shot, coins and bits and scraps of metal.

She walked over to it and knelt down, leaning her rifle against the barrel. She picked up flint and the curved piece of steel used to start the tinder burning. She began to scrape the steel crescent with the flint chip, holding it close to the tinder in the little box kept dry and out of the rain.

"I'll open those front doors for you when you've got the fire started." The voice startled Caroline and she dropped the steel into the tinder box. She turned and saw the shadowy silhouette of a man framed in the opening at the back of the barn.

"Martin?"

"Yes," he said.

"You—you're back?"

"And so are the Apaches. I saw them before I rode down. They're singing their war chants, getting ready to ride down that hill."

"You came back," she said numbly.

Martin strode up to her, picked her up by the arms and drew her to him. She smelled his manly scent and crumpled in his caress.

"Oh, Martin. I've missed you so."

"I've missed you, too. And Anson."

"Anson? He should be back any day now. He—he . . ."

"Shh, don't talk. Get that fire going. I see you brought the big rifle. Good."

"I—I can't start the fire now. Will you?"

Martin smiled. He knelt down and struck sparks off the steel. They flew into the tinder. He picked up the ball of dry shavings and blew into them. The fire caught and he set it back in the firebox, added faggots that began to blaze.

"I'll open the door just so," Martin said. "And you get ready to put fire in the hole. It's all loaded?"

"Yes," she said, staring at him as if he was a dead man come back to life.

Martin opened the front doors of the barn wide enough so that the cannon would have a wide field of fire, but not so wide that the Apaches could see inside.

"Now let them come," he said.

70

L ISTEN," JUANITO SAID. Joselito leaned closer to hear what the dying
man had to say. It was difficult to catch his words with the jouncing
of the cook wagon, the noise of the cattle and horses in the small
caravan.

"Yes, I am listening," Joselito said, but he wondered if Juanito
could hear him.

"Can you hear the leaves of the jacaranda tree rustling?"

"I hear them," Joselito lied.

"I can hear the jaguar prowling in the cordillera; I can hear his
soft purr as he seeks his mate. Ah, the mountains and the wind blowing
across the pampas. I can hear my father calling me."

Joselito could barely hear. Juanito's voice was only a whisper and
then it was still. The boy leaned down to listen for a breath, but there
was none. "Alonzo," he called, tears filling his eyes. "I think Juanito
has died."

"Then he has died," Guzman said. "Be quiet. There is something
up ahead. The men are stopping."

"But Juanito has died."

"He will keep," said the old cook and then the wagon groaned
and the steers came to a halt. The wagon settled. Joselito looked down

at Juanito Salazar. The Argentine's eyes were closed and there was the trace of a smile on his face.

"*Adiós*," Joselito said. "*Vaya con Dios.*" It was very quiet in the wagon, and he heard shouting and cheering. "What is happening?" he asked Lonnie.

"It is Anson and the man called Roy Killian. They have just joined us."

"Let me see. I want to see," Joselito cried, and then he was scrambling out of the wagon and running toward the head of the column. He saw Anson Baron and Roy Killian surrounded by Ken Richman and the vaqueros. They were clapping them on the back and pouring water from the canteens over their heads.

"How in hell did you get way down here?" Ken asked.

"Blind luck," Roy said.

"Juanito guided us," Anson said.

"Juanito? I don't understand." Ken blinked his eyes in bewilderment.

"Oh, just a joke between us, Ken," said Anson. "Give us some water to drink, will you?"

"Sure."

Joselito stepped forward then. "Juanito has just died," he said quickly, then bowed his head and took off his hat.

"Juanito is dead?" Anson asked.

"I didn't know," Ken said. "I knew he was going to die, though."

"Damn," Roy said. "Don't that beat all? How'd he die?"

Ken pointed to the prisoners whose horses were roped together behind the cook wagon where two Box B vaqueros held rifles at the ready. "He was shot by one of those rabbles there. Or maybe Mickey Bone. We found out Bone was their leader and he lit a shuck when he saw we were going to win the fight."

"Who are those men?" Anson asked after taking a deep swallow from the canteen. "They're not Indians. What's Bone doing coming after me?"

"Mercenaries," Ken told him. "Hired by Matteo Aguilar to steal the proceeds of our drive. I also found out that Matteo made a pact with the Apaches."

"What kind of pact?"

"The Indians are going to burn you out and Matteo will take back the land."

"Like hell he will," Anson said. "Come on, let's ride to Texas."

"We're already in Texas," Ken said. "But where are the horses and mules you bought?"

"Probably gone to Texas, too," Anson said, and everyone laughed.

In minutes, after Anson and Roy looked in the wagon and shook their heads at the sight of Juanito's still body, the two lost men were mounted on fresh horses and leading the way back to the Box B.

Along the way, Ken gave Anson the letter Juanito had wanted him to have. "He said he wanted to be buried on the Box B."

"I'll read the letter later. I'm worried about my mother. She's all alone. If the Apaches come while we're gone . . ."

Anson didn't want to think about it. He was saddened by the death of Juanito and thought of him as they crossed the Nueces and rode the trail home, pushing the horses faster than they should, pushing themselves almost beyond endurance.

"I've got Matteo by the balls now," Anson told Roy. "You'll get yourself some land out of this, wait and see."

"I would be in your debt, Anson."

"We made it this far, Roy. We can make it the rest of the way, you and me."

Roy grinned. He wanted the land now. Not for his father's sake, but for his own. He looked at Anson Baron and marveled at his luck in meeting such a man. And he too thought of Juanito with sadness and respect. Such men, he reasoned, do not come along very often. I am lucky to have met them.

It was just before dusk when Anson and the others passed Baronsville as the lanterns were being lit. They heard the boom of a cannon as they neared the Box B headquarters. And then they heard the screams and the yipping of Apaches like fiery streamers on the evening air, and the sound of gunshots popping like Chinese firecrackers.

And then they all were galloping down the hill to La Loma de Sombra, their rifles gripped tightly, the manes of their horses flowing in the wind.

71

APACHES LAY DEAD at the foot of the hill and along a path leading to the front of the barn. Others staggered about, wounded by shrapnel. A pall of white smoke hung in the air like a cloud, tendrils of it floating off across the plain. Martin shot one brave who was knocked off his horse from the impact. Caroline picked off another at close range.

Anson and his men rode into the melee, shooting their rifles, dropping Apaches all around. They fired and reloaded. Then the remaining Apaches, at Culebra's order, rode away, carrying the body of his father, Cuchillo, on the back of a pinto, back up the hill and out of sight.

"Daddy?"

"Hello, Anson." Martin stepped away from the barn. His face was blackened by black powder blowback. "Glad you got back safely."

"I don't know what to say," Anson stammered.

"Light down and give me a handshake."

Anson bounded off his horse and stepped up to the father he thought he had lost forever. "I'm glad you came back, Daddy. How come you did?"

"It's where I belong, I guess."

"Well, things have changed since you left, Daddy. I own the Box B now. And this money I got is going for more land."

Caroline's eyes widened. She pressed her lips tightly together to keep from saying anything. But she watched the two men, one her husband, the other her son, as they squared off against each other in the deep silence that cropped up between them.

"That's good, son. You done good," Martin said. "I didn't come back expectin' to pick up where I left off." But something had happened to him on the long ride to the ranch. The land had gotten into him, and when he saw cattle grazing where once had been mesquite and an empty wilderness, the tug of the land had brought him back to his dream, his and Juanito's dream. And as he rode, he left behind the sea and drank in the beauty of Texas with its long sky and endless expanse of land just made for growing cattle and a family. He had almost thrown it all away in the blindness of his stupidity. Now he wondered if he could ever have it back again, all of it, the way it had been when he had first gazed upon the Matagorda coast and seen beyond to the lush virgin valley of the Rio Grande.

"Well, you ain't," Anson said in a firm tone.

Martin felt as if he had been slapped in the face, and the hurt went deeper than the sting of Anson's words. He had been an outcast and he still was. He bit his lip, though, and did not say anything, for he understood how Anson felt. The land belonged to who claimed it, not to those who rode on through and left it behind. Anson had taken charge and Martin was proud of him for that. But his son's words hurt, nevertheless.

Finally Caroline could contain herself no longer. She stepped between the two men she loved and held out her arms as if to separate them before they started fighting with their fists. Then she turned to Anson.

"Your father came back because he heard from Sam Maverick that we were in trouble. Your grandparents and your uncle were killed by those same Apaches you see lying on this bloody ground. If he hadn't come when he had, I'd be lying there, too. So you treat your father with respect, young man, or I'll give you a hiding you won't forget."

"Yes'm," Anson said meekly. Then, he turned to his father. "I'm sorry, Daddy. I—I just thought . . ."

"Son, I can see you're all haired over and growed. You've done well by the Box B and I want no quarrel with you. I got me some money and I aim to sell the boat and settle down. Maybe try and make up for the years I left you and your mother alone. I can buy land from someone else or I can help you build up the Box B. It's your choice. I won't get in your way."

Anson pondered what his father had said for several seconds. Then he grinned and held out his hand again. "Daddy, I—I'd like

you to come back and stay. We could work together and make the Box
B the biggest ranch in Texas. I didn't mean no disrespect, nohow.''

Caroline smiled and pulled the two men together. She put her
arms over their shoulders. "You two," she said.

Anson and Martin shook hands.

"Why, you're old enough to call me Dad, aren't you?"

"Sure."

"Welcome home, son," Caroline said. She slipped her right hand
from Martin's shoulder and embraced Anson.

"Mother. We got a good price for the cattle." He reached in his
pocket and pulled out a fifty-dollar gold piece, placed it in her hand.
"I had the quartermaster issue me a demand note for most of the
money. Good at any bank."

"That was smart of you, son," Martin said.

"I loaded sacks full of old horseshoes and washers and whatever
metal scraps I could find. The mules ran off with all that junk."

Roy laughed. "You sure had me fooled," Killian said.

"That was the idea," Anson said. "I wondered if any of our vaqueros would get greedy, or if you might think about all that money and
do me in."

Roy's face twitched as though he had been stung. "You didn't trust
me?"

"I didn't trust nobody, Roy."

"That's good, son," Caroline said. "Are you hungry?"

"We all are," Anson replied. "We rode a long way." He told his
mother and father about the fight with the mercenaries sent by Matteo
Aguilar. "We'll get all the land we want at a good price now," he said.
"We've got Matteo dead to rights. Either he sells to us, or we . . ."

"I don't think it will come to that, son," Martin said. "Matteo's
just about at the end of his rope. He's hurting bad now and I don't
think he'll give us any argument." He looked around. "Say, I thought
Juanito was with you. Your mother told me he went on the drive with
you."

"I almost forgot, Dad. He—he's in the wagon. Dead. He wanted
to be buried here on the Box B."

Anson was not prepared for his father's reaction. Martin stepped
back and turned his head and then began to sob. His body shook and
then he stopped crying and stood up straight, brushed the tears off
his face.

"He was the best man I ever knew," Martin said.

"Yes, Dad. The best any of us ever knew. He died bravely. Oh,
Juanito left us a letter. Ken gave it to me, but I haven't read it yet."

"I'd like to see it," Martin said.

Anson walked back to his horse and took Juanito's letter from the saddlebag. He took it to his father, handed it to him. "Go ahead, open it."

Martin opened the letter. It was written in flowery script and in English. Tears welled up in his eyes and streaked down his face as he read the letter.

"Do you want to hear what he wrote?" Martin looked at Caroline and Anson.

"Yes, we do," Caroline said.

"Go ahead, Dad. Read it to us."

Ken Richman and Roy Killian walked over to listen. The vaqueros were busy looking at the dead Apaches, checking to see if any were still alive, taking from them souvenirs to show their families.

"Here is what Juanito wrote," Martin said, and then began to read.

Dear Father:

Thank you for giving me life, as you give life to all things. You are the fragrance in a flower, the light in every star, the song from a bird's feathered throat. You are the air I breathe, the earth I walk upon, the fire from the sun that sleeps inside the tree, the wind in my sails, the blood that flows in my veins.

I have seen you in the eyes of children, on the wrinkled faces of the old ones, and in the smiles of the wolf and the raccoon. I have heard your voice in the symphonies that soar from your heart, in the sad chords of a Spanish flamenco and from the dark melodies of a *son huasteco*. I have seen your shadow on the face of the moon and felt your handshake from every stranger whose path crosses mine. I have tasted the sweet water from your well, enjoyed the food of you at my table, and I have often looked up to the sky and felt your presence.

I carry your spirit within me and it has made me strong and given me faith to see beyond the bends in the road and find peace in solitude and silence. I have heard your whispers in the wind, and touched your soul with mine when I pray.

I am grateful to you, Father of All, for the abundance in my life, for the prosperity in my heart. I give thanks to you for all I've seen and done, for all I've loved and cherished. Friendships die, but the time that they live between two people, they can never be taken away.

I thank you, Father, for the friendship you gave me with Martin Baron. That is what lives, and it lives forever. I pray that you keep this family together, that you heal their wounds as you have healed mine over the years. I am leaving them behind, but I want your spirit to stay with them as your spirit stayed with me all my life.

I give my self to you, not in sorrow, but in gladness. I give my spirit back to the source whence it came.

Muchísimas gracias a Usted, Dios mío.

Your loving son,
Juanito Salvador Salazar

Anson wiped tears from his eyes. He looked at Ken and Roy and his mother. They all were crying.

"I will miss him," Caroline said, and then looked around. Esperanza and Lázaro had come out of the house and were standing nearby.

"Who is Juanito?" Lázaro asked in Spanish.

"A good man," Esperanza said. "A holy man."

"What is holy?" asked Lázaro.

"Someday I will tell you," Esperanza said.

"He was a cattleman," Martin said. "The best in Texas."

"The best in the world," Anson said. "Dad, let me read the letter again."

Martin handed Juanito's letter to his son. Anson read it quickly, then looked up. "I never knew he had a middle name."

"Neither did I," Martin said.

"Salvador," Anson said and his voice was hushed as if he was praying.

"It means 'savior' in English," Esperanza said.

"I know," Anson said.

"We'll bury him where he wanted to be buried," Martin said. "And he'll always be a part of Texas."

And then Martin walked over to the abandoned cook wagon and looked inside. He pulled the blanket from the face of Juanito and looked at the withered visage of his friend.

"I never got the chance to apologize for accusing you wrongly," Martin said, the tone of his voice soft, just above a whisper. "I'm awful sorry. I know you'd forgive me if you could. I wondered if I could forgive Caroline for what she done, but on the ride back to the ranch, I thought of something you told me, Juanito. You said we were all one, that we needed and depended on one another, and I guess if there was fault in what Caroline done, there was fault in what I done. I left her by herself even when I was in the same room with her and I didn't listen to her when she was calling out to me. Like you said, we're all part of the same thing, and I was part of what Bone did to her and I don't blame her none. I—I forgive her, and like you told me, I got to forgive myself now."

He thought of Cackleberry Jack McTavish, the mate he'd had when he first came to Matagorda. Jack had been killed when the *Mary E* got caught offshore in a violent storm. Jack had taken a long time to die, and during that time Martin had listened to him babble. The babble had finally made sense when Juanito explained it all to him. Jack had found his spirit during his dying days, had found something deep inside him that was eternal and pure and good. Perhaps Juanito had died as Jack had, at peace with himself and unafraid of the darkness.

"Tell Cackle Jack I said hello, will you, Juanito?"

And it seemed to him he could hear them both laughing. And when he looked through the fresh tears in his eyes, he saw Juanito's slow smile.

He would carry that smile in his heart forever.

Peabody Public Library
Columbia City, IN